The Wyrde Woods Chronicles

LORD OF THE WYRDE WOODS

BOOK TWO

DANCE INTO THE WYRD

NILS VISSER

Lord of the Wyrde Woods Book Two
DANCE INTO THE WYRD
International INGRAM/SPARK Edition
March 2015 Amsterdam

ISBN: 978-90-823229-9-6
Netherlands NUR-CODE 336

A C.B.S. Green Man Publication
Cider Brandy Scribblers
Burnham-on-Sea, Somerset, England

Text copyright © 2014 Nils Visser
The Wyrde Woods Chronicles TM

Registered at the *Depot van Nederlandse Publicaties*
Koninklijke Bibliotheek, Den Haag, the Netherlands

ABC Edition first published in print in Amsterdam in 2015 as:
(Lord of the Wyrde Woods Book Two) DANCE INTO THE WYRD
ISBN: 978-90-823229-5-8

BNB Edition first published in print in Amsterdam in 2015 as:
(Lord of the Wyrde Woods Book Two) DANCE INTO THE WYRD
ISBN: ISBN/EAN 9789402128246

First published digitally on Amazon Kindle in 2014 as:
Lord of the Wyrde Woods Book Two (DANCE INTO THE WYRD)
ISBN 978-90-823229-3-4

Instructions for use: Start at the beginning and read all the words one after the other until you come to the very end and then stop. Holding the book the right way up will enhance the quality of reading. Not suitable for microwave, washing machine, dishwasher or toaster. Do not read and cross the road at the same time.

This book is dedicated to

Marguerita Bär

Thank you for trusting me

It made a whole world

of difference to me.

Table of Contents

One for Sorrow

Two for Joy

Three for a Girl

Four for a Boy

Five for Silver

Six for Gold

Seven for a Secret

Never to be Told

Prologue

It's late and I wonder and ponder and doubt if I should continue to write all of this down. Joan and Rob said I should. It's been seven years already since that fateful summer and memories can fade fast they said.

It was a struggle at first because there were so many things I had tried to banish from my thoughts over the years but once I got started it was like opening a flood-gate; it all came back in vivid detail. Some of it painful but moments of triumph and delight as well.

So far there were surprises too. Living in Nowhere Place (the Odesby Juvenile Care Home) in the run-down Neverland Estate was not something I had been looking forward to recalling because of the terrible things that happened there. However, there were nice moments too; being mates with Sharon and Biggs for one. Small victories also when we managed to outsmart the system or the really big ones when Joy and Willick came out of the Wyrde Woods pretending to be my grandparents and whisked me away to freedom not once but twice.

The Wyrde Woods were far harder to bring to life again. Recalling those first meetings with Willick, Joy and Puck, remembering the warmth and laughter, the stories and the songs, the first explorations of the woods, experiencing a home for the first time in my life…those first kisses…it all filled me with wonder again. But the pleasant memories are bittersweet too because I now know it was all borrowed time. We were already living under the shadows of Malheur Hall even if we didn't know it at the time.

Sometimes the sense of loss is overwhelming. I'm not sure if I can do the next part. I'm not sure if I can stand to go back to that heart of darkness in our tale. I'm not sure if I can stay away from it either, not now that the memories come flooding back and I search for answers.

My dear sweet Puck, what have they done to you my love?

Part Catterah: Five for Silver

20. The Faery Bridge

The fox lay by the base of a towering ash basking in the sunshine, its coat a warm red in the sun's light. When it spotted us it stared at us but remained where it was for a minute or two before casually getting up and ambling into the woods at its ease, not the least impressed by us.

"It's beautiful," I said, thrilled by the encounter.

"I suppose so," Willick answered carefully.

It was Saturday and Willick had shown up at the Owlery in the morning to ask if I cared to see some more of the Wyrde Woods. I had been delighted of course and we were now heading south-east towards Roreford.

"You don't like foxes?" I asked in surprise.

"I doant mind Mus Reynard when he sits beneath a tree in the sun," Willick explained. "But him be full o' sly mischief Mus Reynard be, and most o' that seems to be unaccountably concerned with mine chickens."

I laughed, feeling as bright as the beautiful morning. A whole week's stay in the Wyrde Woods, I could still hardly believe it. The weekends had been magic already.

"What I like be badgers," Willick continued. "There be many setts in the Wyrde Woods."

"Setts?"

"Aye, those baggas dig into the ground I dunnamy tunnels and chambers and live there, a whole clan o' them in each sett."

"I have never seen a badger," I said regretfully.

"Well that be something to remedy, surelye," Willick said.

"I thought they were really hard to spot."

"Ole Brock be shy all right. But naun if ye know what ye be doing. Evening times be best, hide near the sett and stay middling quiet," he gave me a pointed look and I grinned.

"Now be a good time as well," Willick continued, "cubs come out to play."

"Really?" I wanted to see badger cubs at play.

"I'll take ye sometime this week to see," Willick promised and I grinned happily.

The ruins of Roreford were spooky. The village was mostly clustered around a small church with another huddle of buildings a bit further on by the Rore River. All the buildings had been constructed with the same roughly cut sand stones I had seen at St. Lewinna's. All that was left of them were empty shells. They looked forlorn with their gaping doorways and windows. The church was relatively free of trees and undergrowth and its walls were mostly intact. The surrounding buildings had been reclaimed by the woods though, covered in ivy and various plants which had found tenacious lodging between the crumbled walls. Some walls were little more than piles of stones. A few former houses had trees growing inside them, an oddity which I liked.

I looked at the broad open space in front of the church and felt a moment of discomfort. This was where Roderick Malheur had the unfortunate village girls stripped and flogged hundreds of years ago and I could imagine the humiliation the poor girls must have experienced before pain and the realisation of imminent death became their sole concern. It made being manhandled to the isolation cell in view of a full common room seem relatively mild all of a sudden. I felt an odd kinship with the girls.

"Is the watermill there?" I pointed at the buildings by the Rore River. Willick nodded and we walked over to the river. As we got closer an odd sound which had been puzzling me got louder, a distant roar of some sorts.

"Is it the Rore River which is roaring?" I joked.

"Aye, tis." Willick pointed south. "The Falls and Fey's Pool be anigh, naun far."

"Is that why they called it Roreford?"

"Mayhap it be," Willick nodded.

There was an ancient stone bridge leading over the river just by the outlying buildings and we walked onto it. The ruins here edged the water. One was bigger than the others and I reckoned I could see where the water wheel had been attached. I shivered, thinking of those poor village girls who were doomed to haunt the scene of their deaths for eternity. Behind Roreford I could see the high ragged walls of Hood's Gorge looming up on either side of the river and I thought of Puck who had promised to take me climbing there. To my disappointment Joy had told me he had gone up north for the weekend and I missed him sorely.

"Disyer be the Farisee Bridge," Willick said.

"The Faere Folk?"

"Aye, that they be called as well. Long time ago there be a knight who lived at the castle. He were called Richard Malheur. Sir Richard."

"He went to fight the Knucker at Devil's Tarn!" I said.

"Aye so he does, ye've been there?"

"Yes, Puck took me."

"Aye, the lad reafes up on Knuckers so he does, tis unaccountable, Knuckers and Faere Folk have taken his fancy." Willick nodded. "Puck tell ye what happened to Sir Richard?"

"Only that he was sorely wounded and that he was taken to Pook Hall."

"Aye, that he was. But there's more to this tale. During hisn sojourn in Pook Hall Sir Richard be much taken by Niada, a Farisee healer. Now Niada she doant be exceptionally beautiful for Farisee standards, naun alikes them Shy Maidens for example, howsumdever, to Sir Richard - Niada be the fairest of them all."

"He fell in love with her?"

"Aye, that he did. And what be more, some-one-time it does happen, Niada fell in love with Sir Richard as well."

I sighed. I liked thrillers and horrors but wasn't immune to love stories.

"This caused middling complication, all-along-o' Sir Richard having to gwaon back to Malheur Hall and it be unheard o' for a Farisee to live amidst humans."

"Unless they are a changeling," I corrected him, having recently examined myself in the mirror to see if my ears had just a hint of pointiness. I had got impatient and squeezed the top ends together which produced satisfying pointiness indeed.

"Unless they be changeling," Willick agreed. "So Sir Richard and Niada, they axe for an audience with the King and Queen."

"King Oberon and Queen Titania!"

"Zackly. Oberon jes laughed and laughed. Him thought Sir Richard be a middling fool for believing there could be any happy ending to such a coupling. Howsumdever, deep in hern heart Titania be touched and twere Titania who relented. Queen Titania decreed that Sir Richard and Niada be allowed one year together, howsumdever, she warns them to be satisfied with that and naun be wanting more; love and the pain o' parting or naun."

I thought about this. Would it be better to share a short period with someone, knowing all the time the pain of separation that awaited you at the end of it, or forego it altogether? How much time would I be given with Puck? If at all. I had no idea yet if those kisses by the bridge were an incidental lapse of reason. I hoped not.

"Willick?"

"Aye lass."

"Can I ask you a personal question?"

"If ye mus," he looked wary.

"If you had been given the choice, back then, knowing your time with Joy would be so short; would you still have done it?"

Willick looked out over the river, mulling this over for a moment.

"I would naun have missed it for all the money in disyer wurreld," he said at a last. "Ourn time be short but middling unaccountable, so twere."

"Do you love Allison?"

To my surprise Willick burst into laughter.

"Shouldn't I have asked that?" I asked.

"Tis naun that, jes that ye be refreshingly direct and forrard." He chuckled and I smiled.

"I need to get used to it some Wenn, but I like it in Joy, so I'll learn to cope with two o' yern kind at the Owlery," he smiled and then hypnotised me with his earnest eyes. "Joy became a good friend Wenn, a very good friend. Howsumdever, Allison naun be a second prize for me, I still feel those butterflies in mine belly every time I sees Allison."

I nodded, pleased that this had been clarified because I had been wondering about it.

"What did Sir Richard and Niada choose?"

"Niada gwoan with Sir Richard to Malheur Hall. He got her with a boy child and for eleven months he were the happiest man in the wurreld."

"And the twelfth month?"

"Niada accepted Titania's decision; hern knowing that to disobey Titania would've meant calling misfortune on hern lover. But Sir Richard be dreading the moment more and more, thinking o' all manner o' wild plans to keep Niada by hisn side. He becomes middling poorly from all hisn worries and naun enjoyed that last month much."

"I can imagine, but to throw it away like that…"

"Aye. One dawn Sir Richard awoke and Niada's side o' the bed were empty. He looks out the window and sees Niada walking out o' Malheur Hall, across the moat bridge and into the Wyrde Woods she goes. Sir Richard grabbed theirn young babe Foster and follows Niada, catching up with hern and pleading and begging, holding up the liddle chavee and axing hern naun to let Foster grow into manhood without a mam."

I felt a stab of pain in my heart.

"They reach disyer bridge and Niada starts to descend into the river, there be a gate to Pook Hall here back in those days. The Water Gate. Sir Richard makes one last try to keep Niada with him and grabs hern shawl. But the shawl comes off and Niada tells him to keep it well and fly it alikes a banner if he or Foster ever needed to summon Farisee help. Then hern disappeared and Sir Richard naun ever sees hisn love again. Tis said Niada visited Foster thrice, but hern naun laid eyes on Sir Richard again."

"That's so sad," I said. "What happened to Foster?"

"Foster grew up and became Lord o' the Wyrde Woods alikes hisn da. There's a painting o' Foster Malheur in the castle."

I recalled that Puck had mentioned Foster when he listed the Malheurs he hoped he took after: Sir Richard, Foster and Oscar.

"And the shawl?"

"Ah, the Farisee banner still be in Malheur Hall, akept in a chest in the Drummer's Vault. It can only be flown twice and naun more. And twere already used once in days o' the Waus. Mind ye, most o' the Malheurs doant put much stock in Farisee tales."

"So if Foster was half Farisee, that means Puck has Farisee blood in him?"

"Aye, but I reckon most folk round here have some o' that, surelye," Willick shrugged as if this were a normal thing. "The Farisee doant live with humans, but mix aplenty in other ways."

Meaning that they like shagging, I thought with a grin.

"Ye be wanting to see the Falls and the Fey's Pool?"

"Yes please!"

§ § § § § §

We followed a path which wound around the Fey's Pool so that we came to its banks on the south side. We faced a sheer wall of rock across the pool, some twenty-five yards high and a hundred yards wide. It was broken in the middle by the Rore River which plunged down vertically in a thundering cascade of foam causing a lively dance of waves around the area where the roaring river crashed into the pool.

The word pool was misleading, the water stretched along the entire length of the cliff and then it was another sixty yards to the opposite bank where we were standing. To our right was a small circular island, about twelve feet from the shore, all of it shaded by a huge weeping willow, the lower branches of which touched the lake's surface.

Willick started telling the tale of the Fey with relish and I didn't have the heart to tell him Puck had already told me. He did add an element to it, telling me that walking around the island widdershins seven times would summon the Fey for those who were keen to be seduced and condemned to spend an eternity watching her bathe.

Like Puck, Willick dwelt on the fact that the Fey bathed nude and it was this that enticed men into the pool to their doom. He seemed quite taken by it. I wondered at the fascination men seem to have with female nudity but had to admit the Falls were a spectacular sight and there was something about the lake in the middle of the forest which did seem magical and the tale attached to it seemed fitting.

On the way back to the Owlery however, it was the story of Sir Richard and Niada which played in my mind. It was even better than the poor old Shy Maidens and the deserved punishment of Oberon and Powke. That was still a good story. Although Titania's revenge had turned out badly for the maidens Titania had at least stood up and fought for herself. Just as Lewinna and Ellette had taken on the Knuckers and Joy had tackled Stubbles. But Niada's story went deeper. It must have been horrible for all three of them; that parting by the bridge. I'd give Puck a chance, but if he didn't come back quickly I would just have to bag myself a fit Faere Folk prince instead. See what conditions Titania would lay down for that.

Willick said his goodbyes by the gate and I went into the Owlery to find that Joy had prepared a shepherd's pie and I ate with relish.

While we were eating there was a distinct "Oehoeh" sound from the living room. I was surprised. Previously I had always assumed that was the only sound owls made. I had never heard one of Joy's owls use it before though. The foursome had an incredible repertoire of sounds and often managed to convey the impression that there were about two dozen owls in the Owlery rather than just the four.

"Oehoeh," the call was repeated.

"Oehoeh," Joy called back.

"You're having a conversation with them?" I grinned.

"Tis Aethel, hern mating call. If I doant answer she gets awful cranky."

"She thinks you're her mate?"

"Tis imprint," Joy sighed.

"Quiddy?"

"Aethel be raised by humans, she never see another owl till she comes here. Owls alikes that, we say they have a human imprint."

"You didn't have her when she was a chick?"

"Naun o' them. Truth be told Wenn, though I love them a load, I'd never gwoan and get an owl chick. Owls ought to be out there in the woods and over the fields. Flying free."

"So where did they come from?"

"Sheere-folk," Joy pulled a dirty face that made me laugh. "Think it would be fun to have an owl as pet. Doant realise ye can't stroke or pet an owl alikes a cat or dog. They be wild animals, instinct to kill and them'll use theirn claws and beaks happily if something aint to theirn liking. Owls be needing a lot o' special care: Beaks, talons, room to fly. All o' disyer owls were poorly when they bring them here."

"And you can't set them free?"

"Some folk gwaon does that and the birds'll starve. Most jes doant cope in the wild anymore and them folk jes doant cope with pellets, poop, ceca and molt feathers."

"Pellets? Ceca?"

"Owls regurgitate fur and bones o' their food in pellets. They aint polite, when it comes out, it comes out, wherever they be. And Ceca is at end o' intestines, they empty it once a day. Looks like chocolate pudding but it smells something awful."

I remembered smelling something awful in the living room once but I had assumed then that Lady had farted. She was a brilliant dog in all ways, but I had never realised dogs have no qualms about farting anywhere at all.

"Oehoeh," Aethel called.

"Oehoeh," Joy answered. "As for ourn talk...?"

She was referring to her stated intention to talk about my habit of getting into trouble.

"Joy," I said. "My mum and dad?"

Though I didn't mind listening to her opinion on the mayhem which I seem to attract like honey draws Pooh Bear she did know more about my parents and I really wanted to know.

"I really need to know," I said pleadingly.

"Aye, I reckon ye does," Joy nodded.

"You said you only knew them shortly. But you read people well, don't you?"

Joy sighed. "Aye, I does. I did meant to tell ye, sweetie, that first weekend."

"I know, there wasn't much time," I smiled. "Just knowing that Dad was from Brighton, and Mum from the Edgelands – it's made a such a difference just knowing that,"

"I know the yearning, Wenn," Joy said softly. After a pause she continued talking, louder this time. "There have been folk tasked with being Guardian of the Wyrde Woods since Roman times."

"Forever ago," I said, "Are you one of..."

Joy raised her hand to ward off my question. "Let me tell the tale, liddle one."

I nodded.

"Mus have been somewhere in '86 I recollects. One o' the Guardians asked me to come to the Raven's Roost. We had spoken of a danger – a darkness in the Wyrde Woods, howsumdever, we couldn't put ourn finger on it. She introduced me to Ashley and Nyle."

Just hearing their names filled me with warmth. I already had a dozen questions but stayed silent.

"They were refugees o' sorts. I doant ken the details, Wenn. The Guardian had offered them shelter. Most-in-general, the talk was about the darkness. Yern mam ken more about it. The next and last time we met was here, in disyer Owlery, about a year later. Twere crisis by then."

Joy paused and looked pained for a moment.

"The Guardian and yern parents were in the midst o' it and came for sanctuary. They spent the night. Yern parents in yern room, ye'll be wanting to know."

I nodded happily.

"The darkness was overcome, howsumdever, at a cost. There always be a price for magic Wenn, always. There be no exceptions."

I nodded again. It sounded ominous but I was focused on my mum and dad.

"I told ye what price they paid," Joy said.

"Ash…Mum disappeared into the Wyrde Woods, Dad was shattered."

"Yern father was a good man, Wenn. Full o' life him were. Alikes most young men he thought himself to be invincible; tmight have been a flaw as he were as reckless as yernself can be, howsumdever, hisn optimism kept Ashley on her feet. He doted on her, twere a sight to see. There be plenty o' men who would have left her to hern own devices all-along-o' yern mam's gift."

My mind boggled and I struggled not to unleash a barrage of questions. I had cursed him at times for his abandonment of me. The way Joy described him though, it didn't sound like he was the type of man to just walk away for no reason.

"Gift?" I dared a question.

"Aye, Ashley had a gift. Ye have some o' it too."

"I do?" I was surprised.

"Ye be very receptive to yern surroundings. The way ye reacted to the Shy Maidens, or Niada's tale. Ye pick things up."

I raised my eyebrows; clearly Puck and Will had related the details of our outings to her. I recalled my reaction to Nan Malone's Chestnut; so I took after my mother in that fashion. I had often wondered as to what they were like as people but this was the first time I realized that I could discover part of their character in myself.

"Tis something to mind," Joy warned. "Ye doant have it as strong as yern mum, howsumdever, the intensity o' it can come and go; and it can grow quick in the Wyrde Woods."

I was pleased to hear that; it reinforced my feeling that I was changing in the Wyrde Woods and took away my doubt that I was just projecting a whimsical fancy.

"She were a troubled soul; kind-hearted as can be, howsumdever, very wary o' the world having learned that dunnamy folks will take theirn advantage o' the likes o' Ashley. She trusted Nyle. She trusted Nyle's friend, young Mackellow. She trusted the Guardian."

"Surely she trusted you?" I couldn't help but ask.

"All-along-o' the Guardian's insistence that she could and should. Twould have taken more time for Ashley to let down hern guard," Joy grimaced. "Yern mam were perceptive to more than the normal eye can see, Wenn. She had learned hernself to shut hernself off. The gift she had were also a curse."

"She saw shims," I said softly, thinking of the nuns I had seen at the priory.

"Saw them, felt them, heard them, smelled them and with some she spoke." Joy said.

"Was that what drove her…" I hesitated. Drove her to the edge of madness? Drove her cray? Drove her to disappear in the Wyrde Woods?

"Tis unbeknownst to me," Joy said. "Howsumdever, it be the most likely reason."

"But after they left the Owlery again…"

"Twere to do battle with the darkness," Joy said quietly. "She won, Wenn. She defeated it. Howsumdever, she doant return."

"The price of magic…" I pondered.

Joy nodded.

"And the Guardian? Maybe she knows more?"

Joy closed her eyes and I could feel that her heart was pained. I felt guilty for breathing life into old memories but at the same time I was selfishly glad that I had; it felt as if I had something to hold on to at last. Maybe it was just clutching at straws but it gave me a sense of peace.

Joy opened her eyes again. She looked much older all of a sudden. "The Guardian disappeared as well, I doant know what happened to Maisy."

"I am sorry," I said awkwardly. I reached out for her hand and folded mine around it; careful to avoid giving it a light squeeze on account of her affliction.

Joy smiled warmly and gave me a grateful look. "It be a shared pain, lass."

I nodded and returned her smile.

"That be all I recollect, Wenn," Joy said. "They were good people, that much ye need know. Both o' them live on in yernself. Ye'll have plenty to be thinking o' now, I reckon. We'll talk more tomorrow."

I nodded happily, glad that she understood I would have to sort out all this new information first. Revel in her judgement that Mum and Dad were good people at heart and do so in the very room where they had once spent a night; a room that was now mine. Transform my worry that I took after them in a heartless fashion into a celebration of Dad's energetic optimism and Mum's empathy…they were me, I was them. My head was spinning as I climbed to my loft room – my home in the Wyrde Woods and my first real connection with my absent parents.

§ § § § § §

On Sunday morning I came down the stairs drawn by the homely smell of fresh coffee. After breakfast I cleared up the dishes and did the washing up while Joy was messing about with dead mice. She bred them in one of the sheds and had fetched four of them which she quickly killed after which she started removing some of the intestines. It looked horrible but Joy did not seem to mind.

"Owl feeding time," Joy said and I followed her into the living room.

The owls knew what was going to happen and launched into tumult.

"Eeeeeeghh eeeeeeghh" Aethel sounded like a lamb with a sore throat.

"Mheeeew Mheeeew" Horsa mewled like a kitten.

"EEEEEEEECCCCCHHHHHH" hissed Bran.

"Ccccchhhhwwwaaaaaaa!" Bronwen rasped.

I grinned.

Joy walked from box to box, depositing a mouse in each. The scritch owls attacked theirs with ferocity, Horsa picked at his carefully as if he didn't trust it and Aethel hid hers beneath some straw.

"Aethel likes to save it for later," Joy explained. "Now, let's yern and I talk. We've had ourn talk about yern mam and da, howsumdever, there were another talk I be wanting to have with ye."

I nodded and we sat down on the couch by the fireplace. To my surprise I was nervous.

"Ye have a knack for getting yernself into trouble lass," Joy sighed. "I doant blame ye, having seen that place they keeps ye. Doant hold much with men who punch women meself. That man be a right scrowse."

"They make me angry sometimes," I admitted.

"Aye, I can understand, but Wenn?"

"Yes?"

"I think that all-along-o' folk like that ye have an imprint as well."

I nodded.

"Ye acts gurt and tough, but I have seen ye be a liddle girl as well. A sweet child when ye be here with me, but I think in Odesby, naun so sweet."

"What do you mean?" I narrowed my eyes.

Joy laughed.

"Look at yernself lass. Ye jes did it. One thing that disagrees with ye, and ye tense up, all vlothered, ready to defend yernself alikes a bagga, scrowing at me, snuffy and tessy. Should I be afeared o' ye now?"

I recalled that Willick had asked the same question and shook my head.

"You don't know what it's like there, it's so bloody unfair sometimes," I said in a small voice.

"And doant ye gwoan cause a scamble by playing disyer hurt liddle girl with me neither," Joy admonished me. "Ye promised honesty."

I looked at her sharply.

"Aye snuffy wildcat," Joy grinned and I relaxed a bit. She was right of course, but cutting so close to the truth that it made me uncomfortable.

"I know ye've been handed a rotten deal lass," Joy continued. "Howsumdever, I doant think ye ought to be telling me nor anyone else that they doant understand what that's alike, surelye."

"Most don't," I protested more vehemently than I intended. "They grow up with bloody parents who bloody well care about them."

"This aint about specifics Wenn," Joy was unfazed. "Ye had yern mam and da taken away. Tis unfair. I had mine child taken away. Tis unfair. Mine son had hisn mam taken away from him. Tis unfair and I doant thinks Nate grew up to be a happy man. Ye think I doant hear Puck be hag-ridden when he stayed here? Scared and shouting for hisn mam in the night? Tis unfair. Even that head-doctor o' yern, Miss Hare…"

"What about her?"

"Lass be from here, Wolfden be where she growed up. Ye doant want to know how oft a time hern mam axed me to come to treat liddle Mary and hern sisters. Blued eyes and bruises, poor liddle girls. Hern dad Bill drink too much, so he does. I dunnamy a time he beat them bloody."

"Mary Hare?"

"Aye, hern escaped to University and learnt a fancy trade, but how much confidence has becoming a head-doctor given hern?"

"None," I mumbled, suddenly feeling bad about how I had played on that insecurity more often than not.

"And still naun healed, for hern attaches hernself to a bully once again at hern work. Look lass, there be a pain in ye, I can see that. I can feel it. And naun matter what Mary Hare tries, tis naun gwoan help much. They try to fix yern head, but tis yern soul that be wounded, aint that so?"

I nodded.

"Yern pain will never gwoan away Wenn, never. Tis up to ye whether ye learn to live with it or naun. If ye does, it becomes easier to cope with."

"What is it to you anyways?" I snapped. I just couldn't help it but I felt like she was laying my soul bare and I didn't like it. This place shouldn't become like Nowhere Place.

Joy looked at me for some time; there was no anger or impatience in her eyes, but none of her empathy either.

"Why does ye think ye're welcome here Wenn?" Joy spoke in a dangerously soft tone. "All-along-o' that ye reckon I be lonely?"

"No, I am sorry," I shook my head.

"Puck sayed that ye liked being part o' us."

"I do, I do."

"Then ye'll have to accept that part of being loved means ye'll have to accept that folk have concerns about ye as well. And have the right to does so. Ye cannot jes want the parts o' this arrangement that ye likes and then get tessy about the rest that be part and parcel of being loved."

I nodded and looked at the floor in confusion.

"Even in Odesby there be naun reason to get tessy about everything. There's real pain that means somewhen ye reacts like that. That mister Scrowse what punched ye hounding ye with Calcott; I would have reacted the same as ye did. But there also be feeling almighty sorry for yernself."

I took this coolly. I didn't like it but had to admit it was true sometimes.

"Puck tells me ye want to fight for the Wyrde Woods."

I was surprised. When Puck had said that he needed to speak to people I thought he meant the Weard Hunt, not Joy. So she was involved too?

"Yes, I do," I said.

"And that be the reason I need ye to pick yern fights with care," Joy said. "Tis Catt Malheur who be ourn main foe in this. And that draggle-tail will fight real dirty. I need to be able to trust that ye doant fly off the handle."

"I understand."

"And will ye remember that if and when ye be pointed at yern actions? Listen afore ye reacts snuffy alikes a wildcat?"

"I'll try."

"Naun, ye either does or doant."

"I will do it." I said, though not without some anger.

"One more thing lass," Joy relaxed and her eyes sparkled again.

"Yes?"

"If ye want things to work out with Puck, tis the same rules. Ye maun scratch hisn eyes out if ye think him be meddling in yern life, surelye."

My eyes grew wide and Joy laughed.

"Well doant look at me as if I have the power o' second sight lass. I naun be blind ye know."

"Oehoeh," Aethel wanted attention.

"Oehoeh," Joy answered. She continued: "Good, well I be glad that's over and done with. Now, I've a treat for ye."

§ § § § § §

The treat was clearing out the owl boxes. This had to happen one box at a time because the owl was released during the operation. This meant the other owls had to have their boxes shut to avoid the bloodbath Joy assured me would inevitably happen if one owl encroached upon the territorial sensitivities of another. Joy inspected the poo at the bottom of the boxes closely, she said they were tell-tale signs of health, and counted the pellets to keep track of them; they told her when it was feeding time. We also removed remnants of mice and chicks –aside from Aethel' last mouse which she hadn't touched yet- because the owls liked to hide bits and pieces of their food for later consumption

20

but decomposing mice and chicks were bad news. I was impressed by Joy's knowledge and began to see how an average family buying an owl because they thought it was cute had no idea what they were getting into.

The best bit of the job was that Joy gave me a thick leather glove to wear and one by one Bronwen, Bran, Horsa and Aethel sat on my hand as Joy put fresh straw in their boxes. It was piff having them this close by, I had already stopped associating Joy's owls with Ufmanna. Joy said that if they got a bit more familiar with me we'd be able to take them outside to fly them which sounded like fun.

§ § § § § §

We had the leftovers from the previous evening's shepherd's pie for dinner. Joy poured us both a glass of her birch sap wine which was semi-sweet with a lemony taste and tasted good.

"I forgot to ask Willick something about Roreford yesterday," I said.

"Well, ye can try mine recollections, but it be Will and Puck who knows most about the Wyrde Woods."

"I think you know far more than you let on," I said. "Honesty right?"

After having seen Joy in action during the meeting at Nowhere Place I was left in no doubt who the natural leader was around here. Her astute questions there showed a far greater awareness of the outside world than I expected, probably because she liked to portray herself as an isolated country bumpkin. I suspected that she knew just as much if not more than the menfolk about local matters too.

Joy regarded me sharply for a moment. "Ye're clever lass, and ye be right, I does owe ye an apology."

I smiled; pleased my intuition had been right. "How was Roreford destroyed?"

"Twere during the Civil War. Royalist and Parliament armies coming to and fro fighting with each other. Naun difference for the common folk. When sodgers came there'd be raping, killing, thieving and burning. Doant matter which side they were fighting for."

Joy stopped for a moment and I pictured a village in flames, screaming villagers, laughing soldiers.

"Folk in all of Sussex had enow, naun jes in the Wyrde Woods. Villagers armed themselves and organised defences. Called themselves Clubmen."

"Good, did they get the bastards?"

"At first, aye. Round here the Clubmen built palisades atop Arthur's Fort, jes as there had been in the Old Days. When sodgers came, men, women, chavees, cattle, pigs, chickens: All hid behind the palisades and were safe. Sodgers what'd come anear were mighty sorry they'd tried."

"People power," I was thrilled; better to fight back than be passive.

"Aye, but in the end, it came to trouble. Neither side wanted common folk learning how to fight. It made war less appealing they said. They made a truce and attacked Arthur's Fort together. They brought cannon; twere a slaughter. Survivors fled to Roreford, hoping the Sheere-folk would naun know theirn way in the Wyrde Woods."

"It makes some sense, but Roreford was…"

"Malheur fambly knew how to find it," Joy said. "It were them that showed the sodgers the way to Roreford."

"Why?" It didn't make sense to me, presumably being landlord meant gathering income from rent and taxes. Why destroy your own income?

"To set an example. This be what happens when ye forget yern place in the scheme o' things. Does ye have history at school Wenn?"

"Yes, but it's not like the stories Puck, Willick and you tell. Not real people. Mostly Kings, Queens, Prime Ministers…that sort of thing."

"Naun much have changed then. Ye never heard o' Willikin o' the Weald? Watt Tyler? The Diggers? The Levellers? The Chartists? The Suffragettes? The Wallies?"

"Only Willikin, Puck told me about him, he hid in a cave in the gorge."

"Aye, that he does. Time and again common folk have raised their banners to protect theirn rights. Time and again their Lordships have used every means they could to crush such unity."

Joy stopped for a moment.

"Diggers, for example, were up in Surrey, at St. George's Hill. They mus have known landowners could naun and would naun allow them to succeed. Yet, they went ahead with their dream o' common land anyway."

"And were attacked?"

"Aye, and defeated. Tis the same with disyer motorway, ye understand? Times have naun changed much. We, the folk o' the Wyrde Woods and the Weald will rise to protect what be ourn. What does ye think will happen?"

"They will try to crush us." I said quietly, thinking of the jackboots I had read about in Puck's hideout.

"And probably succeed. Ye understand? I axe all-along-o' ye need to know what might happen."

"Even though you know winning is unlikely, you will fight anyway," I said softly.

"Tis a fine tradition of common folk, we maun ever stop trying. Remember that, whatever happens ye mus always keep trying."

"Then we fight."

"But naun tonight," Joy smiled. "Tis bedtime for me, I be hurting a liddle."

I stood up and kissed Joy on the forehead and then went upstairs to my room.

§ § § § § §

I was still up about an hour later looking at the ceiling. I had tried to read by candlelight but couldn't focus on the words; there was too much going on in my head as I tried to digest the day. Specifically about Joy's talk on my *I-don't-take-anything-from-anyone* attitude.

What Joy had suggested was that I was transferring this habit to my life in the Wyrde Woods. You can't just take the bits you like; it's all part of the deal. I noticed with a wry smile that even now something in me immediately resisted the notion of being told by anybody what to do, even if it was a suggestion rather than a command. I was like those Clubmen and Diggers really, asserting independence even though I knew the system always won and I had no real freedom to speak of. But my habit was so deeply ingrained that I was confusing Joy and Willick for the system. They weren't, Joy had specifically said that it was part of being loved.

I smiled ruefully. I basically did not know what it was like being loved. It had never happened to me before. The ex-boyfriend just played me to get laid and I had gone along with the game because it seemed the thing to do, a status of a kind for the both of us but there had been no real affection. Biggs adored me, but that was different too. He wasn't 'company', for him everything revolved around that worship. I was fond of him in a funny way but that was it. Puck was different, he seemed to actually enjoy my company and I liked his. There was a mutual appreciation there and though I had doubted it then I now realised he had been dropping hints that he wouldn't mind more than just that but had left the decision up to me. Not quite like being swept off my feet by manly resolution but just wanting to be near him was something that was beginning to ache.

Then there were Joy and Willick too. Thinking back of all the trouble they had gone to a second time just for my sake meant that they did really care. They had made a real effort. The closest I had been to someone making an effort for me was Michael, but that was just the effort of listening to me and setting me challenges because he had known that triggered me. Thinking back I realised he had set challenges to achieve but never challenged me in my thinking. Joy *was* challenging me and I had so nearly ruined everything when I started snapping at her; because for me it was an easy step from there to the anger I couldn't control. The very fear Willick had voiced in the car that day when he brought me back to Odesby.

Being loved, I decided, was difficult and something I was going to have to work on before I pushed those offering it away.

There was a rasping at the window which I only dimly perceived and ignored at first as I was trying to work things out in my head. The rasping became a gentle tapping and I rolled over to see what it was.

PUCK!

Puck's grinning face was outside the window. I opened it and he clambered through, I caught him as he more or less fell onto the bed and I kissed him fiercely.

"How did you get up there?" I whispered when our mouths parted.

"Ivy," he whispered back. "Old thick stems."

"Where's Lady?"

"At Rob Hornsby's farm, picking her up tomorrow."

"And where the hell have you been?"

"I weren't in the alus missus, and I does only drink one pint in there while I doant be there."

I grinned happily and poked him in the ribs.

"Ouch," he said, and then added, "Up north in Yorkshire."

"But I wasn't up North, I was down South," I reprimanded him.

"When I couldn't find you in Yorkshire I came straight back," Puck nodded in all seriousness.

I surprised myself with the extent to which I was totally delighted by his unexpected appearance. After we talked some more he started unlacing his shoes and unbuttoning his trousers. Even his bloody boxers were green I noticed with a grin. I was already down to my knickers and singlet and when he crawled under the covers in his boxer shorts and t-shirt I felt some trepidation because I wasn't sure what he was expecting.

If he had wanted to take the kissing further, even all the way, I would have. But only to please him really. I wasn't quite ready for it myself. My worries were unnecessary though, Puck was happy to just lie with me in his arms like that first night in his hideout. It was comforting and I relished the touch of his arms around me. I felt safe and sheltered and figured I had more or less scored my Faere Folk prince; green boxers, glasses and all.

21. Pathfinders

"Wenn sweetie," Joy's voice called from far away. I opened my eyes slowly and smiled when I realised I was at the Owlery. My smile widened when I realised I was spooned up against Puck, his chest warm against my back and arm wrapped around my middle. I wriggled till I had turned around and saw that he was still asleep. I traced his earlobes to check if there was any sign of Faere Folk pointiness. They weren't quite rounded at the top, more square-like, definitely not Elfish though. I ran a fingertip along his eyebrows and the ridge of his nose.

"Wenn, time to get up." Joy called again.

Puck slowly opened his eyes and smiled when he saw me.

"Coming Joy!" I called out and then whispered. "That silly beard of yours, shave it off."

"Never," Puck whispered back.

"Puck it looks like you have pubes stuck on your chin."

"You have a filthy mind Elfin," he whispered with a cheeky grin.

"And ye might save yernself a climb on the ivy and jes come down the stairs Puck," Joy called up.

Puck and I looked at each other with wide eyes and then burst into laughter.

§ § § § § §

We trooped into the kitchen looking sheepish. The table was set for three and there was coffee, as well as a fresh loaf of Joy's bread, Smoked Ashdown Forester, tomatoes and onions.

"I reckon it'll be a fine day today," Joy declared when we sat down. "There be some clouds out yet, but they'll clear away afore noon, the sun she will shimper surelye."

"Joy," I said, kind of worried. "We ..."

"Naun o' mine business," Joy shook her head. "I doant want to know."

Puck and I grinned at each other.

"Now if ye doant want the lad in yern room, kick him out. Could have been hisn room, howsumdever, the ungrateful rogue chose to live alikes a middling wodewose in the woods instead. Tis unaccountable. Tis yern room now Wenn, to share or naun. Jes remember there be a fine sack o' straw in the tool shed that suit Puck jes fine also."

"I'll keep it in mind," I said smiling.

"How were yern jaunce to the Sheeres?" Joy looked at Puck.

"Productive."

"Is this about the road protest?" I asked.

Puck gave Joy a questioning look. She nodded.

"Yes, it is." Puck answered.

"Ye'll know most there is to know afore the week be out Wenn," Joy said and I realised she had decided to let me join.

"Most?" I asked.

"She doesn't miss a thing, does she?" Puck asked Joy and I was pleased to hear pride in his voice.

"Far too clever by half," Joy agreed.

We could suddenly hear a mobile phone go off. It was strange to hear the electronic sounds in this setting, just as strange as watching Puck pull out a phone.

"Goodfellow here," he said.

I smiled; he was using a code name. So this is what he had meant with the cloak-and-dagger stuff.

"Okay, thank you." Puck punched a button and put the mobile down on the table.

"Well?" Joy asked.

"It's begun," Puck answered.

§ § § § § §

"What has begun? Where? When? What are we going to do about it? Why did you use a code name?" I rattled off my questions as Puck and I left the Owlery about ten minutes later, heading east.

"It's nothing dramatic yet," Puck said. "We'll just go have a look after we pick up Lady, see what is happening."

"Yes Mr. Goodfellow," I quipped.

Puck stopped for a moment. "Has Joy told you what we're up against?"

"Lady Malheur."

Puck continued walking and I followed suit.

"Road protests have been going on for a while now Wenn. There are detective agencies specialised in them. They scout the area, look for potential troublemakers, try to infiltrate groups, tap phone lines."

"Tap phone lines?"

"Sounds farfetched, but we know landlines are tapped, we don't know if they have access to the technology for intercepting mobile communication, but best to assume they have."

"But there is not even a protest yet, so how do you know they are already…?"

"Because we know that Aunt Catt hired the services of one of those agencies two years ago when Friends of the Wyrde Woods was set up."

"All that time!"

"Information is power, Wenn. That's why we use the code names on the phone, but better not use them elsewhere okay?"

A brief flicker of irritation, that was all. I made it go away. There, I had been corrected without aiming a bazooka at someone. Achievement unlocked.

"Okay Puck, sorry."

"No worries. It's crazy how far they'll go really, hard to believe sometimes."

"So they're monitoring the Weard Hunt as well?"

"Oh you bet Wenn, those they consider far more dangerous. They are the ones who look like they'll be setting up a protest in the woods."

"Look like?" I was intrigued.

Puck grinned, "This is Top Secret, okay?"

"Sure."

"Might be stupid, my aunt might have sent you to spy on me."

"I get paid by the hour and bonuses for kissing," I answered. "I need the extra cash so you're in trouble mister."

"I'll gladly help you out there," Puck smiled happily. "Looking forward to it."

"See, putty in my hands," I said with satisfaction. "Now tell me all your secrets."

"All of the anti-road groups are connected," Puck said.

"Friends of the Wyrde Woods and Weard Hunt?"

"There are more."

"More!"

"Top Secret?" Puck looked concerned.

"I can keep a secret Puck, okay?"

"Friends is the most public group, and intentionally designed to keep a low profile where action is concerned. They are the folk who will appeal to the broader public."

"Pfff, if you think you can drag that public away from behind their tellies."

"You'd be surprised Wenn. Englishmen live quiet lives but touching something they care about is like waking a sleeping lion. Anyhow, that public may admire but doesn't necessarily want to be associated with the more radical stuff."

Radical stuff. I liked the sound of that.

"And that would be Weard Hunt" I asked.

"Yes and no," Puck answered. "'Weard' is an old word for protect, defend. So the name suggests a kind of aggressive protection."

"Oh, and then the Wyrde Woods: The protection woods? How strange."

"No, 'Wyrde' with an 'e' at the end is the old word for 'word'. Then there is also Wyrd, without the 'e'."

"The Word Woods. All very weird," I laughed.

"Ask Joy about the Wyrd," Puck said. "The Highway Agency wants as little fuss as possible and this is a hugely controversial project already, what with a motorway being planned right through the Weald. So, we expect, that when things heat up, they'll swoop in and think of just about any reason they can to disable the Weard Hunt, cause that's the group they think will take the sort of direct action that will slow the work and get into the media."

"Why isn't there a camp already?" I asked, thinking of *Fierce Dancing*.

"Because they will try to get the camps evicted as soon as possible. And Aunt Catt, as landowner, is going to press that. Setting up camp now and having it evicted before the work starts gets us nowhere. It's when those chainsaws start tearing into trees that the newspaper and telly start to pay attention and that gets public attention. It can work you know, there are projects which have been stopped because politicians got cold feet."

"Okay," I nodded. "That makes sense. So will the Weard Hunt set up a camp?"

"Yes, they will do what the Highway Agency expects them to do. At some stage that involves setting up a camp."

"But they are a decoy," I guessed.

"Yup," Puck said. "There is another group. You could almost say 'professionals'. Some of them have been playing this game since the Newbury Bypass. They'll build the real camp. One that will take days to evict so we get maximum attention which may or may not swing the tide of public opinion in our favour."

"And you are part of this group?"

"Used to be. Remember, I said I got involved in local politics up north? That was a road protest."

"So that's why you went to Yorkshire?"

Puck nodded. "I am like a liaison between groups."

"But not really a member?" I was intrigued, this was all much more secretive and well-organised than I expected. I thought we'd squat a farmhouse somewhere, wave banners, have a laugh, get into trouble with the law and after that I'd get back to being institutionalised. That was, till Joy had warned me it would be serious business. Puck was confirming this by filling in the details.

"There is a fourth group I am member of now," Puck said. "But very few people know about that. The Highways Agency and, especially Aunt Catt, mustn't find out about them. She may act like Sheere-folk and barely spend time here, but she knows the Wyrde Woods much better than we'd like."

"It's in her blood."

"Yes," Puck nodded. "The Wyrde Woods are in Malheur blood."

"Who is in the fourth group?"

"You will meet them this week," Puck said. "Now, about those bonuses you want to earn…"

He stopped and reached for me, folding his arms around my lower back and I grinned.

§ § § § § §

The walk seemed to take forever and I realised I had never really walked the entire length of the woods before; my trips had always been incursions from the Owlery or some part around the woods or other and then back again. Joy had called those places the Edgelands and I liked the name because it suggested the Wyrde Woods was a centre of sorts. This time, I felt like I was travelling from within and it made me feel like less of an outsider. We passed through Roreford and crossed the Farisee Bridge where I stopped Puck for another kiss. I didn't explain it to him because I was afraid he would think it was silly but I liked the symbolism of kissing at the place where Sir Richard and Foster had last seen Niada. It made me feel that I had become part of the story now rather than a spectator.

We continued on our way and Puck being Puck launched into a cheerful folk ditty.

Bees! Bees! Hark to your bees!
Hide from your neighbours as much as you please,
But all that has happened, to us you must tell,
Or else we will give you no honey to sell!
Marriage, birth or buryin',
News across the seas,
You must tell the Bees.

We entered the edge of the broad stretch of oak woodlands, skirting Willick's cottage and from there walking to the towering Halfhollow Oak. We didn't linger there this time, though my fingers were itching because the oak so clearly invited a climb. We headed straight for the grim Blood Stone instead and then into the birch woods, halfway through which we took a right turn rather than following the path to the Carfax. The birch trees thinned out somewhat as the path dropped into a vale. Puck pointed out a whole line of magnolia trees two thirds up the other slope and said these were the offspring of magnolias planted by Oscar Malheur.

"These are late bloomers," he said. "Few more weeks and all of them will be bright pink and it'll smell like heaven here."

Not long after reaching the top of that hill and walking down again we reached the Edgelands where the Wyrde Woods ended abruptly to be replaced by a coloured patchwork of fields surrounding a small farm house in the distance. I realised this was the agricultural enclave I had seen from the bus on my way to Carfax not long ago.

"Hornsby Farm," Puck pointed at the farmhouse and as we crossed the fields on a public footpath I recalled Ellette Hornsby's bravery in outwitting the Knucker. We were about halfway across the fields when a streak of black and white hurled towards us.

"Brace yourself" Puck grinned, just before he was almost knocked over by Lady who had taken a great big leap towards him. He caught her in his arms and she wagged her tail, licked his face, whined, wriggled herself loose and then assaulted me with her frolicking madness before rushing Puck again. We laughed.

"I guess she's glad to see us," Puck said happily.

Lady barked and kept up her excited greeting rituals for another good ten minutes as we approached the farmhouse.

A man had emerged from the main farmhouse, a long thatched brick building that was sagging with age and surrounded by ramshackle barns and sheds. I could smell manure and heard a cow mooing from behind one of the larger barns.

"How do Puck?" The man said. I looked at him curiously. He was in his forties; heavyset but his broad shoulders suggested quiet strength. He had an amiable open face and greying untidy long hair on top of which was perched a white cowboy hat which looked at odds with his grimy blue overalls and green wellingtons. I realised he was scrutinising me with his sparkling eyes just as I was him and we both grinned in recognition of this.

"Middling, how do Rob?" Puck answered. "Lady give you any trouble?"

"Naun, Lady be a fine dog," The farmer gave Lady a stroke over the head. She looked absurdly happy, tongue lolling out of her mouth and her eyes bright as she looked from one of us to the other.

"I am Wenn," I stuck out my hand.

"Rob Hornsby," He folded a great big hand around mine and for a moment I was afraid he'd crush it but he was surprisingly gentle. "So ye be Joy's lass, I've heard about ye."

"My lass too," Puck said shyly, placing his arm around my shoulder and I was so pleased I could have kissed him there and then. Rob raised an eyebrow and smiled.

"You're all much mistaken," I said cheekily. "I belong to myself. Free woman."

"I am not a number! I am a free man!" Puck laughed.

"Woman," I insisted.

"I will naun be pushed…" Rob began and he and Puck finished together: "…filed, stamped, indexed, briefed, debriefed or numbered!"

"I knew Puck was daft," I said. "But you too Mr. Hornsby?"

"I won't be druv; naun o' Sussex will be druv." Rob said. "Willick be saying ye had spirit lass. Ye'll need it with this scoundrel here. He be quite a handful."

"She'll cope. She's a changeling we reckon." Puck said.

"Lass mus be, no Sheere-folk could have charmed ye bunch o' wodewoses that quick." Rob nodded. "Well, we'll be needing all the help we can get, including Faere Folk. Ye be welcome here Wenn o' the Farisees."

He said that last in a strange formal manner and I smiled.

"Thank you Mr. Hornsby."

"Rob if ye please. Jes a farmer me."

"And an archer I heard," I said.

He brightened instantly, "Ye shoot?"

"She wants to learn," Puck supplied.

"Well, I can spare an hour. I'll get ye kitted out, so I will. I have a 35 pound hickory-boo bi-laminate somewhere, good for starting, and some 26 inch streales, looks about yern draw length, surelye." Rob rattled enthusiastically.

I had no idea what he had just said apart from the fact that he seemed eager to teach me how to shoot a bow and I nodded happily.

"Not today Rob," Puck said regretfully. "It's started. I got a call."

"Where?" Rob's smile vanished instantly.

"Lusty Giants, Pathfinders are out today."

Rob threw a glance at me and looked at Puck questioningly.

"She's alright, she's in."

"Well, they be bound to be starting. Got me Notice to Treat somewhen t'other-day."

"Your land too?" I asked, recalling the Compulsory Purchase law I had read about.

"We'd be standing right in middle o' the middling M33 now if it gwoan ahead," Rob nodded. "Leaving me nought but the old farm and a third o' mine fields."

He pointed along the driveway which ran from the farmyard to the A267 on a southerly course and I saw a clustered group of small grey buildings about halfway along.

"I am sorry," I said, not knowing what else to say. He had sounded pretty bitter about it and it seemed to me that it must be terrible to lose the lands you and your family had worked since the dawn of memory.

"Ye be heading out there?" Rob asked Puck.

"Yeah, we came to get Lady first."

"I'm sorry, but there be work here needs doing, I'd come with ye if there weren't. I can give ye a ride to the Earl's Barrel if ye want."

"That would be swell," Puck nodded.

"Well, the kit be in the house, ye'd better get it."

Puck nodded and walked away while I stood smiling and nodding as Rob enthused about a shooting competition he had attended in a language full of archery terms that was mostly Greek to me. Puck returned with a green satchel and then we bundled into Rob's Land Rover and drove off.

It was weird driving by the north side of Odesby. I could see the tenements of Neverland in the distance, a landscape which I knew as well as Puck knew the Wyrde Woods but which had never seemed so remote. From here they just looked like another bunch of ugly flats and I was glad when we hit the Nickleby road and left them behind.

§ § § § § § §

"Well, well, well," Joan stood by one of the tables in the Earl's Barrel which she had been wiping with a cloth and watched Puck, myself and Lady come through the door. The pub was empty but for her. "Young Puck and Wenn and Lady. On a regular day o' the week, playing truant naun doubt."

"It's half term," I said.

"Puck's been saying that for two years now, schooling be unaccountable different nowadays I reckon."

Puck grinned. "How do Joan?"

"I would be tessy and throw ye youngsters out o' mine establishment but unfortunately I be needing all the custom I can get," Joan winked. "Ye'll be wanting some lemonade surelye."

"Yes please," Puck answered. "Pint of Arundel Trident flavoured lemonade."

"Ye can have half a pint," Joan said, "To ease mine conscience and leave the door to heaven halfway opened at least. But set yernself down in the far corner jes in case. Pump Bottom Farmhouse for ye Wenn, if I recollects?"

I smiled and nodded.

Puck led me deeper into the pub than I had been before, taking me through a veritable maze of nooks and crannies. We sat down in an alcove, half concealed behind a supporting beam.

He took some coins out of his pocket.

"How do you get money?" I asked curiously, "You can't sign on yet."

"I plundered the savings account my father had set up for me before things went awry," Puck admitted. "Hypocritical isn't it? Turn my back on society but leech off it none-the-less."

I shrugged, if it was due to him it seemed no major transgression to me.

"I live very frugally though," Puck added, "Trying to make it last."

Well that I knew, having spent time at his hideout in the woods. Joan showed up with three half pints and sat down with us. She threw a quizzical look at me.

"Wenn knows, she's in," Puck said and I realised that Joan was one of our allies.

"Well, I suppose Goody Whitfield knows what be good," Joan said, "Naun offense Wenn, but I doant knows ye that well."

"None taken," I said quickly.

"Pathfinders," Joan looked at Puck, "Two pairs o' two. Parked at the Lusty Giants Visitor Centre and one pair o' them headed east into the Wyrde Woods."

It occurred to me that it might have been Joan who called Puck this morning.

"Okay," Puck said thoughtfully, taking his phone out. "Can you let the Hunt know? Wenn and I will deal with it today, but from tomorrow onwards we'll need folk out there every day. I'll tell Jukes and Tink."

Joan nodded, and emptied her glass.

"Ye can keep yern coins Puck, drinks be on the house," she said as she stood up.

"Bethanks Joan," Puck said, and then punched in a number on his phone.

"Goodfellow here," he said when someone answered. "Thunderbirds are Go."

He disconnected and looked at me.

"And so it begins," he said. "I am glad you're on my side Wenn."

I smiled, thrilled to bits with all the secrecy. So far, life didn't seem capable of being boring with Puck around.

§ § § § § §

We lay on our bellies in the undergrowth on a low ridge peering at the path below; Arthur's Fort behind us and the Lusty Giants to our left. Two men were down there, wearing bright yellow coats. One carried what looked like a metal rucksack with an aerial attached to it and both were fussing over a tripod on which rested something that looked like a short stubbed telescope.

"Pathfinders?" I whispered to Puck. He nodded.

"Surveyors. That pack the one has got on his back is for satellite positioning, the thing on the tripod is a theodolite and they probably have a prisma reflector somewhere too."

"So they're taking measurements?"

"Very, very precise measurements. They are going to be mapping out the specific route."

"Shouldn't we go down and stop them?"

"Then they'll be back tomorrow with security and we will have only won one day."

Puck opened the satchel he had collected at Rob's farm and took out an Ordance Survey Map and some markers as well as a pair of binoculars.

"Today is going to be dead boring Wenn. Observation only."

I nodded, I was just happy to be in the woods. If Joy and Willick hadn't pulled off their latest stunt it would be a dead boring day at Nowhere Place today. Instead, I was free, the sun was shining and I was in the company of a boy in whose arms I had slept last night. Besides that, we were on a secret covert spying mission. I had never had it so good.

I looked at the map which Puck had carefully unfolded. It was incredibly detailed, showing the contours of the land, paths and many other Wyrde Woods landmarks which I hadn't found on maps elsewhere. I could see the Owlery and Willick's cottage marked, as well as the layout of Roreford and the Tuckersham Church. The Giant's Grove, the Blood Stone and the Shy Maidens were present as well. The abundant patches of green on the map even indicated if the woodlands were coniferous, deciduous or a combination of the two.

"So, tell me." I whispered. "What do we observe?"

Puck was just scribbling the date and day in the top left hand corner of the map with a red marker.

"Different colour tomorrow," he grinned. He handed me the binoculars and pointed down at the path. One of the men was bending over the tripod which stood on a patch of grass just off the path; the other had walked ahead carrying some other sci-fi implement.

"Find the man with the theodolite," Puck said softly.

I looked through the binoculars, they were good, when I found the theodolite bloke I couldn't even get all of him in my sights at once, just half, and the details were incredibly sharp.

"Got him," I told Puck.

"Good, now look around the legs of the tripods. Probably dead centre."

I moved the binoculars by a fraction too much and was suddenly examining the leaves of some shrubs, but I found my target again and checked out the tripod's feet.

"What do you see?" Puck asked.

"There's something sticking out of the ground. Brownish, I think it's some sort of metal."

"Bingo!" Puck said happily and I lowered the binoculars.

Puck let the marker hover over the map. "Do you reckon that's about the spot of the metal rod you saw?"

"Fraction of an inch to the left," I suggested. Puck marked the spot. "What is it?"

"Base station. They also call them triangulation pillars. There's a concrete foundation block beneath it. They usually leave them above ground, but with controversial road works they bury the blocks below the earth. They buried these here about two years ago. There will be one every three hundred feet or so."

"What do they do?"

"The surveyors use them as a base to take measurements from. Without these measurements the constructions chaps with the chainsaws and bulldozers have no idea where to go." He was grinning from ear to ear now, fully in his element.

"So if we can stop them..."

"They'll have to start all over again. So what we do today is mark every base station they measure from so we know where to find them later. The Weard Hunt will join us tomorrow so we can send two teams out and follow both sets of pathfinders about."

I nodded, Puck's glee was contagious and it really sounded like he knew what he was doing. This road protesting business was promising to be interesting and I was glad the Wyrde Woods had committed defenders.

Contrary to Puck's warning I didn't find the day boring. There was a certain monotony to it because the surveyors and our little team kept on repeating the same action but there was a definite thrill too. Every time the Pathfinders had finished their measurements at one base station and moved on to find the next, Puck, Lady and I had to move through the forest without being seen. Lady was under strict 'heel' instructions and behaved impeccably.

I was enjoying myself, I felt like a hunter stalking prey and I sensed that Puck was quietly content. I suppose that after years of preparation it must be something of a relief for him to finally get to the practical execution of the plans. The Hornsby farm satchel included a bottle of water and biscuits so every now and then we treated ourselves to refreshments.

The surveyors stopped their work around fivish and trailed back in the direction of the Lusty Giants. We took the path over Arthur's Fort to get back to Nickleby. It was remarkable how different the area on the other side of the summit was, it had dried out and we had none of the difficulties I had encountered when I had first climbed Arthur's Fort.

Puck entered the Earl's Barrel through a side door as there were a fair number of cars on the car park and we emerged in the pub's kitchen where we could hear the buzz and laughter from the pub itself. We handed over the map to Joan for safekeeping and then caught the bus back to the Owlery.

Joy was curious as to how we had managed and I regaled our adventures in excited detail whilst Puck nodded and looked pleased with himself. To my relief he made no attempt to head back to his hideout and came up the stairs with me at bedtime as if it were the most normal thing in the world.

Perhaps it was, I reflected as I snuggled into his arms, I could get used to this.

22. Catherine Malheur

"I be thinking," Joy announced at breakfast the next morning. "That it might be good for ye, Wenn, to see what we be up against."

I nodded, curious as to what she was going to propose.

"Howsumdever, ye mus gwaon with Rob Hornsby, better if the rest o' us naun be seen there."

I threw a glance at Puck; I had been looking forward to stalking the pathfinders with him again today.

"Why can't you guys go?" I asked, trying not to sound plaintive.

"It's the last appeal to the local council," Puck said. "Most interested parties will be there. FWW, Weard Hunt, Concerned Citizens, landowners and people from the Highway Agency."

"Tis bettermost if that brabagious draggle-tail codger doant see Puck or myself there," Joy added.

"Lady Malheur?" I asked.

"The very one," Puck confirmed. "That detective lot I told you about will be there as well. Taking pictures, observing. I don't think they'll pay much attention to you because they won't know you at all. But we don't want to focus her eyes on the Owlery. Rob is a known opponent on account of his farm, he will be expected to be there."

I nodded, picturing a huge eye made of flames directing a fiery beam over the Wyrde Woods in search of stray hobbits.

"Is there any chance the council will say no?" I asked.

"Even if they do, it'll just cause delay," Puck said. "They will be overruled from above, there's too much at stake now. It's really just one last presentation of all the arguments."

"The council be in the pocket o' that middling minx anyways," Joy added.

"Then why bother?"

"To show we exhausted every possible means outside of civil disobedience," Puck said.

"Civil disobedience," I tasted the words with anticipation. "Okay, I'll go."

I wanted to have a look at Lady Malheur and it would be interesting to see some of the stuff I read about in the newspapers from up close. Puck advised me not to wear my rambling gear, the mainstay of my incredible lack of fashion these days, but put on the blue skull summer dress which he had seen casually tossed into a corner upstairs.

"Don't you like me in my rambling outfit?" I challenged him.

Joy chortled as she watched us. She nodded at Puck: "Yer up to yern lips in moil now lad."

"Sure I do," Puck retained his confidence despite his grandmother's warning. Not for long though.

"So you don't like my summer dress?" I placed my hands on my hips.

Puck looked thoroughly confused for a moment.

"Doant answer, tis a trap." Joy grinned. "Jes tell Wenn why ye silly lad."

"You dear Wenn," he declared solemnly. "In your rambling attire, look like the most fabulous and stunning…eco-terrorist."

"Ah," I said, realisation dawning on me. Puck nodded and then left to replenish the firewood by the hearth.

I looked sheepishly at Joy.

"I was being tessy wasn't I?" I asked timidly. Two days with Puck and I was trying to light the fuse already.

To my surprise Joy burst into laughter.

"Wenn sweetie," she said still chuckling. "There be tessy all-along-o' yern soul-pain and there be tessy all-along-o' feeling sorry for yernself. I does forget to tell ye there be a third kind also."

"What's the third tessy?"

"Tessy all-along-o' being a woman. That one be jes fine, ye're naun to worry about that. Now gwoan upstairs and dight-up."

I went upstairs to change my clothes, relieved that I hadn't screwed up. I was also pleased because Joy had called me a woman. I loved the 'sweetie', 'little one' and whatnot, I really did. But 'woman' was the best of them all, I decided.

I went back downstairs wearing my shoes and dress, feeling light as a feather because the rambling gear I had got used to was heavier - especially because all the pockets were stuffed with gear I might need if I ever got lost again- and not wearing heavy boots made my step lighter.

"A butterfly in mine house," Joy greeted me.

I did a little twirl and was pleased that Puck seemed to be admiring me.

§ § § § § §

When Rob drove into Odesby it was strange that we did not take a left at the High Street to head to Neverland but went straight on to the southern half of Odesby, the much posher side of town.

The Council had hired the auditorium of a posh school , the sort of place where the likes of me were shunned. It was housed in an expansive old monastery; gothic arches and spires lent it an aura of wealthy elegance.

I felt well out of place and I wasn't the only one.

"Place be fancy enow," Rob said, frowning. He had tried to dress smart and was wearing a suit but it looked like it had been bought for a special occasion more than a decade ago when he had been a few sizes smaller. The whole wasn't helped by the tropical pith helmet he wore.

"Take off the helmet Rob," I suggested. "You'll feel less distinct, surelye."

"Folk alikes me, we doant be made for these places Wenn," he confessed. "Naun matter what I wears. They jes sense ye doant belong here."

"Well Rob," I gave him an encouraging grin, "Same as the place where I live. We never get invited for a cup of tea here."

"Well, then ye know how I feel," he nodded.

"Are you going to take that silly helmet off?"

"Naun, I likes mine hats," Rob said defiantly.

"Good," I stuck out my arm, "Escort me thither Master Hornsby and let's show these cretins how proud common folk can be."

It was good that we had walked into the auditorium arm in arm filled with pride for it kept our self-confidence from plunging too deep. The whole place was filled with swanky people engaged in polite conversation. Both Rob and I headed instinctively for the stairs that led to a low gallery at the back of the auditorium and we took place in the corner.

I looked around at all the suits and fancy dresses and felt like I had walked into the lion's den. They all looked so respectable. I noted that the corner on the other side of the gallery was filling up with young people wearing a mixture of rambling gear and alto stuff and guessed that these were members of the Weard Hunt. They looked just as out of place as I felt.

At some signal which must have escaped my notice the Respectables broke up their conversations almost simultaneously to disperse to their seats, like a school of fish all taking a sharp angled turn. When they were seated the threads of conversations that were picked up again were carried out in a low murmur.

This ceased when a hush fell over the auditorium as a small group of people filed in. They were headed by a woman who wore a business-like black skirt that reached up to her knees and a matching black jacket beneath which was a blue blouse; the men who followed her were dressed in well-cut grey and blue suits and carried briefcases and bulging files.

"Lady Malheur," Rob whispered.

"Really?" I had expected an ogre who whiffled and burbled and whose eyes shot flames. Lady Malheur looked to be in her forties and extraordinarily beautiful, with long brown hair and flawless smooth skin. Most of the women I knew of that age lived in Neverland where aging well was a rarity. I half expected Lady Malheur to project arrogance by ignoring everybody but she made frequent stops to greet people and exchange short pleasantries. I could see that those she stopped by felt honoured and were pleased to have been singled out.

"She's crafty," I whispered to Rob, who nodded and then made me giggle by crossing his eyes.

The procession reached the front of the auditorium where a row of seats had remained empty. Before she sat down Lady Malheur turned to regally sweep the audience with her eyes. She spotted Rob, who was kind of hard to miss, and now I saw the arrogance I had expected, for she smirked for a brief moment, a dismissive and slightly triumphant little sneer before she gave Rob an sarcastic wave.

Rob stood up, clicked his heels together and gave a perfect military salute. Lady Malheur's mouth fell open and I burst out in laughter which sounded really loud over the ebb of murmur which had resumed in the hall. Almost everybody turned to stare. Lady Malheur fixed her eyes on me for a moment, disapproving and then dismissive.

She sat down and Rob fell down back on his seat, seemingly not at all embarrassed.

"Nice one Rob," I grinned at him.

"So much for naun drawing attention to ournselves," Rob said as he adjusted his pith helmet.

The meeting started. A number of experts were called upon by the representative of Friends of the Wyrde Woods, an elderly gentleman with medals pinned to his jacket.

"That be David Masters, ex-army," Rob told me.

Masters talked passionately about the Wyrde Woods and their place in the history of Odesby. Not all the experts who had come to plea for the woodlands, migratory birds, otters, pole cats and sizable deer population were as eloquent. Some were frightfully dull and Lady Malheur led the audience in chatting through their testimonies which was annoying because they really had clever things to say about the wildlife habitat, emphasising that the Wyrde Woods were a remarkable place.

The next speaker began to talk of the number of badger setts in the Wyrde Woods and how the badgers were threatened by the motorway.

"BTB!" someone in the audience shouted in a local accent. "BTB ye chuckle-headed puck stool."

"That's right!" someone else voiced loudly. "Never mind baggas! What about ourn cattle?"

"Bovine tuberculosis is a very low risk," the speaker tried to counter. "There is a scare factor at work and..."

He was shouted down by a number of men in the audience whose suits generally looked as ill-fitting as Rob's. They in turn were shouted at from the Weard Hunt corner after which general mayhem broke loose.

Rob looked dead unhappy.

"Some o' mine neighbours," he said. "Farmers alikes me."

"Are the badgers that dangerous?"

I threw a glance at the front where Lady Malheur seemed unperturbed by the uproar; she was talking to some of the suited men around her who had been busy taking notes.

"Tis different on a farm Wenn o' the Farisees," Rob said. He had to speak loud to overcome the tumult. "I doant hold much with them what want to save each and every wild animal. I'll eat wild robbut happily; I reckon it keeps the population down to manageable. If I catch Mus Reynard preying on mine chickens in mine farmyard, it be a dead fox, ye understand? But there be no need to gwoan cull them in the woods."

"So you're against culling?"

"I mostly be middling sad, that good farmers used to be managers o' the countryside. Looked to both theirn farms and the hills and woods. We managed for centuries like that Wenn. Afore the Malheurs came the Wyrde Woods were what they called *Maene Wudu*, it belonged to everybody and no-one. We were all the caretakers of the Wyrde Woods. Now Sheere-folk from Lunnon and thereabouts come to tell us 'do this' and 'don't do that' and they be disagreeing with each other in an unaccountable manner. Howsumdever, I reckon naun o' them know much about farming at all. And some farmers forget as well. Or work lands owned by Catt Malheur."

I nodded, it made sense to me. He was being tessy because people were telling him what to do without having a clue. This was something I could easily relate to; school was like that all the time.

The crowd had relapsed in a sullen silence and the speaker rushed through his notes. It was the turn of Odesby Concerned Citizens to take to the floor next. When they started to explain how the M33 would increase local economic prospects some of the Weard Hunt people started booing, then one shouted "Slavery!" and ushers rushed up the gallery and into the corner to escort the offender out of the hall. Other arguments received similar treatment and the whole flow of the pro-road lobby was broken up. This disruption caused the Respectables to employ a whole repertoire of expressions of disapproval. It was a good thing they seemed to have so many of them, for the continued breach of etiquette caused a great deal of Respectable annoyance. I thought it was hypocritical after they had suavely chatted through the FWW speakers themselves.

The Weard Hunters were the last to present their case. One of the few left -much older than the rest- took to the floor with zeal, presenting the complex network of interests that were involved on the pro-side in a clear and articulate manner which most of the Respectables probably did not expect from someone with a red Mohawk and the chain that dangled from a piercing in his nose to his ear.

"Mad Judd Mack," Rob told me.

Mad Judd Mack started to make allegations with regards to money being sluiced to and fro, pointing out that Lady Malheur owned Odesby Chemicals Ltd. which made sizable donations to political campaigns and as major shareholder stood to gain if Duguth Construction's bid for the road work was successful. This on top of the sale of land in the Wyrde Woods which she ought to protect, not destroy. Rob and I gave him a standing ovation, as did some others.

Somebody thanked all the speakers for coming and then said that everything would be taken into consideration and a decision would be made the next week. I frowned, knowing that work had already begun. Maybe surveying didn't count as such.

I filed out after Rob. "Was that all?"

"Aye, were ye expecting more brawling?"

"Well, yes. Why did you come?"

"To see who weren't clapping for Concerned Citizens. A fair few o' them. Tis encouraging."

"Mister Hornsby," an elegant voice called behind us. We turned and stood face to face with Lady Malheur.

She was surrounded by her lackeys and doting Respectables and looked at Rob with an enigmatic smile. Her eyes shone with barely concealed triumph. She clearly believed she had walked out of the building a victor.

"How do Catherine?" Rob said casually, drawing a sharp frown.

"I noticed you brought a young friend, who might you be?" She gave me a haughty look.

I stared back into those cool calculating eyes. She was even more imposing from up close; she seemed to exude wealth and power which gave her a rock solid confidence I envied. Still, I couldn't believe this was Puck's aunt, how on earth could they be related?

"Mine niece, from Lunnon," Rob explained, using the cover story we had agreed on.

"I'm Carol, you look dead fit in that outfit innit?" I put a little rising pitch into it.

Lady Malheur regarded me coolly, her steel blue eyes traveling up and down before she ignored me and turned to Rob again. "I just wanted to say Mr. Hornsby that I do so regret that I will be losing a neighbour soon. It must be terribly hard for you."

She spoke in a sweet tone laced with poison. I sensed Rob tense up beside me. She had gone straight for the jugular.

"But ye be misagift Catt," he countered. "I be fitting out the old farmhouse for living in. Turning out middling cosy so it is. I'll scratch-along."

A little crowd had gathered around us now. I noted that many just fawned over Lady Malheur, but there were a handful who seemed to be rooting for Rob. David Masters and Mad Judd Mack were among them.

"I realise that financial insight has never been the strength of the Hornsby family," Lady Malheur said with a sweet smile. "Surely a third of your *former* land, right next to a motorway, will not suffice to keep you afloat."

I saw Rob's face stiffen and stepped closer to him, grabbing his hand.

"Oh but Uncle Rob has a business plan innit?" I beamed. "No more farming, but a boot camp. You know, those what got busted for dealing and theft. Give inner city kids a chance to explore the countryside and all. They'll think it's bear sic, and Odesby is close enough for visits, innit? They'll really like this town."

Some of the Respectables around Lady Malheur paled at the thought of it. Lady Malheur didn't look fazed though.

"Shush Carol," Rob admonished me. "I told ye to keep that mum."

"I look forward to seeing your planning permit application for such an endeavour in the Council," Lady Malheur said dismissively. "Good day Mr. Hornsby."

She turned her back on us and immediately engaged in conversation with some of the Respectables behind her. We were clearly dismissed from her presence and walked away.

"Phew," I said.

"Ye can say that again." Rob nodded, adjusting his pith helmet. "That were a nice try o' yern though. But that woman be as cold-blooded as a Knucker."

"She's middling brabagious," I snorted and Rob laughed.

23. An Unforeseen Meeting

We drove to the Earl's Barrel because Rob said saluting toffs was thirsty business. I wholeheartedly agreed and was pleased to be back at the Earl's Barrel with half a pint of cold Pump Bottom Farmhouse in my hand. Rob ordered a pint of Longman's Best Bitter. Rob launched into a funny story about his attempts to try horseback archery with his longbow. Although he had been really keen his horse had been less happy and Rob told me that the side of his barn still had some arrows lodged up real high. I was still laughing when Mad Judd Mack walked in.

"Judd!" Rob greeted him jovially.

"Rob, great performance today," Judd walked over and pulled up a chair.

"Naun as middling as yern speech," Rob conceded. "Judd, this is Wenn o' the Farisees. Joy's grandchild."

Judd shook my hand. I wondered how old he was, his face was drawn with the premature lines of a life lived to the max and he had an unhealthy pallor. His grin was infectious though.

"How do Judd?" Joan came to take his order.

"A whole lot better with a pint of Dark Star Revelation in my hands Joan," Judd winked.

"So what did you think Rob?" Judd turned to the farmer.

"A lot more support than I expected, surelye," Rob nodded.

"That's what I thought too. I saw your run-in with the Minx afterwards."

"Aye," Rob nodded.

"A boot camp! Wicked!" Judd nodded at me approvingly.

Joan brought Judd his pint and he raised his glass.

"Sussex wun't be druv!" He toasted.

"Sussex wun't be druv!" Rob and I raised our glasses.

"Best pub in all of Suth Seaxna Lond this is Wenn," Judd said solemnly as if he was entrusting me with a great secret. "Only local breweries are served here, none of the Sheere-folk imitations of real Seaxna brewskis."

I nodded happily, since finding out where my parents hailed from I had been proud that I came from the place that had the best mud in England.

"Wenn o' the Farisees," Judd studied me closely. "An odd name."

I nearly choked on my cider.

"As if! I hear they call you Mad Judd Mack," I countered.

"Touché kid," Judd shrugged and grinned good heartedly. He ran his hand through his Mohawk. "Judd Neville Mackellow is my proper name. I prefer Mad Judd Mack though."

Mackellow, the name sounded familiar, I had heard it recently but couldn't place it.

"Wendy Alice Twyner," I said. "I prefer Wenn o' the Farisees."

"Twyner?" Judd cocked his head, half a smile on his face. "I thought you looked familiar. You're Nyle and Ashley's girl, aint ye?"

I thought my heart stopped beating for a second. My eyes grew large but Judd didn't notice. Rob did, he looked at me with concern.

"By Oak, Ash and Thorn!" Judd continued happily. "Last time I saw you, you were just a grub, all tiny and squirming. You tried to piss on me, but lacked the apparatus to do so properly."

Judd looked at me appraisingly while my mind was spinning, Judd had clearly known my parents and I was in total flabbergastation.

"By the gods Wenn," Judd nodded approvingly. "You're the same stunner your mum was. I always thought Nyle was a lucky bloke. How is your old man?"

"I…I…" I was stammering, looking for words. Rob reached out for my hand and gave it a gentle squeeze.

"Judd, Wenn has naun memory of hern da," Rob said, his eyes trying to tell Judd to tone down a bit.

Judd looked confused for a moment.

"Of course, I am sorry Wenn, I knew that," his buoyancy was deflated, but only for a moment. "Well, would you like to meet him?"

I stared at him.

"I'm naun sure if tis a good idea?" Rob directed his question at me.

"When?" I asked tensely.

"As soon as I finish me pint," Judd smiled.

§ § § § § §

Judd had a tiny red Mini that looked as weathered as he did. The inside was a rubbish tip and Judd invited me to sweep the candy wrappers and empty beer tins off the front passenger seat and onto the floor. He drove like a madman even though the car started shuddering and rattling whenever it went faster than 20 mph. I would have grinned happily throughout the madcap dash to our destination in Stancaster but I was stunned into near silence, even the usual rush hour in my mind was blanked out by one single thought that kept repeating itself.

I am going to see my dad.

"Look Wenn," Judd explained as he overtook a lorry, swerving the car right in front of it to avoid the van that was rushing towards us on the other lane. "It'll be hard okay. Nyle is not the man he used to be. The last few times I went to visit he didn't say a word."

I nodded.

"But it'll be hard whether you see him today, or another day. No matter how much you've been warned I reckon," Judd shrugged.

"It's okay Judd, I just want to see my father," I answered.

"And he'll be glad to see you, even if he doesn't show it Wenn," Judd said.

I looked out of the window at the houses of a small village we were racing through and blinked back a tear.

"I am not sure about that," I said softly.

"He used to be my best mate Wenn; he loved you to bits, him and Ashley."

"Funny way of showing it then," I could not keep the bitterness out of my voice.

"I understand it must have been hell for you," Judd's face turned grim. "I truly do. But this wasn't their choice. Please believe me."

"What happened?"

"People have a breaking point," Judd sighed, he looked weary all of a sudden. "Some of us just keep on going and going, even if we don't know why. Others break. Your mum broke. Losing Ashley drove your dad to the edge. When you were taken away he became undone."

"You knew about me," I said in an accusing tone which I regretted immediately.

"Mea Culpa," Judd said softly.

"I am sorry," I said.

"No, you're right. I did show up once, Nyle asked me to, he was still somewhat coherent then, you must have been about six, in that place in Brighton?"

I nodded, I remembered the place; I used to wander off whenever I could to sit on the shingle beaches and stare at the sea, or look wistfully at young parents taking their kids for a walk along the promenade. "I don't remember seeing you."

"Looking like I did? They wouldn't let me near you; they must have thought I had rabies or something." Judd laughed bitterly. "Only family were allowed near you. The problem was, Nyle was the only family I knew of and he was in a bad way. I lost track of you after that. I didn't know Joy was related to you, or else I would have asked for her help."

"She isn't."

"Oh?"

"She lied to the people at the care home. To get me out of there and into the Wyrde Woods."

Judd's face transformed to one of wonder. He shook his head chuckling.

"That's one hell of a remarkable woman."

"Yes, she is," I agreed. "Don't tell anyone though. Rob and Puck know."

"I won't. She and Rob are important folk you know," Judd said. "They keep the Old Ways alive for the rest of us."

"Rob too?" I was kind of surprised but then again Rob's roots in the Wyrde Woods went back forever and longer.

"Yeah," Judd smiled. "You might not think so on first sight, but there's a lot more to him. Anglo-Saxon to the core, and well versed in the old lore."

I nodded; I had already concluded Rob had more depth than he liked to show. Just like Joy and Willick. My thoughts turned to my father again though. I stared out of the window, my mind blanked again by that single thought but my body swaying with a wide range of emotions.

I am going to see my dad.

§ § § § § §

Nyle Twyner was in the back, they said at the reception of the institution, a non-descript concrete multi-story building on the outskirts of Stancaster. The receptionist clearly knew Judd because we were waved through without ado. Judd led me through a common room where various adults shuffled around aimlessly like zombies, barely registering us as we passed.

Medication. I thought bitterly. This was one of my possible futures.

The grounds of the institution were a remarkable contrast to the depressing building, a broad and deep lawn with various groupings of coniferous trees breaking up the monotony of the fresh green grass. Judd pointed to far corner of the grounds where I could see a man sitting on a lawn chair by a yew tree, his broad back turned towards us, slovenly unkempt dark hair hanging listlessly over the collar of the shirt he was wearing.

My heart beat in my throat when I told myself that this was my father. Part of me wanted to turn tail and run. I was filled with trepidation.

The man was pale and flabby, his facial features partly concealed by fat and listless dull eyes staring at the tall brick wall that enclosed the grounds.

"Hey there Nyle," Judd said in a surprisingly gentle voice.

"Nyle," the man managed a brief nod but there was no animation.

"It's me, Judd. Good to see you mate."

"Judd," there was a slight movement now, one of Nyle's mouth corners twitched in what might have been an attempt to smile.

Judd gave me an anxious look to see how I was coping with the sight of this near empty husk of a man.

I nodded. My throat felt parched.

"I brought someone to see you Nyle," Judd said softly. He stretched out his hand and I stepped forward hesitantly to take it and face my father.

Nyle slowly lifted his head. When he saw me his eyes lit up for a moment and his face finally showed a sign of life, transformed briefly into a look of wonder. I bit on my lip.

"Ashley?" Nyle asked, staring at me as if he had seen a ghost. "Ash?"

I shook my head, afraid I'd go emo if I tried to speak.

"Nyle, this is Wendy, your daughter," Judd said, speaking loud and slow.

Nyle didn't say anything, just stared at me. Then a single tear rolled down his cheek and he slowly stretched out his hand to me. I walked forward and took his hand in mine, sinking to my knees by his feet.

We just sat there staring at each other. Now and then a tear would roll down his cheek or the corner of his mouth would twitch as if he were trying to smile or speak. My cheeks were wet too and I clung on to his limp clammy hand as if I were drowning.

I don't know how long we sat there. Judd was in no rush, he settled against the yew tree, half turned away from us, and smoked roll-up after roll-up.

I felt strangely calm; I was emotional but content to be here. There was no need for speaking, just holding my father's hand, being near him, was enough for now. I had dreamed of this moment so often and although that had always been in the context of a whirlwind of mutual joy I felt no disappointment. Seeing him I realised he was in no fit state to chase my migration through the myriad locations of the Youth Care system. I hadn't been casually forgotten for any reason at all. Right now just the fact that he was alive and holding my hand seemed miraculous.

After a long time one of the staff came to inform us it was time to leave, Judd scrambled up and I stood up too. My father refused to let go of my hand though, somewhere he found the strength to increase his grip.

"Wendy?" He said in a tone of wonder.

"Yes," I answered, and then hesitantly added: "Dad."

"My faery girl," Nyle shook his head again, as if he were trying to shake off the cobwebs to see into the past. "Please come again?"

He sounded like a little boy when he said that, pleadingly.

"I will Dad," I nodded. "I'll come back to see you."

He nodded gratefully, managing something approaching a smile this time, before his face fell back into a vacant lack of expression.

Judd and I left the member of staff with my father and walked up to the building. I reached out for Judd's hand. I needed the support and if he had been my father's best mate he was practically my uncle. He folded his hand around mine and gave it a comforting squeeze.

"Thank you Judd," I said.

"It was the least I could do," Judd said, embarrassed. "For you and Nyle."

§ § § § § § §

"He called me faery girl," I said wondrously as Judd sped back to Odesby in reckless fashion. The gentleness I had seen in the institution was gone now; he was a bundle of barely restrained energy again.

"Your mam," Judd said. "Her parents were quite old when they got her. Old-fashioned God-fearing Seaxna farmers. They never understood her. Ashley was…different. They, and just about everybody in Nickleby thought she was a Farisee changeling."

I smiled sadly. So it wasn't me, it was her.

"She went mad Wenn," Judd grimaced. "Completely lost it and she fled into the Wyrde Woods."

As I have done.

"She was never found. I like to think she went back to Pook Hall where she belonged," Judd shrugged. "You saw what it did to Nyle. He lived for her, breathed for her, she was his all."

I nodded. Love comes with a sharp-edged cruelty attached to it.

"Can you drop me off at Rob's farm?" I asked Judd. He nodded his agreement and started another death-defying venture onto the opposite lane to pass a double-decker bus, his car's engine roaring as he went to full speed to avoid being squashed like a bug against the front of a large lorry that sped towards us. I began to whoop wildly in encouragement, releasing pressure, and Judd laughed.

24. Heorttreów

It was a long haul from Rob's farm to the Owlery but I liked having the woods to myself and I was beginning to know my way around. I found that Willick's advice to experience them, rather than just see them as passing scenery was becoming easier and easier. I soaked it up: Every twig and leaf, every quiet rustle in the undergrowth and the serenity of the old oaks. All the while I was thinking of Nyle…my father. I thought of my mother as well, she had disappeared into these very woods. The presence of the woods made it easier; this was the first time ever that I thought about my parents without descending into morose gloom. It was kind of ironic because I had discovered that both of them were more or less lost to me in their own way, but just knowing meant I felt much closer. He had called me his faery girl. I decided that Wenn o' the Farisees suited me just fine; I had Faere Folk blood just like Puck. I belonged here. My round ears were just a genetic mutation.

During one magical moment a small deer crossed my path, emerging from a copse of younger oak trees about thirty feet in front of me. I was half concealed by a turn on the broad path I was following and froze instantly. The deer did not notice me and crossed the path ahead of me, a fawn following her with dainty little steps. I waited until they had disappeared, enthralled by the sight, and then continued towards the Owlery.

When I got home Joy made me a Brighton Blue cheese sandwich and added a glass of homemade elderberry cordial. "I doant mind sharing a drop o' stronger stuff with ye, howsumdever, evenings only Wenn. So what did ye think o' it?"

"The pro-argument is only about money."

"Aye, there'll be economic benefits alright, they be right in that. But jes for a few o' them, they'll be spending it quick but the woods be lost forever."

"Yes, we are really taking on the local establishment aren't we?"

"Aye. What does Rob say?"

"That he was pleased to see not everybody agreed with the Malheur lot."

"Good. Did ye see hern Ladyship?"

"Aye, talked to her and all. She got tessy with me."

Joy laughed and insisted on hearing the full details of our encounter. I told her about the verbal clash with Lady Malheur, and then about meeting up with Judd in the Earl's Barrel. How I had discovered that he knew my parents and that he had taken me to see my father. That was the news I had really wanted to share with Joy.

"I saw my dad Joy; I held his hand and he cried."

"And how does ye feel about that?" Joy asked curiously.

"Right now, I feel middling good about it," I said. "Like I finally belong somewhere, surelye."

"Answers be better than jes axing questions all the time," Joy nodded. "Even if the answer aint always the bettermost possibility."

She was right but I knew there'd be plenty of food for thought to digest over the next few days. Except, this time I wasn't afraid it would lead me to the edge.

"Puck said something about a tree," I said, changing the subject to explore something that had been bugging me.

"Most-in-general he'll does that," Joy said fondly.

It struck me that her bond with Puck must have been influenced by the past. She had lost a son, almost as if he had died. Then decades of wearing that burden later, her grandson shows up, it must be a compensation of sorts. I thought of the manner in which Puck had picked her up by the well when she had fallen and wondered up to what extent Joy filled that dreadful hole that had been gauged out of his soul by his mother's death. Maybe I was just projecting, having just added a father and uncle to my rapidly expanding 'fambly'.

"He said he had a bad feeling about it."

"Be that so?" Joy sounded surprised. "Puck were feeling bad about a tree?"

"Nan Malone's bridge, the chestnut there."

"There be more folk who feel like that at Nan Malone's bridge," Joy nodded in recognition. "So I understand."

"I didn't know about Nan Malone when I first met the chestnut."

"When was that?"

"On the first night in the Wyrde Woods. I wasted a lot of time there, because I didn't really know I was lost yet. So I climbed the tree, then fell asleep when I was down again."

"Naun a waste o' time to climb a tree, I does wish I could climb one again." Joy said, and then looked thoughtful for a moment. "And twere dark when ye awoke?"

"Yes, and it's going to sound funny...actually it won't, not to you I think. I was really scared; I'd never been out in the woods at night before. You saw the tenements, near the home, I am not easily frightened there and it is a jungle, especially at night. But in the woods...there was no light. Naun at all."

"Ye were near Nan Malone's tree?"

"I fell asleep with my back against it, and woke up in the same position a lot later, which was strange I guess but I didn't pay much attention to it...all the noises in the dark...the cold...that's what had my attention. And the funny...the thing was, I wasn't scared of the tree. It was the only thing that felt safe, like it was a friend. And that feeling happened another time too. Then I saw it recently after the...with Puck, and he told me about Nan Malone but even then...I practically hugged it. I felt sorry for it."

"So ye be hugging trees now?" Joy asked with amusement. "Feeling sorry for them?"

"Well, yes." I shrugged. "But not any old tree, that one is special."

"Tis time I show ye something Wenn. But ye maun tell anyone, not even Puck. And naun the bees either."

§ § § § § § §

Joy led me into the back garden and then into the orchard. There was a small opening to a path in the low wall at the very back of the orchard which I had not seen before. We followed the path into the woods which consisted mostly of larch trees but gradually these were replaced by slender yew stems. These offered a sharp contrast between their reddish scaly bark and spiky rich green leaves. These colours were enhanced by clusters of yellow wood spurge and the white flowers of star shaped wild garlic and woodruff which spread their sweet scent in the air.

As the trees became older and larger there was too much shade for these flowers to grow and they were replaced by a low shrub with green leafs which looked like small spear blades and the plant bore red berries which complemented the yew berries above.

"That be butcher's broom," Joy pointed at the shrubs, "They does likes it here in the shade of yew trees."

"Are the berries poisonous like yew berries?"

"Naun, butcher's broom be handy for medicine. But yew snottgogs aint poisonous neither, the seeds within are, but naun the flesh o' the snottgog. Yew be giver o' life and bringer o' death in one. Used properly other parts o' yew can be used for charm-stuff as well, howsumdever, ye maun be careless or it kill ye, surelye."

The yew trees began to increase in girth and height, the straight trunks of the younger trees now replaced by gnarled curves and outgrowths. The swirls formed hideous scaly faces, some of them complete with hair and beards which was effected by the vines of a climbing plant which had green-white flowers with long fluffy sepals and climbed high, garlanding the higher branches with silky strands. Many of the yews had lichen cascading down their branches as well.

"Sheere-folk calls it old man's beard or traveller's joy. Most-in-general we calls it tom-bacca," Joy answered when I asked her what the vines were called. "The lichen some folk call devil's guts and others the Norn's weaving. I use that last name."

"Why?"

"Ye've heard of Yggdrasil?"

I shook my head.

"The yew pillars, the Wurreld Tree. It holds entire wurrelds on hern branches and at the roots sit three wise maids, the Norns, a-weaving. Each strand o' silk the Norns weave links one thing with another. Jes like the Norn's weaving on disyer yew trees. We say they weave the Wyrd."

We were now passing into an area where the yews got larger yet, some of them were hollowed out leaving just petrified looking skeletons of the old trunks. These were palisaded by younger trunks that grew out of the old and supported the immense mass of the crowns above.

"Puck told me to ask you about Wyrd. He said it wasn't like our 'weird' or the Weard Hunt."

"Naun, Wyrd be something entirely different, a life force if ye will. Ye said that today ye see connections in Odesby, atween folk standing to make money out o' the motorway?"

I nodded; Judd might as well have taken a paint brush and painted red lines from one to the other.

"Connections alike that, according to the Old Ways, exist everywhere. Atween every living creature: man, Farisees, bees, beast, tree, stream, hill and all."

"Streams and hills are alive?" I raised an eyebrow.

"They has a sprite attached."

"Sprite?"

"**E'enamost** likes a Sheere-folk spirit."

"Like a shim?"

"Naun, yetner a shadow o' life alikes a shim, jes a critter o' sorts attached to a stone, a stream, and a hill amongst others."

"Is Ufmanna a sprite?" I asked.

"Aye, a scrowse sprite who be somewhen tiffy and then skreels. Naun all sprites be like that," Joy said.

"So these Norns decide who to connect with what?"

"Aye, or which threads to cut. Tis linked to yern fate. *Wyrd bið ful aræd.*"

"What does that mean?"

"Fate be unyielding. It means ye cannot avoid it."

I stopped in my tracks when I saw that we were approaching yet another transformation of the yew trees. A long line of massive trunks whose lower boughs had grown so heavy that they had drooped like arched doorways, reaching the ground some six feet away from their parent. They had sprouted new trunks there, already considerable in size. It seemed impossible this had been nature's doing for the boughs all drooped at roughly the same height and for the same distance, creating a tunnel effect.

"This be the bettermost place in all o' the Wyrde Woods," Joy said.

She had come to a halt beside me in front of the yew tunnel's entrance.

"Was it arranged like this?"

"Tis unbeknownst to me, I think so for the tunnel turns at the end there and then loops around in a circle that keeps gwoan innards to the centre."

"Like a maze?"

"That be what we calls it aye, the Whychmaze."

"Can we go in?" I asked eagerly.

Joy nodded in response and we entered the otherworldly tunnel.

"But if fate is unyielding that means we're just puppets on a string, everything is decided for you." I continued, frowning.

"I doant believe that," Joy said. "I believe that the Norns brings ye ta places, people. Howsumdever a web being a web, there be more strands to follow from there. If ye be naun aware o' it, and jes head straight onnards all o' time, then that's yern path. If ye are aware o' it, ye be the one who choses which strand to follow. But once on that path, the Wyrd be unyielding. Ye chose it and mus walk it to the end, or to the next crossing where it meets other strands."

I pictured a tiny me crawling along the strands of a spider web that stretched for hundreds of miles.

"So we have alternate fates?" I asked.

"Aye. Ye think twere a coincidence that ye came to the Owlery?"

I thought about that. One the one hand there was the fact that it seemed so normal to be there, that it seemed so much like a home even though it was bloody strange of course. In that way it seemed like it was something that was meant to happen. On the other hand, it could just be a series of coincidences.

"I could have chosen not to come into the Wyrde Woods that day," I said carefully.

"Could ye really? Does ye make a considered decision or were ye *willed*, mayhap something pushed ye?"

We continued winding down the tunnel which was getting more narrow now and curving earlier as we walked towards the within. I thought about No-tooth and Broken Nose. About losing my way, then the spontaneous urge to lose myself on the boughs and branches of my chestnut tree. The connection I felt to Nan Malone. The new connections I had to folk like Judd which had in turn led me, at long last, to Mum and Dad.

"I doant think twere by-the-bye, I think, one way or another, ye would have come to the Wyrde Woods, the woods are in yern blood lass, by ways of yern mam. She be a changeling ye know, from Pook Hall."

"She told you that?" I asked.

"Naun. But I can tell," Joy said simply and I believed her.

"Twere yern choice to come back or naun Wenn," Joy continued. "Some folk can learn to have power over theirn own fate, if and when they recognise those moments o' choice."

"By being tessy or not." I said quietly.

"Aye, in yern case that plays a part. Doant get me wrong, for if ye stormed out in a state I'd welcome ye back again. But ah doant think ye could does that yernself, I think once ye'd run, thread be cut for ye. And that be yern very own Wyrd being unyielding."

I nodded; I was stubborn and headstrong and would no doubt conclude that being lonely and miserable was the better option.

"With all these threads binding us lass: Yernself, yern mam, myself, Puck, Willick, Lady Malheur and even Ufmanna, what be the central thread? The one that binds us all?"

"The Wyrde Woods," I said immediately, that was easy to answer.

"Aye and here we be, at the very heart o' the Wyrde Woods."

The yew tunnel ended in a large clearing. In the centre stood the biggest yew tree of all. It was hard to estimate the girth of the bole as there were drooping boughs here too, all around the central trunk like cathedral buttresses complete with branches forming pinnacles and bulbous outgrowths taking on the appearance of gargoyles. Some of the bough limbs which rose upwards had interlaced with higher branches and seemed to help support the humongous crown for the main bole was hollowed like a nave, some 15 feet high. At first I disbelieved it but when I blinked and looked again I saw there was an actual tall standing stone upraised within the hollow of the yew.

"Does it have a name?" I asked, thinking about the Halfhollow Oak.

"Heorttreów. It means Heart Tree in the old tongue."

Joy started reciting as we started to circle the tree to see it from all sides.

> *Nine the green daughters o' Mother Erce who point the way.*
> *Eight the legs o' Sleipnir, foal o' giant stallion and mare.*
> *Seven the worlds, for gods, giant, elf, dwarf, man and souls lost.*
> *Six times young Leef and Leefthrasir sky-clad renew life in hollow tree.*
> *Five greybeards, with silver in their hair. Four stags with antlers royal.*
> *Three Norns weaving man's Wyrd. Two ravens flying high and spying low.*
> *One pillar o' yew supports them all, disyer Heorttreów tall.*

"So one of those seven worlds would be where the Faere Folk have their halls?" I was dazzled but thrilled by the strange names which had just passed me by; it reminded me of the elven realms of Middle Earth.

"Aye, Pook Hall be one. Some count nine wurrelds, they adds two wurrelds of elements to it. Howsumdever some also reckon these wurrelds be disappearing one by one and the last wurreld be the wurreld o' the souls lost in death."

> *Nine were Norns' sisters,*
> *Then nine came to be eight,*
> *and the eight seven, and seven six,*
> *and six five, and five four,*
> *and four three, and three two,*

"Lotta counting going on," I said.

"There be magic in telling numbers."

"So what about the one you and Willick talked about at the Owlery?"

"Quiddy?"

"One for sorrow, two for joy," I recalled. "Three for a girl, four for a boy. I overheard that too."

"Five for silver, six for gold," Joy continued. "Seven for a secret, never to be told."

"What does it mean?"

"Tis an old nursery rhyme chavees learn to tell when they sees magpies. The number o' magpies foretells yern what awaits ye in the future."

"But it is older than that?" I guessed. "You two seemed to set a lot of stock by it."

"Too clever by half," Joy declared with a chortle and we finished our circumference of the gargantuan yew tree, ending up by the entrance to the hollow again. "Gwoan, think Wenn, figure out the rest yernself."

"Seven for a secret, never to be told," I said aloud and wandered closer to Heorttreów, resting a hand on the scaly bark of one of the outer trunks and peering inside the hollowed main bole. There was something oddly familiar about the shape of the standing stone concealed within its murky interior, like I had seen it before.

I turned around.

"Seven for a secret never to be told," I smiled broadly.

Joy waited for me to continue.

"This is the seventh Shy Maiden!"

"Aye, tis her." Joy looked pleased with me.

"But Puck said nobody knew where Titania had hidden her!"

"Puck has never been here. Naun o' ourn menfolk have."

"But surely…they're like wodewoses you said, they know every inch of the Wyrde Woods."

"Heorttreów be hard to find, very hard," Joy gave a secretive smile.

"Never? No men ever?" I was astonished.

"Nor menfolk o' the Farisees. That be why we doant tell the bees about Heorttreów."

I was thrilled, who said women couldn't keep secrets?

"You really are a witch, aren't you Joy?"

Joy ignored the question.

"I axed Puck to tell ye about the secret groups."

"He did, the veteran road protest people he knows from Yorkshire. And another, he said I would meet them this week."

"Ye met all but one," Joy nodded. "And naun o' the other groups know about the Waer-Wyrd. They know a few o' ourn folk, howsumdever, naun about the group."

"Waer-Wyrd?"

"Cautious o' speech, careful with words, that be what it means. If them others fail, we be the last line o' defence, the last Guardians o' the Wyrde Woods," she paused and then gave me a pointed look. "There be six o' us now Wenn."

Seven for a secret, never to be told.

"You need seven?"

"This be the moment where threads meet Wenn, along yern path." Joy spoke with the authority she had used at Nowhere Place, "I see yern paths here and now and I will tell ye what they be. Then ye mus make a choice yernself. Knowing what there be to win, knowing what there be to lose. Ye mus think carefully, ye've seen yern da now, and know yern mam is lost in the woods. Tis a risk ye might naun want to run. Both could happen."

After which Joy spoke of secrets of the Wyrde Woods and like Niada and Sir Richard I had to make a difficult decision.

§ § § § § § §

Puck returned late, he said that he had gone through the plans again with Mad Judd Mack at the Earl's Barrel after shadowing the pathfinders. Judd had already told him about my dad and Puck seemed pleased for me, he asked loads of questions and I was glad I could talk about it.

That evening, when we had retired upstairs, I snuggled up to him and laid my head on his shoulder as he wrapped his arm around me. I chose my words carefully, making sure I didn't mention the Whychmaze or Heorttreów.

"Joy told me about the Wyrd today."

"Ah, your initiation into the Waer-Wyrd," Puck said sleepily. "Welcome aboard Elfin."

"Sorry about the word choice, but the Wyrd seems weird. Just the idea that some weavers out there are making all these decisions for us and all."

Puck turned his head to look me in the eyes.

"I like to think you're my fate Elfin," he murmured suavely and I pinched his nose. "Ouch!"

"Do you think it's true, that we're all connected, caught in this massive spider web like?" I asked as he rubbed his nose.

I really needed to know. When Joy spoke of it, especially in a setting like the Whychmaze, it made sense and was believable. But thinking back on it later, I began to doubt again. She also believed she needed magic plants to keep the pixies from coming in the house to pull out the owls' tail feathers. By now it wasn't only Ufmanna who had convinced me there was more to the Wyrde Woods than met the eyes, there had been a few moments when I felt I had brushed the edge of magic. But the way Joy portrayed it the edge I could believe in was but the outer layer of something far larger than my imagination could conjure up.

"Yes I do," Puck spoke without hesitation. "It's an old way of thinking; it used to be all around our ancestors, the Wyrd. We lost some of it; other parts have never really gone away. Many places have had all wonder in them destroyed, but others, like the Wyrde Woods, have magic in them yet. Much of Sussex does in fact."

I recalled my thoughts on kids today who still knew not to accept food or drink from the faeries, even if they had grown up in places like Neverland.

"They've been making a lot of advances in understanding human consciousness," Puck continued. "What happens in the brain, in the mind, it's all connected to intuition, the power of imagination, altered states of consciousness. And all that is connected to how we think, behave and feel, which in turn connects us to the way we interact with others. Even trees, there is a vibration in them that we pick up, subconsciously to be sure, but touching a tree actually causes physical reactions in you Wenn. So that's science backing up the core of the Wyrd concept. It's all about connections, and for some it's possible to influence those connections."

"Joy asked me to make a choice," I said softly, looking at Puck's face. I had been aware of his absence all day like I was missing a part of myself.

Puck looked pained.

"Time might be short Wenn," he admitted hesitantly. "I made my choice before I met you. Aunt Catt wants to destroy the woods, my father is not going to oppose her. But one of the Malheurs should try to protect the Wyrde Woods. It's a duty, an obligation. If that motorway comes here; the magic, it'll be gone. I can't back out of that commitment, no matter how much I'd like to just be with you. Can you...do you understand?"

"I understand," I said softly. "I made my choice too Puck. I wouldn't have met you if it wasn't for the Wyrde Woods. Or Dad. I feel like I owe the woods something. Besides, my mum rests in these woods somewhere I think. It sounded like she deserves that rest."

"*Wyrd bi∂ ful aræd*," Puck nodded. "At least we're travelling down the same path Elfin."

"Yeah well, we'll see how unyielding it is. I reckon the Norns haven't encountered Wenn o' the Farisees yet," I grinned, trying to brighten up some.

"Oh but they have Elfin," Puck smiled. "You've been woven into the woods by the Wyrd Sisters."

"So how I feel about you is Wyrd?"

"No," he said with utter sincerity. "It's perfect."

25. War Plans

"Oehoeh"

The sound was out of place, I was dreaming of that hilltop again, lit by untold bonfires around which people resembling savages were dancing fiercely to the beat of drumming. It had been a dream devoid of noise so far making it all the more surreal: I saw skins stretched over the drums vibrate under the steady impacts of drumsticks in complete silence and tall flames reaching high without a single crackle to be heard. The wild dancers opened their mouths to utter soundless whoops when they welcomed a strange procession of raggedy creatures. The air rushed by me without a whisper as I flew circles over the whole scene, stark naked on an old-fashioned broomstick which I could barely control, veering desperately to the side to avoid the flames from a particularly large bonfire as the broomstick chafed my inner thighs.

"Oehoeh"

I came out of the dream groggily, one part at a time and for a moment the sleeping and waking world mixed: Parts of the hilltop blacked out by patches of darkness in my room while a few corners of that same room seemed to light up with the red glow of bonfires. Then the dancers and drummers dissipated altogether, the fires died down and the bright sparks in the heavens faded one by one until I was all that was left; that and the broomstick. I tried to make sense of the world, and came to three realisations at once: Aethel was hooting her mating call downstairs, the darkness told me it was nowhere near morning yet and the hard length between my thighs wasn't a broomstick but Puck's erect cock, straining against the thin cotton of his boxer shorts.

I lay still as a mouse, apprehensive, wondering for a moment if Puck was trying something before I registered that his steady breathing and the deadweight of the rest of his warm body against my back indicated that he was fast asleep. I shifted my body just a little and felt his thing tremble for a moment, drawing a soft moan from Puck who was undoubtedly having a delectable dream, leaving me to deal with this awkwardness on my own, the selfish git. I suppressed a nervous giggle but made no move to extract myself from his embrace.

"OEHOEH" Aethel was persistent but Joy had been feeling pain after our walk and had taken an infusion so she could sleep through the night, leaving Aethel to her lonely business of calling out her instinctive yearning for a feathered mate who would never show. I was far more fortunate because my mate was right next to me, possessed now by the same bodily instinct that drove Aethel to continue calling in vain and now that I was waking my body too was obeying its biological instinct. I was hot and glowing and my nipples stiffened to attention. I had to admit to myself that it felt pleasant and the fact that Puck was asleep made it less threatening.

Focusing I could place the edge of the bulbous tip, a low ridge that broke the otherwise straight shaft. I was amazed how much heat radiated from it, answered by my own and perceived that the slightest movement would send pleasure spreading through my lower belly.

This was new to me. The others had used theirs as weapons of war; swords to lunge, thrust and parry with and they had been eager to launch straight into battle to hasten the delivery of their wet and sticky coup de main as if I were an enemy to be conquered. I had just been a passive recipient, there had been no longing, not like this.

Puck had tried nothing sexual yet, restricting his hands to my neck, shoulders and back when we kissed and otherwise seemingly happy to just hug and sleep in each other's arms at night. I wondered if he was inexperienced or shy or both, though he certainly didn't kiss like he had no idea what he was doing.

Right now, I thought, would probably be a good time but that was only biological. I knew it was childish and girly, but after my experiences with the selfish assholes I wanted the first time with Puck to be special.

No Wham-Bam-Thank-You-Ma'am this time. Wendy might have suffered through it, but Wenn deserved better.

"Oehoeh," Aethel's next call sounded forlorn.

"Puck," I hissed. "Puck, wake up."

Puck remained in his dream world and I hissed at him again, this time digging my elbow into his side.

"…mweuh…trying to sleep…" came a muffled protest.

"Wake up, I want to talk."

"Now?...middle of night?" He yawned and stretched but suddenly became aware of the state he was in and was instantly wide awake, making wild un-coordinated movements as he pulled away from me in a frenzy, gyrating crazily until he had entirely cocooned himself in the blankets leaving me without any.

"Oi," I giggled. "You're hogging the blankets."

"Oh God, Wenn, I didn't mean to…I didn't realise..." Puck was in a panic.

"Hey, hey, it's okay. You were sleeping, I know."

"Yeah, sleeping." I couldn't see him in the dark, but I was sure he was bright red.

I started unrolling him from the blanket, it was chilly and I wanted warmth again. Puck turned to his side, away from me, and I snuggled against his back.

"Is that what they call morning wood?" I was curious.

"Erm, yeah."

"Every night?"

"I think so."

I thought about this for a moment.

"Must be bloody inconvenient some times."

Puck laughed now, recovering from his embarrassment.

"Yes, that's an understatement actually."

"Puck?"

"Hmm?"

"Do you think about sex?"

He made an odd choking sound.

"Seriously, we should be able to talk about these things you know." I admonished him.

"Yes I do."

"Like all the time?"

"It's a bit of a myth that we think about it non-stop Wenn, but yeah, a lot."

"With me?"

"Yes, of course," Puck was quiet for a while. Just as I thought he had fallen asleep again, he added: "A lot."

"Sooo…Why haven't you made a move? I mean, it's not like we have to wait for parents to be away for a night or something."

"I wanted to wait until you were ready, I figured you'd let me know," Puck said softly.

"Okay."

"No wait, that's not really true Wenn, just the half of it."

"What then?"

He was quiet for a moment again and then spoke awkwardly.

"You'll laugh at me. It's silly."

"I won't laugh, I promise."

"I wanted it to be special," he admitted hesitantly.

I stayed quiet making Puck nervous because he added:

"There, who's a big girl's blouse now?"

I realised that he felt embarrassed in his manliness in this. I raised myself and kissed the side of his forehead.

"It's a good answer Puck. Thank you for being honest. You may go back to sleep now."

I lowered myself again and shifted about to get my snuggle just right.

"Thank you Your Highness," Puck mumbled. I smiled and was happy.

"Oehoeh," Aethel called.

§ § § § § § §

I pulled the arrow back and was a little apprehensive of the bow's upper limb bending backwards towards my face. It was strange how wood, which I tended to perceive as a pretty solid substance, could bend like that. I released the string with the three fingers I had pulled it back with.

The bow snapped back into a more or less straight shape and I saw the arrow fly.

Thwack.

The arrow hit the very edge of the target and I was pleased. At least I hit something this time.

"Good, better," Rob encouraged me, and briefly shifted the bowler hat he was wearing to scratch his head. "Ye got the stance jes right this time."

I nodded. It had taken a while to learn to not keep turning my upper body in the direction of the target, but this time the line of my shoulders had been aligned with the target and the loose felt much smoother.

Thwack. Thwack.

Puck sent two consecutive arrows flying in the bull's-eye. He turned to me and beamed.

"I am not impressed," I growled.

"Puck, stop showing off, tis unaccountable," Rob frowned.

"I wasn't," Puck protested.

"Pull the other one," I said, and blew him a kiss.

"Two things Wenn," Rob handed me another wooden arrow fletched with barred turkey feathers. "Naun, three. When ye draw the streale, ye'll be wanting to pull it to same place every time. A good place be the corner of yern mouth, so when ye feels the tip of yern index finger against it, ye know ye got it right. Yern eyes and hands start learning how to work together for the aim, howsumdever; it'll naun happen if the position of the streale keeps changing."

I nodded. *Index finger. Corner of mouth.*

"Second, try to use yern shoulders when ye draw the bow, bring the shoulder blades together, ye're using yern arm too much. And third, doant release the streale straight away, hold it in place for two, three seconds."

I assumed the correct position and tried to think of everything at once. I managed the index finger thing and I think I used my shoulders more, but I still released the arrow too quickly.

Thwack.

This time the arrow was quivering in the outer ring and I grinned. There was something immensely satisfying about releasing an arrow and watch it hurl itself into a target.

"Very old Wyrde Woods tradition, archery is," Puck said. "The Weald had some of the best archers."

"Aye, with ourn Anglo-Saxon yew bows, the bow of the Gods," Rob nodded.

He turned back to me. "That were better. Now try again."

I did and this time I waited a few seconds before I released. My effort was awarded by a hit right at the edge of the bull's eye. I cheered.

"Excellent," Rob beamed.

"Well done Elfin," Puck said.

I grinned happily, I liked this archery business.

Lady gave a soft warning growl and Puck looked up.

"Here they come," he said.

§ § § § § §

Jukes and Tink, as they introduced themselves, were not at all what I expected from the advance party of Puck's secret road protest group, they didn't look anything at all like the Weard Hunt people I had seen in Odesby. They arrived on bicycles which were nearly invisible underneath all the bags attached to them. They were in their early forties but looked and acted much younger. This was aided by the fact that they were both incredibly fit. They wore those tight cyclists' shorts and singlets so there was little doubt about the fact that they were both annoyingly muscular, slim and perfectly tanned. They looked like some sort of perfect Californian couple and I wasn't the least surprised to hear Jukes speak in a distinct American accent when he opened his mouth. He was right butch; with a square jaw, hazel eyes and a sumptuous mane of brown curls which fell to his shoulders. In contrast to Puck's uneven tufts of facial hair Jukes had a perfectly maintained goatee. Tink had short boyish red hair and alert hazel eyes. Her thin eyebrows formed a perpetual frown. She wasn't American and spoke with a northern accent.

They both greeted Puck affectionately and I could see that my boy was pleased to see them, so decided to make an effort to be friendly, even though their arrival felt a bit intrusive. I realised there were going to be more moments like this in the near future and that Puck would probably be too busy to spend as much time with me as he had been doing. It would be a tessy minefield for me but I was encouraged by the fact that I seemed all grown-up in recognising this beforehand. Maybe I could control it this time.

"Hi, I am Jukes," the tanned god beamed with that exaggerated American mannerism as if meeting me was the highlight of his week. It was actually kind of nice. He had a firm grip when he shook my hand.

"Wenn," I said.

"That's a great name! I'm very pleased to meet you." Jukes smiled showing a perfect set of white teeth and then directed his attention at Rob whilst Tink greeted me somewhat cooler.

Rob was succinctly reserved; I guessed that he shared Willick's aversion to Sheere-folk, something I often forgot because I was neither fowl nor fish myself. Having been born in Brighton made me somewhat of an outlander because the city was seen as a 'Lunnon' enclave by most locals and on top of that I talked funny, as Joan had pointed out. Then again my mother hailed from the Edgelands, which were considered part of the Wyrde Woods. Puck had told me that the Waer-Wyrd knew that Joy had talked to the bees about me and had accepted that as a final say in the matter.

Jukes and Tink wanted to get straight to work rather than have refreshments first and all of us walked down the access road to what Rob had called the old farm. This consisted of a small cottage, a barn and a number of sheds arranged in a square around a courtyard. They were all made from the same rough sand stones I knew from St. Lewinna's, Tuckersham Church and Roreford, though here the buildings were still intact. Rob said that he had spent some time repairing the deteriorated shingle roofs. He added that the last time people had lived there was during the war, when it had been used to shelter a family which had been forced to evacuate from the coast in the face of the threat of a German invasion.

"When I loses the rest o' the farm to the road," he said with fierce determination, "I plan to make my stand here. Be a bit less comfortable but it served mine fambly for hundreds o' years."

I wondered if this was the place where Ellette had baked her pie and prepared her father's cart for her journey to the Devil's Tarn and as I thought about it I could envisage the whole scene in the small courtyard.

"The advantage of it," Puck explained, seemingly eager to impress Jukes and Tink, "Is that these buildings and the surrounding land don't fall under the Compulsory Purchase, so as long as Rob gives us permission, we can't be evicted here."

"Has Puck warned you?" Tink looked at Rob.

"Scores o' Sheere-folk, aye," Rob nodded. "All-along-o' that their plans to save the Wyrde Woods mean they're also fighting for mine farm they be more than welcome."

"It'll really feel like an invasion Rob," Jukes said. "If it starts bothering ya, come talk."

Rob nodded.

"So this is Base Camp?" Jukes asked Puck. "Most awesome dude."

Puck grinned happily and started to explain his plans.

"Barn is big enough for a field kitchen and tables to seat thirty. There's a hayloft that's big enough for about twenty people to sleep. Those two sheds can be converted into bunk houses and serve as sick rooms. That one might make a decent shower room, though the water will be cold. There's an unused field behind the barn where we can make compost toilets."

"There be two small fields as well," Rob said. "For more folk to camp on."

"We'll only do that when it becomes absolutely necessary," Tink said.

"Local authority planning restrictions allow for a maximum of 28 days of camping a year," Jukes explained. "After that you can get into legal trouble Rob."

"Staying in buildings doant be a problem?" Rob wanted to know.

"They might send in a team of Environmental Health officers," Puck said. "They'll check out the latrine arrangements, catering and washing and stuff like that. But Jukes and Tink will make sure they'll have nothing to complain about."

"Ye want to see inside the house?" Rob asked.

We trooped into the small cottage. There was a small bedroom with a double bed in it as well as an ancient wardrobe, an even smaller bedroom with a single bed in it and a much larger room with a hearth, aging kitchen facilities in the corner and a huge oak table as well as some other bits and pieces of furniture.

"I understand that the two o' ye will be moving in now?" Rob asked. "I hope the house'll do. I installed electricity and the taps work. There's an outhouse out back, naun a bath. Naun television or internet. Howsumdever, if ye be needing to get online, yern two are welcome to use mine computer at the house. Puck'll show ye."

"Rob my man," Jukes looked delighted, "We've never had it so good. This is sheer bodacious luxury dude."

Rob looked chuffed.

"It's not bad at all," Tink agreed. "And this will make a fine office too. Internet would be great. We'll only use it for the campaign. Puck, what about the other camps?"

Puck walked to the table and folded out an Ordance Survey Map of the Wyrde Woods. It wasn't the one we had used for surveillance because there were no markings on it.

We all pored over the map. Puck had brought some dice in different colours. He placed a green one on the Hornsby farm.

"This is where we are now, Base Camp." he said. "And there is the Giant's Grove. Those trees…" he paused.

"As grand and tall as a temple," I supplied. "They're middling extraordinary, surelye."

"And the hill they be on is to be levelled for the motorway," Rob added.

"A good focal point for the campaign then," Tink said. "What's the ground like, I can see a lot of contours, are they on a hill?"

"Yes," Puck said. "It's an ideal place I think. The main camp there." He placed a red die at a spot to the west of the Grove. "Then the climbers into the trees and the diggers further below the main camp. Drainage is good, it's all higher than the Taunflow River there. The river has very clean water, no habitation upstream. It just needs to be carried uphill."

Puck marked the other locations with dice.

"And the decoy camp?" Jukes asked.

"Well here," Puck pointed at the rough location of his hideout, "Is too close to the main camp. So I thought at the west bank of the Rore River."

"Why not there?" Tink pointed at Tuckersham Church. "Looks like there is some kind of building there too, be a good place to set up."

"Naun a good idea," Rob hastily said.

"It's a bad place," Puck nodded.

Tink frowned.

"It's an old church, you'd be setting up a camp in a graveyard," I put in my penny's worth.

"Okay, so the Weard Hunt here," Jukes took the last die, a yellow one, and placed it on the west bank of the Rore.

"What's happened so far?" Tink asked.

"Main building activity between Sevenoaks and Royal Tunbridge Wells in Kent," Puck said. "Along the lines of the current road already there. They haven't started in the Weald yet; we already suspected they were going to start right in the middle of the route between Royal Tunbridge Wells and Stancaster, because these are private and not public lands or a nature reserve."

"And the more M33 there is, the stronger the apparent need to link the various elements of it." Tink nodded.

"Well, we were right, Pathfinders started on Monday, along this route." Puck traced the area from the Lusty Giant's Hills to the west bank of the Rore. "One team has been working south-westwards out of the Wyrde Woods, towards Stancaster, the other east towards the Rore River. We expect that they will reach the Rore on Friday."

I looked at him with some pride. It felt like we were some secret special operations task force planning a military raid and Jukes and Tink, who obviously knew what they were on about, treated Puck with respect and agreed with the plans he had made.

"Using base stations?" Tink asked.

"Yes," Puck said. "Wenn and I followed one of the two teams on Monday, and we've had two Weard Hunt teams in place on Tuesday and today. They'll observe tomorrow and Friday we'll have mixed teams. We've marked all the base stations on a surveyor's map."

"Security?" Tink asked.

"Not yet, everyone's been real careful, we haven't been spotted yet."

"Good man," Jukes smiled.

"I be surprised they still be using them base stations," Rob said. "I'd have thought they would have that new-fangled digital mapping with lasers and GPS measurements."

"That's the beauty of it," Puck explained. "GPS doesn't work too well when there is dense tree cover."

"Well plenty o' that still in the Wyrde Woods for as long as we slow them down," Rob said, scratching his head again. The bowler hat suited him better than the pith helmet I thought.

"They'll win in the end," Tink shrugged. "They'll have to use a helicopter with laser scanners combined with GPS. It's not as accurate and bloody expensive, so the constructor and the Highways Agency won't be too pleased. They'll get it done, but with weeks and weeks of delays and a lot of extra cost."

"I'll settle for that," Puck said cheerfully. "I thought Saturday night would be good for a dig, moon is full and should be out."

"Print-moonlight all right," Rob nodded.

Jukes nodded.

"Sounds good to me, can we see this Giant's Grove today?"

§ § § § § §

The Giant's Grove was still impressive. Rob had stayed behind so it was just the four of us and Lady. I wandered through the grove recalling my first visit when the Wyrde Woods had just been a blank on the map. I was amazed how much had changed in such a short period of time. I had come here a refugee and now I had something resembling a family and just as important, I had Puck too. Now and then when I looked at him I just couldn't believe it and felt intense happiness.

I had also been a townie then, I managed to appreciate the beautiful parts of the woods but now that I was beginning to develop a sense for the Wyrde Woods' geography and it's abundance of life my perception of the Wyrde Woods was changing. The familiarity of some of the locations now gave a sense of belonging. I was still a townie of course; my understanding of this new world was only starting to develop. I couldn't help but swagger just a little bit though, as Puck, Lady and I led these newcomers into our woods. By the sound of it they were experienced in surviving in woodlands but still, I suddenly understood the territorial urge to sing or piss against a tree. Not because it was mine but because I belonged to it. I wondered briefly if Puck, with his tendency to fill the woods with song, might not resemble that caffincher we had joked about more than he realised.

"Wheee-oo fink-fink," I said cheerfully.

Puck grinned and gave me a peck on the cheek.

"Oehoeh!" I responded imitating Aethel's permanent surprise.

Puck mewed like Horsa and we both laughed.

Tink looked at us as if we had gone mad but I didn't care.

Jukes and Tink liked the grove. Jukes was the most enthusiastic, a continual source of exclamations expressing his wonder. Tink just kept on saying 'It's perfect' but I suspected she was viewing it from a road protest perspective only because she also kept on adding that the place was media friendly. This reminded me that the Giant's Grove was scheduled for destruction, a prospect which filled me with anger. How could anybody in their right mind take a chainsaw to a place like this?

We walked down to the area which Puck had designated as the main camp.

"Why a main camp away from the trees?" I asked.

"Because we want the Lost Boys in the trees," Tink said. "And in the ground. There's bound to be a whole bunch of people showing up, we need their numbers and enthusiasm but it's better if they kind of stay out of our way unless they know what they're doing."

"Lost Boys?"

"That's what our group is called," Jukes explained.

We walked down the hill to inspect the slopes below the area of the main camp; these were somewhat steeper. Jukes and Tink seemed pleased enough and once again complimented Puck on his selection of the terrain. He was really pleased. I was happy for him and suppressed the soreness I felt at having to share him when I so wanted him to be wholly mine.

"So we heading out to the Pathfinders tomorrow?" Jukes asked.

"Nope," Puck said.

"Why not?" Tink asked.

"I take it you brought your climbing gear?" Puck asked.

"DUH, dude!" Jukes answered.

"Well, then I'd be grateful if you could help me keep a promise I made Wenn. We can head out to Hood's Gorge and do a little climbing."

I was delighted, pleased that he had remembered but Tink frowned.

"We're here for the road Puck," she said.

"The Weard Hunt has got the surveillance under control," Puck shrugged. "Too many people observing just increases the risk of getting noticed. Besides, we now still have the luxury of some free time so you two can get an idea of what you're fighting for here, and quite frankly, I'd like to spend some quality time with Wenn now that I still can."

Tink raised an eyebrow, looking from me to Puck and back.

"Most excellent dude," Jukes enthused. "Come on Tink, when's the last time you had a day off?"

§ § § § § §

"FAAAAAAAAAAAAAAAAAAAAAAAAAAAAAAAAAXXXX!" I screamed as I lost my footing on the minute ledge, a good eighty feet above the ground, and plunged down along the almost vertical rock wall.

"…aaaaaaaaxxxxxx…aaaaaaaaaaaxx," Hood's Gorge echoed back.

The safety rope gave a big jerk on my harness and knocked the breath out of me for a moment and then I just hung there in the air.

"WHEEEEEEEEEEEEEEEEEEEEEEEEEEEEE!!!!!" I shrieked as Jukes and Puck began to slowly lower me back to the ground. I ignored them and spread my arms as I slowly turned in the air, high above the ground with a spectacular view of the rock faces of the gorge. Some of these were relatively smooth like the area Jukes and Tink had picked to climb but elsewhere rugged outcroppings jutted outwards and climbed up to divide into sleek pinnacles, like the ends of claws reaching for the sky. At one end the gorge broadened and I could see for miles; Roreford and the Faery Bridge just beyond the place where the rock walls descended into the woods at a steep angle and way beyond that the grassy dome of Arthur's Fort.

"…eeeeeee…" My echo died.

"GERONIMOOOOOOOOOOO!!!!" I ululated back at the gorge.

"…IMOOO…oooooooooo…oooooooo…"

I was totally pumped up on adrenaline, this was like flying! I tried to sway my body so I could get a little swinging motion into my slow descent through the air.

"Oi, keep still you daft Farisee changeling!" Puck shouted from below.

I looked down and grinned. Jukes was as cool as anything but Puck looked concerned. Tink, who had also been climbing, had reached the top of the cliffs before I had fallen and was looking down at us, arms folded and shaking her head.

I liked Puck's worried look. He cared about me. Somebody genuinely cared about me. Me! Ha.

"OEHOEH, OEHOEH" I imitated Aethel' mating call at Puck in a wanton mood and laughed like a maniac. If Jukes and Tink hadn't been there I would have ripped Puck's trousers right off that skinny bottom of his the moment I got down. In my current state of exhilaration I wanted all of him.

"The trick is to try to reach the top Wenn, not to imitate Spider-man," Jukes called, eyes laughing when my feet touched the ground and Puck rushed to me.

"Wenn, you okay?"

I laughed again and clutched on to Puck, relishing his touch.

"That was FUN! Wenn wants to go again!" I said jubilantly.

"You worried me with all that screaming and hollering," Puck said a bit unhappily.

"I'm cray, you knew that. Now shut up and kiss me," I ordered and he obliged me like a gentleman.

§ § § § § §

"So this area isn't near the planned demolition and construction is it?" Tink enquired when she had got back down and we had settled on the Rore's bank for something Puck called Coager, the usual bread and Cheese –Sussex Slipcote- but this time with a big jug of cider.

"No," Puck shook his head, "One of the arguments from the pro-people though is that the motorway will bring more tourists into the area. There are plans for building a holiday park yonder, just beyond the west edge of the gorge and this place will feel less magical anyway because you'll hear the motorway from here day and night."

"I am amazed the area is not more well-known," Jukes said. "You'd think it would be crawling with ramblers, climbers, bird-watchers and the like."

"The Weald is large, filled with pretty marvellous things which aren't that well-known. Besides, this is private property," Puck explained, looking at me quizzically as I started untying his bootlaces. "Owner doesn't encourage people to come and visit; it's just Malheur Hall and the Lusty Giants in the brochures."

"That's a shame, if it were better known it would raise more public concern," Tink said.

"Well," I said, "get somebody who knows how to use a camera to make a photo portfolio of the Wyrde Woods. Not holiday snaps, proper ones, around sunrise and sunset, or if it's misty. Spread it around on the internet and stuff."

I started to tie the bootlaces of Puck's boots to each other.

"Well I'll be damned," Jukes enthused. "That's a really fine idea; I'll make some calls tomorrow. My pal Corin would do a great job."

"Wenn, what exactly are you doing?" Puck asked me with raised eyebrows.

"Tying your bootlaces together," I explained.

"I can see that Elfin, but why?"

Therapy, I thought. I was trying to contain an irritation I had before it grew into more, like being tessy. I was all for putting up a fight for the Wyrde Woods, but the road protest was all that Jukes and Tink talked about. No matter what subject came up, it was turned to that again. I admired Puck for the way he handled himself with these people, the way this suggested that he could turn thoughts in that clever head of his into action as well. But admiring someone was a rather one-sided activity, I missed the interactivity of having fun together, that had been the eye-opener for me. Surely we could do both? I was directing my energy away from feeling annoyed by making a head start.

"Everybody should do it," I grinned. "That way, when the zombie apocalypse starts, it'd be one hell of a laugh."

Jukes laughed and Puck smiled but Tink just looked at me expressionless.

"So at some point we'll have to bring the Lost Boys in," she ventured, changing the subject away from Puck's green bootlaces.

"We don't want to set up the camps too early," Jukes warned.

"Notices to Treat gone out yet?" Tink asked.

"Yes," I said. "September. But those are the properties beyond the Wyrde Woods, eastwards. So I assume they expect to start here earlier."

Tink looked surprised. Well, I wasn't all stupid, I thought, I could be mature about this stuff too. I turned my attention back to pinching Puck's fingers as he tried to reach for the laces. He'd pull his fingers away and try to sneak them back again, evading my parries. He had got the message and I was pleased as I pinched him again.

"Ouch. It'd be good to have the Lost Boys on standby early," Puck said, his eyes still following the epic duel by his boots. "We're working with the Weard Hunt now, but pretty soon we'll need to separate from them if our plan is to work. Ouch. We know that the construction people are debating the holidays."

Puck upped the stakes and starting pinching my fingers back. "Pros for them are that many people will be away, cons that the press doesn't have much to report on and is more likely to show up. Plus a bunch more anti-road people might show up because they have free time on their hands. Ouch. Besides that, they are hoping to surprise us by releasing the dates that work in the woods is due to begin and then start a few weeks earlier. The surveying work was publicly scheduled to start two weeks from now."

"That's good info you got there dude," Jukes said. "How do you know?"

"We have someone on the inside," Puck said. "That's just between us okay?"

"We?" Jukes grinned. Puck just shrugged.

The insider was news to me and I was just making a note to grill him on this later when Tink resumed.

"When the Lost Boys come, Maimie will be there as well." Tink looked at Puck, and then indicated me with a small move of her head. "Will you be okay with that? She really wants to come and we need her."

Alarm bells went off in my head.

§ § § § § §

"Wenn, come to bed?" Puck asked.

We had got ready for bed and he had already crawled under the covers. I sat at the head of the bed, knees drawn up, lips pursed and staring out of the window.

"Wenn?"

"Who the hell is Maimie?"

"My ex-girlfriend. Are you going to ask me if she was pretty next?"

I was, actually, but jumped to my next question instead.

"Why didn't you tell me about her?"

"Have you had boyfriends?"

"Blissfully few. One tosser and then a bloke who dresses entirely in green and prances around with a longbow in the woods playing Robin Hood."

Puck smiled.

"Was the tosser handsome?" He asked. "Square jaw-line, broad chest? Why didn't you tell me about him?"

"He had a six-pack too. But I didn't tell you about him because he was a tosser."

"Well, I didn't tell you about Maimie because she was a mistake."

We stared at each other for a moment and then laughed.

I crawled into bed. Puck stretched out an arm but I kept a bit of distance. I wasn't ready to surrender yet and lay on my back just outside of his reach.

"Then why did Tink specifically mention that it might be a problem for you if she came?"

"I dunno, complications. Maybe you would try to tie Maimie's shoelaces together?"

"Oh definitely," I answered. "So she was a mistake?"

Puck sighed.

"It was at the road protest. I really liked her and she seemed to like me so we got together for a while."

"What happened?"

"There was a bloke there," Puck stalled for a moment, he sounded despondent. "Socialist-Revolutionary type, which is fine of course. But he was consumed by class warfare and he liked Maimie."

I wanted to make a joke about an epic duel at dawn with drawn pistols, but Puck was clearly finding it painful to tell the story so I kept my mouth shut.

"He started talking around that I was a bored upper-class kid going through a temporary green phase."

There was a dull resignation in his voice now. I turned to face him and laid my hand on his arm.

"Kept repeating that, and also insisting that the upper classes could never really mix properly with working folk. Stupid bugger was middle-class himself, the accent was a dead giveaway but that got overseen. He was convincing when he talked, the sort of chap who seems to know it all and people fall for it."

I thought about Stubbles, I knew the type.

"You could have pointed it out?" I asked.

Puck looked at me with a combination of a smile and sad eyes.

"Then I'd be playing the same game, wouldn't I? I don't like those kind of games. Waste of time and they serve no positive purpose whatsoever. Anyway, the label stuck, the bloke could be convincing as hell and Maimie broke up with me because she decided I wasn't committed to the cause enough."

"And got together with the tonguewagger?"

"Of course."

"And if he shows? Will you tie his shoelaces together?"

Puck shook his head.

"I was angry with him, but in the end I concluded that if Maimie was so easily influenced, I wasn't really that important to her was I? I loved her I think, but I don't think she really loved me. So…it was a mistake."

I nodded. We blew the candles out and then I snuggled up against Puck. I could sleep now.

26. The Night Diggers

Puck and I stayed at the Owlery on Friday. Jukes and Tink had been looking forward to observing the Pathfinders and had tried to talk Puck into coming along when we had walked out of Hood's Gorge. He had said again that too many people increased the risk of being seen and also told them that I was due at school again next week and repeated that he wanted to make the most of our time together this week.

"Tink didn't like it," he said at breakfast. "She expects everybody to give 100% commitment like she does, she's really dedicated."

"Won't that get you into trouble again?" I asked, thinking back of our conversation the previous night.

"I am not a member of the Lost Boys anymore," he shrugged. "It's different now. Besides, I have you and grandma to be committed to as well."

"Well, no commitment issues, that's a relief," I said.

Joy laughed.

"Ye can both gwoan and be useful for the protest I doant mind."

"Don't be ridiculous Gammer." Puck shook his head. "You're hurting today, I can tell. And you didn't casually mention the chores that really need doing for no particular reason last night. You can use a hand today."

Joy and I exchanged a glance. I think we were both secretly pleased. Joy because she would not have to force herself and make a bad day worse, and I because I liked the prospect of a day at the Owlery with just the three of us. And a dog, four owls and a whole bunch of chickens and mice of course.

"This is what happens when ye allow a man in the house Wenn," Joy berated me. "He starts telling the both o' us what to do."

"Giving orders like a Sheere-folk Field Marshal," I nodded. "Can it be trained out of them?"

"I be afeared naun, tis easier to potty-train an owl than knock sense into a man's head."

Puck smiled, he looked really happy.

We spent the whole of the morning and the early afternoon working in and around the Owlery, cleaning the owl boxes, weeding in the garden and adding compost around a number of plants which Joy said needed some feeding as well as drawing water from the well to water the plants.

After we had done we went to the grassy expanse out front and I sat on the ground with Lady next to me and watched Joy and Puck fly the owls. These were brought out one at a time and attached to a line. Both Joy and Puck wore sturdy leather gloves and fed the owls a bit of chick each time they flew some twenty feet from one glove to the other.

Horsa was the first and seemed unsure at first but once he spread his long rounded wings and took to the air with rapid wing beats he screeched a protest when he had to stop. The scritch owls couldn't wait to start, both Bran and Bronwen eagerly flapping their wings as soon as they were out of the front door and they flew with apparent relish. Watching them sail gracefully through the air with the black eyes in their pale ghostly faces fixed on their target was incredible. Even more so when, after Bran had been brought back inside and it was Bronwen's turn, I stood next to Joy wearing the glove and the scritch owl landed on my hand a couple of times. Aethel had to be coaxed, it seemed she didn't know what was expected of her and Joy and Puck stood much closer together, trying to entice Aethel with the bits of chick which they tapped against their gloves. When she did fly it was unsteady and she often got the landing wrong, coming in too low.

"Tis early days yet," Joy said with some regret. "Tis a shame, to see a long-eared owl in flight be impressing, they be lamentable nimble in the air."

Puck went into the woods with Lady, his longbow and quiver of arrows while Joy fussed over Aethel some more and I went upstairs to find my hoard of tampons for I had started to feel dreaded familiar cramps in my abdomen.

When Puck came back Joy and I were in the back garden where Joy was selecting vegetables and herbs for dinner. Puck carried two wild rabbits in his hands as well as his bow.

"Better not tell Jukes and Tink about this," he said as he unstrung his longbow. "They'd think it was cruel."

"Poppy-cock," Joy grumbled. "We eat them or they eat mine vegetable garden and we eat naun. Will ye paunch the robbuts for me Puck?"

Puck nodded and Joy went inside. I watched with a combination of fascination and revulsion as he sat down on a broad tree stump, placed the first rabbit's head between his knees with its stomach facing outwards and tail facing downwards, after which he folded out a pen knife and made an incision in the stomach and started to carefully pull shiny coils out of the stomach cavity. The smell was revolting.

"I always thought meat grew in supermarkets," I joked, feeling a bit queasy but unable to take my eyes off Puck's handiwork.

"Wrapped in plastic and all. Welcome to the countryside." He paused and gave me a concerned look. "You don't have to watch Wenn, the first time I saw Joy paunch a rabbit I nearly passed out and then threw up."

I nodded, mostly hearing a challenge, something I could surpass Puck in.

"I want to watch," I said stubbornly. Puck shrugged and laid the rabbit on a chopping board made from a broad wedge of tree trunk and swiftly sliced off the paws. He then inserted his hands into the cut he had made earlier and started pulling the rabbit's pink and glutinous body out of its furry coat.

"I think I'll go inside," I said quickly. Puck grinned without taking his eyes off what he was doing.

"Feeling a mite squimbly?" Joy asked when I entered the kitchen.

Another of those wonderful words I had never encountered before but was a perfect description none-the-less.

"Very squimbly," I agreed. "But it's not the rabbits."

"Oh?" Joy looked up at me.

"It's that time of the month," I explained and Joy nodded her understanding.

"Ye have bad ones?"

I nodded.

"Well naun nausea I reckon, or Puck'd be picking ye off the ground already, what with them robbuts. Is it a heavy flow?"

I shook my head.

"Very little as usual and bad cramps."

Joy scrutinised me.

"Always that bad?" She asked.

I nodded.

"Ye speak to yern doctor about that?"

"The G.P. who does Nowhere Place is kind of old-fashioned I think, he says that it's mostly between my ears in an attempt to get out of school."

Joy snorted and walked to the shelves near the sink to start rummaging about with jars and tins.

"I'll make ye something to increase the flow," she said. "Motherwort, calendula and ginger. And then I'll put a big pot on Rayburn with a motherwort, chamomile and sweet woodruff infusion. That'll fix yern cramps. Chamomile be good too, but alikes the woodruff also better for the taste, motherwort be mighty bitter."

"Thanks," I said.

The motherwort was bitter as Joy warned but I sat at the kitchen table and made myself finish her concoctions, willing to try just about everything not to be bending over with cramps for the remainder of the weekend.

Puck walked in with what was left of the two rabbits which he laid on the counter next to the sink. He spotted the kettle.

"Tea, lovely!" He exclaimed. Joy and I giggled as he poured himself a mug.

"Well that's about it for today," Puck said, turning around with the mug in his hand. "And I smell pretty rank now. Do you want to come down to the stream Wenn?"

I realised he was asking if I wanted to come for a wash. His timing was well off. Had he asked me yesterday after my epic flight through Hood's Gorge I would have dived down the Roreford Falls with him stark naked, singing "Country Roads" and juggling Medlar fruits all the way. Right now I was plugged and feeling bloated, not the kind of state to be wanting to take your clothes off in front of a boy.

"I'll go later," I said.

There was a flash of disappointment on his face.

"I'm having my period," I clarified.

"Oh, I see." The boy who had just been disassembling two rabbits with his bare hands without flinching now visibly paled. "Never mind then."

Joy and I exchanged a conspiratorial sisterly glance.

"It's made him feel squimbly," I quipped.

"Aye, wind shaken grummut be ampery all o' a suddent, e'enamost swymy."

"It's a good thing I didn't understand a word of that Grandma," Puck smiled. "I will happily stay ignorant of this unholy alliance you two seem to be concocting."

He took a sip from his mug and then pulled a face. Joy and I laughed heartily.

§ § § § § §

The motherwort did its job well and by the time Willick drove his Land Rover up the lane I was feeling a whole lot better. Willick walked into the kitchen and inhaled the smell of the rabbit stew that I had helped Joy prepare with pleasure on his face.

"Yer timing, as tis most-in-general Will, be driven by yern appetite," Joy chuckled. "Will ye join us for a meal?"

"I've already et," Willick shook his head. Joy ignored this and asked me to set the table for four and Willick had himself a big helping of the delicious stew.

"Ye still want to see baggas?" Willick asked me when we had finished eating. "All along of tomorrow being digging work?"

"I'd love to!"

"Can I come too?" Puck asked.

"If ye leave Lady here. I know ye've trained her well but Ole Brock'll sooner put up a fight with a dog round."

"Lady can stay with me, naun problem," Joy said and it was settled.

§ § § § § §

We walked in a south-westerly direction through a dark pine forest till we came to Willikin's Drove. This was much less deep and broad than Hood's Gorge and only occasionally walled by jutting rock faces. We took a narrow path that zigzagged down into Willikin's Drove and crossed the stream at its bottom by hopping from one rounded boulder to another to keep our feet dry.

"Watching a badger sett is really magical Wenn," Puck said dreamily as we climbed back up the other side of Willikin's Drove into an area where ash and beech trees were broadly spread.

"Ole Brock be the most ancient Briton o' English beasts," Willick nodded. *"Hals is min hwit, heafod fealo, sidan swa some. Swift iceom on fethe, beodowaepen bere."*

"Part of a Saxon riddle," Puck explained. "My neck is white, my head is tawny and so are my sides. I am swift in my stride. I bear weapons of battle."

"Weapons of battle?" I asked.

"Aye," Willick grinned. "Ole Brock have impressive claws. Baggas can be fearsome if cornered. They will try to intimidate critters many times theirn size to protect what be theirn."

"Like us," I decided and both Willick and Puck nodded in understanding of my reference to the M33.

"Will they attack us?" I asked thinking of those claws.

"Naun, howsumdever, them'll be unnecessarily afeared if they detect us." Willick stopped. "We be near now."

Willick lifted his head and tilted it to the right and then to the left, sticking a finger in his mouth and then into the air.

"Wind," Puck saw my bemusement. "Badgers have an acute sense of smell, we need to approach the sett downwind from them or they won't come out at all."

"And a certain giggle-some lass gwoan be lamentable quiet," Willick's eyes laughed at me as he spoke. "For a long time too, we'll need to be patient, tmight be a good hour or two afore they pokes their noses out."

I nodded.

Willick made a decision and led us in a wide circle around a low hillock. He pressed his fingers against his lips and Puck and I nodded. I felt the same thrill which I had enjoyed from the stealth with which we had shadowed the Pathfinders earlier in the week as I followed Willick up a narrow path. He walked slowly, placing his feet so that he didn't step on anything that would advertise our approach. At one point he stopped and pointed at the ground right next to the path. There was a small hole there, around six inches in diameter and it was filled with poo. We snuck on for another minute or so when Willick stepped off the path and sank to his haunches behind some low undergrowth and indicated that we should follow his example. Puck and I both kneeled down next to him.

About fifteen feet in front of us were several mounds of freshly dug earth and these were surrounded by various holes in the ground, a great many centred around the piles of earth but some in a wide circumference around that. Most of the ground immediately around the sett was trampled into a monotonous brown and there was a strong musky fragrance in the air. The only activity that could be noted was the bright bird song in the foliage above us and we waited for a long time. I didn't mind, Puck had reached for my hand and our fingers were entwined and we kept on gently squeezing them or stroking bits of each other's hands. I could have sat there for hours in the woodland surrounding, silently enjoying the game of lovemaking that our hands were playing but as the sun started setting and twilight set in there was a movement by one of the larger holes.

At first it was barely visible, just a black nose with nostrils that opened and shut, then a slender snout emerged, followed by the rest of the head that was white except for two black bars, wider behind the ears and narrowing down to sharp points well down its snout. When the badger clambered out of the hole the rest of its body looked oddly out of place with the lithe black and white head. It was bulky and covered in grey shaggy fur. The badger looked like it had really short legs, but as it scuttled away from the hole it raised itself on its paws twice and I saw that it was much taller when it chose to be. The badger started feeding and was followed by another two of the creatures before four cubs emerged from the hole. They were about a third of the size of the adults and had the inherent cuteness of young animals that was endearing. For a while the whole clan busied themselves feeding but when the cubs had had their fill they became playful, running circles around the patient adults and occasionally rushing them. Before long the cubs rediscovered each other and twirled around in circles before engaging in mock fights.

I was amazed by the amount of noise the four cubs produced while they played out their mock battles: Chittering, chirping, clucking, cooing, squeaking, wailing, growling, snarling, yelping, barking and snorting in quick succession as they dodged, pounced, jumped, ran, wrestled and submitted. It was absolutely captivating and we sat there as long as the twilight lasted. Just as dusk was setting in Willick signalled that it was time to go and we went back to the Owlery in silence, still enraptured by Ole Brock and his family.

§ § § § § § §

I took my time in parting from Joy. It was late on Saturday afternoon and I had packed my things with a sinking heart for the end of midterm was getting ever closer. The plan was that Puck and I would go to Rob's farm after the planned sabotage mission this night and that Willick would pick me up Sunday evening and bring me back to Nowhere Place.

"I'd take ye in Wenn," Joy said after a long hug. "Permanently like. But I doant think it can be done. They'll dig much deeper in those records o' theirs. What there be now, tis good for weekends and holidays. If we takes it any further, we risk losing it all."

I nodded. She had lifted the veil of my deepest desire alright and none of the hundred arguments I could think of could measure up to Joy's accurate assessment of reality.

"Tis gwoan be hard for ye lass, to be back there after a week in the woods," Joy continued shrewdly.

I just nodded; it was a fear that had been preying on my mind. Readjusting to Nowhere Place would be a tough nut to crack.

"Remember what be at stake," Joy concluded. "Naun jes ourn Puck and the Owlery, but all secrets of the Wyrde Woods. Tis bettermost ye see it as a quest, a middling challenge. If ye mus fight, pick yern battles wisely."

"I'll do it," I said, though without full conviction.

"Twill be summer soon," Joy promised and I nodded again but it seemed far away. "Ye remember now, at that place, try naun to be…"

"Tessy," I answered.

"Ye been doing middling well Wenn," Joy said with pride.

We watched Puck say goodbye to Lady who was to stay with Joy for the night.

"It's bloody hard," I complained.

She laughed and gave me a last hug and then it was time to go. Time to go to war.

§ § § § § §

Willick came to collect us in his Land Rover. He had a small open goods trailer attached to it filled with bulging jute sacks and a pile of tools.

There were some paths in the Wyrde Woods which were just about wide enough to accommodate a vehicle. Puck explained that most of these were the old roads between Nickleby, Wolfden, Roreford, Tuckersham Church and Malheur Hall and were kept open as fire lanes. It was on these dirt roads that Willick drove us down to the ford which linked the dirt road between Tuckersham Church and the Lusty Giants' Hills. I threw an anxious glance at the top of the squat tower of the Tuckersham Church. It was just visible and to my relief we would come no closer to it that night.

Rob arrived ten minutes after we did, just around sunset; his Land Rover was also equipped with a trailer. Rob stepped out first; he was wearing his overalls and a broad brimmed leather hat that was in some sort of brown reptilian skin pattern. He looked ready for a walkabout in the Ozzie Outback, I liked it, it was pretty piff.

Jukes and Tink emerged next and the two newcomers were introduced to Willick, who immediately resorted to his grumpier self upon meeting the Sheere-folk.

"Any chance of visitors?" Jukes asked Puck.

"Very slight," Puck answered. "As far as we know they haven't spotted our surveillance so the constructor isn't worried yet. The information we have says that they expect trouble to be initiated by the major tree felling."

"Locals?" Tink asked.

"The only local who sometimes heads out in the woods at night, except for us, is the Malheur Hall groundskeeper, Fluttergrub."

"Fluttergrub doant be out in the woods tonight," Willick said somewhat grimly.

"Sure?" Jukes asked. I saw Willick react coolly to that.

"If Willick says so, it be the truth," Rob said curtly.

"Good man," Jukes beamed at Willick. "I won't ask you how you fixed that."

"I'll tell ye," Willick was somewhat pacified. "Tis something o' everything, and everything o' something, surelye."

We got to the Land Rovers and retrieved claw hammers, spades and crowbars from the trailers.

"Last chance to leave," Puck pronounced. "This will count as criminal damage."

"Les get started," Rob swung a spade over his shoulder and Puck used the surveillance map to lead us to the first base station. I experienced a small thrill; this was definitely a step up from stealing tampons from the supermarket.

"Three here," Puck said. "Two to dig, the third to keep an eye out and change places now and then. We'll dig out eight, and then start shifting them."

Rob, Jukes and Tink stayed behind and Puck, Willick and I went to the next base station where Willick and Puck started digging. It was hard going; each base was about four feet high and two square feet at the bottom, inclining inwards slightly at the top.

Willick said we were lucky they had only been buried two years ago because that meant the bigger roots had been removed back then, otherwise it would have been sheer hell to hack four feet down into the forest floor. Both man and boy were soon covered in sweat and I insisted on taking my turn with the spade, pleased that they didn't try to convince me otherwise. I wanted to play an equal part in this mission even though digging in dry compact earth around a concrete block was far harder and more intensive than shifting the compost heaps at the Owlery had been. We rotated when one of us started striking the concrete too much, a sure sign that concentration was being affected by the backbreaking work. I was glad I had filled my thermos with Joy's motherwort infusion and drank from it sparingly, hoping it would see me through the night because the cramps had only been minor so far.

When the first eight base stations had been uncovered Rob and Willick fetched the Land Rovers. The crowbars were used to lever the concrete blocks out of the holes and then Jukes and Rob, the strongest amongst us, lifted them into the now empty trailer behind Rob's Land Rover. In the meantime the rest of us got sandbags from the other trailer and filled in two thirds of the hole we made, covering the last third with the earth we had dug up. We then stamped down the earth and threw bracken, twigs and leaves from other bags in the trailer over the ground to disguise the former location of the base station as well as we could.

When we had done this eight times we all piled into Rob's vehicle and drove slowly through the woods towards the Falls, using only the fog lamps to light up the dirt road. The road passed close to the top of the Falls and here Jukes and Rob manhandled the liberated base stations over the edge into the lake below where they disappeared with a big splash. Willick had concealed piles of sand and bracken bags in a nearby clump of trees and we loaded some of these onto the trailer to replenish the stuff we had already used. Then we drove back.

Driving up and down was pleasant and we all went along because it gave us some rest from the digging, there was no way any of us, barring Jukes and Rob maybe, could have kept at that non-stop. When we got back we had a break with a drink and something to eat and then repeated the whole process over again.

"What about tire tracks?" I asked during our second such break, the Land Rovers were bound to leave tracks on the dirt roads we were traversing that night.

"Only on disyer stretch o' the road. Ground on road to the Falls be too hard. Both Willick and myself have a replacement set o' four tires each, for the trailers too," Rob answered and bit into another cold chicken leg.

"Change them first thing tomorrow morning," Willick nodded.

I thought of the piles of sandbags and bracken, the tools and the new tires and was impressed by the level of organisation. They must have been planning this for some time.

"Not brand new ones, surely?" Tink asked. "That would be suspicious."

"Naun, they aint brand new," Rob said. "We're naun middling chuckle-headed."

I lost track of the amount of times we drove up and down to the falls. Each time I picked up a spade it seemed to have got heavier and I was aching badly and my shifts became shorter, as did those of Puck and Willick. I was determined to prove my usefulness though and managed to continue driven by will-power alone.

At long last the eastern sky began to grow brighter. We were within easy distance of the Lusty Giants and it was decided to stop. Though the chance was small, we could not rule out the possibility that some fanatical jogger or rambler would visit the hills just after sunrise and Puck estimated that we had removed some 80% of the base stations between the Lusty Giants and the Rore, more than enough.

We drove back to the Falls for the last time and watched our last captured base station plunge into the water with quiet satisfaction.

"I reckon someone'll be in for a surprise somewhen Monday morning." Rob grinned wearily.

"Yeah man, bodacious," Jukes added. "It'll take them a day to figure out what the heck happened, and much longer to mark and recalculate. We've won a good few weeks here."

"Yes," Puck said. "But they'll also know somebody is actively sabotaging them now. *Alea iacta est.* There's no way back now."

We contemplated that for a sober moment and then it was time to go. Willick drove home alone over the dirt road that led to the Falls; Rob took the rest of us to his farm by way of Nickleby. It was light by the time we arrived and for a while the farmhouse was bustling with activity, people preparing a big breakfast with tea, toast, bacon and sausages and all of us taking turns having a hot shower in the bathroom. After breakfast Puck and I crawled into a commandeered bed together and slept like logs.

27. Five for Silver

Being back at Nowhere Place was a struggle indeed. It was hard to concentrate; my heart and mind were in the woods continuously. One benefit of my mental absence in Nowhere Place was that most of the daily drama and new policies devised by Stubbles and his lackeys passed me by in a haze. I sat through a session with Stubbles and Hairy Mare offering lacklustre co-operation. I had nothing to gain from fighting here anymore; the battles that mattered would be taking place north of Odesby, not in the consultation room. Stubbles made the occasional attempt to bait me, talking of Calcott again, offering his opinion that Joy was a loony-tune and such, but I did not rise to the occasion. I set no stock by his opinions. He was just a douchebag. Recalling what Joy had told me about Mary Hare's past I flustered the shrink by giving her a genuine smile when I left.

That first weekend I got a day pass on the Saturday and met up with Puck on Arthur's Fort. Puck was weary and I felt emotionally drained. Lady seemed sensitive to our mood and lay down with a sigh, skipping her usual exuberant greetings. We barely spoke at all for the first hour or so. I just wanted Puck to hold me. I had missed him so much: The optimistic cheer in his voice, the lively beacons of his green eyes, his smell and his touch.

Having been somewhat comforted at last I sat up and peered at the Lusty Giants. The view had changed. Puck told me that Monday had been pretty much hilarious as the surveyors had turned up and headed out into the woods only to spend much time walking around in confusion. Then the car park by the Lusty Giant's Hills had filled as Duguth Construction sent representatives and the police had arrived to investigate. On Wednesday Duguth had shown up in force; a convoy of lorries had spilled out workers who proceeded to cut down a swathe of trees around the car park and then erect chain link fencing over an area of half a square mile. The next day two bulldozers had shown up to level the earth where the trees had been felled and the workers started erecting porta cabins and storage sheds. All day long lorries had driven into the compound filled with supplies and that evening the compound had been manned by security guards who patrolled the fences with Alsatians. The fences were lit up by the security lights installed at regular intervals. By Friday afternoon the compound had been more or less completed and from our viewpoint on Arthur's Fort the whole formed an ugly grey and brown blot amidst the greenery that surrounded it.

"We caused that," I murmured, leaning my head on Puck's shoulder.

"We caused them to build that weeks before they planned to. Which means a significant increase in cost for the company. It was a blow well struck."

"What'll happen next?"

"We expect that the surveyors will start work again on Monday, this time accompanied by security guards and to judge by all the extra fencing they brought in, they'll probably fence in every square foot of land covered by the surveyors now. It will slow everything down a lot."

"So no more digging up base stations?"

"Nope, plenty of other stuff though. Can you come out next weekend?"

"Yes, Terry is on duty, I can stay out late. I was hoping to go Joy."

"Excellent, come to Rob's instead, in the morning, as early as you can. We'll head out to Joy's after."

We walked down the slopes of Arthur's Fort and headed east to the Water Meadows where we had Coager. Inevitably the fun drifted back in and the afternoon was lighter in mood. We talked and joked till Puck walked me to the bridges at the edge of Odesby.

"Home leave weekend soon," Puck tried to encourage me as we parted. I nodded, but it was another two weeks and it was hard to settle for fleeting moments when we seemed to have had it all the week before.

§ § § § § § §

On Sunday I had a good think. I remembered what Joy had said about feeling sorry for myself and forced myself to change tack. I could have wallowed in misery during all those weeks in Nowhere Place and assume that I'd miraculously come to life on the occasions I was granted my freedom in the Wyrde Woods, but I knew myself well enough to know that I couldn't just snap out of a down. I'd take my morose negatons with me and become tessy sooner or later. I realised that being a member of the Waer-Wyrd meant that I couldn't just go about making unreasonable emotional demands on Puck and Joy and the rest. There were seven weeks to go before the summer holiday with only two home leave weekends in them so I decided to accept that Nowhere Place needed to be an active part of my life, just as much as the Wyrde Woods had become. I made an effort. I tried to hook up with Sharon again and we had some laughs but most of her time was still devoted to shagging Thomas.

I ended up spending a lot of time with Biggs and Jasmin instead. It was actually uplifting to be with them. The two of them were an item now and radiated a quiet happiness that was pleasant to be around. It turned out Jasmin had a big thing for board games which I had previously always dismissed as 'bored' games but the games turned out to be good fun, they required enough thought to distract me from longing to be in the company of Puck and Joy. We spent every evening of that week playing games in Jasmin's room. Jasmin was delighted; she admitted that she had previously played the games on her own.

Getting to know Jasmin better was nice too. She wasn't half as vacant in the privacy of her room as she made out to be, though she still existed in something of a world of her own and would sometimes say the strangest and vaguest things. What I liked especially was that she, in contrast to Sharon or Biggs, was genuinely interested in my experiences in the Wyrde Woods. I had to choose my words carefully, emitting a great deal of detail, but she loved the things I did tell her about; especially the animals. She asked me to tell her about Joy's owls and the visit to the badger sett again and again and I found that being able to talk about the Wyrde Woods made exile easier.

Recalling Biggs' desperate and pathetic attempts to get into my knickers I was kind of worried about what pressure he was putting on her, she was only fourteen after all and much younger in other ways. I was relieved when she shyly admitted that nothing had happened yet though she was worried about what was expected of her.

"Has he been pushing you?"

"No, not at all, he's sweet," Jasmin answered. "We kiss and stuff but that's all. But I am not sure if we're supposed to…you know."

"Do you want to?"

"No, not really. I just like being with him, the kissing is nice and he is really funny. He makes me feel better about myself. Special. Nobody has really taken an interest before."

I felt a stab of guilt as that included me. Who else but me to know how much of a difference a bit of interest could make for a Forlorn Hoper. All the difference in the world.

"Well don't, only do it if you want to. When you're ready."

"But what if he is ready?"

"Boys are always ready," I said dismissively. "They reckon all you need is a boner and they have those all the time."

"What if he dumps me because of that?"

"If he loves you he won't. If he does it'll hurt your feelings but it really does mean he's not worth it. Plus, we'll kick his ass."

She didn't look convinced, she was really keen on him, I realised and I decided it was time to interrogate Biggs. I caught him in his room reading a comic. His room was a worse mess than mine and smelled of stale socks. He was totally embarrassed when I asked him what the deal was.

"It's not that I don't want to," he flustered. "But Jasmin is so…innocent. I don't even know how she tolerates me near her. I am nobody. I don't want to hurt her. She is special."

"She is special," I agreed. "Don't put yourself down though Biggs, you've really made a difference for her."

"Really?" He brightened.

"So you're okay, waiting?"

"Yes," he shrugged. "Other things are more important."

I smiled and he suddenly looked worried.

"Don't tell anyone, okay?"

I realised he wasn't embarrassed to talk to me about it, but embarrassed because he figured it somehow reflected badly on his manhood. I really didn't get boys on this. What he had just told me was beautiful. How could he think this reflected badly on him? This was just like Puck thinking he was a wuss because he wanted it to be special.

Impulsively I walked up to Biggs and planted a kiss on his chubby cheek. He looked at me in wonder.

"You're a good man Biggs," I said, stressing the 'man', and then left the room.

§ § § § § §

I arranged things with Terry and the next Saturday morning I caught the earliest possible bus to the Carfax bus stop, the nearest one to the Hornsby Farm. Although it wasn't much past seven in the morning the traffic on the A267 was already picking up and I yearned for the solace of the woods so I took the path into the birch woods. I took the left turn just past my chaffinch nest; walking into a shallow dale and then up the somewhat steeper track which climbed the last low wooded ridge before the Edgelands started. The broadly spaced birch trees stopped two thirds of the way up to the slope and were replaced by the magnolia trees I had seen a while back. Their lotus-like cups had opened fully since then and were gloriously pink in the rays of the early morning sun.

When I got to the magnolias I stopped just to breathe in the rich sweet perfume of the blooms. I then looked up and noted how incredibly dense the branches were, they traversed about each other in crisscross patterns that were just irresistible. The magnolia closest to the path had a low bole and limbs within reach and I was up in a jiffy. This time I wasn't really aiming to reach the top, instead I wriggled my way through all the passages offered by the swirls of the branches, trying to go through every combination possible and I thoroughly enjoyed clambering around, especially upside down, hanging on to branches with my arms and legs.

When I finally tired of it I settled on the lowest bough overlooking the birch forest below me. I buttoned open my army shirt and joggled the short-sleeved black t-shirt below at the neck to waft in some cool air. My eye was drawn for a moment by the glowering silhouette of the Blood Stone on Gallows Hill to my left and then -from the corner of my eye- I spotted movement on the opposite slope, just about the same time I heard a faraway voice singing. The green-clad lanky body starting a descent into the dale was just about unmistakable but for good measure I saw the black and white flash of a dog racing to and fro along the path which would lead the two to the Hornsby Farm - and me of course.

I wanted to jump off my magnolia and race down the slope to greet them but Puck launched into another song and I loved to hear him sing so I figured I would stay where I was and just listen for a moment. He had disappeared underneath the foliage but I could follow his progress by the sound of his voice. The song that came closer in this manner was hauntingly beautiful and deliciously morbid.

As I was walking all alone
I heard three ravens cry and moan
The one onto the other did say
Where shall we go and dine today?

Out beyond that old high dike
I know there lies a murdered knight
And no-one knows that he lies there
But his hawk and his hound and his lady fair.

His hound is to the hunting gone
His hawk to fetch the wild bird home
His lady loves another knight
So we may make our dinner sweet

Lady came racing past below me and rushed on. Puck emerged into view, singing in his rich voice with a volume that seemed odd coming from his scrawny slenderness. I smiled with delight when I saw that he had shorn his ridiculous beard off, it made his facial features sharper. He was only twelve feet away now; his eyes fixed ahead of him so he still had no notion I was there.

So you may sit on his white thigh
And I'll peck out his bonny blue eyes…

I jumped out of the tree landing right in front of him and for a moment he was startled.

"HALT," I roared and made a pistol shape with my hand which I pointed at him. "STAND AND DELIVER!"

"Please don't shoot kind sir," Puck squealed. "I am just a poor lad with no riches to my name!"

"That's what they all say, hand over your valuables. NOW."

Puck grinned strangely for a moment, then reached into a pocket just as Lady came bounding back down the path to happily greet me. I bent down to pet her some and when I straightened again Puck had an awkward look on his face and pressed something in my hand.

"Sorry Wenn, I am not very good in this," he apologised.

I looked down and saw a fine silver chain with a gorgeous silver pendant attached to it; a filigreed abstract representation of a swan swimming on two wavy lines and surrounded by reeds which swept up to encircle it. It was cleverly done, using a minimum of lines to achieve recognition of what it represented and it sparkled fiercely in the sun.

I looked up at Puck, speechless.

"It's for you," he clarified, all his usual confidence melted away.

"Puck, you can't afford this…"

"I didn't buy it," he said quickly. "It belonged to my mother."

I went all gooey, swept away like in the books.

"I can't take it…" reluctantly I tried to hand it back to him but he took a step backwards.

"I want you to have it Wenn," he was stumbling over his words now. "I wish we had more time, it's been so good. I love you Wenn."

Upon hearing those magical words I fell into his arms. For a moment, we were in a world of our own, hidden by the shelter of the luscious magnolia blooms and enveloped by their sweet fragrance, our souls momentarily unburdened of all their ugly scars. For that one instant all seemed perfect.

Lady re-appeared and circled us barking frantically; wanting in on the action and the spell was broken. We laughed and both knelt down to include her in the embrace and Lady happily wagged her tail.

"You put it on then," I beamed at Puck, handing him the necklace and turning around. I felt his warm hands around my neck as he fastened the chain and the pendant slid down to its new home, the silver cool and comfortable on my chest.

§ § § § § §

We announced our presence at the Hornsby Farm. The main farmhouse was deserted. Jukes and Tink told us that Rob had gone to a nearby cattle market to sell his stock. It had been a hard decision for him, Jukes told us, but if we were to fail in our attempts to thwart the motorway his remaining land would simply not accommodate the animals. Buying extra feed wasn't a financial option for Rob so he had decided to sell now.

We had a cup of tea in the old farm cottage and then headed west. We took the path to the Giant's Grove and then onwards to Nan Malone's bridge where I ran to my chestnut for a greeting after which we went straight onwards to Tuckersham Church. All the time I was aware of the Swan on my skin and kept on touching it, finding it hard to believe I had received such a gift.

Though it was broad daylight it was the first time that I had seen the church and graveyard at Tuckersham Church up close since that April full moon and I began to tremble as memories of Ufmanna surfaced in vivid sequences. I clutched Puck's hand and held it tightly as we walked past, trying to retain my cool as much as possible. I was getting a distinct impression that Tink had problems taking me seriously and saw me mostly as an unnecessary distraction for Puck. Flipping out now would reinforce that notion a thousand fold. Puck knew what had happened here and switched his hands so he could throw his arm around my shoulders. He held me firmly like that and passing Ufmanna's haunt became easier to bear.

We crossed the Rore and found ourselves on the dirt road where we had started digging up the base stations and about two thirds of the way to the Lusty Giants we began to see the first major impact of the construction work as the path had been quadrupled in breadth by the felling of trees and the ground had been ripped up by tire tracks. This whole area was surrounded by temporary chain fencing but Jukes said there were no dogs or guards out here yet.

Puck pointed out two kinds of survey markers to me. Some of the trees around the fencing were marked by black spray-painted crosses and within the fencing there were wooden stakes marked by various colours at their top end. We split up. Tink and Jukes took cans of spray paint out of their bags and started painting similar crosses on the nearest dozen trees around the ones marked by the surveyors. Puck used a cutter to cut a small gap in the chain fence, told Lady to stay and then slipped through with me.

"They'll figure this out and have to purchase sturdier fences now," he grinned happily. "More costs, and they'll need more security."

"So what do we do?"

"The survey markers show them what they planned to do."

I understood and the two of us began to run around gleefully pulling stakes out of the ground and repositioning them elsewhere at random. I thought of the difference in attitudes within the Waer-Wyrd. The older inhabitants of the Wyrde Woods seemed to have resigned themselves to the inevitable with regard to the M33, their conviction lay in making that last symbolic stance. What happened after that was anybody's guess; they had decided surrender was not an option and hoped for a miraculous rescue by the Wyrde Woods themselves. Puck on the other hand, genuinely believed that the project could be called to a halt if the motive of making money was sufficiently undermined by rising costs. Jukes and Tink, though members of another group, shared that belief. They had talked enough about road projects elsewhere which had been cancelled for precisely such reasons, though Tink had pointed out that this was by far the most ambitious project in recent times. Moreover the government had a stake in it as well. If they got away with this one, audacious as it was, they would initiate a new road building policy hoping that the public would accept lesser schemes more easily. Possibly though, they had picked the wrong place. There were a lot of determined people who wanted to show that the maxim *Sussex wun't be druv* wasn't a hollow phrase. It wasn't a clever advertising slogan either; the attitude had been born more than a thousand years ago when the Saxons had founded their Kingdom of Sussex. It was tradition. There was much at stake for everyone.

Repositioning the survey markers became tenser as we worked our way towards the compound and we had to stop when it came within sight, knowing it was guarded day and night now. We met up with Jukes and Tink again, they had emptied a score of spray paint cans, and there were large black 'X' marks on hundreds of trees. We walked back to the Rore where we said goodbye to Jukes and Tink and then headed north towards the Owlery.

§ § § § § § §

It was good to see Joy again and great to be at the Owlery where everything was so familiar, though it was somewhat odd that I wouldn't be climbing the stairs to my room that night but catching the bus back to Odesby. Joy had prepared roast chicken and potatoes for dinner and we spent most of the evening around the kitchen table sampling some more birch wine -amber this time and less sweet- talking and joking. I noted anticipation in their talk with regard to the next weekend. It would be Midsummer on Saturday and I gathered celebrations had been planned. I was glad it would be home leave weekend so that I would be able to join in.

When Puck went out back to collect firewood to replenish the diminished pile by the hearth in the living room Joy laid her hand on mine.

"So mine scoundrel's given ye hisn Swan," she said.

"Yes, today, it's beautiful isn't it?" I looked down to admire it for the umpteenth time. "He said it belonged to his mother."

"Aye, mine son Nate gave it to hern. Hisn Gammer, ole Priscilla Malheur passed it to him. Hern were mad as a bat folk said but she were always kind to me and took a liking to mine Nate, so she does. Cilla hated Catherine, doant want hern to have it. The Swan been in the Malheur fambly for a long time, it has."

"Really?" I looked at the pendant again with awe. "Do you know how old it is?"

"Tis said," Joy had a sparkle in her eyes, "That Foster Malheur were given it by hisn mam."

"NIADA?"

Joy nodded.

"But that would mean…it's Farisee?"

Joy nodded.

"Can silver get that old? In such a condition?"

"Farisee craft, aye. Mind ye, ye'll have ta polish it, if ye doant I'll paunch ye alikes a robbut with mine own hands."

She would too, I had no doubt. Puck walked me back to the bus stop, we were both silent, there was so much to say but I was oppressed by the thought of our renewed parting, even though it would only be for a week this time. We'd have all of the next weekend together.

We kissed passionately by the bus stop, and again more urgently when the light beams of the bus flickered between the trees. Then I got on the bus and as the Wyrde Woods passed by I kept on looking at the Swan. Rob had dubbed me 'Wenn o' the Farisees' and I had liked the name, but that night, heading back to exile, knowing I was the daughter of a Farisee changeling and wearing Niada's necklace, I truly began to believe I was.

28. Fierce Dancing

I spent most of Sunday playing Settlers of Catan in Jasmin's room. I kept on losing as my game strategy was to go for settlements around the woodland tiles to prevent Jasmin and Biggs building roads through them, meaning I had a big shortage of other resources. Jasmin had a similar approach but she focused on the meadowland tiles and talked dreamily of the flocks of sheep which grazed on these; inventing names for the sheep and describing the odd characteristics of her favourites. Biggs focused on the ports and the remainder of the resources, obliging us to trade with him at rates which left him with a wealth of resource cards and he gleefully won game after game.

I got called into pastoral care at school in Monday and was told I was flunking big time.

Doant be tessy, Joy's voice kept on repeating in my head when I started to fume and I touched the Swan and calmed down. They were just stating facts after all, not launching a personal attack and I accepted the offer to help me make a work schedule. I surprised myself by sticking to it and threw myself at schoolwork with vigour, motivated by the thought that Stubbles was monitoring my behaviour. Any missteps would be ammunition for him to show that Joy's influence on me was counterproductive. Sometimes the thought of five whole weeks in the Wyrde Woods filled me with intense happiness but most of the time I didn't dare to conceive of it as being real. I was afraid that if I set too much stock by it the downer that would follow cancellation for one reason or another would be a bad one. School was one of the things I could work on though, to make that summer more realistic.

Stubbles did remark on school during our session that week, saying that he had received a call from pastoral care to inform him that they were pleased with my change in attitude.

"That's really good of you Wendy," Hairy Mare nodded encouragement.

"Thank you Miss Hare," I smiled, genuinely pleased with the compliment.

"Much too late of course," Stubbles torpedoed. "And looking at your record, well, we'll just have to see how long you can keep it up this time."

I glared at him, then took a deep breath and just smiled sanguinely.

"You are right of course Mr. Dagle, time will tell."

When the session ended I went to the common room, feeling a bit proud that I had kept my anger under control. Despite this I felt bitterness too, Michael would have been delighted by such a phone call from pastoral care and offered me all the encouragement he could.

I spotted a copy of the Odesby Gazette on the low coffee table in front of the telly and picked it up. The main headline read: ECO-TERRORISM IN WYRDE WOODS. The accompanying article was written in tabloid style, filled with outrage at work-shy scroungers resorting to criminal activities. The journalist didn't specify the activities, just reported them to be mindless acts of vandalism and quoted a local police officer who had said that criminal behaviour would be treated as such regardless of motivation. The journalist implied that the police already knew who was likely to be behind the actions. He ended with outspoken fear of the despicable hordes of feckless layabouts who were likely to invade Odesby over the next few months and called for Odesby's residents to unite against these invaders as they had done in the expectation of a Nazi invasion back in 1940.

I put down the paper and hoped that Puck's plan to deflect attention to the Weard Hunt was working, realising with a mixture of dread and glee that I was one of the feckless layabouts spoken about. The allusion to the Nazis had me fuming though.

When Joy and Willick came to pick me up on Friday afternoon I was in the hallway already, backpack packed and ready to go. We were stopped at the front door by Hairy Mare.

"I just wanted to say," she said nervously. "That I think you were right Mrs. Whitfield. Wendy has been behaving much better; school has called to say so too."

"Well that be mighty kind o' ye Mary," Joy beamed and I resolved to never call Miss Hare 'Hairy Mare' again.

§ § § § § § §

We drove to the Earl's Barrel where Joan greeted us warmly. Puck was seated by the great big hearth, in animated conversation with a woman in her late fifties. She was lissom and slight, medium long grey hair framing a sharp face that held a hint of sadness. Lady was by their feet.

Puck actually beat Lady in getting to me and we lost ourselves in a prolonged hug.

"Will ye unwrap yernself from that lass Puck ye young scaddle," Willick grumbled when Joan came to take our orders. "Joan be awaiting."

"Let them be," Joan laughed. "Ah knows theirn drinks."

"Young love at Midsummer is naun to be denied," the willowy woman Puck had been speaking to said as she approached us.

I let go of Puck reluctantly and gave Lady a quick greeting. She had given up her energetic scampering and sat by our feet looking up with large sad eyes. Then I turned for an inquisitive look at the woman.

"Allison this be Wenn I spoke of," Willick said. "Wenn, Allison, mine wife."

"So ye be the pretend grandchild o' mine Will?" Allison looked at me curiously.

"Erm," I looked at Willick who looked embarrassed. "Yes. He's really helped me and stuff."

I felt a bit awkward. She was an outsider to the little make-believe family unit I had constructed in my mind, but I liked her instinctively even though I didn't want to because in my mind she had stolen Willick from Joy. I quickly reassembled that notion, reminding myself that it was Mortimer Malheur who had stolen Joy from Willick. I also noted that there didn't appear to be any tension between Joy and Allison, something I would have expected, especially thinking of that Maimie creature.

"Ye've made him a happy man," Allison said with a smile. "We're naun blessed with chavees and he's always wanted a grandchild o' hisn own."

"Really?" I was surprised, though it explained the way Willick behaved sometimes. I looked at Willick for confirmation.

"Tis nigh on midsummer and that sets women all hare-brained with fanciful notions," Willick grumbled.

Allison and Joy laughed. I gave him a grateful smile.

"So what is all this Midsummer business?" I asked when I had sat down.

"It be Summer Solstice tomorrow," Joy supplied.

"Longest day of the year," Puck added.

"We've celebrations each year," Joy's eyes gleamed with mischief. "Howsumdever, tomorrow be extra special."

Then they told me of their plans to let the past echo loud and clear in the Wyrde Woods the next day. We were going to unleash a weapon of old. We were going to summon a legend back to Sussex.

§ § § § § §

"Wenn, wake up." A voice materialised in my dreams of flying out of Hood's Gorge and over the expanse of the Wyrde Woods. I tried to ignore it and hold on to that glorious feeling of flying through the air.

"Wake up Wenn," a hand gently shook my shoulder.

Grumbling protest I opened my eyes. It was still dark outside but Puck had lit a candle. He was on his side, propped up on his elbow, his face close to mine and I looked up into those amazing eyes of his.

"There you are," he smiled warmly. "It's time to get up Elfin."

"Oehoeh," I said and grabbed his face and pulled it down for a kiss. He responded but after a while disengaged and sat up fully, pulling the covers away, robbing me of the cosy warmth that sustained my sluggishness.

"Oi," I protested.

"Big day today Wenn," Puck replied cheerfully. "But you'll need to get out of bed first."

"I didn't give you permission to pull the covers away mister Green Man," I admonished him, lifting myself up and wrestling him on his back.

"Are you bossing me around now?" Puck usual grin faded when I repositioned myself so that my hips were over his groin. I gyrated slowly and smiled with satisfaction as I felt him stiffen in response.

"Have ye naun control young scaddle?" I asked wickedly.

"Naun," Puck managed a shake of his head.

I bent over to brush my breasts against his chest, the Swan cradling on his neck and whispered in his ear: "Puck's a bad boy then."

"Oh my god, Wenn," he moaned as his hips jerked upwards but then he gently pushed me up.

"We can't, not now, everybody's downstairs already," he said regretfully.

I clambered off him with an evil smile. "Well, if you don't want me…"

He snorted and grumbled a denial as we both started gathering clothes. I slipped on my rambler's gear and giggled as I watched him struggle with his trousers, he was still erect and it was refusing to be helpful.

"You have to tuck it in," I suggested earning myself a withering look.

When we got downstairs the living room was much more crowded than usual; besides Joy a sleepy looking Willick sat next to Allison and Joan was there too, all sipping coffee.

"Don't we have to wear something special?" I asked Joy as she led Allison, Joan and myself into the garden and then into the orchard. I had half expected to be fitted into a mystic gown. It was still dark though a band of grey stretched along the eastern sky.

"Naun," Joy chuckled. "We'll leave that to the Sheere-folk what be at Stonehenge this morning."

"Be plenty o' time for dramatics tonight," Joan nodded.

I followed the other three into the yew forest. By the time the yews grew gnarled faces bearded by Norn's weaving it had grown a shade lighter and our progress was marked by a host of eerie yew countenances.

I knew what we were going to do, having been filled in by Joy and I had mixed feelings. On the one hand it was thrilling, on the other it felt silly, though the sense of belonging overrode any second thoughts I might have had as we wound through the yew tunnels towards the within. We reached Heorttreów as brightness in the eastern sky announced the imminent arrival of the sun and Joy allocated us positions around the great big tree.

"Wenn to the west, Allison north and Joan south. Wenn, make sure yern Swan be uncovered."

I unbuttoned my army shirt so that the Swan was revealed and went to my assigned place. When the top of the sun peeked over the horizon

134

the others raised their arms sideways and up and I followed their example.

We stood there for what seemed a long time as more and more of the sun became visible and was greeted by an increase of bird chitter. Joy waited for the first proper beam of light that penetrated the clearing. It shone straight on me, causing the Swan to reflect its brilliance.

"Father Heorttreów, Norns thrice, hear us," Joy intoned in a loud and solemn voice. I suppressed an involuntary giggle at the weirdness.

"The Seven be complete," Joan and Allison answered, speaking in bright and clear voices.

"One for sorrow," Joy spoke opposite me.

"Two for Joy," Allison spoke.

"Three for a girl." It was my turn and I surprised myself with the solemn tone of my voice.

"Four for a boy," Joan said.

"Five for silver," Joy continued.

"Six for gold," Allison said.

"Seven for a secret," I spoke.

"Never to be told," the other three said in unison.

We became silent then and I was kind of disappointed that nothing seemed to happen. The birds continued their songs, the sun seemed unperturbed and Heorttreów continued to be its impassive spectacular self.

Joy turned and walked back into the tunnel and the rest of us followed. I caught up with her when we left the tunnel.

"Was that all?" I asked, somewhat incredulous.

"Ye were expecting something spectacular?" Joy chuckled.

"Well, yeah. Fireworks, the seventh Shy Maiden to dance out of the tree, stuff like that," I admitted.

"The words were spoken, that be what were needed," Joy smiled.

I nodded but was not entirely convinced, I had really expected to be swept off my feet by some cosmic force, to feel all alive and a-tingle like Puck had made me feel that morning.

"Doan't be worried," Joy chuckled. "There will be a gurt deal more afore the next dawn."

§ § § § § § §

We got back to the Owlery where Willick and Puck were carrying a bunch of boxes from Willick's Land Rover to the back garden.

"Where'd you go?" Puck asked curiously.

"Can't tell you," I answered mysteriously and laughed when he pouted. "Women's business," I added proudly, oddly pleased that there was a part of the Wyrde Woods I knew about and he didn't.

Rob arrived soon after. There was a horse trailer behind his Land Rover and he coaxed out a roan gelding with brown mane and white socks. The horse was called Beowulf. I had never seen a horse up close before but decided that I loved them as I stood next to Rob and stroked Beowulf who looked at me with eyes which seemed intelligent and friendly.

"You okay Rob?" I turned my attention to the farmer, who had been looking at Beowulf with obvious affection. He was wearing a John Deere baseball cap today.

"Aye, why wouldn't I be?" He raised an eyebrow.

"I heard about the cattle market," I shrugged but kept eye contact. "Must have been hard for you."

He swallowed, his Adam's apple going up and down as he did so. Then took off his baseball cap and looked down as he scratched his head. He wiped one eye dry when he put the baseball cap back on.

"Tis all part and parcel o' being a farmer Wenn," he said in a gruffly tone.

"I don't believe a word of it Rob," I smiled and laid my hand on his arm. "But if you say so."

"Bethanks lass."

Shortly thereafter after the dirt road opposite the Owlery filled with more vehicles as the Chanklebury Bedlam Troupe arrived, twelve men and women who spoke the Broad Sussex dialect and greeted the others with pleasantries that made clear they were acquainted. They had four dogs with them, large shaggy wolfhounds which made quick friends with Lady.

The Troupe unpacked their vehicles, adding more boxes and bags to those already deposited in the little courtyard behind Joy's kitchen. In the meantime their leader, a robust man with cheerful red cheeks called Tim, consulted with Puck, Joy and Willick while I helped Joan and Allison prepare a big lunch for nineteen people: Soup, loaves of homemade bread, Saint Giles cheese, chicken, potatoes, string beans added to which were bottles of homemade cider which Rob had brought.

The newcomers prepared themselves while we cleared away the meal after eating and then gave us a performance of Morris Dancing on the grass out front. I had only ever seen brief snatches of Morris dancers on telly which had left an impression of men dressed in old-fashioned outfits adorned with bells hopping about in the incongruous setting of familiar High Street shops signs and display windows.

The Chanklebury Bedlam Troupe however, was something entirely different. Their costumes were knee-length coats to which had been sown hundreds of strips of fabric, the bottom ones of which fell down to the dancers' calves. Ten of the coats had strips which were predominantly black, with various hues of grey thrown in. The eleventh was predominantly red with hues of orange and yellow and Tim's coat was adorned with strips of every possible variation of green. They donned headwear, shaggy manes and beards of fabric strips making their heads appear twice as large. The headgear was completed by elegant Venetian carnival masks with beaks and snouts for those in black, flames for the one in red and oak leaves for Tim.

The friendly jocular troupe was gone at once when the masks came on, replaced by ragged creatures that exuded a subtle menace. The dance was complex, the interaction between red and green in the centre –one of changing attraction and conflict- surrounded by a circle of black, the members of which frequently changed formations all the while beating the short wooden staffs they held. These made a surprisingly loud bang on contact with the other staffs. The rhythm of the dance was created entirely by the staffs and I was thrilled by the ominous volatility the troupe established by dancing themselves into a frenzy - whooping and hollering- and then drawing back and outwards just as this reached a violent apex.

"Marvellous isn't it Wenn?" Puck was mesmerised. "This they brought over with them from their homelands across the North Sea fifteen hundred years ago. They danced this at the time they successfully resisted the Roman Empire: Woden's dance."

When they finished we applauded and Joy nodded approvingly.

"Ye be sure she be at the castle tonight?" She asked Willick, who nodded. "Good, let's get to work."

Work consisted of extra similar costumes coming out of boxes and bags and much fitting. All the Waer-Wyrd got black, but I got red and Puck green. I was beginning to think he'd display a violent allergic reaction if he ever had to wear any other colour and grinned. It was a suitable outfit for my very own Green Man. They told me my outfit was that of the Red Queen and that was brill so I beamed regally.

Late that evening the sun was setting into Midsummer's Night and threw a warm glow over the woods around Malheur Hall. Nineteen people –the Chanklebury Bedlam Troupe and the Waer-Wyrd-, five dogs and a horse were concealed in the woodlands near the grassy slopes which faced the imposing front entrance of Malheur Hall.

I got goose bumps when I looked at Rob, astride Beowulf. He had the most spectacular headgear of all, a black rugged beard that reached to his belly, and a simple mask that was entirely black and on top of his head were two large raised antlers.

"Herne the Hunter," Puck said admiringly.

"Ready to declare war?" Rob asked. We nodded and Rob raised a great big horn to his lips, blowing three long signals which were followed shortly thereafter by further horn calls made by some of the members of the troupe who had smaller horns. As if this were a signal the wolfhounds started barking and howling and Lady happily joined in. Rob blew on his horn again and Allison and Joan started tapping on two large round drums they had been practicing with during the late afternoon. The rest of us started ululating now, long shrill piercing whoops that completed our cacophony. Those with staffs beat them together in rhythm with the drums. I felt self-conscious at first but soon found that screaming at the top of your voice with no restraints whatsoever was absolutely brill, and I took to ventilating years of frustration with the fanaticism of a new convert.

Our procession started to move. Rob in front on Beowulf blowing his great horn, flanked by the dogs barking ferociously and followed by the drummers who preceded the rest of us with the other horn blowers making up our rear-guard. Dancing rather than walking came naturally to me now and I lost all inhibition.

We emerged from the woods just as the sun was setting and began to traverse the slope's top end, the sight of Malheur Hall a signal to increase the frenzied blowing, drumming, barking, howling and screeching.

The lit windows of Malheur Hall remained impassive but someone must have noted us because when we reached the end of the grassy slopes we could hear police sirens in the distance.

We ceased our ruckus and melted away into the woods, making for the place where we loaded an assortment of vehicles. Willick led the convoy through the woods as we made our way to the back of the Lusty Giant's Hills where we spilled out of the vehicles and reformed into our procession. We climbed up to the slope of the male giant's hill and when we reached the summit and could see the lit compound below Rob raised the horn to his lips again and once more we made an otherworldly hellish din. We circled the summit thrice and then descended into the saddle between the two hills before climbing the female giant's hill. Below, in the compound, the Alsatian guard dogs were going apeshit, barking for all they were worth and we could see the figures of security guards running to and fro in some confusion.

We made our way south from the second summit and stopped making noise. We came to the broad band of felled trees where dark figures were cutting holes in the fencing so that we could carry on walking. I thought I recognised Mad Judd Mack amongst them but couldn't be sure as they rushed before us to assault the next line of fencing on the other side of the ravaged woods and then preceded us. When we got to the bottom of the slopes of Arthurs's Fort they started running before us shouting at the top of their voices.

"THE WILD HUNT! THE WILD HUNT! THE WILD HUNT!"

Herne blew his horn for the third time that night and we resumed our ruckus as we started our ascent. A flicker of flame was ignited on top of the summit, the sleek flames licking upwards and spreading till there was a huge conflagration which revealed hundreds of people on the top of Arthur's Fort. Smaller fires were lit and it soon appeared as if the entire broad summit of Arthur's Fort had caught fire.

"THE WILD HUNT! THE WILD HUNT!"

By now my voice was already hoarse and I was sweaty and sore but all of us increased our efforts, spinning more wildly, screaming like banshees and when we were halfway up our noise was picked up on the hill where dozens of drums started to beat. Part of the gathering up there came streaming down, mostly young men and women dressed in nothing but loincloths, their bodies daubed in red paint and waving torches to light their way down.

"THE WILD HUNT!"

They surrounded us, casting light upon the last stage of our procession, twisting their almost naked bodies wildly and screaming along with our own yowling. The crowd above parted to let us approach the great central fire but when we reached the last of the embankments Rob stopped and raised his hand and all of us stopped and froze. A creepy silence replaced the clamour we had been making and our group stood there like statues lit by the flickering torches of the red-painted ones that surrounded us.

I saw the crowds now, illuminated by the fires that lit up Arthur's Fort, and was surprised by the amount of people from all walks of life. It wasn't a surprise to see a large number of young folk in the Weard Hunt outfits, or just completely over the top alto, but there were many older folk there too, like David Masters wearing his medalled blazer and others whose usually normal outfits looked out of place on this hilltop on this night. I thought it was sirageous, I hadn't expected so many adherents of the old culture.

Rob raised his horn and blew as hard as he could, the low deep call seeming to spread in all directions. As one we detonated into a…

ROAR…;

the spectators on the hill, the red painted ones and we: The embodiment of the Wild Hunt. I had never heard anything as loud as that sustained bellowing. It was a primordial blast that was as ancient as the land and also a deafening outcry of defiance. We the people were here and would make our stand. Suth-Seaxna-Lond wun't be druv. The roar was an appeal to our ancestors and all that ever had roamed or still roamed the Wyrde Woods.

When the roar began to die down the drums picked up again and we continued our procession up the hill where our group merged with the red-painted ones and we danced our way widdershins around the great central fire, surrounded by the crowd, many of whom joined in what was becoming a collective frenzy, urged on by the fierce drums.

I lost sight of the rest but Puck was beside me so it did not matter. We had removed our head coverings because it had become far too hot, somebody had taken them and pressed bottles of cold ale in our hands from which we drank greedily. Puck laughed and I laughed back, looking at all the swirling madness around us. I downed my bottle and threw it aside after which I took off the ragged coat, Puck did the same and we launched into a wild dance, improvising steps as we gyrated around the great fire, seemingly bonded by a single will as we anticipated each other's every move and response, twisting, turning, spinning and rotating in fierce tempo. I let myself fall fully confident that Puck would catch me in his arms, setting me upright and then leading me to the next fall in the other direction, stopped by his firm grip around my midriff and then lifted up like I was flying. I was laughing all the while now, I felt free in a way that I had never felt free before. My green man with his bright green eyes and keen intelligence momentarily dissolved the chains that bound me and I felt like I was walking in the air and swimming in the sky. I let go of all abandon now and danced wilder, spun faster, jumped higher, rotated quicker, gyrated crazier, fell freely, twisted madly and turned again and again to find those green eyes to drown in each time: We were in a world of our own.

At last we spun to a halt at the edge of the crowd, sweating and panting. Every muscle in my body ached and I was grinning madly.

We were given more ale and I became aware of the crowds around us again, dancing around the fire or further out, looking and clapping with looks of joy on their faces. I downed my bottle all at once and then decided I wanted to be away from the crowd.

I grabbed Puck's hand and pulled him away into the dark fringes of the night below the illuminated summit, my heart racing to the beats of the drums and my blood hot.

"Wenn..."

I shut him up by kissing him fiercely. There was a time for talking. This wasn't it. I probed his mouth with my tongue and he responded instantly, running his hands up and down my back, lingering over the top of my buttocks. I pressed myself into him and suddenly felt hindered by my clothes and started tearing mine off. We then became entangled in frenzied attempts to undress, giggling and chuckling some over the sudden intransigence of our clothing before we succeeded and, sky-clad, sank into the soft grass and resumed our kissing, still driven by the beating drums.

It was, as we had hoped, more than a sequence of who did what to whom when and in which way. As the locals say there was everything of something and something of everything. But most of all it included coming together, being as one, moving as one, and complementing the other like we had when we were dancing so that our scarred souls were whole for a while. When we were finally done we cuddled up on the grass without dressing, spent, sweaty and in a tight embrace. That is how we fell asleep and peacefully ventured into our respective Midsummer Night's dreams.

Part Wheelah: Six for Gold

29. The Lost Boys

Jasmin wanted to know all about my weekend when I got back. I could hardly tell her much about the Midsummer's day and night and Sunday had passed by in a haze of lazy recuperation after clearing up the debris at Arthur's Fort in the morning. Instead I tried to paint a picture of daily life at the Owlery and added things like my encounter with the deer in the oak woods between the Halfhollow Oak and Roreford. She soaked it all up and I realised how little of the outside world Jasmin actually saw, it was like I was living a life for her.

I devoted most of my week to school work, relieved that Joy had supplied me with her motherwort concoctions for I barely noticed my period this time. The Odesby Gazette ran a piece on Midsummer's Night at Arthur's Fort, saying that eco-terrorists and occultists had held a depraved orgy of sex and drugs on the hilltop after which they had committed new acts of vandalism and tried to intimidate the security guards at the compound. He added that the so-called nature lovers had left Arthur's Fort looking like a rubbish tip, which I knew to be untrue. Well, I grinned, he was right about the sex anyway. In the evenings I went to bed early, listened to music and thought about my Midsummer's Night with Puck.

I used my day pass to go to the Owlery on Saturday, getting the earliest possible bus and arriving there just after eight. Joy was pleased to see me; she was still in bed and told me she'd had a bad few days. I busied myself making us both breakfast and coffee and then cleaned out the owl boxes. The owls allowed me to take them in and out of their boxes now and Joy called out instructions from the bed. Puck arrived before noon and we shared a moment in the kitchen where I was preparing a vegetable omelette for lunch.

Joy insisted on getting out of bed and joining us at the kitchen table. Puck's mind was on the road protest and he brought me up to date. He and others had tried to sabotage the surveyor's markers again on Monday evening but then had to run like hell because security patrols now extended along the entire line of fencing which was now stretched two thirds of the way to the Rore. Duguth Construction had hired a new security firm for off-base operations, and these included rapid response units, small teams in Land Rovers who were veterans in dealing with road protests. The Weald Hunt had countered this by setting up a permanent observation post on Arthur's Fort, nothing more than a concealed tent or two since it could be evicted, and this was working well. The view of the construction terrain was good and the observers phoned when they spotted trouble coming, which meant actions could continue but not prolonged ones, just pin-pricks.

Duguth Construction had spent most of the early part of the week replacing the old fences around the construction area with heavy-duty steel ones as Puck had predicted and then work had got into full swing again. Surveyors protected by security guards at work at the far end of the corridor and construction workers felling trees at the beginning of the compound to widen the corridor. It seemed as if there was a drive now to push the work ahead as fast as possible.

"Well, then, they are spending a lot of money, aren't they?" I asked.

"Yes," Puck nodded. "Drawback is that there is no time to set up a Weard Hunt camp on the west bank of the Rore. I met up with Mad Judd Mack at the Earl's Barrel on Wednesday. He said that a number of the prominent Weard Hunt people are being shadowed now."

"The coppers?"

"He thinks it's that private detective agency, but you can be sure they share information with the police."

"So what does that mean for us?"

"Can't mix anymore. The Weard Hunt will carry out their own, more visible actions but the rest of us will stay away from them. Friends will continue to inform all those people who attended rallies or called in support. They're doing a lot of fund-raising too. Jukes and Tink have called in the Lost Boys; they'll be arriving late this afternoon. Next weekend, everybody starts building their camps."

"Where will the Weard Hunt build their camp then?" I asked, thinking of Ufmanna.

"Around my hideout," Puck said. "It's on the route but before it crosses the Taunflow to the Giant's Grove."

"I thought you said it was a bad idea to mix with them," I asked puzzled.

"I'll have to move out," Puck shrugged. "Rob has offered to come pick up my stuff."

"Where will you go?"

"Robin's Cave. I've always wanted to be a caveman."

"Young scaddle will be dragging ye around by yern hair if ye aint careful," Joy smiled.

"Pfff, I'd like to see him try," I answered. "Joy can I ask you something."

"Aye lass."

"Next home leave weekend is in two weeks. Do you think I could bring someone?"

Puck frowned and Joy looked thoughtful.

"Tis naun the best o' times but who'd be yern guest?"

I told them about Jasmin, who never got to leave on home leave weekends and who had been fascinated by my stories about the Wyrde

Woods. I shared my hope that spending some time there might make her really happy.

"You didn't tell her about the road protest I hope?" Puck asked.

"No, I'm naun chuckle-headed," I shot him a look.

"It's not like grandma is some kind of circus show you know, you can't just bring people out here to have a gander. You know we're in the middle of something big." He shot me a look back and I was genuinely puzzled, not understanding why he was suddenly being obnoxious.

"Ah doant think Wenn had a circus in mind," Joy said thoughtfully.

"I didn't, honestly...I just thought that it would help Jasmin...," my voice trailed off and I looked at Puck. "You know what it's like Puck. To have no one, no place to go home to."

He shrugged.

"Tis kind to think o' others," Joy said. "If the lass stays here hern doant be anywhere anigh the protest camps."

"Well, you two obviously agree on it," Puck said resignedly. "I'll go feed the chickens and fetch you some wood grandma, I have to be back at Rob's on time for the Lost Boys."

He stood up and left. I looked at Joy.

"Now he's being tessy," I said, looking down at the table wondering what I had done wrong.

"I think tis the idea o' having to share ye," Joy said.

"But I have to share him with his road protest friends," I objected.

"Aye that ye does. But they doant visit at night."

"Quiddy?" I didn't get it.

"If yern Jasmin comes to stay, Puck doant be sharing yern bed lass," Joy explained patiently.

"Is that what this is all about?" I made to get up and go outside to give Puck a piece of my mind. I thought he was different but if that was all I was good for…

"Wait," Joy held up her hand. "Sit yernself down lass."

I hesitated for a moment, then fell back onto the chair.

"I remember," Joy stared into a time long past, "With Will. I were walking with mine head in clouds most days. Couldna believe how special he made me feel. I felt I was the luckiest lass in the whole wurreld."

She paused and I nodded. I had tried to berate myself for thinking of Puck too much, surrendering my hard-fought fortress of indifference because he looked proud of me or said something sweet and I'd just turn into a silly little girl fawning over a lad like Sharon did over Thomas. But this negative reflection never lasted long, overturned by this daze of cray happiness which sometimes took hold of me.

"Other times…" Joy continued, "…twere different. That naun believing, it took over. I doubted Will, I doubted him were sincere. Naun cause o' him mind ye. Cause o' me. How could Will love me, I being what I was. Will and meself went to school in Wolfden and I were different. Different from farm chavees, different from village chavees."

I could hardly picture Willick and Joy as school kids.

"Me mam being what she was, living in the woods, knowing all about yarbs and plants. Twere considered unnatural. And me naun having a da and all. Will doant care; neither do mine friend Maisy and the Hornsby chavees. Nor this sodger I met in the Wyrde Woods. The rest called me a witch."

"But, surely you had a father?"

"I were chance-born, conceived at the Midsummer Night's fires, Wenn, me mam had liddle use for men, except for that. There be much love making at Beltane and Midsummer." She grinned mischievously and I nodded with a knowing grin of my own.

"Ye know how chavees can be, downright cruel. I was pointed at and called names. I jes ignored it as well as I could, likes I doant care at all. But deep inside…"

"…it hurts," I nodded. "I know this; it's the same for me in Neverland."

"Aye, when Puck carried ye in that first time, alike a fledgling thrown out o' the nest, twere like seeing a shim o' myself at yern age. I doant offer to share mine home with strangers out o' habit sweetie."

"It's like a family," I confessed softly, afraid she might laugh, or even chuckle.

Joy grabbed my hand and held it tight.

"Fambly be naun always blood liddle one, ye understand? Maybe…" She looked at the door to the back garden where we could hear Puck rummaging about, "…ye'll be fambly one day in a proper sense, but to me ye already are. I had one proper friend back then. Maisy were like a sister to me and hern Gaffer and Gammer made me feel at home on theirn farm. I know a liddle how tis lass. Then Will a-came running into mine life down a path in the Wyrde Woods one day."

I nodded. She had spoken aloud words I had despaired of ever hearing. I had a fambly.

"So," Joy let go of my hand. "I appreciates that ye want to bring that Jasmin here and as yern friend hern be more than welcome. I could not say that ye may think o' the Owlery as yern home and then refuse ye guests. But doant be hoping that it'll be the same for hern. Ye understand?"

I nodded.

"As to the disbelieving," Joy had the faraway look again. "There were times I got tessy with Will, who naun understand, him doant care what they said at school. But sometime I believe them and accuse Will o' claiming to love a chance-born lass who could naun ever be loved."

"Insecurity," I was totally following the rollercoaster of emotions Joy was describing.

"My point being, tis easy to be so focused on yern own insecurity that ye doant see hisn own."

"Puck? Insecure?"

Joy laughed heartily.

"Lad learned to carry hisnself well doant he? Appears to know everything and strolls around alikes he be Lord of the Wyrde Woods. Tis his Gaffer's blood. But inside…when Puck comes here he were in a worse state than ye were Wenn. A proper grummut. Him be most-in-general doubting everything, and most o' all hisnself."

"Really?"

"He be outside now a doubting what ye sees in him. Assuring hisnself that ye made a mistake and found out."

"Just because of the sex thing?"

"Lad his age? It be important to him, aye."

"Pfff, boys."

"Be it naun important to ye Wenn? Times mus have changed, twere most I thought about when mine teats were perky. Jes in different way from the lads, but that were all the difference."

I looked into those bright eyes of Joy's which were sparkling mischievously.

I stood up.

"I gotta go talk to Puck."

"Ye does that lass, ye does that. One more thing though."

"Yes?"

"Ye'll have to arrange permission for this Jasmin o' yern to come yernself, Will and I naun gwoan arrange that for ye."

I nodded, that was fair enough. I went outside to find Puck standing at the edge of the courtyard staring at the flowers. I joined him and grabbed his hand.

"Hey," I said, looking at him and thinking about Joy's assurance that he was far more insecure than he let on.

"Hey," he said miserably. "I am sorry Wenn, didn't mean it like that."

"Is it about Jasmin sleeping over?" I cut to the chase, making Puck look even more miserable.

"I thought…I was hoping…"

"So was I."

"Really?" He looked at me in surprise.

"Really," I nodded.

"I thought, maybe…I wasn't…it wasn't…"

"Puck sweetheart," I took his chin and lifted it so I could look in his eyes. "It was wonderful, truly wonderful."

"Oh," he looked bewildered still but pleased now. So far I had mostly viewed him as mature beyond his years, but I saw the little boy now and smiled. It was here that I could take the lead perhaps, not follow in his footsteps.

"We will have all summer," I promised him and gave him a kiss. "All summer my love and I can't wait."

He looked relieved and managed a quirky smile after which we both went back inside.

Little did I know that our time was almost up.

§ § § § § §

I felt like Bilbo Baggins must have felt when all the dwarves Gandalf had invited over came tumbling through the front door of Bag End.

A large red van had rattled and shaken itself up the access road to Rob's farm and shuddered to a halt besides the old farm buildings. I stood in the courtyard with Puck, Jukes, Tink and Lady and watched as the side door slid open and, one after the other, the Lost Boys came tumbling out of the van and introduced themselves to me in quick succession.

"Hiya, I'm Tootles."

"Hey, Nibs."

"Hallo, Slightly."

"Hi there, Twin One."

"And that makes me Twin Two."

The driver got out as well.

"Good day, Curly."

Apart from Curly, whom I estimated to be in his early twenties, the rest were older, somewhere in their thirties.

"Puck!" The passenger door opened and a girl a little older than I was stepped out. She was tall and nubile, with long black wavy hair like a gypsy, an image reinforced by the fact that she wasn't wearing rambling gear like the rest but a colourful skirt and a white bohemian blouse which advertised her cleavage. She bore herself with a cool reassurance that was totally intimidating and threw herself into Puck's arms in an exaggerated fashion. I tried to smile but felt an intense dislike. How could I possibly compete? She looked like one of those models in Sharon's fashion magazines. I felt myself becoming very small.

"Maimie," Puck said and stepped back out of her embrace.

"I'd like you to meet Wenn." He stretched out his arm and I placed myself by his side. He gave my shoulder a light reassuring squeeze.

Maimie cocked her head and regarded me full of bemusement.

"So you found yourself a little girlfriend?" she asked Puck.

"No," Puck said, and for a fraction of a second I saw Maimie's dark eyes light up. Puck turned and looked into my eyes with a warm smile. "Wenn is my soul mate."

And that was the end of that.

§ § § § § § §

I was summoned down from my room at Nowhere Place around noon on Sunday. When I walked down the stairs I saw Mad Judd Mack talking to Terry by the office door. I hastened towards him.

"Is my dad okay?" I wanted to know.

"Nyle's fine," Judd answered smiling. "But he's has been asking for you."

"For me? He's talking?"

"You...He's been remarkably talkative, but all he talks about is his beautiful faery daughter."

"I was just telling this gent that you used your weekly day pass yesterday," Terry told me.

I nodded and tried not to pout. Terry didn't like games and saw through them in an instant.

"Mr. Mackellow wants to take you to visit your father today," Terry continued. "I was just about to give him permission. Seems important enough to me, Wendy. But you stay out of trouble and make damn sure you're back on time. After that party of yours this is my job on the line and if you mess up I will tell them you ran away. Sorry kiddo, but I need to cover myself."

"Yes! I will, thank you Terry!" I gave him a hug. Terry was definitely one of the good guys.

Judd drove to Stancaster in his usual haphazard attempt to flatten the both of us somewhere along the way. When we arrived -in one piece- Judd and I checked in at the reception and Judd led me through a corridor, up a stairway and down another corridor before knocking on and then opening a door.

The room was large enough to house a bed, closet and a desk with a chair. It was remarkably uncluttered; in fact, it was devoid of any personal effects whatsoever. Nyle was sitting on the bed staring vacantly at the wall and for a moment I felt disappointed. Then he turned his head and when he saw me he smiled, not the twitching attempts he made last time, but a genuine smile. His eyes remained dullish but at least they were responsive.

"Wendy," my father said and smiled again. "You're back."

"Hey Dad," I answered, relishing the word that was so unfamiliar to my tongue.

I went and sat next to him on the bed. For a time he remained silent, he seemed to be drifting off again. I took his hand, it was limp like last time but slowly it came to life and he applied gentle pressure. I squeezed back.

"I am so sorry," Nyle slowly turned his head to look at me. "I am so sorry for everything Wendy."

"That's okay dad," I answered, amazed at the ease with which I lied.

"Has it been hard?" He asked.

I swallowed. It had been hell. Pure hell. But it was different now.

"I cope," I lied again.

Judd gave me an encouraging nod. I had gathered from his conversation in the car that he had picked up on some details from Puck and Rob. He knew I was lying.

Nyle relapsed into a long silence again but he hadn't drifted away this time. He continued looking at me as if he was searching for answers. I looked back and did the same.

"You look so much like your mother," he said at last. He still spoke slowly, disconnected, but wasn't slurring his words anymore.

"I didn't know," I answered, pleased with this information. Judd had said so but to hear it from Nyle was different somehow.

"That's a nice necklace," Nyle added.

I smiled, my hand automatically went to the Swan and I touched it with my index finger.

"Somebody gave it to me."

"A young man perhaps?" My father asked me with a hint of a grin on his face.

For a moment I felt daunted. He knew absolutely nothing about me and I knew nothing about him. All I had to go on was the biological connection and the knowledge that it would take a long time to establish any sort of meaningful contact. I also realised that, contrary to my hopes, this was one parent who had not shown up to take care of me and protect me. That would be my task if I took this any further. I took a deep breath and decided to follow my heart.

"Yes," I nodded. "His name is Puck."

Nyle's face darkened for a moment.

"A Farisee name," he commented sadly. "Is he good to you?"

"Very good," I nodded empathically. "I...he's the best thing that ever happened to me."

Judd smiled.

"I'd like to meet him someday, maybe?" Nyle said shyly.

It was my turn to smile. He was showing signs of various emotional reactions. I was beginning to see the shadow of the man he might have once been and resolved to find that man. I would have to exercise patience, not my strongest suit, but I had little to lose here, I only stood to gain.

"I will bring him," I promised. "He would like to meet you too."

I had no idea if Puck was open to such a meeting, but knew he would come if I asked him, however he felt about it.

"Did you bring it?" My dad focused hopeful eyes on Judd.

Judd nodded and produced a small camera.

"Nyle…your father would like to have a picture of you two…" He half asked me.

"I'd like a copy too," I nodded. I hesitated for a moment, and then I shifted over to lean against my father. It was awkward for him too; I guided his arm so that it was wrapped around my shoulder. I closed my eyes for a second, feeling his arm around me. My father's arm. Despite the state he was in it felt protective. A feeling of regret started surfacing; why had I been denied what should have been so normal till now? I gritted my teeth and banished the feeling. I had it now. Enjoy the now, I admonished myself.

"You have to smile dad," I said softly.

Judd then took my first ever first family portrait. He showed us the picture on the little screen on the back of his camera. It was odd, it looked just like a regular snap -we were both smiling a bit foolishly- without giving a hint of the awkwardness and unfamiliarity, or the sterile depersonalised space around us. Nyle was absolutely delighted though, even more so when Judd promised to bring him a printed framed copy within a few days.

When we started to leave at the end of the visit my dad looked at me, almost sharply.

"Wendy," he said. "I don't deserve a say, but please be careful with the Farisee. Please."

I nodded and then followed Judd out of the institution. I was in a daze again on the way back to Odesby.

"You've made him very happy Wenn," Judd said as he casually waved his middle finger at another driver who was going too slow for his liking. "I haven't seen him like this for years."

"That's good," I answered softly.

"Will you be okay though?" He looked at me and I read concern, something odd to register on a face that spoke of a roughness and toughness which was further emphasised by the Mohawk and nose chain.

"Yeah," I nodded. "It's a bit overwhelming, but I'm really pleased."

"Good, good!" Judd beamed. "Wenn, can you do something for me?"

"Sure." I figured I owned him big time.

"With all of the road stuff going on, there's a good chance I'll be arrested. In fact, I'll be disappointed if I am not," Judd grinned. "But I go to see your old man at least once a month. I might not be able to visit him for a while if I get into trouble."

"You want me to go instead?" I asked.

Judd nodded. "I know it's a lot to ask, I can't even imagine what you're going through Wenn. But the Nyle we saw today, I haven't seen him like that for years. You're good for him."

"I'll do it," I promised. "But get me a copy of that photo, please Uncle Judd?"

He turned his head and looked at me sharply. I was sure I saw his eyes go moist.

"The road! Look at the road!" I urged him for we were hurling towards the intersection with the A267.

When he dropped me off at Nowhere Place I leaned over and gave him a kiss on the cheek.

"Thank you Uncle Judd," I said. "Take care, okay?"

"I'm still irresistible if I get kissed by the likes of you Wenn-Wendy Twyner." He beamed. Then he stepped on his gas pedal and roared off down the street. I stood there till he was out of sight and then, with a sigh, I walked back into Nowhere Place.

30. Underearth and Overbranch

I approached Miss Watson on Monday because asking Stubbles was just about the surest way of getting a no. I was hesitant at first, trying to recall that one instance when I had seen Watson let down her guard, she had been beautiful and kind then. When I asked to talk to her she was her guarded wary self. I couldn't blame her, she knew the game and had seen me playing it often enough.

I explained to her that Jasmin had shown a great deal of interest in my stories about my grandparents' cottage in the Wyrde Woods. How I felt that it might be good for her to come along the next home leave weekend, seeing that she never left Nowhere Place during those weekends. As soon as I had spoken I felt foolish. There were plenty of people at Nowhere Place who were trained to know what was good for Jasmin even though that mostly involved drugging her to kingdom come and back.

"Well Wendy," Watson began and my hopes started to sink. "I will talk to the Head Supervisor about this today, we will have to call her parents of course, you understand. They will need to give permission."

I was surprised.

"You mean you think it's a good idea?"

"Not only for Jasmin," Watson nodded. "But for you too Wendy."

"Me?" I was puzzled.

"Don't take this wrong please Wendy," Watson showed that soft face for a moment, and I nodded. *Doant be tessy.*

"This is the first time in the two-and-a-half years that I have known you that you are thinking about somebody other than yourself."

My mind ran riot but I steadied it, knowing that Watson was right and meant it as a compliment.

"Thank you Miss Watson," I said meekly.

§ § § § § § §

I picked up the Tuesday Odesby Gazette to see if there was any word about the Wyrde Woods and found much more than I had bargained for.

The headline ran: OCCULTISTS IN WYRDE WOODS.

The accompanying article picked up on the previous report on the Midsummer Night's celebrations at Arthur's Fort, claiming that further investigations had revealed that elements of bizarre Satanic rituals had been part and parcel of the deviant and twisted festivities, including the appearance of the 'horned one'. This, concluded the article, was the perversion which the law-abiding citizens of Odesby faced with the arrival of more and more occultists who had seized the road protest as an opportunity to enact upon their unnatural desires.

The second page ran an article entitled: DUGUTH CONSTRUCTION JOB PROGRAMME and waxed lyrical about the great opportunities the construction company was offering the Odesby unemployed, a miraculous benefit of the planned M33, if the reporter was to be believed.

The fourth page ran a short interview with one of the surveyors on the site, who admitted that their work had been delayed by vandalism and acts of crime. He expressed his disbelief that this included dozens upon dozens of heavy concrete blocks which had gone missing. "It's almost as if there was magic at work here."

Towards the back of the paper, in the Odesby Social-'Lite' section, there were interviews with six national mediums, all of who claimed they had sensed a strong vibe coming from the area between Odesby and Stancaster over the last month or so, expressing fears that ill-reputed charlatans were playing with a fire which might have greater consequences than they realised.

I frowned, folded the paper and put it away in my school satchel.

§ § § § § §

"I talked to the Head Supervisor Wendy," Watson said when I got back to Nowhere Place on Wednesday. "He called Jasmin's parents."

"And?"

"They were absolutely delighted, they see it as a breakthrough, do you want to tell her the good news?"

§ § § § § §

Puck had warned me to be careful with text messages. He had said that I should assume they were being read by others too. I formulated my message to him with due care.

Can U meet Thursday afternoon? URGENT

The reply was uncharacteristically prompt.

time and place?

I was pleased that he had responded so quickly, I wanted to go tell Jasmin the good news but really needed to arrange this with Puck after I had woken up in the middle of the night with a bad feeling.

Five pm where we first kissed

He was still monitoring his phone because the reply came immediately.

I'll be there, surelye

§ § § § § §

"REALLY?" Jasmin's eyes were wide.

"Really," I nodded, feeling pleased with myself.

"REALLY? REALLY?"

"For real," I grinned.

"But my…parents…" Jasmin looked downcast.

"Have given their permission. You can ask Miss Watson, she arranged it for you."

"REALLY? REALLY? REALLY?"

"Really." I had to laugh; her facial expression was comical, shifting from disbelief to total joy and back again.

"Oh!" Jasmin threw her arms around me and hugged me tight. I hugged her back and we sat there for a while, Jasmin was apparently not going to let go of me soon. I started to grin, but then I felt her shoulders shaking and warm tears running onto my neck, so many that they started soaking my t-shirt.

"There, there sweetie." I stroked her head and then cried a little too.

§ § § § § §

On Thursday morning, going to school, I passed a building plot which had been vacant as long as I could remember, barring the grass and weeds which poked through the cracks in its pavement slabs. It was completely different now. A long double row of men, young and old, queued in front of the gate of the fencing that surrounded the plot. Hundreds of them. Most of them looked like Neverlanders. They were signing in at the entrance and then walked towards a row of coaches which had been parked on one side of the plot. There was another table halfway to the coaches and the men stopped there and were allocated a bright yellow coat from one of the many cardboard boxes piled up there. Most of the men put them on straight away and I could read the lettering on the back: SECURITY.

With a sinking feeling I realised the coaches were headed for the Wyrde Woods. Neverland was coming to my refuge big time.

§ § § § § §

Puck was at Make-out Corner as promised. I greeted Lady and then kissed Puck long and hard.

"If that is what was so urgent," he smiled wickedly, "then it was worth it."

I smiled and shook my head.

"I wanted to show you something. It's been bugging me. It might be nothing, nothing at all, but I have a bad feeling about this."

I showed him Tuesday's Odesby Gazette. He looked amused when he read the article on the front page, but his bemusement was replaced with a frown as I pointed out the other articles.

"I dunno, but it seems like it's on purpose," I ventured, hoping I hadn't made him walk all the way to the edge of the woods for nothing.

"Yes it does," Puck nodded.

I gave him the Wednesday and Thursday editions as well.

"There are more articles here and there, and the Dear Editor letters speak of nothing else but what some call the Wyrde Woods Witches."

"You know who owns the paper I presume," Puck asked.

"Lady Malheur," I guessed and saw that guess confirmed by Puck's grim nod.

"Might just be a bit of mud-smearing," Puck pondered. "But it might also be a hint that Aunt Catt knows more than we think she does. Or wants us to believe that she does. It was good of you to bring these Wenn. I'll talk to the rest as soon as possible."

"One more thing," I added. "The vacant plot on Angel Street, just on the edge of Neverland. It's where they load the security guys on the buses in the morning."

Puck grinned.

"Check," he said. "I'll let Judd know."

§ § § § § §

There was much ado on Friday morning on Angel Street, the queue was just as long as the day before, but nobody could get in. Somebody had wound seven extra sturdy chains around the gates, clamped together with heavy-duty locks.

§ § § § § §

On Saturday morning I caught the earliest bus to Carfax. Puck and Lady were waiting for me and we walked to Hornsby Farm through the birch woods and past the magnolias where Puck had given me Niada's Swan.

"So what's the plan?" I asked.

"Mad Judd Mack will establish his camp with much ado, he's invited the press. In the meantime, the Lost Boys will work on the two sub-camps of New Rivendell."

"New Rivendell?" I smiled.

"The site for the main camp, but that won't be built for a while yet, it'll draw too much attention. They'll start work on Underearth and Overbranch today; actually, the digging has already started on the sly. It'll be quite spectacular today, but if the police or anybody shows up, you and I leave, immediately."

"They chained the new security coach park fences yesterday," I grinned.

"That'll be Judd's people," Puck laughed.

"Did you speak to the Waer-Wyrd about the papers?"

"I did," Puck frowned. "Opinions are divided as to what my aunt knows and doesn't know. Most think she's just trying to frighten the public, but we agreed to be extra careful."

"Oh."

"You expected more?" Puck gave me a sideways glance.

"I am worried about Joy," I said.

"So am I," Puck agreed. "But I know her well enough, she's not going to run and hide. We'll just have to hope for the best."

"Okay," I said with reluctance.

"I thought you'd be inundating me with questions about Maimie," Puck pulled a face.

I stopped, grabbed his hands and looked him in the eyes.

"I trust you," I said earnestly. "Besides, the brabagious broomstick was wearing boots."

He raised his eyebrows quizzically.

"No shoe laces to tie together," I clarified and made Puck laugh.

§ § § § § § §

The old farm buildings were bustling with activity. About another dozen experts had shown up to reinforce the Lost Boys. Although Jukes and Tink had discarded their sporty gear just as Maimie had dropped her gypsy act, none of these protesters resembled the grungier look the Weard Hunt had. They all wore professional looking outdoor wear with belts that were adorned with pouches, clip-on hooks and other gear I didn't recognise. When we got there they were all packing hand-pulled carts and wheelbarrows with tools, rolls of tarpaulin, coils of rope and other bits and pieces.

"What do I do?" I asked Puck.

"Nothing, they've got this down to the smallest details. Just watch and enjoy."

I nodded; I reckoned I could cope with that.

Jukes came over to greet me fondly.

"I'll have a treat for you later Wenn," he smiled broadly. "I think you'll enjoy it."

"What?" I wanted to know.

"We're going to play squirrels," Jukes beamed.

The anti-road protestors divided up into two teams at the farmhouse. The Underearth group left first, consisting of Tootles, Nibs, the twins and three of the new people. Puck and I left fifteen minutes later with the Overbranch group which had Jukes, Tink, Maimie, Slightly, Curly and five newcomers in it.

A handful of people stayed at the farm. Puck told me that the base camp would need to be manned continuously from now on. With the influx of all the new people it was only a matter of time before the location was spotted and the detective agencies especially had burgled protest offices and camps in the past.

"And these new camps? Will they be spotted?" I asked Puck.

"Not for a while I hope. Both camps will be somewhat hidden and until the Weard Hunt camp is cleared there won't be a main camp. If we're lucky we'll have a week or longer before they catch on."

"Why can the Weard Hunt camp be cleared quickly and not these new camps?"

"You'll see," Puck grinned.

"Puck!"

"Okay, in the good old days any camp would take a long time to evict. They had to serve you a Notice to Quit first and give you 48 hours to comply. If you didn't, they had to apply to the courts for a Possession Order. But that meant someone from the camp needed to be summoned to court and if that person showed up with a good law team you could contest it, sometimes for weeks. If they do win, you can still appeal. But you do need law people who are willing to put in the time and who know what they are doing."

"Do we have a good law team?"

"Yup, David Masters arranged that, he's pretty respectable and has the right connections."

"So it could take months!"

"That depends, we hope so. The most successful protests fought half their battles in courts, rather than in the woods. But if they want to play nasty, they can."

"How?"

"The CJA -the Criminal Justice Act- gave a lot of powers to the police. If they claim that protesters are damaging private property or harassing the landowner they can start arresting people on the basis of Mass Trespass. Obstructing someone from carrying out their work is also cause for arrest. This means we have to be careful planning actions, because these days we'll usually lose those protestors. They can even arrest you if they *suspect* you're intending to do something, even if you haven't broken any laws."

"That's unfair," I frowned. "I always thought you were innocent till proven guilty or something like that."

"Not anymore," Puck said. "Anyhow, there will be a bunch of arrests, which is why we have to stay clear of it if we can. The Waer-Wyrd has other plans and needs us for those. Duguth Construction will also try to evict the camps, but are under obligation to do so without causing unnecessary bodily harm."

"And you can delay that?"

"Yes, the Underearth camp will literally be under the earth. They have done a lot of digging already at night, there are tunnels. Those will be manned day and night. When the surveyors and construction workers cross the Rore and start approaching the Taunflow we'll give them a rough indication where the tunnels are and they won't be able to drive machinery over them. They'll have to burrow in and remove the protesters there one by one. They'll probably have tunnelling specialists for that, we call them Potholers."

I shivered; I would hate to be locked up in a narrow confined space.

"And Overbranch, it's in the trees?" I asked.

"Yup, high up in the Giant's Grove. It's going to be one hell of a job to remove protestors from there. They usually use cherry pickers, but those only reach so high, nowhere near as high as Overbranch will be. This means they will have to send climbers up. Those are like specially trained bailiffs."

"Spiff." Being high up in the trees appealed to me a great deal more. "But in the end, they will remove everybody?"

"Yes, you can only hope the media picks up on it. And even then, you saw how the Odesby Gazette portrays us, like a bunch of rabid radicals. Almost all the media in this country are owned by big co-operations. But the Giant's Grove might be just too tempting for them to stay away."

§ § § § § § §

The first thing Puck and Tink did when we got to the Giant's Grove was to go to the site of the main camp and I trailed along, carrying a pile of small light stakes which had different colours painted on the end. Puck and Tink used these to mark the places where they could later build a kitchen area, fire pit, benders for sleeping in, storage areas, compost toilets and paths.

When that was done Puck and I went to visit Underearth. We ran into Nibs who cleared a patch of the forest floor and used a stick to draw a rough overview of the sort of tunnel system the Lost Boys liked to build.

"We don't like it straight. Narrow with curves because us lot tend to be a lot slighter than the bailiffs. It gets confusing down there if the direction changes or tunnels go up and down."

"So how do they get through if the tunnels are too narrow?"

"The potholers make them bigger, but they have to shore up these bigger tunnels of theirs too, it takes time. So the bigger the tunnel system, the longer it takes them. Curves, side tunnels, ups and downs, all make their work harder. Trap-doors and reinforced gates too. Basically we are just going to keep on digging' till E-day. If we're given the time, we'll work our way around the entire hill."

"So you guys sit in the tunnels and wait for them to come?" I decided that I would definitely get claustrophobic.

"Not in the tunnels themselves, we build little rooms too, cubby holes. They have plastic pipes going up so there is an air supply. Plus bedding, food, water, torch, batteries, a good book, toilet paper, a car battery for fairy lights, empty bottles for pissing in and empty bags for crapping in."

"Lock-ons too," Puck said.

"Yeah, Curly showed me at the farm," I answered.

Curly had demonstrated a number of ways a protestor could chain a hand or a foot to solid immobile objects and then make access difficult by surrounding it with a length of piping or whatnot. I could well imagine that in cramped tunnels it would be hard for these bailiffs to move around some protester who had chained him or herself in a way they could only reach by doing more tunnelling. It all came down to delay again.

I was glad Nibs didn't invite us for a look in his subterranean world and Puck and I went back to the Giant's Grove where the Overbranchers were already hard at work. Jukes and Tink, the most experienced climbers, were using climbing slings to tape-climb up the redwoods, a climb that took a long time.

"Foliage starts at about 120 feet," Puck was stretching his neck like me to look up. "That's higher than that rock wall you tried to climb in Hood's Gorge."

When they were all the way up they lowered strings weighted down by small rocks and the other Overbranchers tied ropes to these which Jukes and Tink pulled up after which the others were able to prussik up and soon bundles of supplies were being hoisted high in the air.

"I want to go up there," I said dreamily. Climbing a California redwood! What tree climber could resist?

"No bloody way," Puck said happily. "Remember falling down the rock face?"

"DUH, that was rock, I've never fallen out of a tree before mister Green Man," I pointed out.

"Wenn, I don't want you up these trees, Jukes and Tink and the rest know what they're doing."

I looked at him angrily. *Doant be tessy.* I took a deep breath.

"Okay Puck, I am not going to be tessy about this, but let's get something clear. You can tell me that you would prefer it if I didn't. I can live with that because then I can ignore you. You don't tell me that I can't. You don't own me."

I folded my arms and looked at him defiantly. I reckoned this definitely counted as that third 'woman' category of tessy, so despite the promise I just made to him I was prepared to get extremely tessy if he couldn't understand my point of view in this.

Puck looked at me for a moment, and then laughed.

"Okay Wenn, I am sorry. I'd prefer it if you didn't, I keep seeing that image of you falling of that cliff."

"Trust me Puck," I put my hand on his arm. "There's a mega-huge difference between a cliff and a tree. Wenn does not fall out of trees."

"You'll have to ask Jukes anyway," Puck shrugged.

Jukes had me in a climbing harness in no time and showed me how to prussik, using sliding knots to climb up 120 feet of rope. The first small wooden platform had already been secured up there. It had a lockable trapdoor to confound the climbers who came to evict the Overbranchers. Sitting on it was like being in a boat because even a tree as solid as these giants swayed in the wind. I was totally delighted and sat on the edge of the platform swaying my legs over 120 feet of nothingness to freak out Puck a little while Jukes showed me how to tie a prussik knot, a figure eight knot and a Blake's hitch knot.

"You might as well make yourself useful up here girl," he grinned. "We don't do tourists. I need a couple of tree boats in this one, thought you might like to do that."

"Tree boats?"

Jukes showed me rectangular hammocks with ropes attached to each corner for extra stability. The ropes needed to be tied to different branches and before long I was shimmying along branches some 130 feet over the ground. It took a lot of effort not to whoop with joy, as that would have ruined the covert part of the operation. Jukes in the meantime was hoisting up porta ledges: nylon platforms supported by aluminium frames which Puck and Maimie had assembled on the ground.

"You guys seriously sleep up here in these things?" I asked him.

"Most seriously," he answered. "It's really swell. Puck used to too. We keep the saddles on though."

I conjured up the strange image of a horse up in the trees.

"Quiddy?"

"Ha! It's the climbing harness you're wearing. Rule number one up here, never ever take off your saddle."

I watched as Tink and Curly lashed joists to branches in the nearest tree busily constructing another platform. Further on the first Twigloo was being hoisted up. Jukes explained it was a tree house with a floor made of strong netting lashed to a frame whilst the top was just a basic bender design, a tarpaulin covering a frame made from young saplings bent into half circles.

"You'll like Twigloos Wenn, when the branches aren't ideal for a platform; we suspend these from the trees, like a great big redwood fruit."

I nodded; I wanted to live in one already.

"How do you get from one place to another?"

"We'll put up walkways next. Just ropes, one above the other, about four and a half feet apart. Clip on the slings of your harness, put your feet on the bottom one, hands on the top one, and hey, presto. We'll hang up cargo nets too, we've got a big one I call the village square."

"It will be like a whole village up here!" I said in wonderment. "A tree top village."

"You bet," Jukes nodded. "Complete with a population and ample supplies. I could live up here forever myself."

"So could I!"

"Ever abseil down a redwood tree Wenn?"

"Sirageous!" I grew a huge grin.

Puck was relieved when my feet touched the ground after I had made big leaps down the giant trunk.

"Puck, let's live in a tree? Please?"

He started laughing but then stopped. "Wenn, where are you going?"

"Why," I looked at him in surprise. "Up the next one of course."

I managed to climb seven of the redwoods that afternoon, making myself useful in the process, helping to hang camouflage netting over the more visible structures so the tree village was practically invisible from the ground. I loved it high up in the redwoods, there were amazing views of the Wyrde Woods and much of the country beyond them and I felt as free as a bird.

31. Jasmin

As the home leave weekend approached I became a bit anxious, suddenly realising that I would be more or less responsible for a girl whose primary reaction upon seeing her parents was to fly at them with outstretched claws and bared teeth. I never did find out why. I did ask Jasmin if there was anything specific that triggered it, just in case something like 'pass the salt' turned out to be words with regrettable consequences.

"It's just my parents," Jasmin shrugged it off and proceeded once again to take me through her check-list. She had been preparing and packing for a week. Since she never spent much of her meagre Nowhere Place allowance she was reasonably well loaded so the preparations involved shopping trips to the High Street where it was a relief that she insisted on paying for everything, it made shopping a lot more relaxing.

"It's just a weekend Jasmin," I explained for the umpteenth time when she showed me a new stash of goodies in a large shopping bag which she had stowed next to a suitcase and backpack.

"Oh no! Oh no!" Jasmin shook her head. "It's so much more."

"Be prepared huh?"

"Yes indeed. Do you think I should buy garlic to keep vampires at bay?"

I looked at her incredulously but she was dead serious.

"Joy keeps rowan, hazel and rosemary in her garden to protect the Owlery, so we should be okay," I explained. "They keep evil away."

"Oh good! I can't wait to meet her!" Jasmin exclaimed.

I left her room feeling pleased; she was reasonably focused just as she was during her preparations for the Hindu feast meals. I remembered what Joy said about not expecting the Wyrde Woods to work for

Jasmin in the same way they did for me but they were already having an effect on her.

When Willick and Joy came to collect us Willick raised an eyebrow at me when he saw all of Jasmin's luggage in the hallway. I shrugged. Jasmin was already engaged in an earnest conversation with Joy about owl poo so Willick and I carried all the luggage to the Land Rover. Miss Watson, who usually had the Fridays off, came to meet Joy and Willick and earnestly tell both Jasmin and myself to behave. I saw Miss Hare looking out of the office window and shaking her head whilst she frowned and suspected that not everybody was pleased that Miss Watson had gone over Stubbles' head to appeal to the Head Supervisor.

We skipped the Earl's Barrel this time round and I was pleased because I wasn't sure what would happen to Jasmin's abundant exuberance if we fuelled it with cider. Willick left after he dropped us off and Jasmin approached the Owlery with the reverence of somebody on a pilgrimage to an ancient relic. I felt kind of proud and I stood there enjoying the sight, forgetting to grumble because Jasmin had totally forgotten about the baggage. When I came in, loaded with all the stuff, I heard Jasmin's voice in the living room.

"And that must be Aethel, and there's Horsa! But how do I tell Bran and Bronwen apart?"

"Bronwen be a mite smaller and naun as grumpy," I heard Joy say. "Would ye like to hold Bronwen?"

Jasmin launched into a dozen positive responses and I started taking all the luggage upstairs. When I upended my backpack in my room I made sure I only used one half of the room, leaving space for Jasmin to dump her stuff too.

Joy had done her best for dinner, she had made a nut roast which was savoury and spiced with the Vietnamese Coriander she liked using. Most of the talk was owl related meaning Joy was in her element and I just relaxed, beaming at the two of them. When Jasmin went to the bathroom I gave Joy a questioning look. She responded with a happy smile.

"Hern chatters more than a caffincher but hern be a liddle dear, reminds me of mine friend Maisy," Joy chuckled. "I think ye does give hern a great gift Wenn."

"You too though," I said. "I don't know how to thank…"

"Doant worry, I'll have a dozzle of duzzicks for yern to outshine Master Dobbs in again."

I had questioned Puck about a reference Joy had made to Master Dobbs before. It reminded me of the house elf in the Harry Potter books. Puck said that folk in Sussex had believed in helpful house elves for a long time, and Master Dobbs was the generic name. So I figured the 'dozzle of duzzicks' indicated household chores I could help Joy with, and that was a fair enough deal so I nodded my agreement.

That night I stripped to my knickers and singlet, throwing my boots, socks, trousers and shirt in a casual arrangement over the rest of my junk and then crawled under the covers. Jasmin folded each item of clothing neatly as she took it off and then put on a pair of pyjamas and pulled a comb through her long black hair. After that she unpacked all of her bags carefully, humming as she started to build neat little piles and stacks. I fell asleep before she was done.

§ § § § § §

When I woke up Jasmin's side of the bed was already empty, her pyjamas neatly folded on her pillow next to the little stuffed bear she carried around with her at Nowhere Place and had insisted on bringing. I found her downstairs, seated on the ground in front of Joy whilst Joy was braiding her hair and looking pleased with her efforts. I felt a stab of jealousy; it never occurred to me that Joy might have liked a lass who was a bit more into girly stuff. Jasmin's look of bliss however, cured me of my selfishness, she had been even more isolated

177

than I had been at Nowhere Place and I still rejoiced in coming to the Wyrde Woods with my whole being. Jasmin was practically in heaven. I decided I was allowed to feel good about myself for bringing Jasmin and made a mental note to bring a few more summer dresses for my prolonged stay during the holiday so I could be girly every now and then to please Joy and drive Puck to the brink of distraction. I could go commando in a dress and then insist on climbing trees. I grinned. That ought to do the trick.

The three of us walked outside after breakfast because Joy had said that the honey which Jasmin had spread on her bread had come from her own hives and Jasmin insisted on seeing the bees.

"She likes animals," I told Joy as Jasmin skipped outside ahead of us.

"Jasmin be like a liddle butterfly, enjoying every moment she can," Joy chuckled; somewhat to my relief as I was still worried that Jasmin's presence might have been a little bit too much of a good thing but Joy seemed to relish Jasmin's delight in just about everything.

Jasmin spotted the garden while we were looking at the buzzy activity around the hives and was delighted. As Joy showed her around the two started an earnest discussion about the use of herbs and flowers in food. Joy seemed to like listening to the Indian recipes Jasmin listed. I heard the thud of horse hooves on the dirt road and wandered around the side of the Owlery curious as to who was approaching. It was Puck and he made a spectacular entrance, cantering down the dirt road astride Beowulf. He had a soft guitar case strapped to his back and I noted that he wore a black riding cap; the first time I had ever seen him wearing anything that wasn't green. Lady scampered happily behind the horse and jumped the low wall when she spotted me. She tried to knock me to the ground first by launching herself at my chest and then trotted over to Joy and Jasmin -who had appeared around the Owlery- to give Joy a much gentler greeting and then sit down so that Jasmin could idolise her.

I walked up to Puck, who had jumped from Beowulf like he did it on a daily basis and then unbuckled his riding cap. He was sweaty and smelled of horse but I didn't mind and mellowed into his hug, my mouth seeking his for a kiss.

"I didn't know you could ride a horse, surelye" I said.

"I am a toff, remember?" Puck laughed. "We learn to ride when we're two months old or something. Just in case we need to buckle on our armour and go rescue a damsel in distress."

For an instant my mental images of Sir Richard and Niada passed by and I ran the tip of my index finger along the graceful lines of the Swan.

"Hmm, I recollect yern lot mostly caused damsels distress."

"Fair enough, but I am trying to break the habit," Puck said a bit standoffish.

"I know, that was uncalled for," I gave him a quick kiss. "Ye're a middling good toff."

"And you my Elfin," he smiled again, "have an extraordinary vocabulary for a girl from Neverland. Especially now that you're starting to mix the odd bit of middling Sussex in."

"Am I really?"

"Oh hey Puck," Jasmin drifted by barely glancing at Puck, her eyes focused on the roan who gave her a friendly nudge with his nose.

"Hello Jasmin, nice to meet you again," Puck answered. "This is Beowulf."

"The Bear-Wolfman," Jasmin said looking puzzled for a moment. "That's an odd name for a horse."

"Yes it is," Puck winked at me. "I'll need to water Beowulf and rub him down some, but I thought you might like to ride him?"

Jasmin's eyes widened, she was even speechless. I squeezed Puck's hand, pleased that he was making an attempt to help me make Jasmin's weekend special.

§ § § § § § §

We left the Owlery; I walked beside Puck who was holding the reigns of Beowulf who patiently carried a beaming Jasmin on his back whilst Lady picked up her usual reconnaissance duties. We took the Lover's Lane route along Hood's Gorge to the Shy Maidens where we had a break. We then headed south to cross the dirt road which connected Malheur Hall and Roreford and then arrived at St. Lewinna's Pool which I hadn't seen yet, a large oval pond with clear water which gave the clearing around it a tranquil ambience. After that we continued to the Guardians, a triple row of standing stones about Puck's height which truly did seem to be guarding the path there.

"Tuckersham Church straight ahead," Puck said, but led us onto a path to our right which led to the Falls and the Fey's Pool. We stopped there and Puck launched into the tale of the Faere Fey who seduced men with the sight of her bathing. I rolled my eyes, this was the third time I heard the story but Jasmin loved it and insisted on walking the little island widdershins seven times after she had waded to it.

She came back looking disappointed for no nude Farisee temptress had appeared. Puck explained that it worked mostly for men, and then usually at midnight if there was sufficient moonlight to illuminate the Fey.

"Yes," Jasmin nodded, "That makes sense."

"It's a good thing naun of them ever drink more than a pint," I grinned, picturing locals stumbling dead drunk from the pubs late at night, lured into the woods by Will o' Wisps and then seeing all sorts of things.

It was actually really nice to tour this corner of the Wyrde Woods with Jasmin. We didn't see much in the way of wildlife because she kept on asking Puck questions and commenting on his replies which meant either one of them was speaking all the time. I grinned as I recalled Willick suggesting that I might enjoy the woods more if I shut up. Well, that wasn't how he had put it, but it came down the same thing. I wondered if he had experienced me like I now experienced Jasmin who was vocally enraptured by every leaf, twig and branch we encountered. I must have been a bit less excitable, I decided, though truth be told I enjoyed every minute of it simply because I gained a great deal of pleasure from the fact that Jasmin was having such a grand time.

We headed back to the Owlery through Roreford where I was pleased Puck didn't tell Jasmin about the cruel use of the water wheel.

Joy employed Puck to start building a fire for she had planned to roast a chicken for dinner and declared chicken tasted the best roasted over an open outdoor fire.

Jasmin, in the meantime, insisted that I accompany her to the stream to bathe. I didn't recall telling her about that but I must have.

"Jas, we'll be back at Nowhere Place tomorrow evening. Whatever else, there are hot showers there."

"Cold streams are far more fun," she pleaded. "Please? Pretty please?"

"Might naun be a bad idea," Joy told me. She pointed at the chicken coop and I realised our barbeque meat still needed to be harvested, something Jasmin might not take well.

We went down to the stream and stripped. The water was cold as ever but after that initial plunge when you just about thought you'd die it became invigorating again. I got kind of worried about Jasmin when she was splashing around the pool as I noted that I could just about count all her ribs and the little she had in the way of hips was bony. I resolved to keep an eye out on her eating habits from now on.

When we got back to the Owlery the bits and pieces of chicken were already sizzling over the fire and Puck and Joy were in the kitchen making a big salad with greens and herbs from the garden.

After dinner, in which Jasmin participated heartily, Puck got his guitar out and we sat by the fire sipping elderberry cordial and birch wine while he tuned it and plucked at the strings some.

"I'd likes to taste one o' yern curries one day Jasmin," Joy said.

"She makes them really well," I said.

"I could maybe come back one day?" Jasmin asked shyly. "I could make you one. Two. Three."

Joy looked at me.

"I'd ask ye to come here in home leave weekends when ye have summer holiday Jasmin, but tis Wenn's room."

I *sooo* wanted to go over and hug Joy; Jasmin would love it, those weekends would make her summer more bearable. Then I looked at Puck, remembering his first reaction to Jasmin's visit.

His glasses reflected the fire so I couldn't see his eyes properly but he smiled at me and I knew it was alright with him too.

"I'd love to have you over Jasmin," I said, absurdly proud that I had a place where I could invite people over to. "With or without curries."

Jasmin was elated and jumped up.

"I have paper and pen upstairs; I'll go plan the meals. I'll be right back."

I laughed. More focus.

I walked over to Joy and sank to the ground next to her and leant my head on her knee. I had never met anybody who was this kind and selfless.

"I'm not sure I say it enough…" I started.

"I know, that be enough sweetie," Joy nodded with a smile. "And ye make me happy too, it aint all one way."

Puck began to play the guitar now, his long fingers plucking the strings and before long he began to sing softly.

Come away, O human child
To the waters and the wild
With a faery, hand in hand
For the world's more full of weeping
Than you can understand.

I thought about the Falls and the Fey's Pool, then the enchantment of being taken to the waters and the wild, hand in hand with my Puck, who didn't just have the blood of cottage and castle in him but that of the Pook Hall too. If there was truth to the stories, I hoped that we could stay here for that interminable time visits to the Faere Folk were said to take. A hundred years would do nicely.

We foot it all the night
Weaving olden dances
Mingling hands and mingling glances
Till the moon has taken flight
To and fro we leap
And chase the frothy bubbles
Whilst the world is full of troubles
And is anxious in its sleep.
For the world's more full of weeping
Than you can understand.

Well that brought back Midsummer Night, I liked this song.

That night Puck was relegated to the bedding in one of the sheds Joy had spoken of. I spent half-an-hour saying goodnight to him outside in the garden. I kept on apologising but he said it was alright; he could see how much the whole visit meant to Jasmin now and was pleased I brought her. When I started to apologise yet again he shut me up by kissing me and that was okay by me too.

Jasmin was already in bed when I got upstairs after bidding Joy goodnight. I thought Jasmin was asleep so I got undressed as quietly as I could and slipped into the bed.

"You know something Wendy?" Jasmin said in her dreamy voice.

"Tell me sweetie," I replied.

"You are really lucky you know. Really lucky."

I stared at the ceiling and suddenly my eyes filled with tears. All day long I had been seeing the Wyrde Woods through the eyes of Jasmin and it had been as if I had got a second chance to experience that first encounter all over again. Now I saw myself through her eyes. And I realised just how lucky I was.

"I know," I whispered.

32. Mad Judd Mack's Last Stand

It was the first class of the day on Tuesday and I sat at the back of the classroom trying hard to focus on what the teacher was saying. I was rapidly failing in this endeavour for every time I glanced out of the second floor window I sat next to I looked down at the luscious foliage of a tree and every such glance was sufficient to transport me instantly to the Wyrde Woods.

We had had an excellent Sunday, Puck and I had taken Jasmin to the Devil's Tarn and the Halfhollow Oak. She hadn't expressed a great deal of interest in climbing the oak but sat in the hollow humming songs whilst Puck and I clambered to the top and back. Joy had made soup when we got back and Willick had brought us back to Nowhere Place in the evening. Jasmin had been unusually chatty on Monday, telling all and sundry of her wonderful weekend and Watson had flashed me a thumbs-up together with an approving nod and that had done me a world of good.

Monday had become even better when Judd had dropped by to give me the framed picture he had taken in Stancaster. He had said he had already dropped the other copy off with Nyle and said that my dad had been over the moon. I had been too and put it on my bed side table so it would be the last thing I saw before I went to sleep and the first thing when I woke up.

When I left the classroom after the first hour was up, trudging slowly to the next class of the day, I was whisked into a broom cupboard by Jasmin and Biggs. Jasmin was so excited she could barely speak.

"Have you heard? Have you heard?" She kept on repeating while Biggs beamed at her.

"What's this about Jas?"

"The Road Protest!" She exclaimed, and for a moment I frowned. I had never told her anything about the M33 and neither Puck nor I had mentioned it in her presence during the course of the weekend.

It turned out that Jasmin had done some research of her own when she had first started hearing my stories about the Wyrde Woods and she had found the Friends of the Wyrde Woods site and placed herself on the mailing list.

"They've called us out!" She said excitedly.

"Called us out?" I was wary.

"Yes, the work has crossed the Rore River today, you know, the one that..."

"I know the Rore River Jasmin," I said. "What do you mean the work has crossed?"

"They've started felling the trees on the east side of the Rore River and Friends of the Wyrde Woods has called everybody to go out there today and protest."

I didn't know what to say. Puck had been reasonably clear that we should stay away from the Weard Hunt activities and I assumed that would count for the Friends of the Wyrde Woods events as well.

"Well, Biggs and I are going. Do you want to come?" Jasmin's eyes shone brightly.

"In the middle of a school day?" I grinned.

"We take the rest of the day off," Biggs grinned back at me.

"I am trying to convince them that I'm a good girl," I protested.

"Just the one day," Biggs shrugged. "They'll probably not even miss you."

I realised that was true. If Pastoral Care came looking for me they'd find out, but most regular teachers at our school didn't bother to be accurate with the attendance list. They frequently failed to note missing students or wrote down the names of students who were present and the administration workers despaired of ever finding out whether a student had been absent, had been present but reported absent, had been absent but reported present or was well aware of the permanent state of collapse of the whole attendance system and made the most of the confusion.

There was still the fact that I shouldn't really show my face there though.

"Come on Wendy," Biggs said. "We need to sneak away before the second bell; it'll be a lot harder walking out when the corridors are empty."

"You're definitely going?" I asked.

"Deffo," Jasmin confirmed.

I decided I would go along, if only to keep an eye out on these two and if things got dicey I could just melt away into the woods I figured.

"Ok, let's go," I said and Jasmin smiled brightly.

§ § § § § § §

I need not have worried about being conspicuous for when we arrived in the woods just north of Tuckersham Church there seemed to be thousands of people there. The trees were sparser here, with lots of clearings and little hillocks.

The chainsaw teams had already levelled a beachhead on the Rore's eastern bank which was defended by a double line of security men. There was a police presence too, but the police had gathered on either flank of the security cordon and were chatting to each other in a most unconcerned manner, just as most of the yellow-coated men in the security cordon were.

The besiegers of the beachhead were manifold and I was absolutely amazed how many residents of Odesby had turned out. David Masters was there leading a small army of people dressed in posh rambling gear: Shiny boots, corduroy trousers and expensive wax coats were prominent. Some bore banners pronouncing them to be members of the birdwatcher societies, a badger preservation society, ramblers and whatnot. Similar groups of posh folk, many of them in their fifties or older, were spread around in large groups or smaller batches of two or three. I saw a few shopkeepers I recognised from the High Street shops. One of them was an elderly woman who ran the book shop and she gave me a friendly nod, apparently recognising me from my frequent visits. I felt myself turning red; I had stolen from all their stores, especially the book shop. I certainly did not deserve friendly nods.

There were groups of young parents –mostly mothers- who had brought their toddlers and mixing amiably with all of them were the Weard Hunters in their mixed rambling and alto gear. There were also many representatives of various subcultures, including New Age Travellers who were just about the only ones who managed to look authentically in tune with nature in their threadbare wool sweaters and trousers and boots. The latter had accumulated so much of the countryside over the years that they seemed to grow out of the ground like trees. These were people like Puck, who had turned their back on the system and created a radically different lifestyle, one of their own and I admired them for it.

I had expected tension with latent aggression from both sides threatening to boil over but the atmosphere was festive. This was enhanced by at least two groups of musicians on either side of the protest lines who were strumming guitars, banging djembes and playing fiddles in impromptu jam sessions which were cheerfully encouraged by bystanders, some of whom danced around the musicians with glee.

The first line of trees in the path of the road constructors were all occupied by a protester or two. Some of them were chatting with the bailiff climbers and Yellowcoats who had gathered around the base of the tree trying to talk them down. None of the trees were particularly tall; I wouldn't have climbed any of them in a spontaneous mood because there was little challenge in it. Occasionally members of the crowd, young and old, would detach themselves from their side and stroll over to the police or security cordon to have a chat or start an impassioned debate, but even in the latter tempers were kept in check.

"Isn't it wonderful?" Jasmin exclaimed and I had to agree with her.

Every now and then a tree would be gently cleared of the protester in it by a pair of climbers at which point a few police constables would come to lead that protester away to one of their vans which were parked nearby. Even these arrests proceeded in an amiable fashion however. The crowd would cheer the protester as he or she was led away and the Yellowcoats would cheer good-heartedly in turn when a chainsaw team brought a tree down. Twice the smaller cordon which the Yellowcoats had formed around a tree that was being evicted like this had too many gaps and to the great delight of the crowd a new protester would dash through and scramble up, forcing the whole process to restart from the beginning. Even many of the police constables and security men laughed when that happened.

I could barely believe the relaxed mood, or the absolute slow pace with which the felling was progressing. At this rate it would take them years to reach the Taunflow I realised with a big grin. Of course it was unlikely that FWW would be able to raise such a turn-out day after day but as it was the residents of Odesby were making a clear statement about their opposition to the roadwork, something I had not expected.

"All this for a bunch of trees?" Biggs asked in disbelief. He looked uncomfortable and I suspected he would rather be in his room reading comics. Jasmin's face fell from happy to disbelief and then picked up again with the fierce determination of a true believer.

"Yer up to yern lips in moil now lad," I laughed at Biggs.

"Huh? What?" Biggs asked before he was overwhelmed by a sermon from Jasmin, who had clearly decided that she had a mission to convert Biggs.

It was an incongruous sight really, the fierce little girl taking on the lumbering form of the much bigger boy who was clearly being browbeaten and looked helpless.

I grinned and walked away, those two were coping quite well without me and I wanted to scope the scene out some more. I halted by the furthest group of musicians and enjoyed the gleeful wild dances some of the Weard Hunters and New Age Travellers were engaged in, much to the delight of the musicians who obviously felt appreciated and increased their efforts. Mad Judd Mack was there too, laughing broadly and clapping his hands to the beat of the music. He winked at me when he spotted me and I gave him a wave.

"I thought we'd agreed you'd stay away from these kinds of things," a voice said in my ear and I spun around to look straight into Puck's green eyes.

I was about to call out his name when I remembered where we were. Though the festive mood made it seem highly unlikely there could still be detectives wandering about.

"Hey there you," I said instead and was rewarded with a quick kiss.

"Isn't it a school day?" Puck asked.

"I'm skiving. There's a bunch of us here." That much was true; I'd seen other kids from school wandering about. "I just thought I'd come and have a gander. Besides, mister, you're not supposed to be here either."

Puck grinned.

"Couldn't stay away, not today. So what do you think?" He gestured at the crowds.

"It's an amazing turn-out," I commented happily. "And the mood is just incredible. I can't believe it."

"No, neither can I," Puck said thoughtfully. "I've seen it before with such a big and varied crowd, but the coppers and security just seem far too relaxed."

"Maybe they're just not that worried?"

"Doesn't fit with Duguth Construction policy so far, they seemed to be in a big hurry. Want to dance?"

I nodded eagerly and we swirled around the musicians and I laughed and was happy. This was turning out to be quite a Tuesday, a day off school and bonus time with Puck.

On our fifth orbit around the jamming band I spotted a faraway movement. I stopped abruptly, frowned, and pulled Puck away up to a nearby hillock.

"What is it?" Puck had become tense.

"There," I pointed. It was far away and the lack of dense tree cover where we were was no help because the distance meant there were a fair few trees between us and the spot my eye was fixed on. Still, we could see them, Yellowcoat after Yellowcoat moving steadily eastwards.

"Oh bugger," Puck said. "Wait here."

He spurted towards the group making the music and spoke a few urgent words to Judd before rushing towards me again.

"Come on." Puck grabbed my hand and we began to run along a parallel course to the far off yellow procession, all need for caution thrown into the wind. I saw others running in that direction behind us as Judd was seeking out Weard Hunters and directing them eastwards.

"It's the camp," Puck panted. "They're heading for the Weard Hunt camp."

We arrived there too late. The security men here were not smiling or amiable. They had just started to tear through the camp, kicking over pots and destroying benders by tearing the tarpaulins from the frames.

They were clearly intending to level it to the ground. I saw a girl with dreadlocks trying to crawl out of a bender and receive the full force of a security man's knee in her face. She fell backwards into the bender in a spray of blood. A few other protesters who had stayed behind scuttled up trees to the safety of the rickety platforms but they were pursued by some of the more agile Yellowcoats. Fierce struggles broke out on the platforms, one of the protesters rolled of the edge and I could hear the cracking of a bone when he landed on the ground. That was followed by a scream of anguish. This was met by laughter and name-calling in the Londonish accent prevalent in Neverland. I was appalled; Neverland had come to the Wyrde Woods, the callous violence of the tenements transferred to my safe haven. My home.

"They knew the camp would be near empty," Puck hissed. "No police, no press...this is bad."

These were the jackboots I had read about in Puck's Hideout forever ago, jackboots in the Wyrde Woods this time.

I saw the security man who had kicked the girl crawl into the bender in which the girl had disappeared and then heard her screaming for help.

Puck had also seen it and was already sprinting for the bender. I followed right behind him and we dove into the bender to start pummelling the security man who was fumbling with the girl's sweater as she screamed and tried to ward him off. The unexpected assault made him flee the bender though he started hollering for help just outside of it. I got my pocket knife out and cut the tarpaulin at the back of the bender while Puck helped the girl to her feet and led her out of the new exit I had cut and I followed. We ran out of the camp - keeping low- and managed to get to a thick clump of undergrowth where we hid. The girl was bleeding profusely but it was a nose bleed, I had been worried that her teeth had been smashed to bits as well. She took off her cotton shawl and pressed it to her nose to stem the bleeding. The girl and I exchanged a look. I wanted to ask what her name was, but I remembered we were not supposing to use ours, even if she was on our side. I looked back at the camp.

Much of it was already unrecognisable, benders and huts had been systematically torn apart, tents trampled into the ground, personal belongings were being rifled or tossed aside. Ropes were tied to the tree platforms and lines of men pulled at the ropes, rendering the platforms asunder. Some of the platforms had not been cleared of protesters, these now tried to get to the ropes attached to the lower joists of their flooring to dislodge them but were pelted by a barrage of camp debris thrown by the howling Yellowcoats. When the structures disintegrated the Weard Hunters had to climb higher up the tree for safety.

Mad Judd's people started to arrive and formed little groups. They were immediately assaulted by vengeful Yellowcoats who used their fists to pummel them to the ground and their boots for kicking those who were down.

"Is this normal?" I asked incredulously.

"It's the Beanfield all over again," the girl said with disgust, referring to the confrontation mentioned in *Fierce Dancing* about which the author had so eloquently regretted the imagery of jackboots and all its connotations.

"Has no one spoken with them?" Puck was puzzled.

"They're not in a talkative mood," I pointed out the obvious.

"Normally we establish communication with the locals who are enlisted for security, make sure they realise that the longer things drag out, the longer they'll get paid," Puck said. "It works well; they aren't stupid and drag their feet as long as possible."

"Who was supposed to do that?" I asked sharply. "The Odesby groups?"

Puck nodded.

"These Yellowcoats are Neverlanders."

"So?" He frowned.

"Nobody talks to Neverlanders. You're one of the few exceptions. Most folk in Neverland are decent people but the worst ones get noticed, they rule the streets, set the precedent. The estate has a bad reputation in Odesby, we're tainted. All of us."

"There was a neighbourhood that we didn't leaflet in," the girl nodded. "Or go from door-to-door."

"That was a big mistake," Puck shook his head. "Now the only info they have is what the construction company tells them about us."

Weard Hunters arrived in larger numbers now, sufficient to make the Yellowcoats back off to regroup. It looked something akin to my notion of a medieval battlefield, two battle lines facing each other and roaring and whooping at each other either to give themselves courage or to impress the opposition, probably both.

I heard sirens approaching along the dirt road which ran close to the camp. Four police vans came to a halt, their doors opened and riot police in boiler suits and visored helmets spilled out. They ran towards the lines, large shields held in front of them and truncheons at the ready. Some of the protesters looked relieved when they saw the police arrive but this relief did not last long as the riot coppers made straight for the Weard Hunters and started indiscriminately lashing out with their truncheons, many of them aimed at people's heads.

Puck growled in frustration. The girl with the dreadlocks was watching the fight in the camp with an open mouth and disbelieving eyes.

"We should go help them," I said.

"No!" Puck said. "They're not in the mood for mercy Elfin; they'll knock us silly and then arrest us. We need to get out of here now."

I nodded; I could see we stood little chance of achieving anything. But then the girl screamed a name.

"RUFUS! NO!"

Before we could stop her she spurted out of our hiding place to the edge of the camp where two policemen were knocking a young dreadlocked man senseless, continuing to let their truncheons fall down long after he had sunk to his knees, eyes dazed and blood streaming from his head.

I dashed after the girl whose screaming had alerted the two riot cops. One of them lashed out at her with his truncheon and then kicked Rufus, who was making a half-hearted attempt to stop him by grabbing the policeman's leg.

The other one raised his truncheon and brought it towards me in a wide swing. Puck jumped in front of me and the truncheon impacted on his head hard enough to send his glasses spinning. Puck sank to the ground without a sound.

I snarled at the policeman who had delivered the blow and caught the end of the truncheon in my hands, starting a tug of war. I was the only one left standing though and the other policeman came round behind me.

"Right girl, you're nicked." He shouted at me as he squeezed his hand down hard on my wrist, and twisted my arm behind my back.

I struggled. I lifted a leg and bent my knee to deliver a kick backwards, but it was ineffective, the copper's boiler suit protecting him from the worst of it. He cursed and bent my arm upwards forcing me to double over as pain shot through my arm. From the corner of my eye I caught the movement of the truncheon as the other policeman started swinging it towards my head.

I braced for the impact, but it never arrived. The world suddenly filled with legs, scores of legs clad in torn jeans and smudgy army trousers and the steel grip on my arm was released. I lifted myself up to see over twenty protesters surrounding the policemen and suddenly Mad Judd Mack was next to me.

"You okay?" He asked with concern. I nodded dumbly; my arm was still stinging with pain.

"Well, by Oak, Ash and Thorn we have just de-arrested you Faery Girl," Judd grinned. He handed me Puck's glasses and then pointed at Puck who was getting to his hands and knees. "Get him out of here, the both of you; go back to the main protest, okay? If it turns ugly there head into the woods, you two know your way around."

I nodded and helped Puck up, he was dazed and confused, blood seeping from his hair onto his cheek.

A score of policemen formed up in a line in front of our group, flanked by security men whose faces betrayed more eagerness to inflict pain.

"GO!" Judd shouted at me and organised his Weard Hunters in a line. I took hold of Puck and scrambled away.

"UT, UT, UT!" Judd hollered.

 The other Weard Hunters joined in: "UT, UT, UT!!!"

I looked back to see the line of police and Yellowcoats charge the protestors. The truncheons rose into the air again and then hammered down and down on the protesters who started to fall. Judd was the last on his feet, still hollering defiance as he was stormed by riot coppers and security men from three sides before he disappeared behind blue and yellow bodies. I hoped he wouldn't be beaten too badly.

§ § § § § §

Puck and I made it back to the edge of the main protest; we stopped for a moment, gasping for breath.

"I'm here with Jasmin and Biggs," I told Puck.

"Jasmin! You'd better find them and get them out of here."

"You think it'll get ugly here?"

"I dunno," Puck looked shocked. "This isn't any protocol I've come across before. They're being extremely heavy-handed."

"They wouldn't attack the likes of David Masters, would they?" It seemed inconceivable to me.

Word was now beginning to reach the main protest as some of the defenders of the camp came limping back, bleeding profusely from head wounds. Someone at the back of the crowd screamed and many people turned to see these walking wounded. The mood changed instantly, the music stopped and people became nervous. The coppers and Yellowcoats around the beachhead stopped smiling and tightened their ranks, ready to receive any incoming aggravation. There seemed to be no surprise on their side.

"I don't think they will," Puck said. His face hardened. "This is Aunt Catt's doing."

He looked fearsome for a moment with that grim look and blood drying on one side of his face. I looked around for Jasmin and Biggs.

"There, I can see them," I said.

We ran to Biggs and Jasmin who were looking confused, unable to place the sudden shift in the mood of the crowd.

"You've got to get back to Odesby," I told them.

"Why? What is happening?" Jasmin asked. "Puck, you're bleeding!"

"Things are turning ugly back at the protestor's camp. We don't know if they'll come here," Puck said.

I saw Biggs take an instinctive step towards Jasmin.

"But everybody was having a good time," Jasmin bit her lip. "I don't understand, everybody was just having fun."

I saw people begin to move away whilst many others were still uncertain, aware of consternation at the very back of the protest but not knowing why, nor knowing why the amiable coppers and security men looked so grim all of a sudden. Somebody began to yell through a police megaphone, urging the crowds to disperse and that caused a ripple of further confusion and concern to spread through the crowd.

"Biggs," I said. "Get her out of here, now."

I pointed southwards and Biggs nodded, he wrapped his arm around Jasmin's shoulder and started to lead her away.

"You go with them," Puck urged me.

"Bullshit mister, I am staying with you," I looked at him with anger in my eyes. He looked as if he was going to argue but then nodded.

"Be careful!" Jasmin looked back at me with pleading eyes.

"I will sweetie, I'll see you back at Nowhere Place," I called after her. Then I looked at Puck. "Where to now?"

"New Rivendell," he said.

§ § § § § § §

Underearth seemed deserted, the hatchways of the entry tunnels firmly shut and not a soul in sight. Puck told me that the Lost Boys would be taking no chances and that the Underearthers would all be in their warrens, ready to slip hands or feet into their lock-ons if the look-outs gave the word that Duguth Construction and the police intended to cross the Taunflow today as well.

"I doubt they will, they'll have plenty of work to do between the Rore and Taunflow first. Besides, they must know that they can't overrun Underearth and Overbranch with the same speed as the Weard Hunter camp."

The main camp was permanently inhabited now and it was odd to see benders, fire pits, paths and other infrastructure where we had once planted stakes. The camp was subdued; a steady number of Weard Hunters were trickling in, some supported by others and many of them bleeding, mainly from head wounds.

Tink was standing by the central fire pit, wearing her climbing harness and shaking her head as a bloodied Weard Hunter was giving her a run-down on the eviction of his camp.

"Hey," she said tersely as she spotted us. "You'll need to have someone look at your head Puck."

"Later," Puck said, "I need to talk, is Jukes…?"

"Overbranch," Tink said.

"I think you should have your head seen to first," I told Puck.

"She is right; you can't go climbing like that. Too risky." Tink summoned one of the protestors who came running into the camp with a first-aid kit.

When Puck's wound had been cleaned and bandaged we moved on. We were spotted well before we came to the base of the first redwood and Jukes and Curly abseiled down with extra climbing harnesses for Puck and me. We prussiked up to the first platform and then clipped onto one of the walkways which led us over to another redwood. Jukes' Twigloo was suspended from one of its massive branches and we lowered ourselves down to it. The bender had been folded back so it was half open allowing for the most incredible view of the Wyrde Woods.

Puck and Jukes launched into an urgent discussion about the implications of today's events, mostly consisting of their surprise at the violence which had been unleashed, the speed with which Duguth Construction was proceeding and their expectation that it would be two or three weeks at most before an attempt would be made to evict New Rivendell.

I wandered over to the edge of the Twigloo's frame and looked at the ugly brown stretch of land which I could see in the distance, stretching from the Lusty Giant's Hills all the way to the Rore and I could see that the road workers were wasting no time after today's blow as they were already enlarging the beachhead across the Rore.

I kept on seeing a vivid slideshow of the naked aggression I had seen today, scene after scene flashed by filled with faces contorted by wild hatred or astonished pain. This is what I had read about in *Fierce*

Dancing, blatant and brutal suppression of any who dared to oppose the system. The Wyrde Woods protest, which had started so well with successful sabotage missions was fast unravelling. Duguth Construction – Lady Malheur- seemed to be anticipating our moves and seeing through our plans. The Weard Hunt camp had been expected to last for a few weeks at least, if not months, allowing the Lost Boys to entrench themselves as securely as possible taking the protest into the autumn and perhaps even winter and spring.

Instead, the stretch of woods between the Rore and the Taunflow now seemed lost in one single blow and I had no doubt that Lady Malheur would fix those fierce eyes of hers on the Giant's Grove next. If that fell, there was little left to protect the Wyrde Woods, just the Waer-Wyrd. I had a feeling that everything was unravelling before my eyes.

I was filled with doubts. Joy's explanation at the Whychmaze had made sense in the shadow of Heorttreów, but after witnessing the violence today I doubted whether a handful of well-meaning locals steeped in the legends of their forebears would be able to stop the ruthless ambition which was blazing a path of destruction through the woods. I felt anger. This was my home, the only one I had ever known and I wanted to fight for it. I wondered if it would not make more sense to just stay in Overbranch, high up in the redwoods, and make a defiant stand here. Hoping that powers which once reigned in the woods had not disappeared but were merely dormant seemed like clutching at straws now. I lowered my head; much as I wanted to stay up here I owed a debt of loyalty to Joy. I couldn't just walk out of the Waer-Wyrd now. That was the course I had chosen and fate is unyielding.

After we had abseiled down the redwood Jukes took his leave.

"If you ever change your mind, you'd be welcome here, you and Spider-woman here. We could use good people like you," he smiled.

"I'll keep it in mind, just remember, you're not alone," Puck smiled back and we left.

Puck walked with me to the railway bridges and we said our goodbyes there. We agreed to meet at the Carfax early on Saturday morning to make the most of my day pass.

Halfway across the industrial estate I stopped and looked northwards. Mostly I saw corrugated iron roofs and chimneys of assorted sizes but I could discern a broken thin green line, the treetops telling me where the Wyrde Woods started. Puck was somewhere there, below the trees, making his way through the woods. I knew I was probably influenced by the savage cruelties which still danced before my eyes, but could not help sensing an impending doom rising over us, like a wave of darkness that threatened to engulf us.

"Be careful Puck my love," I whispered towards that thin green line, and then hastened back to Nowhere Place.

33. Every Time a Bell Rings…

The trouble started on Wednesday afternoon after school. I was in the common room hogging the computer to read up on the road protest and a dozen or so Forlorn Hopers were lounging about looking bored out of their skulls. Then a shrill scream shattered the air, shortly thereafter followed by another. The sounds came from the direction of the hallway and we crowded to the hallway door just as a handful of Lifers and Snooties came running out of the office and others –both staff and Forlorn Hopers- gathered at the top of the stairs.

There was another scream, barely human, an otherworldly banshee shriek that came from one of the consultation rooms. The door flew open and Jasmin burst out of the room. I could barely recognise her, her usual pretty face was twisted into a contorted mask of horror. She opened her mouth to utter another scream of terror and I saw that her blouse was open and her bra pulled down so that one of her small breasts was exposed.

Jasmin saw me and ran to me. I caught her in my arms and she clutched on to me as if she were drowning, her small body was tense as a steel wire and she was trembling badly.

Stubbles came running out of the room; he stopped in his tracks when he saw the hallway filling up. The Forlorn Hopers near me instinctively formed a protective circle around Jasmin, the staff who had emerged from the office walked closer to us and people started to spill down the stairways.

"She went absolutely mad, lost it altogether," Stubbles shouted at the staff.

I caught a glimpse of Watson's face, she was next to our group now and she was giving Stubbles a hard stare. I glared at him, he always acted as if he was so clever, he probably believed it himself, but this was just plain stupid. Stupid and evil.

"Jumped on her chair, ripped her blouse open and started screaming," Stubbles continued.

I looked down; all of Jasmin's buttons were still on her blouse. It hadn't been ripped open, they had been undone. I fidgeted with her bra to cover her boob. Jasmin let me. Stubbles stared at the staff, none of whom had responded yet.

"I want her sedated and in the Reflection Room," Stubbles yelled, spittle flying from his mouth. "NOW!"

Jasmin started to hyperventilate, eyes turning in her sockets.

"Miss Watson," I spoke urgently. "Jasmin needs a doctor; she's going into some kind of shock."

Miss Watson turned to me and Jasmin with immediate concern. She gently took hold of Jasmin by the shoulders and tried to look the girl in the eyes. Jasmin was panting like Lady after a run now, quick successions of shallow breaths and her trembling had progressed into violent shaking.

"SEDATIVES! NOW!!" Stubbles roared.

"Quick, call an ambulance," Watson ordered one of the Snooties who pushed himself through the crowd towards the office.

"YOU FAXING BASTAAAAAAAAARD!"

Biggs had been halfway down the stairs with some others and had put the pieces of the puzzle together. He took a few leaps down the stairs, then swung over the barrister with surprising agility and landed on his feet.

Stubbles took a step backwards but it was too late, Biggs charged him like a bull, his momentum easily throwing aside the hands which tried to stop him. Biggs launched himself at Stubbles, the force of the impact knocking them both to the ground. There was a brief struggle which ended with Biggs sitting astride Stubbles and using his fists to pummel

Stubbles' face. He had surprising strength in his arms and put all his considerable body weight in his punches.

The sound of breaking bone and a shriek of agony from Stubbles spurred the staff into action; half-a-dozen of them rushed towards the fight and struggled to pull Biggs off Stubbles. Biggs began to holler obscenities and tried to continue punching Stubbles. He got two more in, despite the fact that he had two staff members hanging on to each arm. More staff rushed in and wrestled Biggs to the ground where he continued to heave and buck to throw them off. Stubbles spat in his face, blood mingled with the saliva.

"NOOOOOOOOOOOOO!!!!" Jasmin screamed at the top of her voice and tore herself loose from Watson to throw herself at the huddle of staff, starting to claw at their eyes. She bared her teeth and sank them into an arm which appeared around her neck, then continued fighting and screaming, the sound of which caused renewed efforts by Biggs to fight off his assailants.

One of the Forlorn Hopers behind me screamed now as well; a shriek of panic. Thomas and one of his friends rushed the entangled bodies to try and pull staff members off Jasmin and Biggs.

A cacophony of vocal mayhem broke out, people shouting, yelling, screaming, crying and on top of that the Snooty in the office had punched the general alarm, which started shrieking in long high-pitched wails, summoning those members of the staff elsewhere in the building and alerting the local police station that trouble was afoot at the Odesby Juvenile Care Home.

Sharon, seeing Thomas smashed in the face by somebody's elbow screamed and rushed into the fray as well.

"No! Sharon, don't!" I hollered at the top of my voice.

I was about to follow Sharon and give it all I got when Watson grabbed my shoulder.

"Wendy, get kids out of here, out of the hall, into the common room."

I roared in frustration but saw the sense of it and attempted to herd the Forlorn Hopers around me out of the hallway. Watson moved towards the fight with two Snooties in tow. She pulled Thomas off the brawl and shoved him into the hands of the Snooties who led him away as Watson tried to get hold of Thomas's friend Dave. Thomas ripped himself out of the grip of the Snooties and launched past her to re-join the brawl. Somewhere below that embroiled mass of bodies Biggs still roared like a bull and Jasmin continued her shrieking.

Watson tried her best, as did I. But most of the Forlorn Hopers refused point blank to leave the hallway, just the younger ones who were in the throes of panic. Those involved in the fight were in such a fury that they appeared incapable of stopping; kids and staff alike. In the end it stopped only when the police stormed in and started untangling the combatants with force.

Ironically the Reflection Room stayed empty. Biggs was sedated and led off in handcuffs by the police, along with Sharon, Thomas and Dave. Jasmin, battered and bleeding now, was tied to an ambulance stretcher and carried outside to a waiting ambulance. I tried to go with her but Watson stopped me. Stubbles was carried out on a stretcher too, his face an unrecognisable bloody mess. More ambulances showed up. The street in front of Nowhere Place looked like an armed siege had taken place. There were ambulances and police vehicles, their sirens were off but the flashing lights were on and these were illuminating the faces of the tenement rats who crowded on the pavement opposite Nowhere Place.

"Miss Watson," I said pleadingly. "PLEASE. I want to go with Jasmin."

"I understand, and if it were up to me I'd let you go," Miss Watson said. "But this is seriously not a time to bend rules Wendy. We'll be under close scrutiny tomorrow."

I nodded miserably. I barely slept that night, staring at the ceiling till dawn.

§ § § § § § §

They called school on Thursday morning to inform them that all the Forlorn Hopers would not be attending the next two days of school. Parents and other relatives had been notified as well because the press picked up parts of the story. I wondered what the Waer-Wyrd would make of it all. I wanted to be with them badly. Extra staff were drafted in from all over the county to talk with us in small groups. It was in this setting that we were told Jasmin was in hospital in stable condition and Biggs, Sharon, Thomas and Dave would make an appearance at the East Sussex Juvenile Court the next day. Stubbles was still in hospital too, they said, and all of us hissed. There would be an investigation, they promised.

Puck texted.

Some of us are worried Elfin. U OK? Can we meet?

I messaged back.

No one is allowed out. Big mess here. I am OK. Jas has been hurt.

He sent another text.

Be strong my love. You're Dragon Slayer material.
We're lighting candles for Jas.
Tell her we're thinking of her please. All of us here.

I concluded that meant he was at the Owlery with Joy and maybe some of the others and I drew comfort from that, picturing them gathered around the Owlery's large fireplace.

Nowhere Place was unusually quiet that day, there was no music and people talked in hushed voices, most of the kids retired to their rooms and everybody seemed excessively subdued.

Jasmin came back on Friday morning, still heavily doped. She was brought to her room and I appointed myself as her guardian, keeping curious Forlorn Hopers at bay and sitting next to her bed as she slept restlessly, tossing and turning as well as moaning softly. I stroked her hair when she became too agitated and it calmed her somewhat. Watson came in to check a couple of times; she said nothing of my presence except to ask me to let her know if anything went amiss. They didn't have time to monitor Jasmin non-stop, although many of the Nowhere Place staff were running extra shifts the external reinforcements had departed again.

Around noon she brought me a tray with a glass of water and some sandwiches and I accepted these gratefully.

"What will happen to Stu…Mr. Dagle?" I asked.

Miss Watson hesitated. "There will be an investigation."

"Her blouse buttons were not torn off you know," I said bitterly. "They were unbuttoned, not torn off."

"I know, I saw," Miss Watson said.

I shook my head and sighed. Miss Watson just nodded curtly in agreement, then looked like she was embarrassed by her transgression and left.

§ § § § § § §

She returned half an hour later with a Snootie in tow.

"Jeff will watch Jasmin, I need you to come with me," Miss Watson said.

I stood up reluctantly; I wasn't ready for any resumption of regular proceedings at Nowhere Place and hoped I wouldn't have to go to the consultation room to explain to some disinterested shrink how I was feeling. I really just wanted to be with Jasmin but followed Miss Watson out of the room.

To my surprise she led us to the back stairs and then into the warren of corridors and spaces in the cellars, an area which was strictly off-limits to Forlorn Hopers. She stopped by a door. When she opened it I saw part of a small room that looked like it was used as office by the maintenance man; a desk, files, plastic chairs, coffee cups and an ashtray. Miss Watson frowned and then closed the door again.

I looked at her inquiringly.

"Do you have a boyfriend Wendy?" Miss Watson was curt and I was momentarily puzzled as I tried to place the question. I also had to grin; nobody used that word in the Wyrde Woods. The elders seemed to regard the fact that Puck and I were together with amusement and approval but nobody had referred to him as my boyfriend yet. I don't know quite what we were but the whole 'boyfriend-girlfriend' sounded immature already.

"Yes, why?"

"What is his name?" She asked and I suddenly felt a flutter of hope.

"He'll either call himself Puck or Peter Malheur. Dressed in green. He wears glasses."

"He was very insistent Wendy," Miss Watson said. "I think he's worried about you but I can't give you more than fifteen minutes, you understand?"

I stared at the door in disbelief.

"No scenes, okay Wendy?" Miss Watson said. "I'm breaking the rules as it is. I'll be here in the corridor with the door open listening. Nothing personal, I think you can be trusted but leaving you alone with someone I don't know is a boundary I don't want to cross. Not right now."

I nodded and she opened the door again and I rushed into the room and Puck was in the corner and he smiled in relief and I flew at him and he spread his arms and held me tight and suddenly everything seemed better.

We stood there like that for five minutes before I drew back at last to drink in the sight of him. He looked so out of place in the basement of Nowhere Place that I laughed.

"You left the woods," I said in wonder.

"I had to see you, I was worried," Puck replied and indicated the open door with his head and a question mark in his eyes.

I nodded.

"What happened? The papers made it seem like a riot took place."

"There was an incident between a member of staff and Jasmin," I said, choosing my words carefully. "It's to be investigated but things got out of hand, badly out of hand."

"How is Jasmin?"

"She was hurt but she's back here now, I am with her."

"Sharon and Biggs?" He asked. I was surprised but then I realised he had met them both.

I shook my head.

"Not good, they were both involved."

"I was afraid you would have got drawn in," he confessed. "I should have trusted you."

"I got tessy but..." I looked at the door again and realised just how much Miss Watson had minded my back during the fight. "...some of the staff are real professionals, kept me occupied."

"Well that's good," Puck said. "Gammer will be proud of that too."

Miss Watson gave a small cough in the corridor.

"Five minutes kids," she added.

I stepped back into Puck's embrace and we just held on to each other. It gave me strength.

§ § § § § §

"Thank you Miss Watson," I said as I followed her back up the stairs.

"You just keep up these changes of yours," she said. "And we forget that this ever happened."

"I will," I said.

She stopped and looked at me.

"I mean it Wendy, this isn't over yet, try to control your emotions. I know you can. Jasmin needs you. I need you. But you need to avoid that bloody Reflection Room or you'll be of no use to anybody."

I nodded and then we went back to Jasmin's room.

§ § § § § §

Late that afternoon the corridors, which had been as quiet as they had been on Thursday, came to life again, filled with a quiet buzz of urgent whispers and hushed exclamations. I ventured out to find out what was happening. The news was from the juvenile court and was bad. Sharon, Thomas and Dave were to be released from custody pending a further investigation to establish if legal action would be taken against them. None of them would return to Nowhere Place though, the court had ordered their transferal to three different institutions in Kent and Surrey effective immediately and they had been bundled into transports straight after the hearing.

My heart went out to Sharon, who was probably being processed in some strange and unknown place at this very moment. We had all been through that before, but that didn't make it any less pleasant. I sent her a few text messages of support but there was no reply.

Biggs had admitted full guilt, defiantly telling the judge that he would carry out the exact same actions given half the chance since nobody else seemed to be bothered by abuse taking place in a care home. Biggs tried to turn it around and demand a criminal investigation into Stubbles' behaviour but the judge wasn't having it.

Biggs was to remain in custody. His fate needed to be formalised but the judge had made clear that the next stop would inevitably be a young offenders institution unless it was decided to try him as an adult in which case he would end up in a maximum security prison. That latter would effectively be a death sentence for someone like Biggs I realised with empty horror and sent him a text message as well, though I doubted he would have retained access to his mobile. It was better than doing nothing anyway.

Watson came up with a nurse towards six o'clock. They needed to clean and feed Jasmin.

"You'd better go now Wendy," Watson said.

"Is it true, what they are saying about Sharon and Biggs?"

Watson nodded sadly. She looked tired.

"You've done a great job today Wendy, but we'll take over from here, okay. I want you to get some rest."

I cast a look at Jasmin, still out of it on her bed.

"We'll check on her every half hour, I promise," Watson said.

I nodded and went to my room where I fell asleep on top of the bedcovers, still fully dressed.

I woke around ten pm, alerted simultaneously by the almost continual beeping of my phone as well as commotion in the corridor. I rushed to the door and opened it to peer outside. A staff member barked at me to keep my door closed, I could see others patrolling up and down the corridors, telling other kids to close their doors again. Some protested, others obeyed. They were containing us, something bad had happened.

I checked my phone and felt my heart stop for a moment. Biggs had been found in his cell at the police station. He had hung himself with his belt. Biggs was dead.

§ § § § § §

I lay on my bed, tears rolling down my face. I had stopped following the stream of information on my phone as the Forlorn Hope really didn't have any further information to go on; it was just continued expressions of sorrow or outrage combined with wild speculation. Instead I kept on repeating an old saying I had heard in the care home where I had spent the first three years of my family exile.

Every time a bell rings, another angel gets his wings.

The text barrages stopped around midnight and the corridor became quiet. Around one I opened the door of my room and peered into the corridor. Terry was there, slouched in a chair and fast asleep. I snuck past him to Biggs' room. It was locked but he had given me a key a long time ago, possibly in the hope that I would decide to visit him some night. Being in his room was bad, he was still very much present, from the smelly pile of laundry in one corner to the collection of comics which had been his pride and joy as well as the empty candy and cookie wrappers which littered the room. Biggs had always been hungry.

Every time a bell rings...

I looked around. They'd probably clear it out tomorrow and I wanted to get something for Jasmin so she would have something of his. I settled for a little statuette of a bear, standing upright with its claws outstretched and roaring. Biggs liked to pretend he was a bear sometimes on his good days, turning his size into something positive. The statuette was tacky, but it characterised him so much that I pocketed it. Another thought struck me and I opened his closet and fumbled around behind his t-shirts till I found his little metal safe box. It was heavy and I sat down on his bed to open it. It was filled to the brim with banknotes, beneath which was a hoard of coins. I stared at the money. I felt bad about taking it, even though I intended to give every penny of it to Jasmin, maybe she could buy a wreath for the funeral or something. Still, it was stealing from a dead person. I closed my eyes. If I didn't the staff would find it tomorrow. I was pretty sure Biggs would prefer Jasmin to have the money. I pocketed all the bills as well as handfuls of pound coins and left the smaller change, replacing the safe-box in Biggs' closet.

I was about to leave when I saw his cell phone on his desk. I frowned.

Jasmin had a phone.

…another angel gets his wings.

I had seen it in her room. It wasn't highly visible, half concealed amidst a pile of nature magazines on her bedside table.

What if she came out of her drugged stupor and checked her messages? I went into the corridor, recklessly passing Terry's sleeping form and went into Jasmin's room.

Every time a bell rings...

Jasmin's phone was on her pillow, its screen throwing a small glare on her open sightless eyes. She had cut both her wrists and I was amazed at how much blood there had been in her small body. The bed was soaked with the stuff and it was still dripping from her saturated sheets into the wide pool of blood that almost ran the entire length of her bed.

…. another angel gets his wings.

I wanted to go to her but realised I would have to wade through her blood. I looked at her again, the open lifeless eyes, the unnatural pallor and immobility of her body. She was dead, just like Biggs.

I remained remarkably calm. I walked over to her desk and placed Biggs' bear there next to the little stuffed bear she always carried around with her.

"Goodbye Jasmin," I whispered and went back to my room.

There I quietly packed my backpack with as much as I could fit in there, including the picture of my dad and I. I snuck downstairs to the washroom and climbed out through the window. The streets of Neverland were quiet and deserted and like a robot I headed north to the Wyrde Woods.

34. The Red King

I wasn't heading for the Owlery, nor looking for Puck who could be in any of half-a-dozen places at any rate. I was aware that I was doing precisely what they had asked me not to do: Breaking the rules big time. If I were found anywhere near them they would be subjected to unwelcome scrutiny. Rather, I headed for the Wyrde Woods because it was the only place I could think of and at least I would be near them.

Staying in Nowhere Place was simply not an option anymore. I had tried hard to make it something of a home at long last but the whole thing had disintegrated. Law or no, there was no way now that I could accept Youth Care had any business running my life. If only people like Michael and Miss Watson got to call the shots it would be a different matter, but they didn't and could only do their best.

I surprised myself by retaining my cool. I knew the woods were pretty busy these days and opted to cross the canal by the Nickleby road bridge so that I would avoid the area north of St. Lewinna's Priory which would be crawling with road protesters and security. Knowing mobile phones could be traced I turned mine off, even taking out the battery so I couldn't accidentally activate it.

The route on the west-bank of the Rore would take me past the M33 route but that was okay, by the time dawn broke I would have passed that area, for safety clearly lay in the northern half of the woods. I had a vague idea that I would head towards the Shy Maidens and try to set up a camp in the woods around it. I had a reasonable idea how to build a simple shelter now, and the northern road offered access to one of the towns up north for supplies. I patted my pocket, thanks to Biggs I had ample funds and if I took it easy I might last for months. I'd find a way to get to Stancaster every now and then to sneak in to see Nyle somehow, other than that I could lie low.

It could have been me.

I walked on in quiet determination but now that I had reached the shelter of the woods I began to feel the full emotional impact of looking into Jasmin's dead eyes. Descent into madness was slow and gradual this time instead of sudden. For a while at least I had been able to seize my grief in a steel vice and refuse to give in to it and even now I felt an odd detachment to my inner self, as if I was floating above myself, watching myself walk, watching the first cracks appear.

I had tried so hard; to control myself, to react with thought rather than immediate action. To love. To be loved. Part of me wanted to run, run to Joy or Puck who had assured me I wasn't alone, and hide in their arms like I had done before, reclaiming a part of childhood which had been stolen from me. Finding a love which I had thought was never meant for me. This path however, was one I must walk alone. It was odd to have the clarity of mind to predict the anguish which would soon engulf me. A solitary odyssey through the mangled ruin of loss. Once that happened thought would cease altogether, all that there would be was my bare psyche, devoid of flesh and blood and covered only by the scars of my already wounded soul. It would be vulnerable and defenceless, surrounded by carrion birds projected by my own flights of fancy. Hideous ugly vultures that thrive on vulnerability and are impervious to mercy. They would circle, crooning hideous calls and then start pecking and clawing, ripping open old wounds and gashing out new ones.

Was this what it had been like for my mother?

It could have been me. It wasn't. It was Jasmin. I felt guilty and no rational thinking could ward off the sinking feeling that I had caused her death. I had chosen to let Stubbles off the hook by not issuing complaint after complaint about his behaviour until someone somewhere finally took notice. I had suggested the solution of misunderstood intentions so I could get what I most desired, trips to the Wyrde Woods to escape from the dire reality of Nowhere Place. Though worried that the predator had set his sights elsewhere I had been mostly relieved that he had been off my back, never mind that his new focus had been set on a girl who was essentially defenceless, having little awareness of the evil mankind was capable of.

For the world's more full of weeping than you can understand. That's what Puck had sung when we were all at the Owlery.

She would never laugh again, that silly goofy guffaw of hers. Never cast a look of adoration at Biggs again. Never smile shyly as he surely but slowly drew her out of her isolation into a wider world. Never look delighted at the sight of an animal. Never cook a curry for Joy. I had killed her. I could have insisted that I stay with her all night, I am sure I could have convinced Watson of the necessity of it. I could have used my brains and removed the telephone or recalled its existence the moment the flurry of messages about Biggs' suicide drove my phone to beep incessantly.

Even now the realisation that it could have been me instead of Jasmin was cause for selfish relief. I could have gone to Joy and Puck but I was not worth it. I had pretended to be for a while, but reality had clawed me back to the shit pit where I belonged.

My last defences crumbled, as surely as a sandcastle is eroded and then washed away by the incoming tide. A cloud of inner darkness enveloped me and it was like being smothered, wanting to scream from the darkest and deepest pits of my being but capable only of uttering a barely audible whimper. I could struggle, kick my legs and reach out for the surface in vain or simply let myself be carried away by a current which led only deeper downwards.

I opted for a third option, hitherto never taken, and turned in the thick mist of madness so that my head was faced downwards and with powerful strokes I launched myself downwards. Out vying the current that tried to drag me under I went voluntarily into exquisite oblivion, welcoming its claws which sank in my soul, surprising the demons by taking a stance amidst them; we were all on the same side now, all on the same self-destructive path. There was power in it and I cackled like a maniac. Control had come at last; I was steering now, confidently setting a self-subversive course for annihilation. I had become undone.

§ § § § § § §

It was in that state of rage and fury that I arrived at Tuckersham Church. My planned route north had entailed skirting the territory of the Owl Man but when I made out the distinctive squat tower I headed east without hesitation, striding towards the cemetery without a pause as I passed through the cold wall of air, impervious to the alarmed screeches of the lesser owls. The moon was half full and cast down enough light for me to make out details as I approached the church and hopped over the low wall into the graveyard. One of the tombs near the far end of the church was larger than the others and on the heavy slab that made up the lid I could see the outlines of a carved dragon. I jumped on top of Ellette's grave and turned my head, scanning the tree lines around the church. It did not take me long to discern the black hunched shape on the limb of one of the larger trees at the far end of the path. He unfolded and raised his face, red eyes beginning to glow. He shrieked a piercing challenge into the night.

"HERE I AM!" I thundered, waving my arms.

Ufmanna shrieked again, louder this time.

"COME ON THEN, COME AND GET ME!" I roared.

Ufmanna spread his wings and shrilled a scream that would have chilled the bones of a corpse. He launched into the air, coming directly towards me, stretching out claws half way through the flight whilst he tried to pin me to the spot with the ruby gaze of his eyes.

He need not have bothered with the hypnotising look. I wasn't planning to go anywhere, this creature was pitiful next to my own demons who had finally been completely unleashed and as Ufmanna entered the final phase of his flight I opened my mouth and released a blast of utter ferocity which exceeded any volume I should have been capable of. Ufmanna shrieked, but this time there was uncertainty and then he pulled up, soaring higher to make a sudden steep turn and dive at me from above.

"FINISH IT!" I bellowed and then uttered another animalistic explosion of noise which once again sent Ufmanna veering off his course, this time back to the tree from which he had launched his initial attack. There he flapped his great big wings and made himself as big as possible, screeching fiercely whilst I shouted at him, daring him to come closer, demanding he sank his beak in my rotten heart.

Ufmanna's shrieks slowly lost volume and then confidence. I jumped off Ellette's grave and strode towards him, stretching my arms out and arching my back so that I was as vulnerable as I could be and demanded yet again that the creature swoop down and finished what he had started in the spring.

Ufmanna reacted with a piteous squeal and I realised he was afraid of me. I threw back my head and roared in triumph before advancing even further. Ufmanna turned and launched himself into the air to fly north in order to get away from me.

I followed him, leaving Tuckersham Church, but soon lost sight of the Owl Man. The eastern sky was brightening and layers of mist twirled between the trees and across my path in slow intricate patterns. I continued striding north, feeling the power of indestructability and howling like a wolf. I was the hunter now, I made creatures scurry to safety or cower in abject terror as I passed. I felt tall, my strides long and confident. All that made me Wenn faded, shrouded behind a dark veil. I came to the rectangular clearing lined with the triple rows of standing stones and even these mighty Guardians seemed to cower in the wake of my passing.

The sheer liberation was absolute. There were no fears, no anxieties nor doubts. Just pure instinct. I howled again purely for the delight of it and came to realise I would never have to go back, never have to relinquish this power, never be weak and submissive again. Instead I could drive mortal fear into others. Fear like Ufmanna had shown.

It was the recollection of Ufmanna's last pitiful squeal which made me stop in my tracks. The creature had been scared, robbed of his defences he had been alone and terrified, just as I had so often been. Is this what I wanted? To inflict onto others what I knew so well myself? To bully others into fearing me? To become Stubbles?

To become Stubbles.

I sank to my knees, shrinking rapidly. I fell on the ground where I curled up and heaved desperate sobs. The rage had passed and all that was left was the weakness which I had just despised with my whole being. I scrambled up at last and stumbled onwards, once again a blind desperate flight into the depths of the Wyrde Woods. I couldn't place what had just happened; surely I had finally succumbed to that insanity which had loomed large behind me like a menacing shadow all my damned life.

The path widened into the clearing surrounding St. Lewinna's Pool. I let myself fall down on the ground next to the water, staring at it with wild eyes, breathing irregularly, my heart beating in my throat and head.

Da-Dum. Da-Dum. Blood pulsing through my veins.

Tears had blurred my vision and I found the razor blade in a side pocket of my backpack by touch, it nicked one of my fingertips and I stared at the welling drop of blood in fascination. It was thick and bright red in the gathering sunlight.

It was pretty.

I had more.

Something inside of me still resisted, and my first cuts across my wrist were ineffective, shallow and producing nothing more than a row of small drops. I couldn't even feel pain and tasted bitter failure. The next cut was deeper and produced a trickle of blood. I raised my wrist to taste the coppery stuff and some of it dribbled down my chin.

I was startled by a sudden sound and half turned my head. A shape loomed out of the mist and for a confused moment I thought Rob had appeared in his Wild Hunt outfit but the many branched antlers were not attached to Rob. It almost looked like a shim for all I could see from my position on the ground was a long elated and broad snout towering over me, flanked by large black eyes and framed by an imposing red mane from the top sides of which protruded antlers that spread and forked into impressive weaponry. The head was slowly followed by the rest of the large buck, a lean and mean body covered by red-brown fur. This animal wasn't like one of the small fallow deer I had seen with their white dotted backs; it was far bigger and projected power. It observed me curiously, not the least bit afraid and I stared at it with wide eyes.

The buck took a few steps forwards, snorting and scraping the earth with a hoof. I remained where I was, awestruck by this encounter with the red king of the forest. The swirls of mist began to thin, revealing the tree line around the clearing. The buck threw its antlered head backwards and actually barked. My lips involuntarily formed half a smile; I hadn't known that deer could bark like a dog. The sound was deep and prolonged and when the buck was done it looked back at me.

More deer emerged from the trees cautiously, smaller does and wide-eyed fawns which made towards the pool. The buck was placed between me and its herd. It made no more sounds or movements, just stared at me regally as it formed a barrier between me and its family. The does and fawns bent down to drink, all but one which stared at me with large eyes.

I began to understand the significance of the antlers Rob had worn on Midsummer's Night as I perceived that I was witness to an age-old scene re-enacted again and again in the Wyrde Woods. In due time this red king would weaken, fall prey to the green men who hunted him or a younger buck driven by instinct to drive the elder from the herd and establish his own dominance. This is how it had always been; this is how it always should be. At that instant time disappeared, it was literally gone. The year I lived in seemed far away, this might have been a hundred years ago, five hundred years ago or a thousand years ago. It was irrelevant from the perspective of the Wyrde Woods. A year labelled by mankind meant nothing, only the uninterrupted continuation of the natural cycles.

My mind filled with the awareness of my own kind; Puck crawling through my bedroom window as Willick had done when Joy had slept in that bed. A Malheur Lord come to claim a maiden in the woods, no matter how awkward and gentle this one had been. Choices made involving love and pain and brutal conquest. People choosing that short moment of happiness knowing that pain would follow again for that too was a cycle. People choosing to fight against impossible odds in the full knowledge defeat would follow, for mankind too struggled for dominance, fought to be king of the heap, Lord of the Wyrde Woods.

The archetypes were all there: Young sky clad lovers, good natured grey-beards, power hungry fiends with ruthless ambitions, human monsters, wise women such as Nan Malone and Joy...I knew from the stories that all of these had always been here and experiences we believed to be unique were just parts played according to a collective subconscious script driven by the same force -the Wyrd perhaps- which drove this buck to place himself instinctively between potential danger and the herd he considered his but was only temporarily in his loan. Nothing lasts for ever. Everything lasts for ever.

I thought of the maidservant who had thrown herself off the Herne Tower at Malheur Hall, was that my part to enact now? I looked at the scratches on my wrist. I thought of the other maidservant who had jumped into the moat to escape, floundering in the water just as I had been floundering in this morning's mist. She had been driven by a will to live.

Flounder in desperate determination to reach the dry bank or plummet down to inevitability?

I looked at the doe which was still staring at me; she was out of focus because I tried to look through a blur of tears. I wondered if my mother had played the very part I was playing now. On her knees in the Wyrde Woods, her mind a mess of madness and her soul torn to shreds. I suddenly felt close to Ashley Pilbeame, knowing intuitively that she would have recognised this scene. What had she done? It was kind of obvious since she had never been seen again. She had returned to the womb that the Wyrde Woods could be. Should I? I doubted she would want me to. Both Joy and Judd had said my parents loved each other a great deal. She must have felt the pain of failing Nyle and I would only compound that failure if I deserted my father now, just as he was beginning to show signs of life again. I could make amends for my mum. Or follow her into hell.

The doe seemed to shake its head. Bloody Hell, I was projecting badly, personalising just about everything. I longed for my chestnut, in the state of mind I was in I was sure the tree would reach out for me with her branches, press me against her barky torso and cradle me like a babe. I snorted, and the buck snorted back. This was, I realised, one of those junctions in the Norn's weaving. This was where I could decide my fate.

"I am a part of the stories now," I said to the buck. "I'll stay a bit longer. I have a part to play here yet, I think."

The buck blinked. The first of the does and fawns began to retreat back into the forest now, disappearing into the woods. I wanted to toss the razor aside, but seeing one of the fawns bend down to nibble at some grass, I put it back into the side pocket of my backpack instead.

The herd left and the buck slowly stepped backwards. It then lowered its head to drink from the pool, the glory of its antlers distortedly reflected in the ripples of the water. I sank my face in the pool as well and drank greedily for I was thirsty. Then I stuck in my head altogether, letting the water refresh my head.

I looked up, the buck was by the tree line now and it inclined its head in a greeting.

"Wyrd bið full aræd," I told it and bowed my head too. The Red King of the forest disappeared.

It could have been me, but it had not been, and it wasn't going to be me now. I chose my fate and stood up. I was not in the least bit surprised when the three Norns came slowly walking out of the mist, shrouded in black capes with hoods that hid their faces.

I walked steadily towards them, stopping when I was about six feet away from them, standing firm on the ground with my dripping head held up high. The three pulled their hoods backwards. They weren't the Norns after all, but Joy, Joan and Allison. I did not rush forwards for hugs and kisses. Nor did they.

"Come sister," was all that Joan said and I joined them after which we walked to the Shy Maidens side by side.

35. Robin's Cave

Puck, Willick and Rob were waiting for us by the Shy Maidens. Rob looked at me with a quirky grin and raised a wool Afghan hat in a salute. Willick beamed. Puck looked incredibly relieved, but neither of us made a move to hug one another. There would be time for that later; this was a war-council of the Waer-Wyrd.

My situation was discussed. Nobody was angry or disappointed. Willick had got a call from Nowhere Place on Thursday about the incident and he and Allison had alerted the others. The events at Nowhere Place had been on the local TV and radio and in the Odesby Gazette. No mention had been made of Stubbles, just of sudden unexpected mass hysteria which had ended in a severely injured member of staff and the arrest and transfer of four children. In the early hours of Saturday the tally had been increased with two deaths and four runaways, three girls and a boy.

I realised that three other Forlorn Hopers must have drawn the same conclusions I had and that Jasmin must have been discovered fairly quickly after I had left. They would have had a room-check and discovered the missing kids. I wondered who had informed the media; I doubted it was an official announcement at that time of the night. I felt bad about Miss Watson, she had really tried and I had broken my promise to her.

The Waer-Wyrd had assembled at The Cottage and their night had been bad, no names had been given by the media, for hours all they had known was that there had been arrests and fatalities and runaways. Willick had tried calling Nowhere Place repeatedly, but had only got the answering machine and I had not responded to my mobile. It wasn't until the early morning TV news that the faces of the runaways had appeared on the screen, much to everyone's relief. They had then assumed that I would be making my way into the Wyrde Woods.

"Does ye know the chavees who died well?" Joan asked me.

"Jasmin and Biggs," I answered.

There was a stunned silence.

"Poor liddle Jasmin, may she rest in peace," Joy said at last.

"Was there really just collective hysteria?" Puck asked.

"There was…" I paused. "There was a wolf."

To my relief I could see that everybody understood without me having to go into detail. I may have crawled out of the pit but the wounds were still fresh and raw.

"Yern picture is all over the TV and in the papers," Allison said pensively.

"I am not going back there," I said with calm determination.

"There be times when it is bettermost to ignore Sheere-folk laws," Willick said quietly. "Naun o' us expects ye to gwoan back."

"I can build a shelter in the woods," I nodded gratefully and explained my plans. "There's naun need for you to get involved."

"But we be Wenn," Joy said. "We look after ourn own."

"You can't stay in any of the houses for long though," Puck said. "The police have already rung Willick's house to ask if maybe you showed up."

"Why Willick's place?" I asked.

"That's the address I filled in on the forms," Joy said. "They be wanting a telephone number and one of them computer addresses."

"E-mail," Allison clarified.

"They might come round there, or Joy's place," Puck continued. "If they ask around then locals will recognise a description of Joy."

"Earl's Barrel be too public." Joan said regretfully.

"Wenn can stay with me," Rob offered.

"No Rob, you have the Base Camp there," I said. "It'll be watched."

"I suppose Wenn could stay with me in Robin's Cave," Puck suggested.

"Suppose?" Willick grinned. "Doant pretend ye're naun delighted lad."

"I am not sure," I smiled at Puck evilly. "Puck is a bit weird."

"We all be Wyrde now, that is settled then," Joy declared. "What be the word from the Giant's Grove Puck?"

"On full alert," Puck said immediately. "Duguth Construction is really trying to speed things up. The Lost Boys are assuming a siege is imminent. They are still carrying out actions, but nobody is allowed to wander about by themselves anymore. The coppers have been picking up lone stragglers, arresting them on the basis of suspicion alone."

"So not a lot of time to alert the public and build up support?" I asked.

"Nope," Puck confirmed. "Any eviction should still take a fair few days. Especially of Underearth and Overbranch. The remnants of the Weard Hunt have moved into the main camp at New Rivendell. There are people watching the depots in Stancaster and the Lusty Giants compound. At the first sign of activity which suggests eviction is imminent they will let Jukes know, gain access and chain themselves to vehicles, machinery, gates. That will buy Jukes some time to notify the press."

"Then we must assume that the Waer-Wyrd will be needed," Joy nodded. "Be prepared."

We all nodded, it looked like the Waer-Wyrd would be going to war.

§ § § § § §

After the meeting was over I walked to Robin's Cave with Puck and Lady. We didn't make a big ceremony about me moving in. I upended my backpack to scatter my belongings in one of the smaller chambers where Puck had set up his pallet bed and that was it.

That evening we roasted fresh trout over an open fire just outside the cave. Rob had brought ample home brewed cider when he helped Puck move from the forest hideout to the cave and it supplemented the trout just fine. I treated myself to a roll-up after dinner. I would have to cut down severely as I only had a limited supply and strolling into the shops would be risky.

I told Puck in detail what had happened at Nowhere Place. He became angry when I told him in what state Jasmin had escaped from Stubbles in the consultation room and said that he understood what Biggs had done.

"I'd hate to think of anybody touching you like that," Puck growled.

I hesitated, and then, stammering, told him about Calcott.

"I seriously don't know what to say," he said when I was done. This was far better than over-the-top sympathy or pity, but did not leave me feeling entirely satisfied. There was something I needed to hear.

"I feel guilty now, for wanting to…you know," he said miserably.

"Maybe I should have told you before," I confessed.

"Why?" Puck was puzzled.

"Because…I am damaged goods," I tried not to play the hurt little girl here but couldn't help it, my lips trembled and my eyes grew moist. I really did feel that I had cheated on him somehow, that I was tainted and had kept that from him.

"Hells Bells! No way Wenn. Those Neanderthals, they're the ones who are damaged. Not you."

"Puck, I am cray, remember?"

"Bullshit, you reflect the daftness of those homes. You're not half as crazy as you think Wenn."

"I have demons…" I whispered, recalling the previous night.

Puck pulled me towards him and kissed my forehead.

"I will introduce your demons to mine Elfin; they can have tea parties and play bridge."

I laughed.

"And now, you ought to go to sleep. You look exhausted."

I recalled that I hadn't slept properly for days on end. When I hit the bed I fell asleep almost instantly, vaguely aware that Puck tucked me in and sat by my side stroking my hair before the sweet oblivion of sleep overtook me. I slept through the night and for a good part of the next day.

§ § § § § §

"They are leaving, see!" I pointed at the three groups of Yellowcoats who had spent the better part of the evening roaming the fringes of the woods around Hornsby Farm, training binoculars and tele-lenses at both the new and old farm buildings. We had taken post in the trees on the northern edge of Rob's farmlands to wait for a safe moment to visit Rob at my insistence. I wanted to borrow a bow and arrows.

"But why Wenn?" Puck had raised his eyebrows back at the cave.

"Because…because…" I had sought to put a feeling into words.

"Ah, an excellent reason," Puck had teased me.

"How can I be a proper outlaw…" I had glanced around our camp in the cave "…without a bow and arrows?"

Puck had looked at me for a moment, and then jumped to his feet.

"Let's go," he had said.

This is one of the things I loved about Puck; he totally understood.

We watched the Yellowcoats melt into the forest.

"I want to wait, Wenn, till dusk," Puck said. "If they have any smarts, there'll be a team there yet, somewhere in the undergrowth."

It was sensible and we waited patiently for the arrival of dusk. Half way down to the farmhouse we heard a commotion behind one of the hedges that separated two fields. We found a fence to jump over and encountered a furious Maimie confronting a bewildered looking Rob.

"Murderer!" Maimie shouted at Rob. I saw that Rob was carrying his own bow and arrows as well as a wild rabbit he had evidently shot.

"But, I'm naun a murderer," Rob protested, shaking his head so that the tall top hat he wore was left askance on his head.

"You killed that poor little rabbit, you're a bloody murderer."

"Robbut?" Rob looked at his catch and back at Maimie. "But ye doant understand lass, I'll be eating this liddle feller for me tea."

Maimie paled.

"Evening Puck, evening Wenn," Rob was relieved to see us. "How do?"

"Middling, how do Rob?" I greeted him happily.

"Puck!" Maimie exclaimed. "This man has shot a rabbit!"

"They do that around here, hunt for food," Puck shrugged.

"Well I think it's inhumane," Maimie complained. She looked at Rob. "Monstrous."

"I reckon ye doant realise that if robbuts are left to theirn own devices they'll breed alike...robbuts. Then there'll be dunnamy o' them and they'll die very slowly, o' starvation or disease," Rob explained.

"I don't care. I am going to raise this at the meeting; we'll soon put an end to this." Maimie was outraged.

"Maimie," I said carefully. "Do you realise Rob is the owner of this land? Your host? You're his guest you know."

"That doesn't give him the right to kill poor defenceless rabbits," Maimie said angrily.

"Maimie," Puck looked at her with some amusement. "It's a normal thing around here; I also shoot rabbits for food."

Maimie's eyes grew large.

"You…?" She began.

Puck shrugged and nodded.

"Tootles was right about you!" She exclaimed. "When it comes down to it you're just another Tory who likes to torture foxes."

"We're not talking about foxes Maimie," Puck laughed. "It's just a damn rabbit."

"That is precisely how your kind of people look at life!" Maimie accused him. She turned and stormed off leaving us somewhat bewildered.

"Shouldn't you follow her?" I asked Puck.

"No, she'll go to Tootles and he'll tell her exactly what she wants to hear," Puck shrugged.

"Tootles is…" I asked.

He nodded.

"And this meeting she talked about?"

"Jukes and Tink are not going to risk the whole base camp because Maimie is upset." Puck said. He looked at Rob. "They'll probably not like it either, but they'll respect that they are your guests."

"Unaccountable," Rob shook his head. The top hat fell off and I caught it before it hit the ground. "Bethanks Wenn o' the Farisees."

"Can I borrow that bow I used, and some arro…streales?" I asked him.

"Aye ye can," Rob smiled at the mention of archery. "But I'll wrap it all up in some sheets, cause if the Sheere-folk see ye wandering around the woods armed, they'll call in an air strike I reckon. Boom!"

"Yeah, or some protest people will lynch us," I frowned.

"Got ye some tobacco as well Wenn, thought ye might need it," Rob added to my delight. He looked at Puck. "I'll gwoan with ye some o' the way back. I reckon I might visit Joy for a few days. Can I borrow yern room Wenn?"

I nodded. Puck looked concerned.

"You don't have to run away from your own farm Rob, it isn't right."

"Naun animals left but Beowulf and the chickens but they'll manage and I'll take Beowulf. Suddent I got me idle time," Rob shrugged. "Aside o' that, I'd feel better if Joy aint left on hern own."

We all agreed with that and later that evening traversed the oak woodlands like proper outlaws, with a horse and bows and arrows.

§ § § § § §

Puck told me that he had spoken to Jukes whilst Rob had been selecting archery gear for me and then packing for himself. Jukes said they were losing people from the main camp daily now. Those who would sneak into the main compound to chain themselves to heavy machinery, or climb into the construction corridor to perch high up in the remaining trees. It had become a war of attrition. Every action was cause for more delay, every delay cost Duguth Construction money but New Rivendell was losing people fast. A few new arrivals trickled in each day, but they reported that many more potential protestors were being detained by the police on the main access routes into the Wyrde Woods.

I wanted to go join the actions, or at least go see but Puck said security patrols had already been seen as far as the Halfhollow Oak, St

Lewinna's Priory, Arthur's Fort and the Guardians. It was becoming too risky.

What followed instead were four days during which we saw nobody else and stayed in Hood's Gorge. We built a compost toilet, practiced archery, did a bit of rock climbing, spent hours watching otters at play, caught trout for dinner in the Rore and drank cider around the campfire. The nights formed a sour contrast to the delightful days. I could not stop the images of Jasmin and Biggs surfacing in my mind. Sharon too, for she was lost to me now as well and I would sink into sadness. No longer the overwhelming type which threatened madness but the grief bit deep.

Jasmin's face most of all; I kept feeling that happy uplift of my heart as I heard the echoes of her laughter and contagious enthusiasm. It had turned out that she had the gift of infecting people with good cheer once she had been released from her solitary bubble. I missed her and as the evenings progressed became gloomy and down. Puck put up with me and either sympathised in silence or would listen patiently as I told him stories from Nowhere Place and Jasmin's visit to the Owlery. It didn't occur to me that he had played a part in a great deal of the stories himself. When I cried in the dark hours of the night Puck would cradle me and whisper words of comfort till I succumbed to sleep.

Our daytime outlaw lifestyle is what I had imagined when I had been looking forward to five weeks of summer before Nowhere Place turned sour. Filled with peace, trout and cider I experienced a freedom that was not as ebullient as the freedom I had felt dancing on Arthur's Fort on Midsummer's Night but made me feel wholesome anyway, even as I was aware that the shadows of recent violence would accompany nightfall.

§ § § § § §

On the afternoon of the fifth day Puck decided to hunt a rabbit and I insisted on coming with him, my borrowed bow in hand and a filled quiver on my back.

We made our way up a steep and narrow path close to the cave and reached the top of the gorge.

"Are you planning to launch some arrows at a rabbit?" Puck asked.

"Heck no. I'm not as good a shot as you," I said. "I don't want to see it wounded and rush away with an arrow stuck in it."

"But you wanted to bring your bow and arrows anyway?" Puck grinned.

"Wenn o' the Farisees is living out her fantasy," I explained. "And you're in them, which is a good sign, my love. Naun need to worry till I no longer include you in them."

"I'll keep that…" Puck started and then looked up. I heard it too, the whinny of a horse.

"It'll be Rob," I said confidently.

"Let's just hide ourselves till we see," Puck suggested and we concealed ourselves in the undergrowth.

It was Rob approaching on Beowulf. He was wearing his white cowboy hat and for once he had got his hat down to perfection; he looked the part as he came riding in like he was on his way to a duel with the Sherriff at the saloon.

Lady barked happily and trotted towards Rob and Beowulf.

"How do Lady?" Rob said and got off Beowulf.

Puck and I emerged from our hiding place.

"By Gemeeny," Rob laughed. "Two Greenwoods outlaws."

"How do Rob," Puck said. "Is everything okay?"

"I was on mine way to see Willick," Rob said. "I met him on the path on hisn way into the woods. Looking for Wenn."

"Looking for me?" I asked curiously.

"Aye, ye have visitors." Rob nodded, "They're waiting at The Cottage, if ye two take Beowulf I'll take Lady and the bows down to the cave and wait for ye to come back."

"Visitors?" I was puzzled. "Do you know who?"

"Naun," Rob shook his head. "Willick jes said to tell ye it were safe."

Puck got on Beowulf first and Rob helped me up. The ride to The Cottage was exhilarating. Till now I had mostly been concerned with Beowulf's head, fascinated by his eyes which held a gentle intelligence. Sitting behind Puck I suddenly felt Beowulf's strength; he seemed to have no problem carrying the both of us and seemed eager to exert himself more.

"He wants a run," Puck turned his head. "You up for a trot?"

I nodded eagerly and wrapped my arms around Puck's middle. Beowulf broke into a trot and Puck had to restrain him from going faster at times. I watched the woods go by and used Puck as a guideline as to how to move along with Beowulf.

"You okay back there?" Puck asked. He couldn't see my face otherwise he would have seen me grinning from ear to ear.

"Can Beowulf go faster?" I asked.

"It's irresponsible," Puck said. "We're not wearing helmets."

Beowulf neighed and snorted and broke into a canter and I laughed. The movement became far more fluid and I swayed along with Beowulf and Puck and felt the wind blow through my hair.

Puck stopped Beowulf around a corner from The Cottage. He got off the horse and then helped me down.

"You'll stay here out of sight," I guessed his intention.

He nodded, "And keep an eye out. Willick said it was safe, so there shouldn't be a problem."

But just in case. We have to be careful, we're both fugitives now. I thought.

I walked down the lane and towards The Cottage curious to see the inside of Willick and Allison's house. The front door opened though as soon as I reached the start of the path through the small flower-filled front garden and I froze when Michael stepped outside.

§ § § § § § §

"Michael?" I asked in disbelief.

"Wenn," Michael smiled. "It's good to see you."

I was speechless. I became even more confused when Miss Watson emerged behind Michael. On the one hand I was wary, she represented Nowhere Place and I was a runaway now. On the other I was surprised by the pleasure I felt at seeing her.

Willick stepped out now and shrugged at me. His presence made me relax a little, I couldn't imagine that he would have betrayed me and I realised his address would have been in the OJCH files.

"Wendy," Miss Watson smiled, I thought I read relief on her face. "Are you okay?"

I nodded, trying to figure out what the game was.

"We don't need to know where you are staying Wenn," Michael said. "We just wanted to know that you were safe."

"I am safe, very safe," I answered. I was still wary, assuming they had come to talk me into going back. It was the only thing that made sense and I made ready to ensure no harsh words would fall from my side because obviously I was going to resist. There was no way that I would go back to Odesby. I calculated that I could outrun Michael to the woods if needed.

"That is good Wenn," Michael smiled. "I am pleased to hear it. Judy told me you had found a place where you felt at home. We were hoping we'd find you here."

Judy? Oh, of course, Miss Watson.

"I met my father," I blurted out. "I know what happened to my parents."

Michael started to smile again and I could see it was a warm smile, he was genuinely happy for me, he knew well enough how that tormented me.

"You forgot something when you left Wendy," Miss Watson said quietly.

There was no recrimination in her voice and I was relieved. She stepped forwards and held out a linen bag. I took it and peered inside. I recognised the contents straight away; they had brought me my medication.

I looked up again with an open mouth and Michael laughed.

"Enough for a month, I can't take too much at once without raising suspicion," Miss Watson said and then asked Willick: "Can we visit again in a month's time Mr. Maskall?"

"Twould be mine pleasure," he nodded.

Miss Watson scrutinised me.

"We have to leave now, but maybe next time we can catch up?" She asked.

I nodded eagerly. "That would be really good."

"Mayhap, if ye call afore, we can share a Coager," Willick suggested.

Michael looked puzzled and I laughed.

"You'll like it," I promised him. "Bread, cheese and cider."

"That sounds excellent," Michael said. "I look forward to it."

I gave them both a hug and then said goodbye to Willick. He searched my eyes and I smiled at him. He had been right to trust Michael and Miss Watson and the medication would help, I had nearly run out. We both nodded at each other and then I demanded one of his great big bear hugs.

I talked excitedly to Puck on the way back about how people could surprise you sometimes. I was also elated by the fact that their visit symbolised an implicit acceptance that I had chosen to do what I deemed best for me. I doubted it could be described as approval but there was an understanding there which warmed me.

Rob greeted us when we returned to Robin's Cave.

"Afore I forget," he said. "I went to the farm somewhen t'other-day, Jukes be asking me to tell ye that Corin's photographs be up on the internet."

"The Wyrde Woods collage," I said happily.

"Drat," Puck shrugged. "We could have seen it at The Cottage."

"We could go back there one of these days?" I suggested. Puck nodded.

"And Joy axed if ye be wanting to come for tea tomorrow," Rob added.

"Yes!" Puck and I answered at the same time.

§ § § § § § §

Both Puck and I were pleased to see Joy again and she enjoyed our company although she was having a bad day of it with the pain. We stayed in my old room that night, it smelled stuffy because the owls had been having a 'poo phase' as Joy diplomatically described it and the whole Owlery smelled of it. Puck opened the window before we went to sleep and the flow of air was refreshing. We also figured that if any official visits were made I could make my way down the ivy and hide in the woods.

We spent most of the next day cleaning the Owlery, for a 'poo phase' involved lots of squirting the stuff outwards from the boxes and Joy was still poorly.

Puck and I cooked dinner and Rob came back in time to join us. Then it was time to go.

"Grandma, Wenn and I are going over to Willick's place. I want to show Wenn the results of the Wyrde Woods photo shoot that Jukes has put up on the internet. We'll come back later tonight and head back to the cave tomorrow."

"Jes be careful, take the smaller paths, avoid the dirt roads," Joy said. She looked weary, having been afflicted by the pain again she had trouble walking.

"You'll be okay?" I looked at Rob who nodded. I saw that he had placed a wooden club by the hearth.

"I'll leave Lady here, she's a good guard dog," Puck said. "Lady stay, stay with grandma."

Lady whined but walked over to Joy who was sitting in her rocking chair and sat down next to her.

"See you later Rob, see you Joy," I said as I followed Puck to the front door.

"Take care chavees." Joy answered.

"Be careful," Rob said in parting.

"Kleak-kleak," Bronwen added.

36. Desolation

"Apparently hern ladyship gave an interview on local television disyer afternoon," Willick announced after Puck and I had seated ourselves behind the computer.

It was in the room he used as an office and atelier, for I saw piles of tree bark in a corner as well as a cutting board and various cutting tools. Two of the walls were decorated by rimless picture frames. These contained astounding collages of bark forming patterns reminiscent of a forest, some of which were oddly aglow with the reddish light which the setting sun cast through the window. The other inner wall was hidden from sight by floor-to-ceiling bookshelves which were on the verge of spilling books for these were crammed into every available space. There were odd items tucked in there too, I saw an old World War helmet and a toy airplane and wondered at these.

Allison came and joined us.

"Kettle be on," she said as she cast a look at the computer screen which flickered into life after which Puck logged in using Willick's user name.

"What channel, roughly what time?" I asked Willick.

"Sussex-on-Four, round six, twere that local news show," he answered. "We missed it ournself."

I took the keyboard from Puck and my fingers flew over it as I directed us to the screen I was looking for.

"Be careful not..." Puck began.

"...to log in under my own name anywhere, yup Mr. Smarty-pants."

The screen filled with small squares representing the programs of that day on Sussex-on-Four and I selected one. It began with national news summary and I started fast forwarding. When the counter was on 00:14:07 Puck pointed.

"There, ten seconds back," he said.

"Well I'll be! Tis unaccountable," Willick was amazed.

"That'll be all-along-o' ye let me does ourn computer work Will," Allison teased him. "I told ye o' digital magic oft enow."

"Aye that ye did." Willick acknowledged.

I found the spot and raised the volume. Two presenters sat on a high beige couch behind a round coffee table, a man in his forties, elegant with a slightly boyish look, and a woman in her thirties with a stunning mane of brown hair and full lips. Both looked outrageously happy to be there, creating an immediate insincerity. The large stylishly modern chair opposite them was empty for two seconds and then Lady Malheur strode into view. She had changed the sharp business look I had seen at the Council meeting for a conservative dress which was designed to make her look desirable without being ostentatiously sexy. The only accessoire was a simple pearl neckless. Her hair had been done up giving a slight regal look. The whole spoke of elegance.

"Our guest this afternoon is Lady Malheur of Malheur Hall near Odesby," the male presenter said as if it was a miracle.

"And we are honoured to have her here of course," the female presenter said Bridget Jones style, failing to get the delivery in a natural way.

"It's a pleasure to be here," Lady Malheur said with a sincere smile. She had changed her accent too, sounding much more like a toff now. This really was the image of old English aristocracy. It would send the young folk of the Weard Hunt into peals of laughter, but she wasn't aiming her message at them, that was clear. I knew that many Neverlanders, for instance, staunch royalists and patriots all, would find this image far more appealing than the business shark.

"I understand, Lady Malheur, that your home is practically under siege," the female presenter pulled this one off, putting in just the right amount of sisterly yet respectful sympathy and stressing the word *home*. Not Malheur Hall the stately palace, but *home*, one just like her audience would have. Now that I had a something of a home, and all the mental comfort that entailed, I realised that I had not even begun to understand how important it really was during the dark days on which I missed a vague notion of home so badly without actually knowing what it meant. Now I knew and it was a powerful opening, many would sympathise with the idea of Lady Malheur being besieged in her home.

"Well," Lady Malheur smiled, "I wouldn't call it besieged; groups of people have appeared outside my home in an effort at very vocal intimidation. I must admit it wasn't pleasant."

We all exchanged glances.

"Indeed, not very pleasant at all to be made to feel unsafe in your home," the male presenter shook his head sadly. They were really pushing that point home, I frowned. It seemed to me be too blatant with all this repetition.

"I had to call the police," Lady Malheur nodded. "I went out myself first of course, to ask them to leave in a polite manner, but they were extremely rude. Crude expressions which I dare not repeat out loud."

We exchanged more glances. Willick and Allison were getting angry.

"That lying draggle-tail," Allison snorted.

"Oh dear," the male presenter said politely.

"Do the police have any indication who these people might be Lady Malheur? We have heard rumours that it might have to do with the road-protestors in the Wyrde Woods," the other presenter said.

"Much as I disagree with the methods of the road-protestors, who are squatting on private property, I have to acknowledge that at least they are clear about their agenda. They honestly believe that they are right to break law after law even when a long democratic process revealed they are not." Lady Malheur gave the poisonous compliment in a regretful tone. She continued.

"There is a more sinister group active in the Wyrde Woods. Unfortunately this unlawful road protest appears to have drawn all sorts of people to it. It is this group which is responsible for threatening the income of many local residents who have found employment opportunities due to the road works. Unlike the road protestors, this anti-Odesby group operate in anonymity, refusing to reveal their identity. Not having introduced themselves, I call them the wodewoses, after the wild brutal primitives of our distant past."

"Well that is bad news for all of those working hard to feed their families," the female presenter shook her head.

"Times are hard enough as it is for all of us," the male presenter answered.

"Indeed, unfortunately that is not all. Their activities seem mostly based on conducting occultist debauchery such as the shameful conduct on Arthur's Fort a few weeks ago," Lady Malheur said.

"We have heard things indeed: Drunkenness, drug abuse, public nudity and other acts of indecent behaviour," the female presenter nodded.

"It's disgraceful, very un-English," the male presenter added. "These people are occultists you say?"

Allison hissed. Puck and I gave each other a look.

"I am afraid that seems to be the case," Lady Malheur agreed. "I have been informed by reliable sources that an investigation is being conducted into activities which resemble those of a sect."

Puck and I exchanged another glance. I heard Allison hissing behind me again. Willick was just shaking his head.

"Good Lord, a sect? Here in Sussex?" The male presenter sounded shocked, his counterpart raised her hand to her mouth to mirror that shock.

"Indeed, they have even been in Odesby to find recruits. They selected the Odesby Juvenile Care Home as a likely source."

At that moment the screen changed and we were looking at footage of Nowhere Place, the building sullen behind its unkempt low hedge.

I felt my heart stop for a moment.

"Why that location?" the female presenter asked.

"Presumably because they think we, as a society, don't care much for the unfortunate children who are there. Perhaps because the so-called Neverland Estate is seen as…easy pickings…I do believe they call it. They have selected a number of teenagers from the estate as their victims, mostly girls." Lady Malheur's voice commented on the footage.

Suddenly the school photos of Jasmin and myself filled the whole screen. Lady Malheur continued speaking.

"These two girls, one aged sixteen and the other aged fourteen, are known to have been out in the woods with the sect. Upon their return there was a series of unfortunate incidents at the Odesby Juvenile Care Home…"

The school photos decreased in size and moved to the bottom of the screen which now displayed Nowhere Place again, this time with ambulances and police cars in front of it, flashing alarm lights emphasising an emergency situation. They had even added the sound of blaring sirens to push the point home.

"…which has resulted in the untimely death of the younger girl, the death of another young male inhabitant of the OJCH in the Neverland Estate and the disappearance of the older girl. It is believed she may have been abducted by the sect. I dare not even contemplate what dreadful treatment that poor girl is being subjected to by these occultists even as we speak. Three other children are still missing and it is likely that they too are in the hands of this cult."

Three more portraits appeared at the bottom of the screen, kids I knew well enough. They were from other corridors but Forlorn Hopers none-the-less.

I fought to repress my rising fury.

"Well I am sure the police will be conducting a very careful investigation," the male presenter said.

"I hope they find the location of these…animals…soon and free that poor girl," the female presenter said.

"As a matter of fact investigation has revealed the Headquarters of this despicable cult," Lady Malheur shared.

Puck and I looked at each other again; there was fear on his face. I felt it too. From the kitchen we could hear the sound of the kettle starting to whistle.

"Well…ahem…that is new information," the male presenter stumbled; it seemed Lady Malheur had wandered off the script.

"I only found out this morning, but assumed it was already public knowledge that it is a place called the Owlery on the North Woods lane."

"The Owlery you say?" The female presenter asked.

"On the North Woods lane," Lady Malheur confirmed.

The kettle uttered a piercing shriek.

We were stunned. Puck was the first to recover.

"Burn the witch," he said slowly.

We both jumped up and followed by Willick and Allison we rushed out of the room.

§ § § § § § §

Willick drove his Land Rover through the internal dirt road network at a dangerous speed, his lights on full as the trees sped by. He slowed down some as we came close to the Owlery and switched to the mist lamps, then turned those off too as we ambled to a halt.

"Disyer be as close as I durst to go," Willick said.

We spilled out of the car and heard distant angry voices from the direction of the Owlery.

We ran through the forest. We approached the side of the Owlery where the ivy stretched to my bedroom window. There was nobody on the grass there, but we could see a group of people by the front door, shaking fists and shouting. The dirt road beyond was full of cars. The back garden contained the far larger part of the crowd around the house and to my horror I saw men and women actively trampling flowers, herbs and vegetables into the ground. There was much hateful shouting here too. Many people appeared to be drunk. Their faces were distorted by anger and hate.

The window by the sink in the kitchen had been broken and I saw smoke billow through.

Puck grunted and made to storm the mob but I pulled him back. He nearly broke loose from my grip but Willick enveloped Puck in his broad arms.

"Puck, did you lock the bedroom window this morning?" I asked urgently.

"What?" His eyes were wild.

"The bedroom window, did you lock it?"

Understanding came into his eyes, he shook his head and we both looked at the distance to the ivy. It was mostly out of view of the crowds on both sides of the house, and covered in a deep dark shadow.

Puck and I dashed forwards as one and raced towards the ivy. We hauled ourselves up; Puck tugged open the window and we spilled onto my bed. There was acridity in the air that suggested fire. We rushed past the chimney and down the stairs. The kitchen door was two thirds of the way shut. We could hear the crackle of flames in there and smoke wafted through the opening. Puck pulled it shut and we then rushed into the living room and froze in our tracks.

§ § § § § §

Joy and Rob had made a stance by the far wall. Joy lay on the ground in front of the wardrobe, a disturbingly large pool of blood around her head. Rob sat half upright against the wall, his chin resting on his chest which was dark with blood. There were feathers everywhere as well as more blood and chunks of…

…Aethel, Horsa, Bronwen and Bran had been literally torn to pieces. There was no sign of Lady.

Puck rushed to Joy and I to Rob. I shook Rob by the shoulders and to my relief he groaned.

"Rob is alive," I shouted to Puck. The fire in the kitchen began to increase in fury and more smoke started billowing in, even though we had shut the kitchen door. There was a roar from the mob outside.

"Grandma is dead," Puck choked. I turned and looked. Joys face was one of frozen anguish and I felt the chasm opening wide. I fought it.

Something ignited in the kitchen with a whoosh that drew a cheer from the mob.

I rushed to Puck's side.

"Puck, we've got to go."

Puck shook his head, stroking Joy's cheek.

"Puck, we have to go NOW." I pulled at him and he resisted.

I brought my face close to his.

"Puck my love, for Joy, do it for JOY. She would have wanted us to finish what she started."

The horror on his face was replaced by dull resignation.

"Come on," I pulled him again and this time he followed me to the corner where Rob was attempting to get up, clutching his bloodied head. We were all coughing now as the room was smoking up pretty badly. Puck and I helped Rob up and supported him towards the stairs. He was moving groggily and we more or less had to push him up the stairs.

We were barely able to breath by the time we reached the window by my bed. Puck went out first and then we both helped Rob out of the window after which I left. We scrambled down the ivy. Rob fell halfway and tumbled on the grass below. There was a roar from the mob and for a moment I was afraid we had been seen, but they were reacting to the fire, the flames of which were spreading fast now.

Puck and I helped Rob up and supported him across the garden and over the wall. When we reached Willick and Allison they caught the three of us as we fell down, all of us coughing.

"Joy is dead," I said gasping for breath.

"The owls too," Puck began to tremble. "I don't know where Lady is."

"She chased some o' them into the kitchen," Rob wheezed.

Willick had gone pale, Allison grabbed his hand and squeezed it but then let go.

"Away from here, now," she hissed and pushed us in the direction of the Land Rover.

She made Willick get in the passenger seat and took the driver's seat herself. Puck and I helped Rob into the back and then crawled in as well.

Allison drove the Land Rover backwards till she could make a turn, and then thundered down the startled Wyrde Woods towards The Cottage. Puck and I clutched each other and began to weep.

37. Six for Gold

Puck rocked on his haunches, his face almost unrecognisable, his eyes red sore from crying and snot running from his nose as he alternatively sobbed and gasped for breath. He had run from the Land Rover when we arrived and I had followed him into one of the sheds which smelled of fresh wood shavings. Just before I entered the shed I had seen Allison and Willick supporting Rob into The Cottage.

I had stopped crying myself and was suspended over the abyss now, my demons howling eagerly below in a dark huddle, their red eager eyes turned upwards and their cajoling calls almost lost in the vast expanse of emptiness I felt. I despaired that they were back. I had secretly hoped I had banished them at last after my meeting with the Red King. However, I was stronger now though, much stronger. I needed to be for Puck. His chest was heaving rapidly and I focused on him, nothing else existed or mattered, he became the focal point of my being. I reached out for him. He struggled but I applied all my strength and pulled him towards me. Puck ceased his struggling and curled his upper body on my lap. I stroked his hair, his neck, his back and arms quietly shushing his sobs. I wanted to tell him it would be okay, but that notion seemed hollow and meaningless to me. He did begin to calm down somewhat.

"Rob said that he would protect her," he suddenly said angrily.

"And nearly gave his life doing so," I said thinking of the brightly coloured Nepalese wool cap Rob had been wearing when we left the Owlery in the early evening.

"Not good enough," Puck hissed.

"Puck, Rob was strong enough to have got away. He stayed."

"She should have never stayed at the Owlery; she should have come to the cave."

"Ssshhh," I said, momentarily unable to speak as I was shaken by a spasm of painful grief.

"I shouldn't have left today, I should have stayed there," Puck said tonelessly.

For a moment I envisaged him there, lying by his grandmother's feet, Puck's lifeless face disfigured by a snarl. I shook my head to banish the image and felt guilty for being relieved that he hadn't been there.

"If you want to blame somebody Puck, blame me," I confessed in a shaky voice. "They used me and Jasmin as an excuse…if I had never come to the Owlery…"

The full realisation left me sucker-punched, unable to breathe for a moment.

"Aunt Catt," Puck hissed with venom and then continued with sudden clarity in his voice, "would have thought of something else. She knew Wenn, she knew all along. Everything."

Puck became silent again but his breathing became more forced and I felt him beginning to tense up, his arms and torso becoming hard as steel on my lap. I continued to stroke him but it was to no avail.

"NNNgggggwwha," he suddenly uttered and sat up, his eyes wild and unfocused. He struggled to get up but I pulled him down again, throwing both my arms around him and pressing myself against him.

"Ssshhh Puck," I said, for a moment totally exposed to his pain which loomed over him like a giant pile of precarious rocks which could avalanche down any minute.

"Gggwwe," he started shaking again but this time with blind anger. How well I knew the desolate place he was in now, how often I had haunted those same paths of incessant fury, feeling like a time-bomb that was relentlessly ticking towards detonation.

"GET OFF ME," Puck suddenly snarled and struggled angrily. I increased my grip and held on to him for dear life.

"I am never letting go of you, Puck, never. I love you." I said.

Puck uttered another angry growl but some of his tension melted.

We sat there all night like that, Puck alternating between bouts of anger, hopelessness and heart breaking anguish which left both of us sobbing and weeping with unspeakable pain.

We did not sleep.

§ § § § § §

Joan's car pulled up in the driveway in the morning. Puck and I stumbled out of the shed to meet her. She took one look at our faces.

"So it's true," she whispered sadly and then hugged us.

We went inside, Willick was sitting at the kitchen table, Allison busied herself with tea, coffee, bread and cheese and Joan and I went to help her while Puck stumbled to Willick. Boy and man looked at each other for a moment, unable to speak. Puck sank down on a chair.

The rest of us sat down too, everybody looked drawn and haggard.

"Rob be in bed," Allison said. "He will be all right physically, but I'm naun sure about hisn mind, he be in a bad way. Blames hisnself."

She looked around the depleted war council of the Waer-Wyrd.

"Question be, what does we choose to do now?" She asked.

We maun ever stop trying. Remember that, whatever happens ye mus always keep trying. I heard Joy's voice loud and clear in my head.

"We finish what Joy started," I said with angry determination. "I am not letting that Malheur bitch have her way."

"Tis what Joy would've wanted, expected o' us," Joan agreed.

"We also have to assume Malheur knows a lot more about us than we thought," I said grimly.

"Naun everything," Allison looked at Willick. "We would've known it if she knew all, surelye."

Willick nodded.

"Problem be," Joan spoke slowly. "That Joy weren't sure how exactly it would be done. She had some notion, places and the like, but never completed hern plans."

"We're going to have to work it out for ourselves," I said. "Start with what we can do now."

"So what can we do now?" Puck asked.

"Gold, six for gold," Joan answered. She looked at the Swan on my chest, it seemed dimmer this morning. "Wenn's got the silver."

"Where is the gold?" I asked.

"Malheur Hall," Allison answered.

"We go tonight," Puck declared.

"How do we get in?" I asked.

"I'll get ye in," Willick said grimly. "But, Allison..." He looked at his wife.

"I'll pack ourn things," she agreed softly.

I looked at them quizzically, no longer following the logic.

"Wenn," Puck laid his hand on mine. "Willick is Fluttergrub."

"FLUTTERGRUB?" I exclaimed.

"Aye, he be the groundskeeper at Malheur Hall," Allison nodded.

"Willick is our man inside," Puck explained.

I was flabbergasted and didn't know what to say. Everybody looked at me expectantly.

I realised that they had deliberately kept this a secret from me. My heart hardened for a moment and I felt pissed off.

"You didn't tell me," I said.

Doant be tessy, I heard a familiar voice whisper in my ear.

"Joy wanted to wait before telling you," Puck said softly. "It wasn't relevant for you to know yet."

"Well it is now. Are there more secrets I should know about?" I said the words without rancour, accepting that I had been the wild card in the pack.

"Naun liddle one," Willick said quietly. "Ye know all now."

"Good and you can get us into Malheur Hall tonight?" I said.

"Aye, but naun all o' us. Too many'll draw attention. Two at most." Willick answered.

"I am going," Puck declared firmly.

"And I am coming with you," I said.

We looked at the others defiantly. With Joy gone and Rob out of action the Waer-Wyrd had got a lot smaller and was essentially leaderless. They would have to accept Puck and myself as fully grown. I could sense that Puck too was ready to combat any references to our youth.

"That is bettermost, I reckon," Willick agreed and Joan nodded.

"I agree on one condition," Allison said thoughtfully. "Ye two look like ye haven't slept at all. Ye must sleep first. I'll naun have ye soodling about that place too tired to think on yern feet."

I nodded, suddenly feeling tired.

"I'll show ye the spare bedroom," Allison said.

"No," I said quickly. "I'll go to the cave."

"Lass, ye can sleep here," Willick said.

"No," I repeated. "You saw the news, they claim I was abducted by…an occultist sect. What if the police come to make enquiries? You're practically Joy's nearest neighbour, they don't even have to suspect that I am here, just come to ask questions about last night. But if they find me here, you two are done for."

"Wenn is right," Puck nodded.

"You can stay here," I told him.

"Don't be a ridiculous Elfin," he managed a first smile. "I go where you go."

§ § § § § § §

"So this be how ye got in," Willick shook his head when Puck led us through the loose end of the chain-link fence and then through the gap underneath the hedge. Willick had a hard time struggling through the small openings; we ended up seizing his hands and dragging him out of the hedge.

The Landrover was parked on the nearby dirt road. We had dropped the trailer off near Robin's Cave; Allison had packed it with all the essentials and things she and Willick didn't want to part from. They were taking no chances, if Lady Malheur discovered Willick's part in the Waer-Wyrd then who knew what retaliation she might come up with this time. Rob had recovered enough to walk about unaided though he was still groggy and withdrawn. He had insisted on going back to the farm but we had all vetoed that. Joan had found Beowulf wandering in the woods near the Owlery and Puck had assured Rob that Beowulf would be looked after. Puck had brought the horse back to the farm before meeting us back at the dirt road where Joan, Allison and Rob would wait in the Landrover until we came back, after which we would all head to Robin's Cave to consider our next move.

Puck retrieved the beam and we crossed the moat in quick succession. It was dark and Puck and I had smeared our faces and hands with mud so as not to reflect any light. Willick wore his Fluttergrub outfit; he was the only one who conceivably had an excuse to be wandering around the grounds of Malheur Hall this night. We crept through the herb garden and then through the butterfly and magic gardens until we reached the Shakespeare Garden. Willick led us to the far wall and produced a key with which he unlocked the gate to the Poison Garden.

"Doant be touching anything ye two," he growled a low warning.

I walked past the flowering greenery with my arms rigidly by my side. Willick turned on the torch he had brought. There was a set of steps leading downwards at the end of the deadly courtyard, it led to a lower gallery sunk some ten feet down and covered by a domed brick ceiling. There were two low tables in the gallery, with neat rows of gardening tools, a water tap, watering cans and sacks of fertilizers by the walls. The far end of the space had an arched doorway. Willick unlocked the door using a key on a key ring that held many old-fashioned keys, large iron ones. A series of steps led us some fifteen feet further down into a chamber. There were some old kegs and crates piled up in one corner, and a ramshackle cupboard with empty glass jars in another.

"This be where they prepared poisons in the old days," Willick said. "Puck, help me shift that cupboard. Wenn, can ye hold the torch and shine it this way?"

Willick and Puck shifted the cupboard to one side, revealing a low door of aged oak. The iron hinges and fittings were rusty coloured, as was the ancient lock. Willick produced another key and stuck it into the keyhole. He tried to turn it and the mechanism resisted at first but then gave way with a loud click and the door slowly swung outwards, revealing a low passage hacked into rock.

Willick took the lead and we followed him down the passage. Both Willick and Puck had to crouch to avoid their head hitting the roof of the tunnel; I was okay, though sometimes the rock overhead would brush against my hair. The tunnel went on forever, sloping gently downwards, sometimes becoming a bit higher and at other times more constricted yet. At some point water started dripping down from the roof, gathering in small shallow puddles on the floor.

"Moat," Willick whispered.

We nodded and continued. The tunnel became dry again and started to slope upwards. It ended at an arched doorway where we encountered yet another aged door. This one had a key mechanism which refused to budge.

Willick cursed and fumbled with the key. Something snapped and Willick hissed in disgust.

"We'll have to force it open, door swings outwards," Willick decided. "Puck, lend us a hand."

Puck nodded and the two threw themselves against the door on the count of three. They thudded into it with a bang and the door creaked in protest. I joined them for the second attempt. This time the thud was followed by a metallic crack and the door swung open. We held our breath, we had made a lot of noise, or so it had sounded like in the confined space we were in, but heard only an ominous silence apart from the faint echo of dripping water behind us.

We walked through the door emerging into a small bricked open space from where a narrow spiral stair began a steep climb upwards. I realised we were now beneath Malheur Hall and felt my heart beating in my chest.

Slowly and carefully we climbed the long stairs which ended in a rectangular space long enough to accommodate twice the length of the door and there was a narrow passage which led away to the right. Willick unlocked the door with yet another key on his key ring. He then took hold of the door handle and began to slide it sideways, the sliding door squeaked softly in protest at first and I held my breath. It appeared at first there was nothing behind the door but more darkness, but shining the torch on it I saw burgundy red with lines and circles of other colours woven into it. It was the back of a wall hanging I realised.

"Ah need to gwoan get something," Willick said to Puck. "Can I have the torch Wenn? Puck, ye know what yern looking for?"

I gave Willick the torch and he detached the key of the sliding door from his key ring and gave it to me.

"Yes, my father told me one time when he was drunk," Puck nodded.

"Shoulda stayed in Sussex, we naun ever drinks more than a pint," Willick smiled and then entered the passage and disappeared from view.

"I'll go first," I whispered, "I'm the smallest."

"Wait," Puck whispered back and gave me a kiss.

"For luck," he explained.

I dropped to the ground and crawled underneath the wall covering, I figured it would be less conspicuous than the appearance of a sudden bulge. I need not have feared because the room beyond was devoid of human occupation. I scrambled to my feet and gasped. The room was square with no windows and only one door to my left, next to a wardrobe which had darkened with age. The room had an absurdly high ceiling, a dome bricked vault some twenty feet over my head. There was a grand hearth in the wall opposite me and to my right stood a huge lacquered desk adorned with rows of drawers and hatches, all exquisitely decorated. The wall behind me was draped by the wall hanging.

Puck scrambled underneath it and joined me.

"The Drummers Vault," he whispered.

"The drummer shim picked a place with acoustics," I whispered back, pleased to see a faint smile on his face.

Puck crept up to the lacquered desk and started feeling under the table edge. He found what he was looking for and pressed some sort of mechanism which clicked. The table top, which had seemed continuous to me, suddenly revealed a lid which had sprung open. Puck opened it further and we peeked inside.

There, in the hidden cavity, was a long rectangular box, some thirty inches long and five inches high.

Puck picked it up with reverence, setting it on the edge of the table. He clicked open the small hooks and raised the lid of the box. Inside was a folded roll of cloth, predominantly gold with silver and red stitching on it.

"Niada's banner," Puck said in awe.

I felt the Swan tingle and opened the top buttons of my shirt, seized by the odd notion that the pendant and banner should see each other. Puck saw me do it and smiled.

"This is hardly the time and place to get your kit off sweetheart," he whispered with something of his old grin returning.

"Peter!" A woman's voice behind us suddenly said.

§ § § § § § §

We spun around to face Catherine Malheur, fully dressed despite the late hour. She was pointing a sleek automatic pistol at us.

"We meet at last Peter," Catherine Malheur said icily.

"Aunt Catt," Puck said resignedly.

"DON'T YOU DARE CALL ME THAT," Catherine Malheur snarled furiously. She raised the gun so that its barrel pointed straight at Puck. I tensed all over, ready to jump in front of him.

"The worst mistake my father made in his life," Catherine Malheur said acidly. "Was to spill his seed in that common hussy from the woods. I rejoiced at the news of the old witch's death."

Puck started and I took hold of his arm.

"Don't," I said, though I was seething inside.

Catherine Malheur looked at me with disgust on her face.

"I see that you inherited your grandfather's poor taste Peter," she said coolly. "I hope you enjoyed screwing your little whore, because you'll never see her again."

This time Puck had to restrain me.

Catherine Malheur laughed.

"Touching, it really is. A bastard's son and his little whore. Covered in mud and dressed like labourers. I would stay where you are though, I know how to use this gun and I will not hesitate to shoot."

"Brabagious murderer," I hissed for Joy's sake.

"Nobody would blame me for defending myself in my own home from eco-terrorists who broke in to threaten me," Catherine Malheur smiled contentedly. "And I am tempted to, those little plans your uneducated brains came up with in that cave of yours have cost me a great deal of money Peter."

"You're supposed to protect the Wyrde Woods, not destroy them," Puck said angrily.

We heard footsteps in the hall.

"Over here," Catherine Malheur called and then fixed her eyes on Puck again. "Don't you dare tell me what to do bastard boy, you have no notion of the responsibility that comes with the family name. Let alone honour. I don't know what weakness caused my father to allow Nathaniel to assume the Malheur name but I do know that a failed scrounging drop-out with a taste for dipping his tiny pecker in common trash does NOT deserve to bear that name. You bring SHAME on the family Peter, and to make it worse you have the audacity to live on my property, sneak in and out of the castle grounds as if you own them and then break into my home and bring your little whore with you."

Puck was as furious as I was and we both glared at her.

Willick's form appeared in the doorway, strangely, he was carrying an old sword. Catherine Malheur glanced at him.

"Mr. Maskall, what are you doing with that sword?"

"I heard a commotion Ma'am," Willick said, looking at us. "Grabbed nearest weapon at hand."

"I would prefer it. Mr. Maskall, if you kept to your duties on the grounds, you have little business in the Hall. I've told you so before. However, as I apprehended these two burglars, you may as well be useful and find a telephone and…"

Her voice died down as she looked back at us and her eyes fell on the Swan on my chest.

"Where did you get that necklace?" she hissed venomously.

"Pu…Peter gave it to me," I answered defiantly.

"So you had to pay the little whore to open her legs for you," Catherine Malheur's eyes shot hatred at Puck. "It was not yours to give Peter."

"Great-Grandmother Cilla gave it to my father before she died," Puck said.

"Unfortunately my grandmother was quite mad; the Swan belongs to the family. It belongs to me. That…" She pointed at me "…*thing* has no right to wear it."

"If anyone is not worthy of wearing it is you," I said calmly.

"Mr. Maskall, call the police if you please," Catherine Malheur's eyes became fierce and then she made the mistake of stepping towards me, gun aimed at me with one hand and the other outstretched to snatch the Swan from my neck.

The sword clattered to the ground noisily as Willick showed surprising speed in stepping forwards and seizing Catherine's gun hand from behind, pushing it high up into the air.

BANG

The shot was deafening in the relatively small room and thundered on in the high vault.

Catherine Malheur struggled to regain control of her arm, turned and drove her knee up hard into Willick's groin. Willick doubled over in pain, letting go of her arm and she tried to level it but then Puck rushed forwards to grab it while I went forwards to support Willick, kicking Catherine Malheur's shin as hard as I could.

"You little bitch," she dripped venom at me.

Willick struggled back up to come to Puck's aid.

BANG

Another shot ran out and we all froze for an instant. Then Willick groaned and slid to the floor, clutching his abdomen, blood seeping between his fingers.

Catherine Malheur took a step back, steadying herself while she pointed the gun at us.

"That is what traitors deserve Mr. Maskall. I should have known you would follow the Owlery witch anywhere you feeble man," she said, and then stepped out of the room, locking the door behind her and calling out for help.

"Quick," Puck hissed. He helped Willick up while I closed the rectangular banner box and picked it up. I then held up the wall covering so that Puck and Willick, who was looking deadly pale, could move through.

"Wenn...the sword..." Willick panted.

"Leave it," Puck said.

"No...Richard's sword...Sir Richard."

I dashed back, picked up the sword and scrambled through the gap under the wall covering which Puck held up for me from the other side. We closed the sliding door and locked it with the key Willick had given me and then moved down the stairs as quickly as we could, Puck leading, treading on the narrowest point of the stairs so Willick could lean on him and I followed. The going was agonisingly slow. I was casting anxious glances behind me but nobody was banging on the sliding door as of yet.

"Maybe she hasn't gone back into the room yet," I said hopefully. "She might just wait for the police."

"Leave me be," Willick said weakly when we reached the bottom of the stairs.

"Never," Puck said, grim determination on his face. We moved through the tunnel quicker now that we had negotiated the stairs.

"We can't get him through the hedge, not like this," I told Puck when we reached the chamber below the Poison Garden.

"Back gate," Willick said hoarsely, "I've got the key."

"Security?" I asked.

"We'll have to risk it," Puck decided.

Every window of Malheur Hall seemed to be lit when we got to the back gate and vehicles were pulling up at the end of the moat bridge, men emerging to run towards the imposing gate house of the hall. The back gate of the grounds, however, was deserted.

We made our way into the woods and followed the fence to the gap and from there went up to the dirt road where Allison, Joan and Rob were waiting for us by the Land Rover.

Allison took one look at Willick and opened the back door. We helped him in and she sat next to him. Puck and I squeezed into the front passenger seat and Joan took the wheel. Once again the Land Rover sped through the Wyrde Woods in the dark of night. We had succeeded in our mission, I was still clutching the box containing Niada's banner to my chest and Puck was now holding Sir Richard's sword, but at what cost?

38. On the Run

"We can't go to the cave," I told Joan as she negotiated a tight corner.

"Wenn is right," Puck added. "Aunt Catt mentioned it, she knows about it."

"We have a head start," Allison said behind us, cradling Willick in her arms. "We can at least get ourn stuff from there. I need it to treat Will."

"We should takes him to hospital," Joan said.

"Naun, naun ta hospital," Willick said weakly. "That be the end o' all things."

"Willick is right," Puck said quietly. "They don't just treat people with gunshot wounds without asking questions, they'll notify the police and Aunt Catt will have told them a likely story already. Whoever brings him will probably be arrested."

"Allison?" Joan asked.

"Naun to hospital," Allison said hesitantly.

"To the cave then," Puck said. "But only to get the stuff. Place will be crawling with police come morning. So will The Cottage."

"And after that? Rob's farm be too obvious, I'd takes ye in, but knowing how much Malheur knows, I reckon they'll come alooking at Earl's Barrel drackly after they search the farm."

Everybody remained silent. We had run out of safe places to hide.

"To the cave first," Puck said at last. "We'll figure out what to do from there."

We hit a bump in the road and Willick groaned in pain. I looked behind me anxiously, worried that we would lose Willick too. How much more of this?

§ § § § § §

Puck, Joan and I made journeys up and down the cliff path that led towards Robin's Cave and loaded the back of the Land Rover with our stuff. We hooked on the trailer and then Joan drove us to Lover's Lane, where we helped Willick out of the car and to one of the trees so Allison could examine his wound and dress him. Joan helped her while Puck and I sat on the hood of the Land Rover. Rob sank against a tree trunk, still in a daze and withdrawn into silence.

The pink and white blooms were gone, as was their fragrance, I reflected sadly.

"A fancy Fluttergrub had?" I asked Puck, indicating the trees.

"He planted them for Allison," Puck said slowly. He looked tired and weary. I realised that we all needed a place where we could rest. Lover's Lane would do for now but the eastern sky was beginning to brighten already. Come daylight we needed a safe shelter.

Joan and Allison walked towards us. I threw an enquiring glance at Allison. She shook her head softly, the wound wasn't good.

"We need a safe place," I pronounced.

"There be naun left," Joan said. "We can set up a camp in the woods mayhap."

I shook my head.

"Wenn, Catt Malheur knows Wyrde Woods, that's clear. Buildings at Roreford and such will be checked." Allison said.

"There is one place in the Wyrde Woods she doesn't know about," I said meaningfully. "A safe place."

Allison and Joan looked appalled and I realised I would need to convince them.

"Where is this place then?" Puck asked.

"Puck my love," I said. "Would you mind joining Willick for a moment?"

He hesitated.

"Just do it," I said. He threw me a wondrous look and drifted off.

"Wenn, we naun gwoan to take the menfolk there," Joan insisted when Puck was out of hearing.

"Tis an ancient law," Allison said, but she lacked Joan's conviction.

"It's the only place," I insisted.

"Joy'd be disappointed in ye lass," Joan crossed her arms. "That yernself, the latest o' a long line o' Keepsters o' Heorttreów would break with yern obligation."

I felt the all too familiar rush of anger but again heard that familiar voice: *Doant be tessy liddle one. Think first. Then act.*

I shook my head.

"I don't think Joy would be Joan," I said carefully.

Joan and Allison waited for me to continue. I looked at the eastern sky which was promising the sunrise soon.

"Is our plan still intact?" I asked. "To rouse the Wyrde Woods?"

"Aye, but we dursn't risk the secret o' Heorttreów."

"What do you think will happen to Heorttreów if and when a motorway rips the Wyrde Woods in two?" I asked.

They remained silent, we all knew the answer.

"Think of the Norn's Weaving. All we know is connected to the Wyrde Woods. And the Wyrde Woods in turn are connected to Heorttreów."

"Well that be right," Allison acknowledged.

"What is the worst that can happen if we bring menfolk into the Whychmaze?"

"Oberon'll finds out afore too long," Joan said.

"Yes," I said. "Oberon will find out. And what does Oberon want? What do all men want, regardless if they be man or Farisee? He will want to reunite the stone with the circle and see the maidens dance for him once again. Don't you see? The seventh secret. *THE* one which must never get told. Why not? Because knowledge is power. But all this time some people have known about this power. People with the responsibility to safeguard this power. Ask yourself why? I think it is because this power would be needed some day. The final step is the secret? Isn't it? Five for Silver, Six for Gold and Seven, us seven, for the Secret. If it was just keeping the men safe, no, naun good enow. But to save the Heorttreów and the Wyrde Woods themselves? The key to warding off destruction lies in telling the secret."

"We be charged by ancient tradition to keep Heorttreów hidden." Joan said stubbornly.

"There be reasons why folk be afeared o' meddling with Farisees Wenn," Allison said. "Tis naun for naught we doant."

"We are charged to protect the Wyrde Woods, whatever the cost," I insisted. "You want to raise the woods? Then let Oberon know, let the Seven dance. MAKE the Seven dance. That will summon the Farisee from their halls. Wake Oberon and Titania will follow and in her wrath there will be strife, strife that will have repercussions. Farisee mischief is destructive for man. You just said so yourself."

"Might be for us also," Allison said.

"Aye, but we've naun much left to lose Allison," Joan said, looking at me with new respect. "Tis like I hear Joy speaking young Wenn. Ourn old friend have learned ye well."

"Then heed the words, please," I looked at Willick, leaning pale and listless against one of his grafted cherry trees.

"How does we makes sure Oberon find out? I doant know how to talk to the Farisee." Joan asked me, and both she and Allison looked to me for the answer as if I knew how to talk to the Faere Folk. I realised with surprise that I did.

"Simple," I said. "We tell the bees."

§ § § § § §

The Landrover stopped about half a mile from the Owlery. We agreed that Puck and I would walk there while Joan and Allison unpacked the vehicle and would back it up into a hollow in the earth within a circle of ash trees and then disguise it as well as they could with branches.

Closing in on the Owlery was hard, Puck and I clutched each other's hand as hard as we could. There was no one there, just plastic yellow police lines around a smoking ruin. The roof had collapsed inwards on the blackened walls; the sheds had caught fire as well and were nothing but smouldering ashes. Not a plant remained standing in the garden; all had been crushed underfoot and now lay pale and withered amidst the mud. Only the orchard served as a reminder of the cheer that had once pervaded the Owlery, the trees had been left untouched.

We walked to the far corner. One of the beehives had been knocked over, the other remained standing upright, and oddly enough for the early hour bees flew to and fro.

Puck handed me his copy of the front door key of the Owlery and I stepped forwards. Ignoring the buzz of curious bees I tapped the key on the hive.

"Bees," I said, and my voice broke. I took a deep breath. "Bees, I want you to know that Joy Whitfield and the owls Aethel, Horsa, Bronwen and Bran, and Puck's dog Lady have passed away."

I could hear Puck trying to contain a choke behind me.

"Bees, the Owlery will be empty for a while, Joy's grandson Puck o' the Greenwoods and I, Wenn o' the Farisees, will hide at the Heorttreów, there where the seventh Shy Maiden is hidden, that is where we will be. In the Whychmaze in the grove of yew trees."

I took half-a-dozen respectful steps backwards and then turned.

"Come," I told Puck and we went back to the Land Rover.

"Did you feel…odd telling the bees?" Puck was curious.

"No," I said.

§ § § § § § §

We slept in the hollow of Heorttreów, building a field kitchen further out in the clearing. There was a sense of rest but we talked in hushed tones, casting glances at Willick who grew ever more haggard and pale. He was delirious at times, mumbling about hidden cities behind white cliffs, Messerschmitt cannon shells and somebody called Jamie. Allison barely left his side.

Rob had withdrawn to the edge of the clearing, looking oddly vulnerable without a hat to wear, and stayed out of the planning. Puck and I wandered over to him and sat down next to him. He looked at us with bloodshot eyes, his face drawn and haggard.

"I feel like I've failed ye Puck," Rob said dejectedly.

"You put up a fight Rob," Puck said, his voice trembled for a moment. "You risked your life for her, what more can I ask?"

"We heard them coming, all those cars. Dunnamy, but too many anyhow, we knew that there was trouble." Rob said, staring into nothingness.

I sought Puck's hand with my own and held it tightly.

"Why didn't you try to make a run for it?" I asked.

"She were in pain," Rob looked at me with dull eyes. "Had trouble walking and refused to. I offered to carry her out the back, howsumdever, hern refused to leave the owls. Said we'd talk ourn way out o' any trouble."

"She would have never left the owls," Puck nodded.

"Them folk made a middling gurt noise when they get out o' their cars. So much anger and hate, it gave us a fright." Rob continued. "I wanted to get my bow and arrows, but Joy said it would just makes things none-the-better."

I thought of the scores of people which made up the mob. They had been far too many, Rob might have hurt a few but he wouldn't have been able to stop the tide.

"Front door held, but they got in by the afterdoor," Rob said. "Big men, half o' them tossicated it seemed. Some local, Bill Hare for one, but many from Odesby I think. More and more came in, shouting for hern blood. Twere over for Joy quick Puck. She stepped forrards, to try to talk sense into them."

Puck nodded. I stared at the ground.

"I held them off with mine club for a few minutes," Rob grimaced. "Yern Lady by mine side, it made it more difficult for them. She were alikes a hell-hound, so hern were. Others what made for the owls met claws and beaks. Owls give it all they were worth. But it just made them madder. Lady chased some into the kitchen though, then I get knocked on mine head."

"I want to thank you for staying with her Rob," Puck said, his voice shaking. "It should have been me protecting her, I am glad you were there for her."

"But I failed."

"None of us could have stopped a mob like that," I said softly. "We saw them outside, tearing the garden apart."

"Rob," Puck grabbed his hand. "You did all you could. You mustn't blame yourself."

Rob nodded; I saw some relief in his eyes. I stood up and walked around to him; I bent over resting my arm on his broad shoulders and placed a kiss on his forehead.

"Bethanks Wenn o' the Farisees," he said.

"There is more to do though Rob," I looked him in the eyes. "I hate to ask it of you after what you have been through, but the Waer-Wyrd has need of you."

He looked up, a sudden determination on his face, "We gwoan ahead?"

"Soon, very soon now," Puck nodded.

"Good," Rob growled.

§ § § § § §

We were completely isolated from the world. We had no idea what was happening out there but there was a solace in that, giving us a chance to grieve for all that had come to pass, and would still come to pass for it was clear that Willick was dying. It also allowed us to finalise the plan for that last defiant stance which Joy had advocated.

On the second morning we held another urgent but hushed debate about the option of bringing Willick to a hospital. He refused point blank.

"One of ye will have to bring me," he said. "And they'll not let that person gwoan back. That'll be end of it and ye all knows it."

We looked at each other, knowing that he was right. The Waer-Wyrd was shrinking fast and all had a crucial part to play. All but Willick.

At the end of the third day I was sitting at the edge of the clearing, leaning against Puck who had his arm around me. We had not spoken for hours but just being together brought some comfort.

Joan walked over to us, her steps slow and laden with sorrow. We looked up.

"Willick be gwaon soon," she said. "He wants to speak to yern two."

Puck and I walked to Heorttreów holding hands and entered the tree.

Willick was deadly pale now, his broad cheeks sunk into his skull, his eyes without their bright lustre, the life seemed to be fading out of them as we watched.

"Chavees," he whispered.

We knelt down by his side. I began to cry.

Willick stretched out his once powerful arms, they trembled with weakness. Puck and I both took hold of a hand. Willick managed a weak squeeze.

"Ye be a good lass Wenn," he said. "I seen ye fight yernself like a bagga fights to defend hern home."

I nodded, tears streaming down my face.

"One more promise lass," Willick coughed, flecks of blood coming out of his mouth.

I nodded.

"Take care of disyer scaddle. Puck needs ye. Doant let him gwoan lass."

"I won't," I promised. Willick turned his eyes to Puck.

"Ye be worthy o' yern blood lad. All o' it," Willick trembled and shut his eyes. Puck sobbed audibly and I laid my free hand on his shoulder.

"Ye be looking after yern lass now Puck. Yern Gammer be proud of ye, never forget."

Puck nodded.

"Joy be proud o' both of ye," Willick managed a feeble smile. "Real proud."

He turned his head to Allison, who looked down on him with pain in her eyes.

"My love," he whispered and saw her smile in response. He then closed his eyes for the last time.

We sat around him all night in a silent wake.

In the morning we buried Willick at the edge of the clearing.

An hour later a bedraggled and singed Lady ambled into the camp wagging her partially scorched tail.

Part Whiler: Seven for a Secret, Never to be Told

39. The Fey's Pool

Puck and I ventured out of the Whychmaze, we had to find out what was going on in the Wyrde Woods, find out if Underearth and Overbranch were even there anymore and if so link up with the Lost Boys.

The Owlery was no longer smouldering and fresh green spouts dotted the wasteland that had been Joy's beloved garden. We paused there for a moment, holding hands and lost in sad thoughts. This no longer filled us with the depths of despair though, only a grim determination to see Joy's will done in the Wyrde Woods. It also reminded us that our foe did not hesitate to use any means at her disposal to combat us. Catherine Malheur, like many of her forebears, was ready to be a harbinger of death to those who crossed her will.

Avoiding the main dirt roads meant that it was better to avoid Roreford altogether, so we went by Lover's Lane to the Shy Maidens where we had a break. I used my last baccy to make a rollie and sat in the middle of the stone circle with Puck, wondering if we truly had the power to make the Shy Maidens dance again. So far no Faere Folk had appeared in the Whychmaze in search of the seventh Shy Maiden as I had half hoped they would. I ran my fingers along the Swan wondering if we were on a fool's errand, clutching at make-believe straws based on fantastical tales told by the locals to amuse each other on long winter evenings while they drank that one pint of theirs. I shrugged, doing something was better than doing nothing.

We headed south, past St Lewinna's Pool where I had seen the Red King, and then the rows of Guardians. The warmth of the sun was pleasant and the air beneath the trees seemed vibrant with life. However, the usual birdsong which had still been prevalent at the beginning of our journey had been joined by the sounds coming from the construction corridor between the Rore and Taunflow all too soon. For the last half hour or so the noise of heavy machinery and the whine of chainsaws had drowned out all other sounds. It all seemed unreal.

We came to the edge of the construction corridor shortly after we left the Guardians behind. A whole swathe of the Wyrde Woods had been flattened, as far as we could see to our left and right felled trees were being loaded onto trucks by construction workers and bulldozers were flattening the uneven ground puffing or roaring like primeval monsters all the while. Security guards patrolled the fences and smaller vehicles sped to and fro. On the other side of the broad swathe of destruction we could see the squat tower of Tuckersham Church, and somewhere in the wasteland to our left was the place where Puck's hideout had been.

Despondently we skirted the new edge of the woods and found a place to wade over the shallow Taunflow. Downriver the east bank of the Taunflow was crawling with Yellowcoats so we walked in a wide circle around New Rivendell until we came up behind the hill which fortunately still proudly bore the redwoods of the Giant's Grove.

We hid in the undergrowth till two of the protestors walked by; Curly and Maimie.

Puck hailed them. Curly was pleased to see us and full of questions and Maimie acted distant though she was still curious. Puck said we had little time and asked them to fetch Jukes or Tink with as little ado as possible.

"Please don't tell anybody else you've seen us," Puck insisted.

Curly and Maimie nodded and went up to the camp.

They came back within ten minutes with Jukes and Tink in tow. There were no loud greetings, just a firm clasping of hands.

"The papers said you two are wanted by the coppers," Tink said. "For burglary at Malheur Hall, it seems some family heirlooms were stolen?"

"We did sneak into Malheur Hall," Puck admitted. "But it's a bit more complicated than a burglary."

"None-the-less," Tink remonstrated him. "It's not good for PR."

I wanted to shake her, tell her that four people had died but I reminded myself that half of that was Waer-Wyrd business and she simply didn't know what upheavals there had been in our world.

"Which is one of the reasons we are here, and didn't stroll into the camp," I pointed out instead.

"The press has linked you with the road protest none-the-less," Tink shrugged. "They depict you two living like wanted outlaws in the wood now."

I wanted to grin at that but smiling seemed odd when I thought of Joy and Willick.

"Trust me, we had a good reason," Puck said. "We're well hidden now, but need to know what's going on here."

"Well you came just in the nick of time buddy," Jukes said. "They have their papers from court now; the judge rushed the case through. We've been given 48 hours warning. The Law Team is trying to work on it, but making little headway. The word is out that the eviction is to take place the day after tomorrow, after dawn."

"That is what the police expect," Tink said. "One of the more friendly security guards let drop that all of them will be working overtime tomorrow night."

Puck looked from one to the other.

"So it's going to get ugly tomorrow night?" He asked.

All four Lost Boys nodded.

"It sounds like they want to start evicting tomorrow night without there being a police presence," Puck explained to me.

I nodded, I had gathered as much.

"Some of our people have seen climbers and potholers at the main compound today, prepping." Curly filled in.

"That's all I needed to know," Puck said. "Tomorrow night it is then."

"You'll be here?" Maimie asked.

Puck nodded.

"We will be here, you might not see us, but we'll be here," he confirmed. "But I have to get back to…"

"We don't want to know," Jukes said.

"Have you heard anything from Judd?" I asked.

"He's in custody, not too badly hurt from what I heard," Jukes answered. "Is there anything else you need?"

"Tobacco," I said eagerly. Curly laughed and reached into his pocket to give me a pack of fags. It was nearly completely full and my eyes grew big.

"Keep it," he said. "I was going to quit anyway."

"Yeah, as if," Maimie joshed him.

"You know what you're doing Puck?" Jukes asked.

Puck nodded.

Just then Tink hissed: "Security!"

We could see a patrol of some dozen Yellowcoats down the path, far away as of yet but Puck and I melted away into the undergrowth immediately.

Jukes gave us a wink and then led the others back up to the mighty redwoods.

§ § § § § §

Puck and I left Overbranch and made our way north and then westwards, avoiding the main dirt roads and sticking to paths which were little more than deer trails. We followed a stream that fed the Taunflow for a while, and then waded across the river again. We reached the Guardians with the sounds of destruction loud in our ears like an apocalyptic orchestra.

"Let's go by way of the Fey's Pool and Willikin's Drove," Puck suggested.

I nodded, it was fine by me. I cast glances at Puck as we walked. Though he still came to me for comfort there was something of a distance now. Though there wasn't a great deal to laugh about these days I missed his smiles and grins and the silly little make believe games we used to play. He mostly looked grim these days, coupled with an unstoppable determination which showed me the man he would become…was becoming. Now and then I perceived infinite sadness in him, mostly when he considered himself unobserved. I wanted to reach out to him at those moments, and though I established the physical contact it was as if I couldn't reach him anymore. I knew that grief was an individual process, given time the Puck I knew would emerge from it again. The problem was, we didn't have the time. We had until tomorrow night, from then on everything became an uncertainty, except for the high likelihood that we would be parted, one way or the other.

I heard the rush of the Falls up ahead.

I shut my eyes for a moment and felt pain when I thought about Joy and Willick. Selfishly this time but I forgave myself for that. I had so been looking forward to five weeks of summer with them, an expansion of that one happy midterm week I had spent at the Owlery. Five weeks of waking up at home, five weeks of hearing stories from Joy and Willick, five weeks of roaming about the Wyrde Woods with Puck, fighting dragons, kissing in the shade of the trees.

I touched Niada's Swan.

Niada had a whole year with her Sir Richard. Tomorrow's end to our tale was the choice I had made when Joy had taken me to Heorttreów. I had opted to know happiness with the people who treated me like I was family, the boy who had professed he loved me. I had known it would end but wanted to experience it nevertheless. Except, in my mind that period of happiness had included the summer. It had all ended far sooner and now it felt that I was starting to lose Puck even before our short time together was up.

I recalled how he had told me he came from the Boulevard of Broken Promises in Busted Dreamville on that day I met him and Lady on Arthur's Fort. There was, I decided, one promise I could keep, wanted to keep.

We got to the Fey's Pool and I told Puck I wanted a cigarette break. He nodded. We sat down and I smoked my cigarette while Puck stared morosely at the Falls. When I stubbed my ciggy out I looked at him.

"Puck my love, I need you to do something for me," I said.

"Anything Elfin," he nodded.

"Close your eyes please, and keep them shut."

He looked puzzled but did as I asked. I walked away from him so he wouldn't hear me and started undressing as quietly as I could. I was filled with doubt. What if I only reinforced the horrible words his aunt had said about me? What if he didn't like the sight of me? My breasts were too small, my belly wasn't perfectly flat and I hadn't shaven down there for over a month so there was a merry little bush there. I knew the list inside out and he hadn't seen me before. That night on Arthur's Fort we had been concealed by darkness and explored each other's bodies with our hands, not our eyes.

Stop doubting, I told myself as I finished undressing and waded softly into the water.

"Wenn?" Puck called.

"Just a minute!" I waded some eight feet into the water till I was knee-deep and turned to face him.

"Okay, you can open your eyes now," I said, my heart beating wildly.

Puck opened his eyes and his face transformed instantly, the haggard look replaced by surprise and then softened into wonder and delight. He likes what he sees I thought with relief. I beckoned him and he shot up and strode to the water.

"No, naun likes that ye chuckle-headed scaddle!" I scolded him. "Take yern clothes off."

Puck grinned and then took his glasses off followed by the rest while I watched. His torso was skinny but not in a weakling way, he was firm and sinewy. When he pulled down his trousers and boxers in one, bending down to relieve himself of the trouser legs I saw his buttocks were tight and when he turned I gave his genitals a curious look.

He followed my gaze but I wasn't embarrassed, he'd been giving me a good look over as well.

We swam out to the falls and then along the cliff to dive down in search of submerged base stations but they had disappeared into the depths. We swam back to the falls to feel the water drumming on our backs, splashed each other, laughed, submerged to stalk each other below the water and then I slowly enticed him to the island where we retired underneath the dome of the willow tree. He was hard as rock when I took hold of him and guided him in me. We made love with a desperate passion. Driven on by the sense of tragedy and belonging we laughed and cried all the way to the surge of ecstasy at the end.

When it was over Puck rolled to his side, propping himself up on his elbow, a sudden shy look as he found my eyes.

I took his hand and laid it on my breast.

"And so," I whispered. "The Faere Fey said, I've made ye mine for middling eternity."

"Forever and longer Faery maid, surelye," Puck confirmed and kissed me.

40. Seven for a Secret, Never to be Told

Allison and Joan were pleased with the chosen night.

"Joy had hoped for Samhain," Allison said.

"Why?" I asked as we sat around the little fire we had stoked by our field kitchen on that last night of our exile.

"Barriers atween the wurrelds grow flimsy at Samhain," Rob explained. "All the wurrelds, naun jes that o' man and the dead, but others too."

"Gods, giants, elves, dwarves, men and the dead," I said pensively. "But now that is not to be."

"Naun, but tomorrow's second full moon o' July," Joan said.

"The Blue Moon," Allison added.

"If we can see it," I cast a look overhead, where low clouds were gathering.

"Doant matter if we can sees it or naun," Rob said. "As long as tis there."

We discussed our roles again, Rob, Puck and I didn't have much choice in the matter. But Allison and Joan did.

"I will take Gallows Hill," Allison said. "I've naun to lose."

"But ye all paid yern dues," Joan protested. "I mus pay mine."

"Please Joan," Allison pleaded. "I beg it off ye, I need to strike a blow for mine Will."

That settled it and we went over the plan one more time before we retired to Heorttreów where I burrowed myself into Puck's arms for perhaps the last time.

Puck had to leave around midday, to walk eastwards to Hornsby's farm with Allison and Lady before he would head south. We had to take our leave and I clutched on to him so tightly I could hear his heart beat in his chest. The sun shone on our parting, there were still a great deal of clouds overhead but it shone through the gaps at times.

"I'm scared Wenn," Puck confessed.

"So am I," I answered.

"Aye, but you've the right to be. Naun knows what'll happen to ye."

"I'll come back to yern Puck," I promised.

"But when Elfin?" There was a ghost of a grin, and then we kissed and it was time for him to walk away, possibly out of my life altogether.

I stayed with Joan and Rob helped them clear our gear out of Heorttreów.

"What if I can't do it Joan?" I revealed my deep fear as we carried the stuff to the kitchen area.

"Ye can lass," Joan tried to reassure me. "Jes think o' Joy. Hern'll be there for ye."

"It doesn't matter that I am not a maiden?" I had asked Joy this many times. She had always chuckled and said that a maid became a woman when she gave birth to a child; virginity had nothing to do with it.

"Only in men's tales lass," Joan said.

Rob and I emerged out of the Whychmaze when the sun had started its definite course to the western horizon as if it were running from the band of storm clouds drifting in from the east. I wore only a simple linen shift and Niada's Swan and shivered for the temperature was falling.

Rob and I met Tim and the rest of the Chanklebury Bedlam Troupe at Lover's Lane. They were dressed in the same costumes they had worn on Midsummer's Night except for their headgear, which they carried in their hands along with the drums each member had brought. They had brought Rob his Herne the Hunter outfit.

I led the way to the Shy Maidens, an odd procession which slowly made its way through the Wyrde Woods which watched us impassively, not yet impressed.

We got to the Shy Maidens as they caught the last of the sun, the sky a contrast between the sunset's hues on the scatter of clouds to the west and the dark billowing storm clouds gathering speed in the east, close enough for us to hear them rumbling. We had a meal of bread and cheese in silence, though I was too nervous to eat too much. I hoarded one of the big jugs of cider instead, guzzling it like it was lemonade and smoked Curly's ciggies one after the other. Nobody said anything about it, they treated me with a wary respect, and they were even in awe of me except for Rob who muttered the occasional encouragement. I was glad he was there.

About an hour after dark the Blue Moon sailed into what was left of the semi-clear sky, now under imminent threat by the booming rolls of the tempest, the edge of which had reached the eastern end of the Wyrde Woods.

It was time.

I took a deep breath and stood up when Rob had finished changing into his Herne outfit. Tim's troupe donned their headgear and surrounded the stone circle all the way, standing evenly apart from each other. They started a slow ominous beat on their drums which sounded for all the world like a heartbeat.

Rob had donned his headgear and held out his arm. I took it and he led me into the circle.

"I feel like the father o' the bride at a most peculiar wedding," he muttered underneath his mask, the antlers towering above us.

"Apart from Nyle I couldn't think of a better man to do so Rob," I said.

"Bethanks Wenn o' the Farisees."

We reached the middle and Rob and I let go of each other. He took his place in the middle of the circle and I walked outwards again, taking my place where the seventh Shy Maiden had once stood. I raised my arms and so did Rob and this was the signal for the troupe to start their slow widdershins march around the circle to the beat of their drums.

When they had completed their first circuit Tim called out the words.

"COME IN THE STILLNESS"

"COME IN THE NIGHT," the others answered.

"Eena for Sorrow," I spoke loud and clear.

I closed my eyes. Panic was screaming at me and my demons were howling with laughter, knowing they were to feed on my fragile soul if I should fail. I banished them from my thoughts and their shrieks of indignation faded away. I didn't have time for them; they would just have to make an appointment.

"COME NOW!" Tim called much faster than I had thought he would for it meant he had completed his second circuit.

"AND BRING DELIGHT," eleven voices answered him.

"Deenah for Joy," my voice trembled when I spoke her name.

I forced myself to keep my eyes closed and my mind's eye summoned the consequences of messing with the Faere Folk. I could turn to stone. I could crumble into dust. I could be dragged kicking and screaming into the Faere Folk's halls and spend a century there whilst Puck aged, withered and died. Or nothing would happen and I would age and wither knowing all the time I let the Wyrde Woods die. I mustn't let that happen. I resolved not to let that happen.

"MOONSHADOWS LONG!" Tim hollered.

"MOONLIGHT BRIGHT" came the answer.

"Dinah for a Girl," I spoke more confidently. Not any girl either but Wenn o' the Farisees, I thought and felt stronger.

Time seemed to speed up for I heard Tim's voice again long before I expected it even though the sound of the drumming told me that they kept on walking around the stones. Around and around.

"STONES STILL AND TALL!"

"LEFT AND RIGHT!"

"Doe for a Boy," my own voice sounded distant as if it came from a long ways away. I envisaged Puck's face in better days, his contagious grin and lively green eyes.

"LET HEART BEAT!"

"AND BLOOD FLOW!"

"Catterah for Silver," I spoke and just then the first lightning struck the Wyrde Woods, multiple forks lighting up the sky and I saw myself standing there in the circle of stones, the seventh Shy Maiden, arms upraised and the Swan flashing as it reflected the lightning. Almost immediately the ground shook and the crash of thunder rumbled over the woods.

"COME NOW!" Tim summoned.

"COME NOW!" the others echoed.

"WHEELAH FOR GOLD!" I called and it was as if I could see my Puck atop Beowulf, an imposing sight on the summit of Arthur's Fort. He raised a long pole and the wind caught the banner which unfolded. A gold banner streaming proudly in the gusts of wind, its metallic embroidery catching the flashes of lightning just as Niada's Swan did.

"COME TONIGHT!" Tim demanded.

"COME TONIGHT!" The rest hollered.

"WHILER FOR A SECRET!" I shouted with all my might and from above I could hear my voice as clearly as the strains of a trumpet over the tumult of a battlefield.

"NEVER TO BE TOLD!" All our voices rang out and the antlered figure in the middle of the circle raised his horn and blew three long blasts.

Lightning struck close by; even though I had my eyes shut I perceived the flash and the boom reverberated around the amphitheatre. I heard strange rumbling echoes of that boom but ignored them. Wenn o' the Farisees started to spin. The troupe increased their drumbeat now, competing with the tempest to make themselves heard. Faster and louder, faster and louder. I waited for the next bolt of lightning to impact the earth and then took my spin sideways, in the opposite direction of the drummers who continued to circle us widdershins, spread out so my ears could hear the circle around me. I fully expected to knock myself into the nearest stone but it simply didn't happen. I resisted the urge to open my eyes to see if I had veered from my course. I danced on instead, leaving the spin now to jump and twist in the air. The movements came naturally.

From above I saw the Norn's Weavings shimmer into being, shining through the bands of rain which now swept over the amphitheatre. They connected me to the other maidens, dressed in similar white shifts and twirling in their circle, graceful and beautiful, surrounded by shaggy wodewoses beating on their drums. The Norn's Weaving, silvery reflections of the lightning, reached inwards to Herne the Hunter and then spread from the seven Shy Maidens to the wodewoses and then out and beyond, jumping from blade of grass to blade of grass until it reached the tree line where it enveloped the watching Faere Folk king and his manservant and then spread from tree to tree. Ever faster it spread, I saw the silver web expand rapidly, cascading down into Hoods' Gorge, Roreford, St Lewinna's Pool and the Devil's Tarn. It then rippled onwards to envelop Lover's Lane, the ruins of the Owlery, the Falls and Fey's Pool, the Guardians and The Cottage. Next were the

Whychmaze, Willikin's Drove, Tuckersham Church, Nan Malone's Chestnut, the Giant's Grove, the Halfhollow Oak and Malheur Hall to be followed by the Blood Stone, Hornsby Farm, St Lewinna's Priory, the Water Meadows, Arthur's Fort and the Lusty Giants.

All was connected now by the Norn's Weaving, a vast silk network that touched every being in the Wyrde Woods, alive and dead or in a state of twilight. Sensing that we were complete I shouted.

"WYRD BITH FUL ARAED!"

"WYRD BITH FUL ARAED!" Puck shouted and raised an ancient Malheur sword into the air next to the Fairy Banner which streamed in the wind, untouched by the rain.

"WYRD BITH FUL ARAED!" Joan repeated, standing in front of Heorttreów with her arms upraised. Her words echoed into the empty chamber of the giant yew for the standing stone was gone.

"WYRD BITH FUL ARAED!" Allison ululated triumphantly at the Blood Stone.

"BY THE BANNER OF NIADA AND MY BLOOD I SUMMON MY FARISEE KIN!" Puck shouted into the night, the golden Fairy Banner dancing wildly in the same wind that tugged at my shift and the seven Shy Maidens continued their wild dance, encouraged by the drummers who were beating their arms lame.

"BY THE ROOTS OF HEORTTREÓW I SUMMON THEE SPRITES AND WILL O' WISPS ALL!" Joan shouted.

"BY THE BLOOD OF THE STONE I SUMMON THEE LOST SOULS!" Allison shouted, after placing her hand on the spiral pattern carved into the Blood Stone. "AND I CURSE OUR FOES!"

"ARISE! ARISE NOW FOR THE WILD HUNT." Rob bellowed and raised his horn again for a blast which stretched for an eternity.

The heavens replied with thunder and a huge horizontal flash of lightning brightened the sky, spreading out wide and branching out again and again like a tree of white fire spreading its protective crown over the Wyrde Woods.

41. The Lord of the Wyrde Woods

My mind's eye expanded now, I could see all of the Wyrde Woods. I was the Wyrde Woods and the Wyrde Woods were me. In the long construction corridor the Yellowcoats surrounding the specialist teams glanced nervously around them as the rain beat on them and the thunder roared at them and the lightning lit their anxious faces. Down in the tunnels of Underearth the protestors huddled in silence as the earth trembled beneath the onslaught from the heavens and up in the redwoods the soaked inhabitants of Overbranch howled at the sky like wolves.

The signal was given and the long column advanced over the makeshift bridges that had been thrown over the Taunflow. Two long flanking columns of Yellowcoats jogged ahead to surround the hill and cut off any escape while a third column walked behind the growling bulldozers. Protestors from the main camp rushed out of the woods shaking their heads at the drivers of the bulldozers but these were implacable, relentlessly driving onwards their machines, onwards straight towards and then over the tunnel systems of Underearth, where soil cascaded down as tunnels and chambers collapsed, the more shallow ones crushed by the bulldozers which sank through before struggling out of the new cavities and moving ever onwards, pushing down trees in an implacable advance towards the redwoods of the Giant's Grove. One of the protestors rushed to stand in front of a bulldozer which simply crushed him without slowing down, leaving a gory red smear in its tracks. The Neverlanders who followed the bulldozers roared their approval, their eyes wild, all semblance of normality gone and they snarled as if possessed.

The column that followed the bulldozers pushed on, only the potholers staying to thrust spades into the collapsed tunnels, pulling out the living wounded and battered dead. The corpses were quickly wrapped in tarpaulins and dumped on a flatbed lorry which had followed the procession.

The protestors in Overbranch looked at each other in disbelief as they saw the smaller trees pushed aside and come crashing down. There was no way the bulldozers could have come so close so fast unless they had simply crashed over the tunnels and this realisation made them pale. New lines had been crossed tonight and the Giant's Grove was now within range of this deadly advance.

At Malheur Hall Catherine Malheur stood behind one of the large windows, looking out over the woods with a satisfied smile as she sipped a glass of sherry. She did not notice the room behind her slowly filling up.

Lightning struck repeatedly around the hill that rose to support the redwoods, crashing into the treetops again and again with deafening fury though the Giant's Grove was spared this fury and the seven Shy Maidens continued to dance.

A new roar was added to the assault on the ears as, above the main construction compound two giants, hundreds of feet tall, tore themselves loose from the hillsides.

An unnatural silence reigned over Arthur's Fort, where an army had gathered to the Fairy Banner which Puck still proudly held aloft. The army was ethereal, shimmering in and out of recognisable shapes. To his left there was a woman on horseback, her long hair bound backwards so as not to be caught in her chainmail coat, shield and sword in her hands. There was also a cart driven by a young girl next to whom sat a boy of the same age, grinning and pinching her bottom. Four near naked girls stood dripping wet next to the cart, their faces set in grim fury and they were flanked by four nuns. A wise woman was to Puck's right side, with a cat on her shoulder and behind her were a host of poachers and highwaymen. More shadows joined this army of shade, a young girl with black hair in pyjamas holding a stuffed bear leaning against an overweight lad. The villagers rent apart by the cannon of the Royalist-Parliamentarian alliance and horribly mutated Lost Boys.

The brightest of the apparitions stood nearest to Puck. To one side of him stood an elderly woman holding the hands of an elderly man. Four owls were perched on their shoulders. To Puck's other side stood a tall gaunt bearded man wearing the armour of a knight and clutching the hand of the only being apart from Puck, Beowulf and Lady who bore the colour of life, a tall woman of incredible beauty who shimmered with an unearthly radiance. Puck handed the knight the Malheur sword and the bearded knight bowed his head in thanks, taking the sword with his free hand.

The Lord of the Wyrde Woods looked over his vaporous ranks and raised the Fairy Banner higher yet. The armoured woman near him lifted her sword as did the bearded knight.

The seven Shy Maidens continued to dance, the wodewoses continued to drum, Herne blew his horn again and again and the vast web of Norn's Weaving seemed to course with live electricity as it absorbed lightning hit after lightning hit. From afar it must have looked like the entire Wyrde Woods were lit up with an eerie white glow.

At the Giant's Grove Maimie screamed as the first bulldozer came into sight. Jukes and Tink exchanged a worried glance. The bulldozer ploughed confidently into the first redwood, but the tree stood its ground and the bulldozer backed off to prepare for another run-in.

The Lord of the Wyrde Woods started waving his banner rapidly left and right and his host streamed down the slopes of Arthur's Fort faster than a flash flood, taking only moments to speed down the construction corridor and falling on the rear ranks of the yellow army still behind the Taunflow. Further behind them two giants, chalky pale, fell upon the main compound, picking up bulldozers and lorries as if they were toys, tossing them into the air and letting them shatter loudly on the ground, stomping on porta cabins, barracks, sheds and vehicles. The noise overpowered the thunder and the rain washed away fires that ignited as fuel was spilled and electric cables were sundered.

An eerie concert erupted around the yellow perimeter that encircled New Rivendell as the men there suddenly found themselves assaulted by ferocious badgers, deer, woodpeckers, boggarts, foxes, owls, otters, hikey sprites, hawks, buzzards, falcons, squirrels, pixies, an angry collie, rabbits, bees, tall elves, ants, mice, elves, ducks, geese, goblins, herons, swans and magpies. The men stood their ground for a moment, ineffectively waving their arms at their assailants and then fled towards the Taunflow –pursued all the while- where a far worse foe awaited to torment their minds and wither their souls, for the Lord of the Wyrde Woods' army had come crashing through and had crossed the shallow river.

The seven Shy Maidens danced on and on whilst Titania slapped Oberon around the ears and berated him, much to the amusement of Powke until Titania's handmaidens started pinching him like bees. Only one of the handmaidens did not join in, she stood to the side of the marital skirmish, dressed in her Farisee garb with tears streaming down her narrow face as she beheld the dancing maidens.

The bulldozers atop the hill, as of yet unaware of the total mayhem which had broken loose around them continued their inexorable advance on the redwoods until they suddenly stopped as two creatures came whiffling and burbling out of the woods. The drivers fled their vehicles screaming as two scaly and terrifying Knuckers sank their teeth in the bulldozer blades, tearing the thick steel slabs like they were paper. The drivers looked behind them as they fled downhill only to see a large black shadow with widespread wings and red glowing eyes swoop down on them, screeching murderously.

And the seven Shy Maidens danced on and on, Allison shuddered as she maintained her hold on the spirals of the Blood Stones, screams rang out in Malheur Hall and Joan watched the Heorttreów shudder and shake as if it too, were dancing.

At long last an hour passed and with it the hour of the witch and wolf.

Soaking wet and gasping for breath I collapsed on the wet grass and was quickly pulled away by the exhausted drummers.

The battle was over.

42. Unconditional Surrender

I stumbled through the woods in the wet rain, slubbering until I was grabby and gormed up. I was cold and shivering but could only think of one thing and that was the Halfhollow Oak where Puck and I had promised to meet afterwards if we could.

I had not turned to stone but as I had hurried southwards I had briefly glanced back to see the seventh Shy Maiden standing in her place as if she had never been away. Ten magpies had been whirling around her in the night's last dance. The last things I had seen with my eyes closed were the vivid images of Allison clutching her heart by the Blood Stone and falling lifeless to the ground -with a smile of happiness on her face- , and the far larger spectacle of the Whychmaze spinning in a swirling vortex flowing faster and faster around Heorttreów until it had come to a sudden standstill, leaving Joan dizzy and bewildered but alive. Rob was on his way to her.

I had not seen what happened to Puck though and did not know if he was alive until I reached the Halfhollow Oak where he was waiting for me. Soaking wet and muddy like myself. He had returned Beowulf and Lady to Rob's farm first he said as we held each other tight.

We took off our wet clothes and crawled into the hollow sky-clad, and there, fatigued beyond belief, we fell asleep in each other's arms, oblivious of the white, yellow and red vehicles that started driving into the Wyrde Woods from all directions, lights flashing in the diminishing rain and sirens barely audible over the screams which reigned supreme around the foot of the Giant's Grove hill that night.

Screams of anguish from shattered minds.

Apart from those sheltering up in the redwoods and the inhabitants of the main camp who had fled to Rob's farm when the first bulldozers had arrived, not a single man or woman on the ground between the Lusty Giants and the Giant's Grove had escaped the wrath of the

Wyrde Woods that night. They had been driven collectively insane: babbling of monster rabbits which flew at their throats; bulldozer-eating dragons, lorry-throwing giants; pixies who had pinched their noses; ghostly figures who had howled their brains into jelly and a large black flying shadow with glowing red eyes. Dozens turned out to be missing and crazed witnesses said they had been borne screaming into shimmering gates by tall regal creatures clad in rich coloured robes. King Arthur himself, some said, had come storming down from Arthur's Fort, tall on horseback bearing a banner that had glittered like dragon scales. The police couldn't tie head or tail to it.

They were also confounded by a call from the security guards at Malheur Hall, who reported that Lady Malheur was wandering around the garden stark naked and babbling about headless horsemen, kitchen boys, drummers, starving children and handwringing young women. They sent an ambulance and found Catherine Malheur in the Poison Garden where she had ripped up the plants and was stuffing them in her mouth. She died in violent convulsions on the stretcher before they reached the ambulance.

The police arrested every protester they could apprehend, including those at the Base Camp at Hornsby Farm. They suspected some kind of manic role play enhanced by hallucinogenic drugs induced in the gallons of coffee and tea consumed by the construction workers and security men before they set out on their final assault. This left them to explain the wrecked vehicles and buildings at the main compound and all along the construction corridor to the top of the Giant's Grove hill. Only a single vehicle was intact and inspection teams could not fathom how the protestors had achieved the level of destruction they found, for the vehicles were crushed like toys or torn apart by supernatural strength just like the buildings in the main compound. The only vehicle untouched was a flat-bed truck on which the police found the wrapped corpses of mangled protestors. The names of those identified were added to the list of missing security men from Neverland.

Puck and I woke up in the Halfhollow Oak and beheld each other in happy wonder. We laughed as we stroked each other's faces, shoulders and chests as if we could not get enough of the sight of the other. The feeling was overwhelming and wonderful but did not last long.

The police showed up and we were roughly hauled out of the Halfhollow Oak.

"Good Lord, they are only kids," one of the police constables shook his head in wonder.

"Stark naked and covered in mud like savages," a sergeant growled. "Your parents should be ashamed of you."

I laughed hollowly and Puck and I fought like fiends to get to each other but we were handcuffed and led to separate cars. I would not see him for another two months.

When I did see him it was at a hearing in some court or other -I lost track of the legal proceedings which took place, there were lots- and registered little of the complaints levelled at Puck, Judd, Jukes, Tink and Maimie. The little I understood was that scapegoats were needed and the ringleaders of the 'cult of violence' had been selected for this purpose. Other than that I just looked at Puck, drinking in the sight of him. It became clear the prosecution were seeking maximum sentences due to the severity of the damage caused. Puck smiled as if to say this was part of the pact we had been part of. A short time of magical bliss followed by the reality of that other careless world. Then he told the judge that the others hadn't been part of the cult, but that he himself was a highly placed member and the sole survivor.

When the judge ordered a short recess the suspects were led away and both Puck and I shook ourselves loose from the grip of the court wardens and rushed to each other. We couldn't hug, as we were handcuffed but our fingers gripped each other so firmly that we could not be pried apart easily.

"Agree with everything they say," Puck said urgently.

"What?!"

"Agree with everything, no matter how hard, you must go free. Please Wenn, for the sake of the future." He glanced down as the Wardens pulled at us.

"How...?"

He was torn loose from me and dragged away.

"The bees told me!" He shouted. "I have Farisee blood, remember Elfin? Just like you. The bees told me."

"I love you!" I shouted before I too was dragged down a stairway into the catacombs of the court.

§ § § § § §

My case came up and I was presented as an innocent victim by my defence, seduced by the promises of an occultist cult headed by a certain Mrs. Joy Whitfield who had lied her way into the Odesby Juvenile Care Home. I agreed to it all in a dull tone, torn by the sense of betrayal I felt. I looked at Puck the whole time as I betrayed everything we had been. He looked back at me, encouraging me with barely perceptible nods and smiles. His eyes spoke only of love. Never before had I realised the full extent of his love for me as at that moment when I betrayed him, denying him and the sanity he had gifted me.

I looked into those eyes as I agreed that Willick and Joy had promised me a place where I could belong but instead forced me to carry out hard laborious tasks. I agreed that they had supplied me with alcohol and herbal substances and, weeping inside, I agreed that I had been sexually abused and now carried the baby of one of the cult members in my womb. I just hoped the little one was too early in its development to hear any of the manifold lies that were told and then wept inconsolably for the rest of the hearing, wept as I was brought to a car and I was still weeping when I was escorted through the door of Nowhere Place where I was formally released and placed into the hands of Youth Care once more.

§ § § § § § §

Puck was sentenced to eight years, the rest to six months, mostly on account of criminal damage; they weren't quite sure how to play all the missing people. The M33 was never built, stopping at Royal Tunbridge Wells and leaving the Weald untouched apart from the scars that blemished the Wyrde Woods, though these soon turned green again as the Wyrde Woods healed themselves.

I gave birth to a healthy baby girl and was allocated a flat in the Neverland tenements. Nowhere Place monitored me for two years and then it was done. I was supposedly free but sometimes felt that I too was locked up.

Puck sent me a letter from jail, asking me to never bring our daughter Jay-Jay there; he could not abide the thought of her seeing him behind bars. I visited when I could, but he had been placed far away from Sussex making the trip an expensive one. Once every month Joan would drive me there and back and before too long that became the established pattern. Puck looked odd not wearing green and though he said he was coping he became more and more withdrawn. After a year he ceased smiling and after another year I could barely recognise the man on the other side of the safety glass window. It was as if his soul had been sucked out of him.

As I had promised Judd I visited Nyle every month and each time I returned he was a little better. He was much taken by Jay-Jay and wrestled himself to increasing normality because he wanted to be there for Jay-Jay as her grandfather and in doing so he was there for me as a father at last. He improved so much that when Judd got out of prison he was allowed to pick Nyle up and my dad would spend his weekends with me. Jay-Jay and I would take Granddad Nyle and Uncle Judd to Uncle Rob and Aunt Joan at the Hornsby farm. Joan had moved in with Rob and the two were happy. Lady lived there too, Neverland was no place for a dog used to the freedom of the Wyrde Woods.

I pretended happiness for Jay-Jay's sake but at nights would stare at the ceiling and feel incomplete, yearning to drown in bright eyes which were as green as the Wyrde Woods in summertime.

43. Seven Years After

I look at my last sentence on the bright screen of my ancient laptop until the words start to blur as my tears flow. I let them, this is as good a moment as any.

"Mummy?"

My daughter stands in the doorway, shyly, she is not used to seeing me like this. She has my brown hair and her father's green eyes and looks for all the world like a faery child. Of course, she is, the blood runs strong in her.

"I think there is something under my bed mummy, can you tell it to go away?"

I quickly wipe my eyes dry.

"I will Jay-Jay, sweetheart," my voice trembles a little bit but I pull myself together for her sake. She looks timid, standing there in her pyjamas, clutching her stuffed owl; my beautiful little girl with her bright elfish eyes.

I walk towards her and pick her up, finding solace as I feel her small warm body pressed against mine. She wraps her arms around my neck and rests her head on my shoulder. She is probably eying my necklace; she has always had a fascination with the graceful Swan.

"I love you Jay-Jay," I whisper.

"I love you too mummy," Jay-Jay answers, then curiously adds "Why were you crying?"

Tomorrow is her sixth birthday, she is growing so fast. Of late her questions about her father have become more determined; she is no longer prepared to settle for my vague explanations about her daddy being on a long journey. I look at the letter on the table. It has filled me with uncertainty. He is to be released early, he wrote, and wants to come straight to Neverland. He signed his letter with the name Peter.

How much will incarceration in prison change a man? Who will come out? Will there be any resemblance to the gawky funny boy I loved once upon a time? The man I visited in prison seemed a shadow of his former self. Puck needed freedom to thrive and locked up had withered away. He did that for me, I can never forget that. But he stopped calling me his Elfin long ago. Can we be Wenn o' the Farisees and Puck o' the Greenwoods again, or would we simply be Wendy and Peter, scratching out an existence in Neverland?

If it's up to Rob and Joan we can make our escape from Neverland at any rate. They visited earlier today and gave me the key to the cottage of the old farm. They insisted that they would help me move in before Peter-Puck was freed, so that we would have our second chance in a proper home. Michael and Miss Watson wanted to help as well.

I banish the fears, it is Jasmin-Joy who matters now, who ought to know both her parents in the way they never knew theirs. I loved Puck with all my heart and I will take my chances with Peter, it is, after all, a promise I made to a dying man. A man who fought for me as if I were his kin.

"Your daddy is coming home next week sweetie."

"Really? Daddy?" Jay-Jay looks at me with wide eyes.

"Really," I smile at her.

"To stay?"

"To stay, he has missed you very much lass."

"Does he love me?"

"More than anything in the wurreld liddle one."

We walk into her small bedroom and I tuck her in, sitting on the bedside.

"I wish he could come earlier!" Jasmin-Joy has brightened, the creature under her bed forgot.

I bend over and kiss her on her forehead and think of the corner of the living room. There is a faded and battered backpack there, just below a framed embroidered gold rectangle of cloth and an ancient sword. I packed the backpack earlier this evening. I haven't dared to go back to the Wyrde Woods since we were dragged out of the Halfhollow Oak. Too many shims. The closest I have got were visits to Jay-Jay's aunt Joan and Uncle Rob and then I looked away from the green fringes of the woods, afraid to behold them...

But tomorrow I will have to face the past. Tomorrow I will take my daughter by the hand and lead her into the green splendour that so haunts my dreams. Tomorrow I will begin to tell her about the secrets of the Wyrde Woods. About Joy, Willick, Jasmin, Allison and Biggs.

I will ask Puck to tell her about Niada, Ellette, Richard, Foster, Willikin and Ufmanna; Rob to tell her of Herne, Oberon, Titania, Powke and the Seven Maidens; and Nyle to tell her about Ashley. Joan and Judd made their own requests already. Joan wants to take her to Goody Malone's tree and Heorttreów and Judd wants to treat Jay-Jay to her first beer in a pub when she turns eighteen many years from now.

"Mummy, I want *the* rhyme." Jasmin-Joy has come to a decision. I have tried to teach her others, but this is her favourite. I recite it by heart and she joins in at three.

> *One for Sorrow*
> *Two for Joy*
> *Three for a Girl*
> *Four for a Boy*
> *Five for Silver*
> *Six for Gold*
> *Seven for a Secret*
> *Never to be Told*

"Why does it stop at seven? Why not go on to ten?"

"It does go on sweetie, there is more."

"Tell me," Jasmin-Joy demands eagerly.

I smile, sometimes she reminds me of myself. I say the words…

> *Eight for a Wish*
> *Nine for a Kiss*
> *Ten for a Time*
> *of Joyous Bliss.*

…and I can only hope it's true.

-THE END-

One for Sorrow

Two for Joy

Three for a Girl

Four for a Boy

Five for Silver

Six for Gold

Seven for a Secret

Never to be Told

Eight for a Wish

Nine for a Kiss

Ten for a Time

of Joyous Bliss.

With Help from My Friends (extended version)

I owe a great many amazing people a debt of gratitude for helping me one way or another. There is a comprehensive list at the end of ESCAPE FROM NEVERLAND; this one is more specific.

A few literary giants to begin with. It was William Blake's painting of William Shakespeare's *A Midsummer Night's Dream* which formed part of my inspiration. Rudyard Kipling's *Puck of Pook's Hill* and *Rewards and Fairies* were also sources of inspiration. The names Oberon and Titania are from Shakespeare's play and my Puck cites his Puck at the hide-out in the woods in a tribute.

A few years ago my friend Marcel was kind enough to drive me to Kent on a literary pilgrimage to the Pearson's Arms in the seaside town of Whitstable (best fish and chips I ever had), where I had enticed author C.J. Stone to show up with the promise of a pint. Two decades earlier I had visited Chris at his flat a few times to discuss what it meant to be a writer. He went and did it and his works are truly marvellous, as described by Puck. I procrastinated for another twenty years first. I saw this visit to Whitstable in the light of Arthurian lore, a noble quest to sit at the feet of a fount of wisdom and be spoon fed the magic which would allow me to write fiction.

Chris gave me the best advice ever, though I didn't realise it at the time. "Find the Wyrd" he said when he figured out that I wanted to touch upon the undercurrent of the English psyche and more or less left it at that. I am not sure if I found the Wyrd or if the Wyrd found me, but we became well acquainted the Wyrd and I. I have tried to convey a sense of it in the Wyrde Woods.

My intention was to write something resembling a Gothic Horror Story in which the supernatural roots would be firmly based on pre-Norman Anglo-Saxon mythology and customs. The setting for this work would be East and West Sussex, after I encountered the Weald during research for an article on the exploits of William Cassingham, an almost forgot English hero.

Fate, however, is inexorable. My characters hijacked the plot. Wenn and Puck insisted that the story became a love story, their love story, rather than my cleverly devised tale of horror. This is more apt, as this story is a rather belated love gift for Zoe, who put up with my egocentricities for a good twenty years before my early midlife crisis created a madness which nobody in the world could have possibly tolerated, apart from myself that is. Wenn is partially based on a slightly younger version of the Zoe whom I met in the early nineties and who swept me off my feet back then and there is some of my friend Janna in Wenn as well. Many of Wenn's thoughts are mine though; especially in the Red King chapter. Been there, done that. Don't like to talk about it but have no hesitation baring my soul in a book. Puck isn't based on me; I suspect that he is a subconscious representation of the kind and gentle man I reckon Zoe probably deserved in lieu of myself.

Just like Wenn and Puck, Joy too played a subversive part in stealing my story. In my original plans she was due to play a short role at the very end of the story, offering Puck and Wenn a place of shelter when the going got rough. Joy told me in certain terms that this plan was balderdash and that Wenn needed a female role model who could help her transformation from Wendy to Wenn much earlier in the story. I conceded and Joy then became an increasingly important character. I found myself frequently consulting my friend Joyce, on whom Joy is loosely based, to seek her approval of Joy's sometimes audacious actions, and she would chuckle, tell me to do as I pleased and drop little predictions as to what would happen regardless of my intentions. Joyce's four owls, whose names have been changed to protect their privacy, are far less forgiving and have promised to squirt their ceca at me during my next visit.

Willick too is partially based on a friend whom I admire much, he was and is to me what Joy was for Wenn, an invaluable guide to the Wyrde Woods and Dave has, albeit unknowingly, supported the creation of this story when he and Libby showed me the real Giant's Grove and taught me that you can't base a story in a woods and just keep on saying 'the woods' and 'the trees' and expect that will suffice as a description. That made the Wyrde Woods into a living character, as did my father Rob who took me for long walks in his own Wyrde Woods: His beloved Veluwe National Park.

Both Joy and Will are to feature as the main characters in new Wyrde Woods novels set in the 1940s (*Will's War, Forgotten Road, Secret Spring*). Priscilla and Oscar Malheur will feature in *Fool's Folly*. Ashley Pilbeame and Nyle Twyner will feature in *Shim's Whispers*. Last-but-not-least Jay-Jay Malheur will set all to rights in *The Owl and the Badger*.

My favourite character is Rob Hornsby who is partially based on my good friend Richard Hornsby. It was Richard's enthusiastic appreciation of his native Somerset that he generously shared with me which was the final key to unlocking the Wyrd, and much of this enthusiasm has been transferred to Rob, Puck, Joy and Willick. The photograph on the front cover was taken at Glastonbury Tor during one of our jaunts in Somerset. The scene of the archery lesson is a tribute to Richard. The hat fetish is something we share; the Pith helmet is his, the bowler hat mine. Much of the Carfax Alus and the Earl's Barrel is based on Richard's local; the Crossways Inn in West Huntspill.

Lewinna the Dragon Slayer is a tribute to sword fighter Willeke and the fight scene by the Devil's Tarn is a tribute to Famke, Jinke and a bunch of bettermost kids called the Fantasten; for we created magic together, real and make-belief rolled into one and sustained that magic for years.

I owe thanks to my mother Marijke, Marcel and Geert for taking me to the Wyrde Woods on more than one occasion. My grandparents Adrie and Dien for instilling a love of the Wyrde Woods in me at an early age, and Marijke, Judith and Marguerita for teaching me to admire strong women. I also owe a great deal of thanks to Jovannah and Nicole for coming to the Wyrde Woods with me. Seeing it through the eyes of two young women was the final push I needed to sit down and write the novel. Jo and Nicole will no doubt recognise some of the places and situations. I forgot to work in the mosquitos (ouch ;-)) though, they will follow in a next book.

Nicky, Dunia, Leon, Bren, Richard, Jacqueline, Geert, Liesel and Heather helped make this story possible by supplying sound feedback and encouraging me to keep on writing and I owe special thanks to author and composer Neal Callen Clarke, fellow Putnam City Pirate. Even though he had his hands full with his own novel (*Firadis (Arena)*), he was kind enough to mentor me, and his professional feedback was so encouraging that it spurred me to complete the book by writing ten chapters in a crazed 72 hour sitting that included little sleep, a lot of coffee and cigarettes and life-saving sustenance provided by a concerned Magén who provided me with shelter during the storm in any case, showing what true friendship is worth. Like Joy said, if you find it, never let it go.

Corin Spinks has also been most helpful in providing the photograph on the cover; I was much taken by it and look forward to working with him in the future. We have already embarked on some of this work. I have also been impressed by the American Book Center in Amsterdam, one of those independent book stores where books really matter. Do support independent book stores when you can, the chains are run by economics now.

For those of you who were hoping for more Faere Folk in the story, do remember that Faere Folk are like badgers, they are hard to catch sight of and notoriously wary of humans. On the other hand, things are not always what they seem, but that will become clear in further books of the Wyrde Woods Chronicles. We will meet Wenn and Puck again, or Wendy and Peter. Time will tell but the other nine elements of the prophecy are all present in the Lord of the Wyrde Woods, which is a promising sign.

Written at Herstmonceux in Sussex, the edge of Amsterdam in the Netherlands and, of course, in the Wyrde Woods in August and September 2014.

SONGS, POEMS & REFERENCES

Cover Photograph
Front: Richard Hornsby at Glastonbury Tor
Back: Carlo Robbé at the Amsterdamse Waterleidingduinen.

The Bee-Boy's Song
Features in Rudyard Kipling's fantasy book *Puck of Pook's Hill* published in
1906.

Nine the green daughters o' Mother Erce who point the way
Inspired by Eleanour Sinclair Rohde's *Garden of Herbs*, published in 1922.

Nine were Norn's sisters
A counting charm in the *Lacnunga*, a collection of Anglo-Saxon medical texts
and prayers as well as spells written in the late tenth or early eleventh century.
It has been slightly adapted.

One for sorrow, two for joy
An old nursery rhyme

The Three Ravens
An old English folk Ballad printed in the song book *Melismata* compiled by
Thomas Ravenscroft and published in 1611. The song is believed to be much
older.

The Green Man and Red Queen
Are often wed during the old midsummer celebrations.

The Stolen Child
A poem by William Butler Yeats, published in 1889 in *The Wanderings of Oisin
and Other Poems*.

Every time a bell rings, an Angel gets his wings
An old folklore saying often heard around Christmas time.

GLOSSARY

abroad - anywhere not in Sussex
abusefully - insulting
afeared - afraid
afore - before
afterdoor - back door
aftername - surname
all-along-o' - because of / on account of
alltsinit - all that is in it i.e. taking all this in consideration
alikes - like
alus - alehouse (pub)
ampery - weak / unhealthy
anigh - near by
atween - between
axe - ask
axed - asked
axing - asking

bagga - badger
bandersnatch - (LEWIS CARROLL) nonsense word from Jabberwocky
bear sic - (SLANG) really cool
beazled - exhausted
beleft - believed
bellick - to bellow
beliddling - belittling
bethanks - thank you
bettermost - superlative of better.
bi-laminate - (ARCHERY) a bow made of two layers
bio-degredibble - (OWN INVENTION) bio-degradable
bostin - (SLANG) amazing
boning - (SLANG) fornicating
brabagious – no translation, but the worst thing one Sussex woman can call another Sussex woman
brill - (SLANG) brilliant
browned off - (SLANG) to irritate/anger
buff - (SLANG) attractive
bun that - (SLANG) forget that
burbling - (LEWIS CARROLL) nonsense word from Jabberwocky
by Geemeny - the exclamation 'O Gemini!' Like: Gee, Wow, Gosh
by-the-bye - by chance

caffincher - chaffinch
callow - bald (derived from the Dutch 'kaal')
catching hot - to catch a cold

catterah - (children's counting rhyme) five
caterwise - diagonally
chance-born - born out of wedlock, or a Farisee Changeling
chank - chew
charm-stuff - 'unofficial' medicine, i.e. not from modern doctor or hospital
chavee - child
chipper - nipper /child
chirpsing - (SLANG) flirting
chuckle-head - idiot/fool
clinker – (SLANG) dried feces attached to the hairs of the buttocks
cloober - (SLANG) 'clooby' derived from bloody, can be used as adj., noun, etc.
cray - (SLANG) mad/crazy
codger - a miser

da - dad
dappens - as soon as
deedy - clever or industrious
deenah - (children's counting rhyme) two
devourously - voracious
dight-up - get dressed up, make yourself presentable
dinah - (children's counting rhyme) three
dingleberry - (SLANG) dried feces attached to the hairs of the buttocks
dishabill - disheveled
dissing - (SLANG) making fun of/ making a fool of
disyer - this here
doant - don't
doe - (children's counting rhyme) four
dooby – (SLANG) very dumb
douchenoggin – (SLANG) friendly insult related to douchebag
douchebaggery – (SLANG) behaviour which is below any sort of par
dour - to put out a candle
dozzle - a small portion
drackly - directly
draggle-tail - a woman of dubious morals
Drefan – (ANGLO-SAXON) trouble
druv - driven. From 'Sussex won't be druv'
duguth - (ANGLO-SAXON) a band of warriors
dunnamy - don't know how many
dursn't - dare not
duzzick - a chore / a day's work

eena - (children's counting rhyme) one
e'enamost - almost

ellynge – miserable / lonely
enow - enough
et – eaten

fambly - family
Farisee – of the Faere Folk (Faerie)
fax - (SLANG) fuck
faxed - (SLANG) fucked
faxing - (SLANG) fucking
fit - (SLANG) in a good shape / sexually attractive
flabbergastation - (OWN INVENTION) own invention for 'flabbergasted'
flaffing about - (SLANG) hanging around
fluttergrub - somebody who likes to potter around in the earth
forename - first name
foredoor -front door
forever ago - (WENN) a long time ago
Forlorn Hoper - (WENN) Wenn's invention for resident of Nowhere Place
forrard - forward
fresh - tipsy
frumious -(LEWIS CARROLL) nonsense word from Jabberwocky
FUBAR - (SLANG) Fucked Up Beyond All Recognition
furriners - foreigners (anybody not from Sussex)

gaffer - grandfather
gammer - grandmother
gark - look at
garm - mud
generally-always - almost always
giggle-some- giggly
Coomony - from the expression 'O Gemini!'
gobbet - a mouth full of something
Goody - a titular address, usually for an older woman
gormed up - all dirty on account of mud
grabby - covered in mud
graft - (SLANG) to fancy
gret - (SLANG) cigarette or hand rolled cigarette
grummut - an awkward boy
grump - someone who is grumpy
gubber - mud
gurt - great
gwoan - going

hag-ridden- having a nightmare
Heolstor – (ANGLO-SAXON) dark

Heortréow – (ANGLO-SAXON) literally Heart Tree
hickory-boo - (Archery) hickory wood, bamboo
hindesideafore - the wrong way round
hot spice - (SLANG) a sexy girl
howsumdever- however (also used as howsumever)
hugger-mugger - in disorder / without system

ike - mud
ingenurious - ingenious
innard - inward
insultive - (SLANG) insulting

jaunce - a (weary) journey
jes - just
jiggered - surprised
jubjub - (LEWIS CARROLL) nonsense word from Jabberwocky
justly - just so

ken - to know someone, from the Dutch 'kennen'.
knucker - dragon / large worm

lamentable - adjective used instead of 'very'
legend - (SLANG) something that is really cool
letbehow'twill - let it be how it will
les - let's
liddle - little
lifer - (WENN) Wenn's invention for veteran caretaker at Nowhere Place
lippy - someone quick to give commentary, not always polite
loped – to run off – possible from 'eloped' or the Dutch 'loopt'
Lunnon - London
Lunnoner - Londoner

mack moment- (SLANG) the moment two people realise they are about to have sex
maene wudu- (ANGLO-SAXON) Man's Wood / Common Wood
mam - mum/mom
Master Dobbs - Sussex name for the household elf
mawkin - a scarecrow
maun - must not
mayhap - perhaps
middling - a commonly used adjective which can mean anything at all

misagift - mistaken
moil- trouble
moist - (SLANG) sad, pathetic
most-in-general - usually / generally
mucked-up - all-in confusion
Mus - master
Mus Reynard - a fox
nary - any
naun - no / not / none
negatons - (SLANG) negative vibes
none-the-better - drunk
no-ways - no way

oakum - nonsense
onnard – onward
Ole Brock – badger
OTF – (SLANG) Opportunity to Fuck
otherwhiles - at other times / otherwise
outlandish - used to describe someone not
from Sussex
outyer – out here

parring - (SLANG) showing disrespect
peert - lively, charming
peg away - to eat or drink enthousiastically
peng - (SLANG) really cool
piff - (SLANG) cool
plaguey - troublesome
poking - (SLANG) making fun of
pranging out - (SLANG) being scared
preggers - (SLANG) pregnant
prensley - presently
primed - lightly drunk
print-moonlight - clear moonlight
puck stool - toad stool / mushroom
pug - mud
purty - pretty

quiddy - What did you say? From French *Que dis tu?*

ravtile - (SLANG) the worst possible insult
you can call someone
reafe up- to get really excited and
enthousiastic about something
real beast - (SLANG) really cool
recollect - remember
recollections - memories
rheummatics - rheumatism though it was
used more generically
robbut - rabbit
rolling about - fornication. Not sure if this
was Sussex but I left it like it was.

safe dreams - (OWN) My own variation of
sweet dreams
scaddle - wild / mischievous / thievish.
scamble - to create confusion
scrazed - scratched and bruised
scritch owl - barn owl
scorching - (SLANG) being disrespectful
scorse - exchange
scrowse - angry, dark, scowling
set - obstinate
shatter - a great number or quantity
Sheeres - the Shires. This would include
places like Surrey, but also Manchuria and
Arizona. Basically, anywhere that is not
Sussex.
Sheere-folk - people from the Shires, i.e. not
from Sussex
Sheere-man - a man from the Shires, i.e. not
from Sussex
shimper - to shine brightly
shims - an apparition, from the Dutch 'Schim'
shirty - easily offended
shruck - shrieked / yelled
sic - (SLANG) cool
sirageous - (SLANG) a widely applicable
adjective expressing something is positive
skag - (SLANG) someone who eats rotten
fetuses
skreel - a scream or a shriek
slab - mud
sleech - mud
slob - mud
slubber - to slip in mud
slurry - mud
smeech - a dirty black smoke or mist
smeery - mud
smoking crow and getting blunted -
(SLANG) smoking pot and getting stoned
snooty - (WENN) Wenn's invention for
optimistic newby caretakers at Nowhere Place
snotgoggs - yew berries
snoule- a small quantity
snuffy - angry
sodgers - soldiers
somewhen - sometimes
somewhen t'other-day - the day before
yesterday / just about any day before
yesterday
some-one-time - occasionally
soodling - a slow meandering walk
spake - (SLANG) a hefty insult, usually used
as a comeback when just insulted yourself

sprite - (OWN INVENTION) spirit. I wanted something that sounded a bit differently.

squimbly - feeling unwell

streale - arrow

stodge - mud

stride - a long walk (usually any destination outside of Sussex)

stuckish - stuck in a manner of thinking

stug - mud

suddent - suddenly

surelye - surely, often used to for emphasis, the spelling is odd but widespread in old texts and Broad Sussex dictionaries.

swag - (SLANG) attitude, arrogance, sense of own attractiveness

swymy - giddy / faint

tarn - small lake

tater - potato

teats - breasts

teddious - tedious

telling - counting (Sussex with Dutch origin)

tessy - to be angry

timmersome - timid

thereaways - there about / that way

there is everything o' something and something o' everything - a favoured explanation for something that isn't really understood.

tiffy - touchy / irritable

tossicated - very intoxicated

trolling - (SLANG) fooling someone

tulgey - (LEWIS CARROLL) nonsense word from Jabberwocky

tmight - it might

twack - (SLANG) insult, not very nice

twere - it were

twill - it will

twould – it would

unbeknownst - unknown

Ufmanna - (ANGLO-SAXON) literally Owl Man

unnacountable - an adjective which can be used for just about anything. Used often.

vlothered - agitated/ flustered

waer-wyrd – (ANGLO-SAXON) to speak carefully, to choose one's words wisely

Waus - (HISTORICAL) from the French nickname for Willikin of the Weald.

wazzock- (SLANG) know it all

weard – (ANGLO-SAXON) protect, defend

well stacked - (SLANG) big boobs

wheelah - (children's counting rhyme) six

whiffling - (LEWIS CARROLL) nonsense word from Jabberwocky

whiler - (children's counting rhyme) seven

widdershins - anti-clockwise

wind shaken – thin, puny, weak

Wodewose - mythical creature of the wood. Ranging from wild man to wood spirit.

wurreld -world

Wyrd – a major part of the Anglo-Saxon belief system with regard to destiny Dr. Brian Bates's *The Way of the Wyrd* is recommended for anyone wanting to know more about the Wyrd.

Wyrde - properly the 'Wyrd' but I wanted it to be slightly different for the Wyrde Woods name.

yarbs - herbs

yetner - not yet

ye can cut yern stick - do as you please

yoked - (SLANG) muscular, well built

Yuletide - Christmas

zackly - exactly